Stork Lake

TALES FROM A WALL OF HATS

L.C. Reid

ISBN: 9781777892500

For the village who raised me.

Lori Reid, 1964

What ever happened to the loveable characters after Stork Lake?

Catch up on their stories, view photos, and more online at

LCREID.ca

TABLE OF CONTENTS

1979

Lori dropped the worn khaki knapsack on the sun-bleached planks of the pier, took a deep breath, then turned around. So this was it. In a little more than an hour, she would leave this place forever, and she did not know how she was going to bear it.

The young woman did not notice the bustle around her, the stream of faceless silhouettes shuffling box after box, transporting bag after bag to a growing pile of cargo on the dock. All she noticed was the place, this storybook place. For as long as Lori could remember, this secluded fly-in resort tucked into the picturesque forests of Northwestern Ontario had been her family's life, their livelihood, the setting for their fairy tale existence. Now, however, the resort was closing, ending the only life she had ever known.

Her senses surrendered to their surroundings. Summer died beautifully here; a rich fall palette of vibrant wines, currants, plums, and gingers painted the landscape, while a concert of golden poplar leaves jingled as they twirled in the late September sun. A cool northerly wind picked up the full-bodied pungency of autumn's decaying leaves at her feet and carried it upward to her nose. Lori turned toward the lake. An endless blue sky dotted with tiny tufts of white clouds reached down to meet the water. Sunlight bounced off the curly waves as they swayed to the rhythm of the wind, ending their dance as little ripples gently lapping the sandy shore. Nearby two islands floated languidly in the sparkling water, their silhouettes spiked with jack pines outfitted in winter green. Overhead a flock of Canadian geese graced the sky in their flowing passage south. On silent wings, they called out a lament for the end of summer.

Suddenly a loud buzz jolted her out of her reverie. From between the two floating islands, an amphibious plane emerged, hovered over the water for a moment, then made contact. It was not an elegant landing; the Canso did not cut cleanly through the water like most float planes. Instead, grunting and groaning, it landed belly first, wallowing in the water. Slowly the plane began to chug toward her, the prop beating its way through the air until it finally reached the dock. There it loomed over the shore like a great grey beast, one that had come to snatch them all away.

Lori's head felt like it was caught in a vice grip as she surveyed the scene in front of her. It seemed surreal, rolling out like the images on an old eight-millimetre home movie. Frame by frame, she watched as the men manoeuvred the heavy wing-tip floats of the plane into place, secured it to the dock, then opened its massive freight doors. For the first time, there were no supplies, no gas, no food or lumber to unload. Instead, the crew immediately began to move the mountain of luggage onto the Canso. The plane's leaden belly sunk deeper into the cradling waves of the lake with each bag, box, and suitcase that disappeared into its cavernous mouth.

Her throat collapsed with emotion. She could not just stand here while these people packed up her life and stowed it away on a plane. This was the place of her childhood dreams, her adolescent hopes. How was she going to get through this? How could she leave, knowing there was no way she could ever return? Tears bubbled in the corners of her eyes, and she turned blindly away. "I can't leave. I'm not ready yet! I don't have everything I need!"

Everything I need. The words had spilled out of Lori's mouth, seemingly unconnected to any conscious source. What did that mean? What had she forgotten to pack that would somehow make everything all right? How could anything that fit into a suitcase make leaving here even remotely okay?

A gust of wind tugged at the brown suede cap on Lori's head. As she pulled the brim back down, an idea came to her. With purpose, she strode up the grassy hill. From the top, she could easily see the sprinkling of guest cabins peering from between groves of pine and poplar. Each was a different shape and size, each was a unique personality. She had witnessed most of them being built, watched their skeletons grow, watched them flesh out as, log by log, the walls grew higher, the floors hammered down, the roofs raised up. To her, they were all special; however, only one of them would unlock the answer she needed—the one she was standing right in front of now.

Shaded by the long lazy fingers of frayed paper birch, it was a square log building, trimmed in a white as brilliant as the sun-bleached moose antlers propped up against it. A large south-facing picture window dominated the front, underscored with a wooden planter box where a few brave yellow and russet marigolds still nodded their heads in the autumn breeze. The cabin had been thoughtfully placed so as to have not only a breathtaking view of the lake below but also a panorama of every inch of the entire resort, from the flag pole on the marshy point on the far left to the fish house squatting over the water on the extreme right. Every boat that pulled up to the dock, every plane that landed on the water, and every guest that wandered the grounds could be seen from this critical vantage point, which was why her family had made this cabin their summer home.

Lori ran up the creaky wooden steps, placed her hand on the doorknob, and with a deep breath, opened the door. Inside, she stepped into what had once been their living room. There was little left to see—the room had been stripped of all its belongings—that is, except for its hats.

Hanging on every wall of the small room were hats of every description. There were striped bonnets and sequined berets, sombreros, and Stetsons. There were baseball caps, ascot caps, engineer caps. There were safari hats, fishing hats, rain hats. There were hats made of straw and wool, felt and fur, canvas, and plastic. There were hats of every size and every shape—from brand new to old and well worn—and in every colour, from emerald green to fluorescent orange to sombre black.

The hats here were no mere decoration. Each one belonged to someone who had visited the resort; each one had a life, each was an integral character with a tale to tell. Every hat here had a *reason*.

"You'll find your answers in a hat." That was the advice she had received during a tea leaf reading just a few days ago. At the time, it had made no sense, but now—perhaps among these hats that were very much part of this place, she would find the answer to what she was looking for.

Lori's eyes darted from hat to hat, coming to rest on a small, faded purple straw bonnet in the corner. Slowly she walked over to it, then reached down and lifted it off its nail and gently held it in both hands. The first time she had worn this hat, her world had seemed so big—and yet so small—

1964

Lori's small face, half-hidden by a purple straw hat, peered in amazement at the scene out the scratched, foggy window of the float plane. She could hardly believe what she was seeing—everything was so tiny! They were flying high above the trees, so high the landscape rolled out like a vast dark green carpet. Rivers, which looked like the squiggly lines she drew on an Etch a Sketch, linked the puddle-sized glimmering lakes. And every so often, a whipped cream cloud floated past the window. It was magical.

The buzz in her ears was loud, but she did not mind. It was all part of the excitement. Lori turned around to see her brother, Phil. She could barely see his blond, cropped head past the large red drums of gas. Several seats had been removed to make room for all the supplies, so while Lori was strapped in between a pile of luggage and a pail of linseed oil, seven-year-old Phil sat in the back of the plane on a carton of frozen meat. His animated face told her he, too, was enjoying the flight. Lori turned back around and continued looking out her window. More whipped cream clouds sailed by. The plane bumped and rolled like a roller coaster ride.

"Oh, Susie!" she said to the doll perched on her lap. "I wish this ride would never end!"

***

"Will this flight ever end?" moaned Lori's mother, Helen, to herself, as she glanced down at her watch. They had been in the air almost an hour; they *had to* be getting close by now. She had never been on any airplane before—never mind a bush plane—and did not like it one bit. Nervously she sat beside the pilot, her hands clasped tightly together, her face pinched and white. She stared straight ahead, not daring to take her eyes off the array of dials and buttons for fear of seeing out the window. The plane seemed too close to the sky, too far from the ground. Here the world rolled out rapidly, an endless sea of blue enveloping her. Moreover, with only a naked metal shell between her and the heavens, she was constantly aware of the frailty of the old plane. How could it still be airworthy? Especially with the ridiculous amount of cargo they had squeezed onto it? And the smell! Her nose stung as she inhaled the fumes drifting from the drums of gas lining the plane's rear.

After a few attempts to engage her in conversation, Neil Walsteen, the young pilot beside her, had given up and turned his full attention to flying the plane. For once, Helen did not feel like talking. Instead she listened to the deafening thunder of the engines, hating the sound, but at the same time praying it would not stop. She tensed at every roll, dip, and bump as the plane rock-and-rolled side to side, up and down.

Suddenly the plane plunged several feet, thrusting her stomach into her throat and causing her heart to almost pop out of her chest. Frantic, Helen looked around for something sturdy to grab onto but was scared to touch anything for fear of sending them plummeting further toward the ground.

For the umpteenth time, she turned around and checked on the kids. Both of them looked like they were having the time of their lives. *Why can't I enjoy this like they are? Maybe if I think about where I am going instead of how I am getting there.* She determinedly turned her thoughts to their destination.

Tucked away in a heavenly slice of Northwestern Ontario, Stork Lake Camp was a fly-in fishing camp designed as a backwoods getaway for rich Americans who wanted to experience Canada at its purest, untouched by roads or industry, towns, or trains. It was a place they could kick back and relax, with no phones, no television, no interruptions or hassles of daily life. And this piece of paradise had just been purchased by Helen and her husband, Al Reid.

Al was a passionate outdoorsman. Fishing was in his blood, and he had always been determined to find a way to scratch out a living doing it. So when the historic Stork Lake Camp came up for sale, he did not hesitate. Al convinced Helen they should buy the camp, sight unseen, for $28,000—every penny they had and more— much more. They'd had to swallow their pride and ask Al's dad for a loan. They'd also had to sell their home and move into a tiny, two-bedroom basement apartment. No, it had not been easy, and Helen knew money would be tight for a while longer. However it was all going to be worth it.

As a city girl, she was not looking for wilderness adventures. Her husband, however, had been so animated, so excited, so sure this was the right move, that she decided to go along with it. Al had left for the camp a month earlier and reported that it was a little rustic and needed some fixing up, but that was okay. She didn't mind painting, and she loved to decorate. After all, if rich Americans wanted to fish there, just how rough could it be? Al had also mentioned they were short staffed so she'd have to help in the kitchen, too. Though Helen had no restaurant experience, what could be simpler than serving up a few meals, clearing a few tables? She was not afraid of hard work. Cooking, cleaning, she could do all that until they got on their feet. Besides she only had to stay until September 1st, when she'd have to return to Winnipeg to get Phil ready for the school year. Two and half months—she could rough it for two and a half months.

Finally, after an eternity in the air, Neil tapped Helen on the shoulder and pointed toward the ground.

"There's the camp," he shouted over the noise of the engines.

Helen drew a deep breath and took a quick glance out the window. Visible below, a crescent-shaped sandy beach outlined a greenbelt freckled with red roofs. Neil banked the plane, then lowered the flaps on the *Norseman* and began to descend. The land tilted sickeningly up to meet them. Helen grabbed onto the door and repeatedly swallowed to regain her hearing. The plane fluttered by the shoreline, past a blur of cabins, until it came to rest on the rippling blue waves with scarcely a bump.

Three figures stood on the dock as the plane taxied slowly toward the camp. A short man with dark curly hair grabbed a strut and held the plane in place while a rubber-booted boy grabbed a rope to tie it in place. The third figure stepped onto the float and opened the freight door. He peered inside.

"There's my pussycat!"

"Daddy!"

Neil slipped to the back of the plane, released Lori's seatbelt, then lowered the little girl into her father's outstretched arms. In one fluid movement, he swung her down to the ground. The three-year-old silently stood in the middle of the dock, her purple straw bonnet framing her pale face, staring up at the husky figure of her father, which was covered in brown paint, from his brush-cut hair to his Kodiak boots.

"Hi, Dad!" Phil squeezed between the gas drums and made his way to the doorway. He eagerly climbed down, jumped onto the plane's float, and hopped onto the dock.

"Well look at you!" Al grinned ear to ear. "I think you've grown since I saw you last!" He reached down and gave him a big hug.

"That was *so* cool! I loved the plane ride, all except having to sit on that freezing box. My bum's kinda cold."

Al laughed. "So you enjoyed it, eh?"

"Sure did!" Phil looked around, seemingly oblivious to his father's paint-splotched appearance. "Wow, Dad, I didn't know this place was going to be so cool! Look at all the cabins. Which one is ours? And look at all the neato-looking boats! Will you take me fishing?"

"Slow down! Yes, we'll go fishing, but first, I've got to get your mom onto this dock! Then I'll show you around."

By this time, a white-faced Helen was slowly negotiating the steps down to the float. Clad in a streamlined shift and open-toed white leather sandals, this was none too easy a task. She stood on the dock for a moment, her ears buzzing and her body still shaking from the plane's vibration. Finally she looked up at the paint-coated man in front of her.

"Am I glad to see you!"

"I'm so happy to see you too, honey!" Al leaned over and kissed his wife. "Enjoy your flight? It's really something, isn't it? An amazing feeling of freedom. I can hardly wait to get my pilot's licence so we can take off whenever we want." Al did not wait for Helen's response to this news; instead he turned to introduce her to the man standing beside him. "This is Albert Vanasse, my right-hand man. I couldn't run the place without him."

"Welcome to Stork Lake!" Albert reached out and pumped Helen's hand hardily with his grease-stained one.

"Thank you," Helen answered, vaguely wondering how the cigarette stuck to his lip through his enormous grin.

"And this is my son, Roger."

A curly-haired boy smiled up at her. "Pleased to meet you, Mrs. Reid."

"Oh yes, pleased to meet you too, dear."

"We've got to get this plane unloaded," said Al. "Why don't you take the kids off to one side. We don't want you getting run over by a gas drum."

Albert and Al dragged a wooden ramp up to the freight door. Neil shifted a barrel of gas on its side, and the three men manoeuvred it down the ramp. Once on the dock, Roger helped Albert roll it past Helen and onto the shore.

"I wish I could help!" said Phil, watching them.

"I wish I could play!" said Lori, gazing at the beach.

"I wish I could go home!" cried Helen, as her stomach settled and she became aware of her beleaguered surroundings.

A handful of pitiful log cabins with peeling red paint lined the lakefront. Only one cabin, perched on top of a small hill, had a coat of fresh brown paint, the same colour that now covered her husband. Old flat-bottomed wood boats, all sporting the same blistering paint as the cabins, were tied up to a second dock that gradually sagged until its end disappeared into the lake. A mud pathway cut a brave trail through overgrown grass and past a sorry-looking garden choked with weeds. Parked beside the weeds was a rusty tractor, a battered wooden cart hitched to it. On a long sawhorse, several old Evinrude outboards hung in various states of disrepair.

This was paradise? This was where rich Americans came to spend their holidays? *This* was what they had spent their life savings on? Where were the meandering stone pathways or the cozy cottages with flowers blooming in the planters? Where were the shiny aluminum boats, the cedar-planked docks? As scared as Helen had been of the plane ride, this place terrified her more. She felt a knock in her heart when she thought of all they had done to get here, and "here" was in the middle of nowhere. She did not just wish she was home—she was going home!

Al dropped a couple of suitcases onto the shore and started back up the dock. As he passed Helen, he smiled and, with a grand gesture, said, "Well, what do you think? It's all ours!" His voice glowed with pride of ownership.

Helen stuffed her purse under her arm, grabbed her children's hands, and then walked right up to Al, nose to paint-spattered nose. In a quiet, steely voice, she said, "What the hell have you done?"

Al looked confused. "What do you mean?"

"I'm taking the children and going home. Kids, come on." She turned toward the plane. She would rather brave another hour in that tin can on wings than stay here a minute longer.

Al chased after her. "Wait a second! What's going on?"

"I'm getting on that plane and going back to Winnipeg!"

"Helen, what are you talking about? You just got here!"

"And I'm just leaving! I can't believe you! We paid $28,000 for this?" Helen's voice rose louder and louder. "We sold our house for this? We borrowed money from your dad! We're in debt up to our necks . . . for *this*?"

Phil had a confused look on his face. Al placed a hand on his golden head. "Now let's all settle down. Roger, will you take Phil and show him where to put the luggage?"

"Sure thing, Al." Roger picked up a couple bags and nodded to Phil. "Follow me."

Phil quickly trotted off after him, apparently relieved to be saved from the erupting war front.

Al turned back to Helen. "Now Helen, for God's sake! You can't go back! Elsie, the cook . . . she needs your help. She's doing laundry, setting tables, serving the guests their dinner."

"I thought there was a waitress here?"

"There's Agnes. But she won't wait on the guests."

"A waitress that won't wait on guests?"

"She's shy."

Helen could not believe what she was hearing.

Al continued. "We've already got our first group of the year in, all big shots working for a company called Twin Disc from Racine, Wisconsin. They got in last night. If we treat them right, they plan to bring twelve more guys up fishing this year and another ten guys moose hunting in the fall. This one group alone could keep us open! But we can't do it without your help."

"I don't care if we stay open. I did *not* sign up for this!"

"Helen, please. You're overreacting."

"Don't tell me I'm overreacting!"

"You knew it needed fixing up."

"This place doesn't need fixing up. It needs tearing down!"

"You can't judge the place just by standing on the dock. You haven't seen the lodge, the inside of the cabins. You haven't met the staff or talked to any guests. And believe me, if you talked to the guests, you'd see we have something here, something special. That"—he pointed to the weathered cabins—"is all cosmetic. We can fix all that. What this place has is soul, and that can't be bought with any amount of money."

She still looked unconvinced.

"Helen, it's too late to turn back now. You said so yourself. Every dime we have is invested in this place. We *have* to make a go of it. Do you understand? If we quit now, we'll have nothing. If we forge ahead, we just might have the chance of making a good life for ourselves. You want that, don't you?"

"Of course."

"Well then, let's give it a shot. Let's not fail because we quit. Please, will you stay?"

Helen looked down and, in a deceptively quiet voice, answered, "I'll stay. But I don't know if I'll ever forgive you."

Meanwhile Albert and Neil had finished unloading the plane, all the while pretending not to notice the argument going on.

"Neil, want to come get a cup of coffee before you take off?"

The pilot shook his head. "Not today, Al, thanks anyways. I've got to get back." He jumped into the cockpit.

Helen sorrowfully watched her last chance to escape taxi away. *Great, I'm stuck here now. I'm stuck in a dilapidated old camp in the wilds of Ontario. What am I going to do?*

Helen's stomach started turning again, but this time it was not from the flight.

"Come on, Helen. I'll show you the lodge and introduce you to Elsie," said Al.

"What about Phil?"

"Don't worry about him. He's with Roger."

"Yes but he's only seven and—"

"Where's he going to go? This isn't the city. There aren't any strangers, and there isn't any traffic."

***

Lori was oblivious to the tension around her. She clutched Susie in one hand and her dad's hand in the other as she skipped along, jumping over the occasional mud puddle. There was so much to see. She loved this place! The path wandered past quaint cabins that looked like the ones in her fairy tale book. All around were trees, some tall and lacy, some all green and pointy, like Christmas trees. It was so open, so bright. What a change from the busy, crowded street their stuffy apartment overlooked!

They continued to wind around several more buildings before they arrived at the main lodge, sweet wood smoke billowing out of its stone chimney. Al opened the squeaky screened door and ushered them inside. Lori gazed around in wonder. Cheerful blankets with square and diamond designs covered the comfy couches scattered around the room, and several funny-shaped tables with green felt tops were set up with cards. In the centre of the room, a fluffy black bearskin rug lay at the foot of a shimmering granite fireplace. Lori looked up. Hanging on all four burnished log walls were the biggest toy fish she had ever seen, complete with glowing eyes and an arsenal of teeth. They were both terrifying and fabulous.

They passed through double doors into the dining area. Large windows ensconced both ends. In fact, windows offered a kaleidoscope of views of the sparkling lake from every room of the lodge, and Lori felt like the indoors was part of the outdoors. The trio stepped toward the adjacent staff room and kitchen. The wide windows here showed a shoreline of tall reeds and bulrushes fronting a tranquil bay, where one tiny island, like a precious pearl, sat squarely in the middle.

The jumbly little kitchen was warm and cozy—and smelled wonderful. Lori had never seen a real wood cookstove before. It sat in the corner, gentle breezes entering through the screen windows stirring up its delicious aromas. In the centre of the kitchen was a funny wood table with a hole in the middle of it. Long shelves of organized chaos stored an array of interesting dishes, pots, pans, bowls, and cooking utensils. Awestruck, Lori decided this was the most fantastical place she had ever seen.

***

Helen had quietly walked beside Al as he showed her through the rooms, barely listening as he droned on and on about the furniture, the mounted fish, the equipment. It was all rubbish to her. She now stood looking at the cluttered shelves lining the kitchen walls, bowed in the middle under the weight of the dishes. A row of mugs that had seen better days hung on a line of hooks. She stared at the bare bulbs with their tin pie pan reflectors hanging from the ceiling; she gazed at the boxes stacked in the rafters and the confusion of dry goods piled on the floor. A huge butcher-block table dominated the room, leaving barely enough room around its perimeter for two people to pass. A pinwheel-sized fan hanging from a nail valiantly spun above the sink but was no match for the old wood stove that glowered in the corner like an angry dragon. She was speechless. How on earth could you cook for guests in a tiny, hot kitchen like this?

Obviously someone could. Hovering over several large pots perched on top of the stove was a short, dark-haired woman in her mid-fifties, a white apron wrapped around her ample belly.

"And here's the heart of the camp! Helen, I want you to meet Elsie, our cook and Albert's wife."

"Helen! I've been waiting to meet you. Al's talked a lot about you."

Elsie hobbled over and extended her hand and a smile so wide that her eyes disappeared into the folds of her crinkled cheeks. For the first time that day, Helen saw something she liked.

"Elsie, hello. So glad to meet you. And this is my daughter, Lori."

"Hello there! Aren't you cute! Look just like a little version of your mom."

Helen said, "I hear you've been almost running this place by yourself."

Elsie gave a little cackle reminiscent of a crow. "Oh, it's not been so bad."

"Don't let her try and fool you," said Al. "She's been run off her feet. The woman never stops working."

"I hope I can take some of the load off." Helen looked meaningfully at her husband. "I'm here to help."

"That'll be good then," said Elsie agreeably.

Just then, Phil came running in the back door with Roger. "Dad! Roger says I can help him do his chores!"

"This must be your boy."

"Sure is," said Al, his voice full of pride. "This here's Phil. Phil, this is Roger's mom, Elsie."

"Hi," Phil absently replied before he turned back to his dad. "Roger says—"

"Yes, yes, Roger says you can be his helper. Sounds like a good idea."

"I don't know, Al. Maybe he should stay with me," said Helen.

Al turned to his wife. "He'll be fine. Besides, Roger probably really could use the help. Look, I know it's not much of an introduction to the place, but I really should get back to work. I need to finish getting that cabin painted before supper. And Elsie *really* needs some help right away. It's been raining for days. That means there's a backlog of laundry. If some washing doesn't get done, there'll be no clean linens for the guests tomorrow. I promise I'll show you around the whole camp later."

Helen looked down at her crisp shift and dainty sandals. "Can't I get changed first?"

"You look fine," he answered absently. "You'll be all right here now?"

"I guess."

"Good. Elsie will get you started."

Al smiled down at his small daughter. "See you in a while, pussycat." He nodded to the boys. "Come on. We've work to do!" And with that, the three of them were gone.

Deserted, Helen looked around. "Elsie, isn't there another girl helping here?"

"Agnes? Yes, she's cleaning the guest cabins right now. You'll meet her at lunch."

"You'll have to excuse me, Elsie. I'm usually not so scattered. This place has been such a shock for me. I'm not sure what I expected, just something more than this."

"Oh? How so?"

"More modern, more . . . I don't know, just more. I think I'm a little out of my element. I don't even know where to start."

As she spoke, Helen plopped her purse on top of the butcher-block table.

"Well I'd start by moving your purse."

Helen grabbed the purse back up off the table. "I'm sorry, is it in your way?"

"Nope. It's just a purse on the table means you'll have a disappointment."

"What? Is that an old wives' tale?"

"Nope. That's just the way it is."

Helen thought of the dingy cabins, the sinking docks, the outdated kitchen and couldn't possibly imagine being any more disappointed. However, she turned to Elsie with a bright face and said, "So I should tackle the washing first? Where are the laundry facilities?"

"I'll show you." Elsie led Helen and Lori through the back door to a washstand outside with a wooden floor and a rickety roof. On it was an old wringer machine, two washtubs, and a mountain of dirty linen.

Helen was incredulous. "You do all the laundry *here*? And with this machine? It looks just like my mother's old gas washer, the one we used back in the thirties!"

"So you know how to use it?"

"I suppose so."

"I'll leave it to you then."

Helen turned to the huge pile of sheets on the washstand.

"Lori, stay nearby where I can see you. You can watch me do the laundry with this funny old machine." Helen filled the tubs with water then stepped on the kick-starter. In a puff of blue smoke, the washer started with a roar as loud as any motorcycle. She jumped back a step. "Oh my goodness! Now Lori, don't be afraid. The machine is just a little noisy when you first start it."

Actually Lori didn't look the least bit afraid. Rather it looked like she was enjoying the whole experience. The fact that the rackety machine was outside—in the sunshine—made it even more fun. She sat on the edge of the washstand, holding her doll, and watched as her mom fed sheets through the wringer.

"Okay now, you just stay right here while I get these sheets hung." Helen grabbed the bucket of clothes pegs and started to hang sheets, but the long lines sagged under the weight. It was getting hot by now, and Helen was frustrated. More than one sheet ended up on the muddy ground and had to be re-washed before she figured out how to adjust the wooden poles to better hold up the lines.

Eventually all the sheets were washed and flapping in the breeze blowing off the lake. Helen emptied the tubs, the soapy water forming rivers of bubbles as it ran out onto the grass.

She stood back, hands on her hips, satisfied with her morning's work. "I think we're finally finished." She then surveyed the large water stain on her shift, her muddy legs, and grass-stained white sandals. "But I'm a mess, aren't I, Lori. *Lori?*"

Helen looked around. Susie, the doll, lay on the washstand, unattended. The purple straw bonnet lay on the grass a few feet away. Helen felt a stab of fear. Where had she got to?

"Lori! Answer me!" As her fear increased, so did the volume of her voice. "Loori, where are yooou?"

"I'm here!" came a muffled reply. She ran around to the front of the washstand but still could not see her.

"Where are you?"

"I'm up here."

"Where up here?" Helen ran around to the side. There was Lori, crawling on top of the six-foot woodpile in the woodshed, which was attached to the washstand.

"What are you doing up there?"

"Climbing."

"You can't climb up there! The wood could all topple over on you! Come down off there right now."

"But Mommy, it's my playhouse! It has a roof, rooms, and stairs. And from up here, I can see everything, even squirrels."

"I said get down right now! It's dangerous."

Lori slowly climbed down her firewood 'stairs,' her defiant look giving Helen the feeling the little girl would climb back up as soon as she had the chance.

"We're done!" said Helen with false bravado as she entered the kitchen with Lori in tow.

"Good! Just in time for lunch." Elsie, who was standing at the butcher block, was busy compiling sandwiches while a slim Ojibwa woman plated them. "This here's Agnes."

"Hi." The voice was so soft, the word cut so short, Helen almost didn't catch it. Agnes did not look at them but kept her dark glossy head bent down, continuing to work.

"I'm happy to meet you, Agnes."

Elsie slapped the top on the last sandwich. "Done just in time. The guys will be here any moment. Why don't you sit? Agnes'll bring you both some soup."

"My goodness, you don't have to wait on us! I'm supposed to be helping."

"It's okay. It's your first day. You sit."

"Okay maybe just today." Thankful to get off her feet, Helen led Lori into the staff dining room just as the door opened and the men filed in.

"Mom!" Phil's face was beaming. "This place is so cool! There's a garbage pit where the bear eats, and a mill where they make wood . . . well, I mean logs from wood. And there's a fish house where they cut the fish all up! Roger says he'll teach me how to do it."

Helen looked up at her husband, who had by now scrubbed off a good portion of the brown paint. Her brow furrowed. "Fillet fish? Al!"

"He's okay. He's just excited. Son, I don't think you're ready to be filleting fish just yet. Maybe you ought to just watch Roger for now."

Phil continued. "Anyways, then they throw all the fish guts into this big tub and take them out in the fish gut boat across the lake and dump them at a place called Fish Gut Island."

"What an appropriate name."

"Roger says the seagulls know every night when you're comin' and wait there. As soon as you leave the island, they swoop down and eat 'em all up before the boat even gets back to camp! He says he'll take me with him when he does his dump tonight."

"I suppose that will be okay, as long as you wear your life jacket."

"Life jacket! Mom, no one wears a life jacket here! Everyone sits on cushions that float."

"You're not everyone. You can't go unless you wear a life jacket. Now why don't we all sit down and have some lunch?"

Once they were settled on the wood benches around the long table, Agnes served them. She moved between them like a whisper, placing brimming bowls of thick ham and pea soup in front of each person. On either end of the table, she placed the heaping platters of thick chicken sandwiches made with Elsie's homemade bread. Helen thought it a shame she was too shy to serve the guests; she obviously made an excellent waitress.

"So what do you think so far?" Al asked Helen as he stirred some sugar into his tea.

"I honestly don't know how Elsie and Agnes have been keeping up with all the work. I've only been here a few hours, and I'm already overwhelmed."

"You've never seen a staff like this. Take Albert here. He's not only the head guide. He's also the chief mechanic, engineer, and building contractor. He keeps the place running on spare parts and shoestrings. If we don't have the right part, he makes one. He is always finding a newer, better way of doing things. And Agnes's husband James . . . he's the best guide in Northwestern Ontario for both hunting and fishing. Guests love him! No, there'd be no Stork Lake without this staff."

"Wow. Al is lucky he found all of you."

"He didn't find us. He inherited us. We came with the camp. Don't suppose he had much choice," said Albert, wrapping his fingers around his sandwich and taking a big bite.

"Thank God I did." Al shook his head. "I couldn't afford to hire the number of people it would take to do all the work you do."

"And Roger? What do you do? Besides help unload planes and dump fish guts?"

"Cut grass, take out the garbage, chop and pile wood." Roger grinned. "And anything else you want me to do, Mrs. Reid."

"Call me Helen." This one was going to be a charmer.

Al smiled at the young boy. "Roger's our camp boy, but I bet by next year, he'll be old enough to go out guiding. Won't you, bud?"

"You bet! I can hardly wait!"

Helen was taken aback. "Goodness, won't you still be a little young to have such responsibility?"

"I'm already 12! My brother Joe has been guiding here since he was barely 14."

"The kids've been fishing since theys was old enough to hold a rod," said Albert. "They knows this lake and where the fish are hidin' better 'en many of them older guides."

Helen turned to Elsie. "What do you think about it, Elsie? Doesn't having your boy out in a boat guiding all day worry you?"

"Not much use worrying about it. Won't change anything."

Helen anxiously thought of her own young son. What was wrong with these people? There was no way Phil was going to guide at fourteen! She decided to change the subject. "So you just have the two children?"

"Gracious no, we got nine!" laughed Elsie. "Roger is the youngest. Rest are pretty much grow'd up and married off. And we got a whole load of grandkids."

"Goodness! What a large family! No wonder nothing fazes you!" Helen turned to Agnes. "How about you, Agnes? Do you have any children?"

Agnes had wordlessly sat in the corner all during lunch, nibbling on her sandwich, washing each tiny bite down with a sip of tea. With the mention of her name, she suddenly looked up and saw Helen watching her. Her cheeks turned red, and her eyes quickly fell back down to her plate.

"Yep."

"How many?"

"Just one boy."

"What's his name?"

"Lawrence."

"How old is he?"

"Four."

"And where is he now?"

"In town. With his grandparents."

"You must miss him during the summer."

"Yep."

Even Helen, who was never at a loss for words, found it difficult to pull conversation out of this sweet, shy creature. She was saved from wondering what to say next by the appearance of Elsie, who had disappeared into the kitchen a moment earlier and now returned holding a meringue-domed lemon pie. She cut each of them a large slab, then sat down and lifted her leg, resting it on the bench. Near the ankle was a large, angry-looking varicose vein.

"How in the world have you been keeping up with all the work with that sore-looking leg? I'm having a hard time with two good legs."

"Oh, you just do. As for the bad leg, well, I'm used to it. Always had one. Was born with a bad hip, which makes one of my legs shorter than the other. That's why I hibble-hobble! This"— Elsie pointed to the black-and-blue roadmap of veins—"this is sometimes annoying, but it's not so bad."

Albert stood up. "Well enough of this chitchat. I got work to do."

"And I've got to unpack and get my kids down for a nap," said Helen.

"I don't need a nap," piped up Phil. "I'm helping Roger."

"You need a nap. You've been up since five."

"Listen to your mom, son." Al stood up, too. "Come on. I'll show you where we are staying."

Al led them into a building overlooking the docks. Built into the side of the hill, the cabin had a dark and damp interior, even on this sunny day. The black linoleum floor was ripped in places, showing the cement floor underneath. In front of the tiny window, a piece of plywood, sitting on two workhorses, served as a desk—at least, that was where a large stack of bills, a stapler, and a couple of pens sat.

The back wall displayed a mad confection of goods. On one side, hanging from a pegboard, was everything a fisherman needed for a day on the lake: sinkers, swivels, and leaders, plus an amazing array of brightly coloured fishing lures of every size. On the other side of the back wall, battered shelves held the rest of the goods needed for a day on the lake: chocolate bars, potato chips, packs of cigarettes, and cans of snuff. On the floor were cases of beer stacked almost to the ceiling. A faded brown-and-black striped sofa chair with broken springs sat in the corner. A corner bookshelf jammed with ancient *Reader's Digest* and *Popular Mechanics* magazines completed the room.

Al led Helen past the shelves of wares and through a dusty purple curtain to a small, breathless backroom. Here the floor wasn't even concrete, just mud. All the luggage Helen had brought with her was piled on a double bed, which was pushed against one wall. Two military cots curled up under a cobweb-lined window. A bare light bulb hung on a cord from the ceiling. That was it—there was nothing else—there was no room for anything else.

Helen was aghast. "You've got to be kidding. *This* is our cabin?" For the umpteenth time that day, Helen's voice rose to operatic proportions. "I'm *not* staying here."

Al scratched his head. "Phil, take your sister outside."

"But Mom said we had to have a nap."

"In a minute. Just take Lori out for a minute, and then you can come back in and take your nap."

"I thought you said we had a nice cabin. With bedrooms," said Helen, once the children were out of earshot.

"But I got chance to rent it out. It's the best cabin, and the guests like it because it has a bathroom—"

"I like a bathroom, too! What are we supposed to use?"

"There's an outhouse just up the hill."

"That'll be convenient in the middle of the night."

"There's a chamber pot under the bed. I keep the toilet paper up here on this nail so the mice don't chew it."

Helen could not believe what she was hearing. "What about showering? If you want me to wait on guests, I'm going to need one before dinner. Do I have to share that, too?"

"You will have to share. There is only one shower in camp."

"One shower? For *everyone*?"

"Yes. And you can't use it before dinner, not unless you want a cold one. There won't be any hot water at this time of day. The water for the shower is heated by the wood stove, and you will have used it all doing the laundry and dishes. Fact is, there is usually only enough hot water for a couple of showers a day, so most everybody just rinses off in the lake."

Helen shuddered. "I'm not bathing in a cold lake. I like a nice warm shower. When is my best chance of getting one?"

"After work, if no one else uses it."

Phil peeked in the doorway. "If we're not going to nap, maybe I could go help Roger—"

Helen snapped, "You'll do no such thing. You come in right now and bring your sister. In fact, I think we could all use a nap!"

***

Helen and Lori arrived back at the kitchen at five o'clock on the dot. She plunked the little girl on a stool, then turned to Elsie. "So what can I do?"

"Just get the tables ready for dinner. Agnes'll show you."

A few minutes later, Roger and Phil appeared. "Mom! We brought ice."

"Oh good. I was just about to get the water pitchers ready," Helen said, then peered into the bucket. "Why, this ice is dirty!"

"It's not dirt, Mom. It's sawdust. We got most of it off."

Helen was almost afraid to ask. "Why is there sawdust on the ice?"

"It's from the icehouse! Mom, it's so cool! They cut the ice off the lake in the winter, and then they stick it in big chunks in the icehouse. Can I help Dad and Albert cut ice this winter?"

"No." Helen then repeated her question, "So why is there sawdust on the ice?"

"They cover the ice up in sawdust from the sawmill so it stays cold. Every night, Roger takes a piece out, wheelbarrows it to the end of the dock, and dunks it in the lake with these big tongues—"

"You mean tongs," said Helen patiently.

"Tongs—and washes the sawdust off. Then he puts it back in the wheelbarrow and chips it all up with an ice pick. I helped. Then we got the wheelbarrow up the hill to every guest cabin and gave them ice." Phil looked quite proud of himself.

"I don't want you using an ice pick. You'll end up stabbing yourself! Roger's a lot older than you so he can do these things."

Seemingly oblivious to her comments, Phil continued. "Now we're going to go down to the docks and watch all the fishermen come back in. Roger says every night they bring in boatloads full of fish, some as big as me! There have to be more fish here than anywhere else in the whole world! I can hardly wait till I catch a muskie!" Then to make sure his mother understood, he added, "That's one of the big fish 'round here."

"I don't know if you should be in the guests' way—"

"I won't be in their way. I'm going to *help* them. Roger says you can get tips for helping them unload their boats. Mom," he said seriously, "they need me."

"I suppose. But when Roger comes for dinner, you come with him. Which reminds me," Helen turned to Elsie, "how does everyone know when dinner is ready? Is there a set time?"

"Not really. When we're ready, we ring the gong for the guides to come. And about half an hour later, we ring it again for the guests to come. Us girls try to squeeze in a meal between serving the guides and the guests."

"When does Al eat?"

Elsie giggled. "Whenever he can. Sometimes it takes him all night to finish his supper. He's always being called away for some reason or another."

Helen had just finished setting up the tables for dinner when Agnes slipped outside to ring the dinner gong. Almost immediately, the guides began to file into the staff dining room, chatting easily with each other as they settled into their spots around the table. Phil marched in with Roger and another teenage boy and squeezed in at the table between them. Helen peered around the kitchen corner at the sea of bronzed faces as Agnes began serving them dinner. Albert, noticing her curiosity, waved her in. "Come! Meet the boys! Across the back, them's Eddie, Charlie, Tommy, and Peepsight, that's Johnny at the head, and over on this side, there beside Phil is our other son, Joe. This here's Al's wife."

A couple of the white guides smiled and mumbled hellos. However the Native guides kept their heads down—except the last one, who had just walked through the door. He was a striking man in his late twenties with wavy black hair, twinkling chocolate-brown eyes, and a huge white smile. He was wearing a beautiful moose hide jacket embellished with intricate beadwork.

"Hello, Boss Lady!" he said, giving her hand a firm shake. "I'm James."

"You must be Agnes's husband! Glad to meet you, James. Just call me Helen."

"Okay, Boss Lady." His big deep laugh resonated through the room. He turned and took his place at the table.

Staff fare was usually a home-cooked soup followed by something simple but wholesome. Tonight Elsie served up savoury stick-to-the-ribs stew and mountains of thistle downy dumplings. For dessert, cereal bowls full of crumbly apple crisp, fragrant with cinnamon and nutmeg, were washed down with several pots of tea. Helen stood beside Elsie in awe. "They eat that much every night?"

"You bet! A day out in the fresh air makes a man hungry! And if you think that's a lot, wait till you see how the guests fill up."

Helen was aghast. "We'll go broke!"

"Eh?"

"We'll go broke serving so much food!"

Elsie laughed. "Don't worry! I know how to stretch a dollar."

Helen prayed she was right.

***

"Why aren't they coming?" Helen asked. "It's been twenty minutes since Agnes banged that gong thing for the guests to come. Maybe they didn't hear it. Should we bang it again?"

The guide table was now empty. Phil had disappeared with Roger for his ride to Fish Gut Island, and Al, having finally found time to squeeze in his supper, took Lori back to their "cabin" to put her to bed.

Elsie, who had been comfortably snoozing at the table with her hands resting on her round belly, slowly opened her eyes. "Could . . . don't figure it'll do much good though. They'll be buzzing from a day of fishin' and several bottles of scotch. I don't think they'll pay much attention to the gong. Best to just let them come when they will."

Helen was astounded. "How can you stand this waiting? Aren't you worried your supper will be ruined?"

"Things either go right or they go wrong. No use worrying about it, is there, Agnes?"

"Nope," Agnes answered without looking up from the necklace she was patiently beading.

"Well I can't just sit here!" Helen jumped up, grabbed a flyswatter, and headed back into the dining room to swat at the flies that, contrary to the guests, had all too happily already arrived for their meal.

It was another half hour before the guests moseyed down to the dining room, most with a cocktail in hand. The slightly intoxicated men were as sunburnt and merry as sailors on leave. When they had each found a chair, Helen smoothed the front of her shift, put on a bright smile, and then froze. She had never waited on tables before and suddenly understood why Agnes would not. While Helen was not the least bit shy, she was not at all sure of her serving skills. She stood for a moment, staring at the twelve fishermen, and then in a high-pitched voice loud enough to instantly quiet the crowd, she shrieked, "Hello everyone. I'm Helen, and I will be your waitress tonight!"

There was a moment's silence, and then, in a booming voice almost as loud as Helen's, a man resembling Clark Gable answered. "Hello there! I'm Jack Yetter, and we're thrilled you're our waitress tonight!"

Helen had worried for nothing. Every morsel was complimented on and devoured. They raved about the soup and the Red River bread. They loved the roast and the roasted potatoes, both smoky from the wood stove. But most of all, they loved Helen. She filled their glasses and served their food, smiled and kibitzed with them— even when she muddled their names, mixed up their soup orders, and forgot to get one gentleman his dessert.

Finally dinner was over, and the guests exited to find their way back up the hill and to the right cabin. Jack was the last to leave. As he stepped through the door, he plucked the stogie out of his mouth and turned around to Helen. "You know, I don't think I've ever enjoyed a day more. I'm so glad we found this place. It's a real treasure!"

Helen gave him one of her bright smiles, waited for the door to close, then turned to the kitchen, where Agnes and Elsie were still attacking the stacks of dirty dishes and pots. "Oh yeah, it's a treasure, all right!"

It was almost another hour before the tables were cleared and reset, the dishes done. Helen knelt down to sweep up the last crumbs off the kitchen floor. Her back winced as she straightened. "My goodness! I don't think I have a muscle in my whole body that isn't screaming at me. I can't remember living through a longer day. Is it always like this?"

Elsie untied her apron. "Pretty much. You get used to it." As she headed to the door, she asked, "Need help to your cabin?"

"That's all right, Elsie. I'd like to shower first. Can you tell me where it is?"

"Just walk out this here door and turn right, and right again. You can't miss it. Good night." And with that, Agnes and Elsie disappeared into the night.

Helen grabbed a towel from the laundry room and tiredly picked her way over to the shower stall. She was just about to enter when James threw open the door, his wet black hair slicked down and clean face gleaming as bright as his smile.

"Night, Boss Lady."

"Night, James."

She entered the tiny cubicle and turned on the taps. They both ran cold. The stove had cooled down for the night. There would be no more hot water until the next day.

All the washing I've done today, and I'm still dirty. I guess I'm bathing in the lake after all!

Helen made her way to the lakeshore to wash off her feet. Sitting down on the dock, she slipped off her sandals and dipped her feet into the cool water. It was near 10:00 p.m., yet the day had not surrendered to the night; the tints of twilight lingered around the edges, staining the horizon a warm golden patina. The whole camp was still, but she could see a couple of twinkling lights coming from the guest cabins up on the hill. There wasn't a sound except the gentle lapping of the waves, the soft movements of the wooden boats rubbing against the dock.

How was she going to last up here until September? One day and she already felt beaten. She leaned over, scooped up a cupful of water in her hands, and tried to scrub off her makeup, rubbing the rest off with the towel. When she was done, she gazed down at the faded towel with the ragged hem. Was there nothing here worth anything?

She did not notice the riches around her—the deep sapphire sky, the liquid gold lake, the silvery birches lining the shore—her vision obscured by fear.

When Helen returned to their small room, Phil and Lori were fast asleep in their little army cots. Al, already in his nightshirt, sat up in bed.

"Better hurry and get into bed before Albert shuts the generator down."

"Why would he want to do that?" asked Helen, as she slipped off her clothes and into her frothy nightgown. She then sat on the edge of the bed, grabbed the roll of toilet paper off its nail, and wound the tissue around her elaborate bouffant hairdo to preserve it for the next day.

"It costs too much to keep the generator running all night when no one needs any power, so we shut her down around 10:00 p.m." No sooner were the words out of his mouth when the lights suddenly blinked out, and the room was flooded in darkness. Helen crawled into bed, punched her flat little pillow, and pulled up the covers. She was so glad this day was over; she just wanted to get some sleep.

But she couldn't. There was this smell—

Helen lifted her head off her pillow. "What's that rotten smell? It's not me. I just washed my feet! Al, is that your feet?"

Al had no sense of smell, so he had no idea what she was talking about.

"Just go to sleep."

"I can't!"

Helen began sniffing around. She followed her nose until it led her to the log wall, right beside her head. The moonlight sneaking in between the cracks in the drapes illuminated a healthy crop of mould and mushrooms growing there. Helen shivered. First thing in the morning, she would attack them both with a bottle of bleach.

She had finally fallen asleep when a rustling near her head wakened her. No sound—not that she could have heard anything over Al's deep snores—just a quiet movement. Her eyes popped open. The movement was not near her head; it was in her hair. She reached a hand up to touch her 'do and saw something scurry away in the dark. Like a bolt, she sat straight up and furiously shook Al's shoulder.

"Al! Wake up! There's something scurrying around! It was in my hair!"

Al rolled over. "It's just a mole, wanting that toilet paper on your hair for its nest."

"*Agh!*" Helen ripped off the toilet paper, shook her head violently, and savagely ran her fingers through her hair. She lay back down but did not go to sleep.

***

The sun was already peeking above the horizon when a tired Helen, her flat hair pulled back in a stretchy white hair band, entered the kitchen the next morning. She found Agnes and Elsie already busy at work.

"Morning Helen! Did you have a good sleep?" asked Elsie.

"Fine." Helen was in no mood to get into details. "So how can I help?"

Elsie scratched her chin. "I got everything ready except maybe . . . feel like getting started on the toast? Them guides will be coming any minute."

"That sounds easy enough. Where's the toaster?"

"There's no toaster. You toast the bread on a grill on the stove."

"Oh boy," groaned Helen.

"Look." Elsie lifted the round lid off the top of the stove and placed a grill over it.

"See? Now you just put the bread on top."

Helen reached for a thick slab of homemade bread and gingerly placed it in the centre of the grill.

"Now just wait a minute, then flip it."

"That's not so bad." Helen took one peek. Satisfied, she reached for a cup and poured a coffee out of the blackened kettle, then took a pair of tongs and flipped the bread. Four black strips stared up at her.

Elsie looked over her shoulder and chuckled. "I told you it just took a minute. It's quicker than a toaster. You have to learn how to boss the stove. Left to right. Left side of the stove is high heat, the middle is medium, the right is low. Right now, you're cooking on high. It's kinda like cooking out over an open fire. Done much camping?"

"None. Believe it or not, Elsie, I'm not much for roughing it."

Several more slices were blackened, and two fingers burned before Helen finished grilling her way through the guides' breakfast.

"Wow!" Helen mopped the sweat from her brow. "That's hot work. I'm soaking wet, and we haven't even fed the guests yet. Do you think they will be as late for breakfast as they were for dinner last night?"

"No chance of that!" said Elsie. "Them's guys want to get fishing as early as possible."

And sure enough, not two minutes after the gong was rung, guests were filing in the door—and so was Al.

"What are you doing here?" said Helen. "I thought you were going to watch the children until after I served breakfast!"

"Don't worry. I told Phil to watch Lori. I can't stay in the cabin all morning. I've got eggs to cook." Al slipped his jacket off.

Astounded, Helen pulled him to the side. "Eggs to cook? Why do you have to cook the eggs?"

"Because Elsie can't."

"A cook that can't cook eggs? That's ridiculous! I watched her cook eggs for the guides!"

"She just scrambles a big batch for them. It's when the guests order them a specific way that she has problems." Al rolled up his sleeves and strode over to the stove.

A specific way. Helen stood there frozen, suddenly realizing she was going to have to remember egg orders! Supper had been difficult enough, and all she'd had to remember was who wanted soup and who didn't. How could she possibly remember twelve different egg orders?

"Dammit," she murmured under her breath. She pasted on a smile and approached the guest table.

"Good morning! How did everyone sleep?"

"Like a baby. All the great fresh air yesterday . . . I was asleep before my head hit the pillow," replied Jack. Helen assumed he had not had any moles dancing around in his hair.

"We've eggs on the menu this morning. How would everyone like them?"

"I'll have mine scrambled."

"Easy over."

"Basted."

The orders came flying at her.

"Okay, you wanted sunny-side up—"

"No, scrambled."

"And you wanted yours easy over—"

"No, poached."

Helen grew more and more agitated. She would never get it right! Noticing her discomfort, Jack laid a hand on Helen's arm.

"Look, honey, don't worry about it! Just give us all one up and one over!"

Breakfast was barely over when Elsie approached Helen.

"What do you want to serve for supper tonight?"

"Supper? It never ends, does it?" One meal seemed to blur into another. "What were you thinking of?"

"I seen some pork chops in that box of meat that came in with you yesterday. It's in the fridge there."

"I didn't know we had a fridge! I thought there was just that old icebox." Pleased she had one modern convenience, Helen opened the propane fridge and pulled out a brown paper package.

"This meat's still frozen!"

"Oh, that's because the fridge is a freezer. Albert converted it."

"Oh boy." Helen banged a knife on the side of the rock-hard package. "Maybe we should take the meat out at night. This might not be thawed by the time we have to cook it."

Elsie nodded her head. "We could do that."

"Now I better go get my kids. Phil is staying with Lori until I am ready to get them. I'm sure he's getting antsy by now."

Helen returned to her room to wake up Phil and Lori. Neither of them was in their beds.

"Phil? Loooori? Where are yoooou?"

She ran to the dock. There stood Phil beside Roger, watching the boats full of guests leave for the day's fishing.

"Phil!"

He could not hear her over the roar of the outboards.

"Phil!"

Finally he turned around.

"Where is your sister?"

"Over there." He nodded his head in the general direction of the beachfront.

Lori, still in her nightgown, was wandering barefoot among the trees beside the lake. As Helen approached, Lori turned to her in rapture. "Mommy, isn't this just like the enchanted forests in my storybooks?"

"It sure is!" squealed Phil, who had come up behind them. "The guides say this lake has the best fishing anywhere! I'm going to be a guide. Imagine getting to fish all day! Roger says he can start teaching me now. And when I grow up, I'm going to help run the place! Dad says he is going to make it into the best fly-in fishing camp in Canada!"

Helen did not have quite the same vision as her children. To her, the camp was a carefully constructed war zone with hidden dangers and traps lurking in every wave and around every tree, diabolical tortures designed just for her.

"Lori, I don't care if you think it's an enchanted forest. You can't wander around by yourself! How am I ever going to keep my eyes on you? And Phil, I wouldn't think about guiding just yet. My Lord, you can't even take care of your sister, never mind a boatful of guests!"

"I was watching her."

"Oh honestly!"

Helen flopped down on the dock, her shoulders slumped, completely defeated.

That's how Al found them a few moments later. "What's happening here?"

Lori shrugged. Phil intently watched the toe of his sneaker dig a hole in the sand. Finally Helen piped up.

"I can't do this. I've only been here a day, and I've lost Lori twice already. I don't know how I'm going to watch her all the time when I'm trying to work. She could end up in the lake or lost in the forest, attacked by bears or coyotes."

"What coyotes?"

"You know what I mean! I can't remember egg orders, I don't remember names, and I don't know how to operate a wood stove. Phil's playing with knives and chisels, and he wants to be a *guide*. I still haven't had a shower, and the fridge is a freezer! Why are we going through all this?"

Al stood beside his wife. "Slow down. It's going to be okay. There are lots of people around to watch Lori. We just have to ask them. You'll get used to the wood stove, and you're great with the guests. In no time at all, you'll be slinging those breakfast plates around like a waitress at a diner. And Phil's not going to play with any knives or ice picks or guide just yet. Everything will work out."

Helen looked unconvinced.

"Come on. Let's take a tour. You haven't even seen much of the place yet. Maybe it will make you feel better."

"Lori's not even dressed yet."

"Who's here to see? I don't think a little girl in a nightgown is going to matter here."

Reluctantly, Helen rose. "I guess I could look at the place."

"Sure, Mom!" said Phil excitedly. "I'll show you 'round. I've seen the whole camp already!" He led the family up the hill.

"There's a great view of the lake from here." Al pointed to a cabin right in front. "This is the house cabin . . . the one that was supposed to be ours. The guests have already gone fishing, so we can take a peek."

Helen opened the door, and they stepped inside. There was a living room with a sagging couch and chair under a window dressed in drab brown curtains. A pot-bellied stove stood in the middle and a pile of wood in the wood box beside it. A card table held a deck of cards, an ashtray, and a tray with an ice bucket and glasses. Beyond was an alcove sporting twin beds with an array of hats hanging above them.

"See, Mom, isn't the cabin cool?" Phil looked around, his eyes shining. "Guests get to stay here, but it's really all ours!"

"Guests *get* to stay in this?"

Al answered, "They're fishermen, Helen. They're here to fish. They're not looking for the Hilton. They just want a nice clean place to lay their heads at night. And believe me, the cabins are clean. Agnes spit-and-polishes them. I dare you to find a cobweb. Besides I plan to build new guest cabins, at least five or six of them. Albert has this fabulous sawmill so we can mill our own logs and build cabins for next to nothing, and they'll all have bathrooms with showers and new beds!"

"And I'll help!" said Phil.

"You bet," Al answered before Helen could. "There's something so satisfying about building from the ground up—such a feeling of satisfaction from doing it all yourself."

Al motioned to the lake, visible through the picture window. "We already have the fishing, and that's the most important thing. This lake is a fish factory! Every time you drop a jig, every time you toss a spoon, you catch a fish. And not just any fish. BIG fish! Why the average walleye pulls the scales down to four pounds, and eight pounds is not uncommon. And the muskies, God, the muskies are monsters here! We just need to fix the camp up a bit. We'll get everything painted so it looks nice and fresh. We'll build new docks and get new boats with twenty horsepower outboards! And I want to build a new lodge, with a brand-new kitchen, a dining room that seats thirty, and nice accommodations for us and the kids. Heck we'll even have our own planes to fly guests out to other lakes for a day of fishing! Just wait. It's going to be great!"

"Where does the money come from for all this?"

"It's going to take a little time, of course. And lots of hard work. But I know we can do it."

"I hope so."

"We will." There was no doubt in his voice.

Helen did not share Al's vision. All she could see was the grime, the bugs, the mice, and the moles.

As they walked out the door, Albert's happy face met them.

"Elsie says she has some breakfast still warming for two kids."

"Thanks, Albert."

"And don't worry, I'll take them. Later, Phil can help me fix an outboard motor that needs a new bottom, and Lori can help Elsie with the baking."

As the two children happily trotted away with Albert. Helen shouted, "But Lori's still in her nightgown!" Then, realizing her protests were futile, she gave up.

"See I told you. It's going to work out." Al's eyes twinkled. "Let's finish the tour."

Helen took a deep breath, then slowly headed down the path with her husband, having no idea where it would lead.

Lori took the wee purple bonnet and hung it back up. She thought of the whole realm of emotions Helen had experienced—fear, anger, shock, hurt. And yet she had somehow made it through that first awful year. However, all the struggling appeared to be in vain the following year, when it looked like Al was going to have to pack it in. Lori removed a large Russian fur hat from the wall—

1965

Al leaned back in his creaky chair. It didn't matter how many times he punched the numbers into the adding machine: the total just didn't get any larger. There was not enough money to pay his staff. He was stretched to the limit at the bank and had run up tabs at every supplier. He could not ask his dad for another loan, and he was too proud to ask anyone else.

He was in serious trouble.

It wasn't the first time he had run short of money. Last summer, he had not been able to pay Albert and Elsie their wages. His intentions had been good; every payday, he tried to hand Albert and Elsie their cheques, and every payday, they refused to take them.

"What are we going to do with a cheque here?" Albert would ask. "There ain't no banks and nowhere to spend it. Wait till the end of the year. You can pay us then."

So every payday, Al would calculate how much he owed the Vanasses and put that amount away so he wouldn't spend it. Only there were so many expenses—so many things needed replacing, so many things needed fixing. By the end of the year, he had only enough money to either pay the Vanasses or pay his suppliers. He could not afford both. To Al, it spelled the end of his dream. Either way, he would have to liquidate to pay off his debts, and the only thing he owned to liquidate was his camp.

When Albert found out about the cash flow problem, he sat Al down. He poured each of them a shot and lit a cigarette. He replaced the pack in his breast pocket of his work shirt, took a puff of his cigarette and a slug of his whiskey, then looked Al straight in the eye.

"Pay off your suppliers. You're gonna need their credit next summer. Elsie and me, we can wait."

"But, Albert, that's the thing. I don't know how long it will be before I can pay you."

"Don't matter . . . don't care if you ever pay us. Don't worry about it."

"Are you crazy? A whole summer's wages? For both of you? What the hell are you working for then?"

Albert tapped his cigarette on the edge of the ashtray. "Look, Al, the camp provides a roof over our heads and food in our bellies for us and our boys. What more do we need in the summer? Like I said, don't worry about paying Elsie and me this year."

"I can't do that."

"Yes, you can. Look at it this way. What would we do if you had to sell this place? The next guy who bought it may not be as good a boss as you. He might not even want me and Elsie workin' here. Then what would we do? I like it here. Elsie likes it here. The boys love it here. I don't have to worry about them runnin' all over town all summer, gettin' into trouble. We want to stay. So that's the end of it. I know you'll make good when you can."

"But what will you live on? You gotta eat!"

"I've got a job at O.C.A. for the winter, fixin' planes. We'll make it through. We always do. And so will you . . . you'll see."

Al was speechless.

Albert's incredible act of charity had squeezed Al through that first tough season. And during the winter, deposits flooded in, more than he ever expected. Word of mouth from ecstatic guests spread, and there were triple the bookings of the first year. Al was able to pay Albert and Elsie all their back wages and even purchase a better generator—one that would run more than just the lights. He would never forget what the Vanasses had done for him, and he promised himself that from now on, they would get paid, no matter what it took.

This year, it had looked like meeting the payroll was not going to be too difficult. The season was going well. Sure, money was tight, but he had managed to stay on top of it all—until he finally got around to opening that week's mail.

There, among the pile of bills, was a note from the Forger Company, regretting to inform him their party of ten had to cancel their trip. The letter was postmarked two weeks ago. Not that things would have changed much had he gotten it earlier. He still would have had no way to fill the gap in bookings at this late stage. Without the Forger party, he would not have enough money for payroll this month. Al had been counting on these ten guests—counting on them because the money they had not yet paid him—and now never would—was already spent.

True, it was a risk to spend money before you got it, but this business was different than most. More important even than running water, Al thought it important to have new boats and new beds. Guests spent eight hours a night in a bed and eight hours a day in a boat. They *had* to be comfortable. The old flat-bottomed wood boats had been slow, they leaked, and they were very uncomfortable. The beds had been lumpy and had a decidedly musty odour about them. Nothing was more important than getting new boats and new beds into the camp.

So after the spring thaw, when the lakes were free of ice, he, along with a couple of his faithful guides, Eddie and Peepsight, tied the six new boats together, filled each with mattresses, and began their journey from Kenora north up the English River. He had not realized that even in the spring, when the waters were high, there would still be so many portages—ten to be exact. And he had never realized just how incredibly difficult it was to carry a floppy, plastic-covered mattress like a hat on your head through the bush.

Still, they had made it. The new boats and beds were a hit, and he had thought all the time, trouble, and debt had been worth it. Till now.

Al was not a man to give up when the going got tough. In the summer, his hectic, fevered existence drove him to work eighteen hours a day, without a day off. And all the while, he never felt down. Dead tired, yes. Challenged, definitely. But not once had he ever felt like giving up on this place. This was his dream. He *knew* he could make it—at least, that was how he had felt in the past.

Today was different. Al rubbed his forehead. First things first. With ten fewer guests, he was not going to need the extra food ordered for delivery on tomorrow's plane. The few necessities they really did need this week, they would have to do without. Being short on a few staples seemed minor compared to the larger looming problems.

Al glanced at the calendar pinned to the wall—July 12. *Happy birthday to me,* he thought as he turned to the battery-operated radio phone and pressed the button on the side of the handset.

"Kenora, Kenora, Stork Lake calling."

"Stork Lake, this is Kenora. How you doing, Al? Over." The operator Ollie's pleasant voice could easily be heard over the sputter of interference.

"Good. Listen, Ollie, can you hook me up with O.C.A.? Over."

Usually Al chatted with Ollie for a few minutes before having her connect his call. In absence of any radio, television, or newspaper, she was often their only lifeline to any news around the area. Today, however, Al was in no mood for any lighthearted banter.

Ollie responded quickly to the new tone in Al's voice.

"Will do, Stork Lake. Have a great day. Over."

After a moment's silence, the voice of Jimmy Adams, the manager of O.C.A., crackled over the line.

"O.C.A. here."

"Jimmy, it's Al. Can you cancel my Frosted Foods order for tomorrow?"

There was a pause. "Al, this connection is a bit fuzzy . . . Am I hearing right? You want to cancel your food order? Over."

"You heard right."

As with Ollie, Al usually chatted with Jimmy for a few minutes before getting down to business. This was a chance for Jimmy to unleash his dry sense of humour. It took months for Al to realize that most of the stories Jimmy told so sincerely and so seriously were nothing but poppycock.

However, Jimmy also had a serious side. The camp owners, who all had radio phones, had no way of contacting suppliers to place their orders. So Jimmy took their orders and passed them on. He never wrote an order down, yet he never forgot one item on the long lists of supplies. He could tell you the exact date and time it was ordered, and approximately how much the order cost. So Jimmy—better than anybody—would have known Al was running low on staples.

"Al, you have only four guests booked on the plane tomorrow, and it's large enough to pick up the ten coming out. There's a lot of extra room for your food order."

That was another service Jimmy provided. He was an expert at squeezing extra cases of meat and beer onto scheduled flights taking guests back and forth, often saving camp owners hundred of dollars in transportation costs.

"I know, and God, I hate to send in a half-empty plane, but, Jimmy, my credit is stretched to the limit there. I've gotta wait until I can get some more cash before I can order anything. I thought I'd have enough, but I just had the Forger party of ten cancel their trip next Saturday. Over."

"Ouch, that hurts."

Al took a deep breath. He decided to be straight with Jimmy.

"I don't know how much longer I can go on. If I cancel this supply plane, then I'll be able to pay my staff for maybe another week. After that, I don't know. Frankly I don't know if I'll be able to pay you any time soon. I don't even know if I'm going to be able to stay open. Over."

"What? Are you sure, Al? I've seen a lot of camp owners come and go, and I can always see why. They don't have the personality, the gumption to stick it out. But I've always felt in my gut you have the right stuff to make a go of it."

"Nice of you to say, Jimmy. And if working harder could get me out of this mess, I'd work harder. But no amount of back-breaking is going to save me this time."

"God, Al. I'm sorry to hear that. I hate to think of you closing down. Tell you what. Don't worry about that Frosted Foods order, Al. I'll cancel it for you. And I'll cancel the planes you ordered for the Forger party. As for your bill here, it can wait a while longer." He paused for a moment. "I hope something works out for you. Over."

"Thanks, Jimmy. Over and out."

Al placed the handset back in its cradle. Over and out was right—over and out of business.

***

Helen, who had entered the office during the conversation, now felt sick to her stomach. She collapsed on the creaky sofa and nervously bit a hangnail. Last year, she would have given anything for the place to have gone under so she could have gone back home to Winnipeg. It had been her hell year, and she was not sure still how she had stuck it out. There had never been enough money or enough hours in the day to get everything done. She had scrimped, scrubbed, slaved, and saved. And she was tired. Every night, she fell into bed in that little mud-floored room behind the office, so tired she ceased to care about the smell of mould or the sound of moles.

This year—well this year was not as bad. Yes, it was still hard, very, very hard. There were nights when she lay in bed, her back aching from carrying heavy baskets of sopping sheets and her fingers aching from being chilled to the bone in the breezes blowing off the lake. And then there were days she would pass out in the heat of the kitchen; the wood stove could never be "turned off," not even when the temperature hit ninety degrees. She had never become friends with that blasted thing—and had burned more toast and more fingers than she could remember. She still routinely lost Lori, and no amount of punishment kept Phil from trying to operate every piece of machinery the camp owned. She missed the city—the stores, the theatre, and "luxuries" like listening to music or reading the newspaper. There was still no money, and there was still no such thing as a day off. And yet—

This year, the family stayed in the house cabin. There was much more room; each of the kids had their own real bed in their own tiny cardboard like bedroom. Al had even installed a shower for her, the first private shower in the whole camp. It wasn't much—just a metal stall shoved through a hole in the wall of the bathroom, the back of it sticking a good foot into Philip's room. Still it was like heaven. She could have a hot shower almost whenever she wanted.

All the cabins were now painted dark chocolate with brilliant white trim. Up on the hill, a new cabin that would house six more guests was taking shape. The footings were poured, and the floor nailed down. Next they would be raising the walls. In the rest of the guest cabins, the old mattresses had been replaced and covered with new checkered bedspreads and fluffy new pillows. Indoor plumbing was just around the corner for everyone—the plumbing lines had been laid, and a new septic tank was in the works.

The docks were repaired and tied up to them rocked shiny new aluminum boats. Agnes had spent her free afternoons weeding the flowerbeds, her hard work revealing a bounty of beauty. Bright orange tiger lilies, their heads hanging down and their petals curling up, snuggled next to buttery yarrow. There were the tall, graceful indigo spikes of lupins and the pretty little faces of pansies. Agnes had also cultivated a garden, fresh herbs, tomatoes, beans, and rhubarb.

There had even been improvements in the kitchen. The chipped cups and saucers had been replaced with white mugs. New oilcloths covered all the tables, and Helen had managed to get all gleaming cutlery and pots from a restaurant wholesaler that was going out of business.

More than anything, however, it was the *people* who were changing Helen's mind about the camp. Al had been right. Once she had started talking to the staff and to the guests, she had warmed to the place.

She loved the chance to mingle and chat with the unique variety of fishermen who found their way up to the backwoods camp. Their warm praise and the looks of joy and contentment on their faces made her feel proud of the retreat she provided. The people that stayed here, whether it was for three days or ten days, all left feeling like friends. The comments in the red vinyl guestbook proved it: *We felt like family, Excellent hospitality, Forged a forever friendship*, and *See you next year!*

Often appreciative guests even sent unexpected gifts after they left. There were new Elkhorn-handled steak knives from a couple of brothers who had caught their first pair of muskies. A huge basket of fresh fruit arrived from the father and son who had forgotten their differences for the week and had actually enjoyed each other's company. A multicoloured double hammock "to entice Helen and Al to take some off time and swing in the breeze" was a gift from a couple with whom Al and Helen had played cards. Most guests from last year had returned again this year, bringing with them more family, friends, and colleagues.

No longer did Helen feel like a fish out of water. She had gotten to know each guide, often joking and kidding around with them. She had found a way to fit into Elsie and Agnes's easy work pattern and now felt like part of the team. She learned how to be a housekeeper, bookkeeper, storekeeper, hostess, waitress, laundress, bartender, fire tender, administrator, and interior designer. She learned how to make a mean martini and how to cut one chocolate cake so it would feed twenty guests. Most of all, she was learning to, if not enjoy, at least willingly accept, every aspect of camp life.

Yes, it was coming together. Al's dream was starting to come true, and she could almost catch a glimpse of it.

Was it all going to blow up in their faces now?

She turned back to Al. "What are we going to do without our food order? We're almost out of rice, and—"

Al quipped back, "Then we don't have rice!" His expression softened when he saw his wife's face. "Look, we're going to have to make do for a while, at least until I can figure something out." However, in his heart, he wasn't sure just what he could do. "We have to go on. There is a camp to run . . . at least for now. The guests must not be affected; no one must guess our problems. The day will continue as usual." He rose from his desk, and Helen followed him out the door into the sunshine.

"Al, can we talk to you for a minute?"

Helen's nephew Ricky and his best friend, Danny, stood there. The two seventeen-year-old boys were spending their summer working at the camp. Worried expressions furrowed their usually happy-go-lucky faces.

"What is it, boys?"

"Ah, there's a . . . a problem with the septic tank we're building," muttered Ricky.

"What's wrong with it?"

"One of the walls kinda caved in."

"What? Jesus Christ! How the hell did that happen?"

"Well when we took the framing off the last side, it just . . . caved in."

"Dammit!"

Helen watched her husband stride off with the boys close behind. She turned toward the lodge and nervously began to bite her hangnail again.

***

A new septic tank would mean all the guests could enjoy indoor plumbing . . . showers, toilets, the works. However, building the septic tank took money—money Al, of course, did not have.

So they had improvised. The most expensive component of the septic was the plywood needed to frame the walls. It couldn't be milled at the camp, so it had to be flown in at great expense. It would have taken six sheets of plywood to frame each wall. Al decided to purchase just one sheet and use it for all six walls. Sand was hauled in by boat from miles away and then hand-mixed with cement in five-gallon pails. Ricky and Danny framed one wall of the septic and poured the cement. The next day, they took that frame off and used it for the next wall. On the fourth day, they poured the fourth side. Now it was obvious they hadn't given the cement enough time to set.

Al now wished he had been a little more specific with the teens, like telling them to check and make sure the cement had actually cured before removing the plywood.

Al peered into the hole. It was a bloody mess.

Glob. Glob. Glob. As they stood there surveying the damage, another side started to slide, then another, and finally, the fourth remaining wall crumbled. The three of them stared in disbelief. There was nothing left but a heap of cement in what used to be a hole.

Ricky stroked his long, sunburned face. "Uh, what do you want us to do now?"

Al thought for a moment. "Scoop it up. We'll have to use it again."

"The same cement?" Danny sounded flabbergasted.

"I can't get more cement in here. Just scoop up as much as you can and remix it. Clean up the plywood and frame it up again."

Astonished, the boys glanced at one another. "Ooookaaay, if you say so, Al," replied Ricky.

Al glanced at his watch.

"Christ, I've got to go guiding!" He ran to his cabin to grab a hat and jacket, then headed to the lake.

There was only one boat and one guest left at the dock. The boat was one of the original flat-bottomed wooden ones, built right at the camp in 1945 from lumber cut at the on-site sawmill. Its boxlike plank hull was the only object left in the whole camp that was still covered with blistering red paint and was only used when there were more than twelve guests. Today there were thirteen.

Al couldn't believe his bad luck. Of all the guests in camp, it just had to be the Colonel that he kept waiting. And it just had to be the Colonel who was going to have to get into and fish from that old boat.

Al had learned that Colonel Becker had acquired his title during the Second World War, and it had stuck during peacetime because he ran his life with the same military precision with which he had run his regiment. Straight as a ramrod, he literally marched down to the lodge in the morning. Al knew that the Colonel expected everyone to be already seated for dinner when he arrived so that when he strode in the door, they would all stand up at attention—all eight of them. The Colonel assigned them their seats at the table; he assigned them their cabins, and he assigned them their fishing partners. It seemed to Al that every detail was meticulously thought out before being carried out.

The Colonel was always immaculately groomed from the top of his precisely parted thinning hair to his spotlessly white canvas shoes, and today was no exception. His slim, 6'2" frame was dressed in neatly pressed khakis and a round-necked navy sweater with a small crest on the breast pocket. He held a windbreaker in one hand and a cap in the other, not unlike that of a marine colonel. Beside him, a couple of rods and a tackle box were neatly stacked on the dock. He would have looked more at home going yachting than fishing—and he certainly did not look like he belonged in that wooden barge.

"Sorry to keep you waiting. It's been a hectic morning." Al hated making excuses. Your business problems were never supposed to become your customer's problems.

"That's all right, Mr. Reid," barked the Colonel. "I like to see my men off first, make sure everything has gone off without a hitch. The last boat just left the dock five minutes ago, so we're not *too* far off schedule."

Al took a quick look at the bottom of the boat to see if it was leaking any water. He had fixed a small hole near the stern the day before and hoped his patch was holding. All looked dry.

"If you'd just like to get into the boat—" Al began to pick up the rods and tackle box sitting on the dock.

The Colonel looked at the boat-shaped object floating beside the dock, not quite believing it was a watercraft. "This one?"

"Yes, sir." Al tried to sound confident as he stacked the gear. If he sounded sure enough, perhaps his guest would feel sure as well.

"Okay then." The Colonel stepped into the boat—and right through it, up to his knees in water.

He looked down at his sodden pants and then up at Al. Coolly placing his cap on his head, he inquired, "Got another boat?"

Al looked horrified. "God, I'm sorry!" He reached down to help extract the Colonel, who with as much grace as he could muster, climbed back onto the dock.

"I'm going to change. I'll be right back." His soggy shoes squished as he marched back up to his cabin.

Al quickly dragged the boat out of the water and turned it upside down on the beach. He then ripped out the broken board with a crowbar, banged in a new board, and pulled the boat back into the lake.

The Colonel returned in an identical pair of neatly pressed, dry khakis. He glanced up and down the dock. Seeing no other means of transportation, he casually asked, "We're using the same boat?"

"It's the only boat I got left."

Expressionless, the Colonel climbed back into the boat and stood for a moment. Deciding it seaworthy, he nodded his assent and sat down, pulling on his jacket. Al climbed in after him, and off they went.

As they passed the first island in front of the camp, the Colonel made a motion for Al to slow down.

"Drop me off here." The Colonel indicated a large rock hanging over the water.

Al looked around. "I'm sorry, I don't understand."

"I'll fish here."

"You won't catch anything big here."

"Doesn't matter. You can pick me up at 11:45 so I can join my men for lunch."

Al felt awful. He couldn't blame the guy for not caring to travel any further in the old boat. He probably figured the next leak would sink them right to the bottom of the lake!

Colonel Becker climbed out of the barge, peeled off his jacket, and spread it neatly on the big rock. Al scrambled to unload his equipment, then slunk back to camp.

He was just tying the boat back up at the dock when Al saw two men motoring up in a strange boat. Prospective guests? With their own boat? Maybe the day was getting better!

He stood up and put on a welcoming smile.

"Hi there!" Al grabbed their rope and tied it up to the dock.

One of the men jumped out. "Hi. Name's Bill Pire, and this here's my buddy, Dan," he said, pointing to a figure in the bow.

"Bill, Dan. Glad to meet you both! I'm Al Reid, the proprietor here. How can I help you gentlemen today?"

"We were wondering . . . Could we buy some outboard motor gas from you?" asked Dan.

Dashed, Al tried not to show his disappointment. "Sure, just pass me your jerry cans, and I'll fill them for you."

***

Bill, however, seemed to catch the look on Al's face. It had that tight look around the corners of the mouth that a man gets when he is trying not to show emotion—when he feels it is indecent to show any sign of weakness or suffering. Few would have noticed, but Bill knew the expression well. He had worn it often enough himself.

"We're actually running two boats," said Bill, as he helped Dan unload the jerry cans. "There's six of us fishermen all together. We heard this lake had some awesome fishing, so we contacted that float base in Kenora. What is it? O.C.A.? Anyways, the guy there suggested we book into your camp, but we really just wanted to camp out on our own. So instead, he had us and all our gear flown into the south end of the lake. He even hooked us up with these boats that belong to some trappers. However, what he didn't do was give us enough gas. I guess he didn't know we'd be motoring around this much."

Al hooked up the first jerry can to the forty-five-gallon drum of gas sitting on the dock and turned on the tap. "How's the fishing been for you? Any luck?" he asked.

Bill answered, "Like I said, we've really done some travelling . . . trying to find the sweet spots! We finally had a great day yesterday. Caught lots of walleye. Haven't found any big northerns or muskie, though."

"The big ones are there, just takes a bit of time to figure out where. There's an island out near where you're staying. Out in the middle of nowhere . . . You can't miss it. It's pure white, not a tree on it. We call it Bird Shit Island."

"Yes, I remember seeing it on the way here," said Dan.

"Try casting on the north side of that island. We've been pulling some monster northerns out of there. You'll catch a few for sure. Just make sure you use a surface bait. They're hunting shallow right now."

"Thanks, we'll do that," said Bill. "Nice place you got here. Been here long?"

"This is my second year."

"The outdoors as your office. What a great way to make a living. My family owns a meat plant in Eau Claire, Wisconsin. Great living, not the best job."

"And this is a great job, just not the best living!" Al gave a little laugh.

Bill observed Al carefully as he finished filling up the jerry cans, his sinister slanted eyebrows at odds with his warm brown eyes.

"How much do we owe you?"

"Let's see, fifteen gallons at forty cents a gallon . . . that'll be six dollars."

Bill fished some bills out of his pocket. "Please keep the change. For your trouble."

"No trouble at all. Come back anytime. We also have a store here if you run short of any supplies. And if you have a hankering for a home-cooked meal . . . well you'll find no better cook in all of Northwestern Ontario!" Al helped them load the cans back in the boats, and away they went. As he stood there, watching the boats roar away, Phil slowly ambled up to him.

"Ah, Dad?"

"Yes Phil?"

"Dad, I *think* the lawn mower is on fire."

Al's jaw dropped. "You think . . . *Where is it?!*"

"Down on the Point. That's the only place Albert will let me cut grass, because it's nice and flat, and there's no tree roots for me to run over."

Al raced down to the Point, Phil right behind. Nothing was scarier than a fire at a camp built out of logs. However, by the time they got there, the fire had burned itself out, leaving nothing behind but a blackened lawn ornament of a mower.

"Sorry, Dad. I . . . I ran out of gas. I know I'm not supposed to fill it myself, but Albert's all the way down at the mill, Ricky and Danny are down in a hole, and you were busy with those guys on the dock. I've seen it done millions of times, so I thought I could do it on my own. Roger does it all the time, and he's only a little older than me. And I did do it! I got most of the gas in the tank, and I only some spilled some over the sides. But when I pulled the handle to start it, the mower just . . . blew up."

Al looked into his son's frightened blue eyes. "It's all right, Phil. I know it was an accident. Just next time come ask for help. You could have been burnt."

Phil face was totally crestfallen. Al's heart went out to the trembling boy. He put a hand on his son's shoulder. "Speaking of help, I could use some. Since I don't have to guide this morning, I figured I'd grab Albert and we'd work on that new cabin for a while. You in?"

Phil's face immediately lit up. "Really? You bet I'm in!"

***

The morning wasn't going very well in the kitchen, either. After Helen's talk with Al, she went straight to Elsie to figure out just what to do about the food situation.

"There's not going be a food order coming in for a while—" began Helen.

"Oh? Is that so?"

"Something's come up, and the plane won't be in tomorrow." Helen had no intention of elaborating. "I'm almost glad there will be only four guests after the Becker party leaves tomorrow. Less to feed."

Elsie seemed unconcerned.

"We'll work it out. I've been in plenty of tight spots before. When most of my kids were still living at home, it seemed we were always just a little short. I always find a way to get plenty of bread on the table."

"Oh, Elsie, I know you do. Nobody can stretch out food as well as you without sacrificing taste. No, it's just we're going to be short on rice. And pork and beans for shore lunch. What's a shore lunch without pork and beans?"

"We can do without rice. And I can make baked beans. I got lots of navy beans and molasses and salt pork. They'll be better'n even the canned ones."

"Okay that solves that problem. But what about eggs? There's only one crate left."

"If we're careful, that'll last the week. We just won't give any to the staff for breakfast." Elsie paused, the wheels turning. "Rhubarb is getting big, so we can have rhubarb and strawberry pie tonight. That won't take any eggs unless you still want me to make Al a birthday cake?"

"We can't spare the eggs. I guess there'll be no birthday cake. Al will understand." Helen took a deep breath. "So there, the problems with the menu are solved for now." Calmed by Elsie's unflappable demeanour, Helen felt better. "I better get on with my work." With that, she headed out the door to conquer the endless mountain of laundry.

***

"No birthday cake?" That was the only part of the conversation that Lori heard. She was sitting at the staff dining room table, drawing a picture of their family on the back of a gin rummy scorecard: her mom, dad, Phil, and herself under the big spruce tree by the lake. It was to be a present for her dad's birthday.

Imagine not having a birthday cake! She couldn't think of anything worse happening on someone's birthday. Her mom always made her nice cakes for her birthday. And she thought how sad her dad would be if he had no candles to blow out if he couldn't make a wish. She decided right then and there she would make him one.

Lori had never made a cake before, but she had watched Elsie whip them up many times, and she had licked out a lot of bowls. She had a pretty good idea how to do it, and it didn't seem too difficult. With Elsie in the pantry kneading bread and Agnes off cleaning cabins, there was no one around to notice her wee figure slip off the bench and steal around the small kitchen.

Lori climbed up on the stool to reach for a bowl. The large mixing bowl Elsie used for making cakes was too heavy to take down, so she chose a smaller one instead and placed it on the floor. She took a coffee cup, dipped it into the large barrel of flour, dumped it into the bowl, and then took the cup and dipped it into the sugar barrel and added it to the flour. Hmm, what next? Butter and milk. She found them both on the staff dining table. Lori added a large glob of butter, along with half a can of evaporated milk. What was she missing? Eggs. Elsie used eggs in her cakes!

Plop. The first egg ended up on the floor. She tried to scoop it back up, but the slimy goo kept sliding out of her hands. The second egg almost made it into the bowl. The third egg hit its target, with just a little shell mixed in. In fact, it worked so well she added another, just for good measure. Now what to do about the spattered mess all over the floor? She grabbed Elsie's soup pot and turned it upside down over the broken eggs—a perfect fit.

With a wooden spoon, Lori mixed all the ingredients together. When she was done, it looked just like Elsie's cake mixture. Pleased, she gazed around for a pan to bake it in. All the cake pans looked so big for the little bit of batter she had. She decided on a small loaf pan. Carefully she poured the batter in then used a spatula to wipe the sides, just like Elsie did. She was careful to leave a little batter at the bottom. After all, what was the use of baking a cake if you had none left to lick out of the bowl?

Now all she had to do was bake it. But how? She was not allowed to use the oven. She would have to enlist Elsie's help. Picking up the pan, she trotted into the back pantry.

"Elsie, can you cook my cake for me?"

Elsie swung around, looking puzzled. "Cake? You made a cake? All by yourself?"

"Yep . . . see?" Lori proudly held up the pan for her to inspect. "It's for my dad's birthday."

Elsie wiped off her floured hands on her apron and peered down at the batter in the small tin pan. "Looks like you done a good job here. Yes sirree, doesn't look like it needs a thing. Except maybe . . . Did you put some baking powder in?"

Lori shook her head.

"Salt? Vanilla?"

Again she shook her head. Her cake was a disaster!

"That's okay. We'll just add a little now." Elsie pulled the ingredients off the shelf and stirred a little of each into the batter.

"You used eggs, didn't you?"

"Oh yes, two of them!" She didn't volunteer any information on the eggs hidden under the pot.

Elsie didn't blink an eye. "Then it's ready for the oven." She opened the door on the wood stove and popped the tin in. Then she set the timer for twenty minutes.

"Now I'm going to go finish kneading my bread. You let me know when the timer goes off. That's when we'll take the cake out."

Lori smiled and shook her head agreeably. The cake was okay after all!

She sat on the stool in front of the oven, intently watching the timer while she licked the batter out of the bowl. The batter tasted good, so she was sure the cake would be good, too. When the bowl was spotless, she placed it in the sink then jumped back up on the stool. She looked again at the timer. *Tick. Tick. Tick.* The suspense was agonizing. Would the cake never be done?

Ding! Finally the buzzer went off.

Lori raced to the pantry. "Elsie, Elsie, it's ready!"

"It is, eh? We better get it out." Elsie grabbed an oven mitt, hobbled over, opened the oven door, and pulled out the little cake.

"Looks mighty good," said Elsie. "What colour would you like the icing?"

"Blue. Bright blue."

"Good choice. We'll ice it as soon as it's cool. We'll keep your cake a surprise for the party tonight, shall we? Even from your mom."

"Oh, Elsie, could we?" There was nothing better than a surprise on your birthday!

***

Al made sure he was prompt picking up the Colonel. At exactly 11:45, he pulled the old barge up to the island.

"How was your morning?" he asked as he loaded up the Colonel's gear.

"Fine." The answer was short and abrupt.

Al didn't know what to say. Obviously the fishing here had not been that great. The two men were silent on the short ride to the lunch spot where the Becker party was meeting up. As they approached, a couple of guides ran up to help them land. The Colonel stepped out of the boat, then turned back to Al.

"I won't be needing you anymore today. After lunch, I will join one of the other boats."

Al felt miserable. He had just screwed up a nine-man account. He knew Colonel Becker would never forgive or forget falling through the bottom of that damn boat.

***

Each night, Al made a point of greeting every single guest in the lodge, feeling that this personal touch was as important as good fishing. So even though his heart wasn't in it tonight, he was determined to get down there and act like an attentive owner, even if he didn't feel much like schmoozing. Al quickly showered and pulled on some clean clothes.

A drone filled the air just as he was leaving his cabin. An airplane circled then landed in front of the camp.

We're not expecting anyone. What now? he thought.

By the time he reached the dock, Ricky and Danny were tying up the bright yellow plane. A heavyset man sporting a brush cut similar to Al's, only in silver, jumped out of the cockpit.

"Al . . . good to see you."

"Barney! To what do we owe this pleasure?"

The two men sauntered off the dock. "It was such a nice evening, I thought I'd take my Cub for a spin. Don't have as much time to fly her anymore. It's just about a thirty-five-mile jaunt from my place . . . a nice little ride."

Al knew Barney didn't just "jaunt" somewhere. There was a reason for this visit. Barney Lamm owned Ball Lake Lodge, the largest, most luxurious fishing camp in Northwestern Ontario. It was a fly-in fishing camp that didn't just offer fishing but also had a dancehall, a chapel, and even a beauty parlour. Barney also owned O.C.A.—the airline that flew all their guests in. Had Jimmy Adams told Barney he was in trouble? Had the owner of O.C.A. himself come to collect on his bill?

Barney's sharp eyes darted around, missing nothing.

"I see you've invested in new boats."

"Had to. The wooden tubs that were here plowed through the water, and there wasn't a one that didn't leak."

"Smart move. Boats are the most important piece of equipment a fishing camp can have. A decent boat and motor, a good guide, and great water full of fish, and you've got it made. You're doing a nice job of fixing up the place. Amazing how much you've accomplished already."

"There's so much more to do—"

"I felt the same way when I first started. Wanted everything done yesterday." He paused. "Listen, Al, is there someplace we can talk for a moment? In private?"

"My office is right here."

Al led him into the tiny, dusty office, refusing to be embarrassed by it. Barney, likely sensing how he was feeling, looked around, then remarked, "Better than the first office I had."

"Tell that to my wife." Al nodded toward the faded curtain. "We lived in that backroom our first summer."

"Tell that to *my* wife," retorted Barney. "We lived in a mink trapper's shack our first summer."

Al laughed, starting to relax. Here was a man that understood.

"Have a seat, Barney." He pointed to the sofa chair with the sagging springs.

"The floor's fine." Al watched in amazement as the big man lay down in the middle of the cracked cement floor.

"Back's been bothering me. I used to be able to put in an eighteen-hour day. Now my back screams after only fourteen."

Barney stared straight up at the ceiling. "Thing is, Al, Jimmy Adams phoned me after he talked to you this morning."

There it was. Al braced himself for the other shoe to drop.

"And—"

"And once I heard about your dilemma, I knew I had to come. I would like to help you out." Barney reached into the breast pocket of his plaid shirt, pulled out a folded piece of paper, and held it out to Al. "Here." Al bent down and picked it up. It was a cheque, blank except for Barney's signature scrawled in the corner.

"Fill it out for any amount, whatever you need," Barney announced calmly.

"I can't take your money," answered Al, shocked. "I don't know when I could pay you back . . . I don't know *if* I could ever pay you back!"

"I'm not backing you. It's not a loan. I'm giving it to you. Take ten, fifteen thousand, whatever you need."

Ten or fifteen thousand! He could buy a whole resort for that!

"I couldn't do that."

"Of course you could, if you truly want to stay in business."

"I . . . I don't know what to say. I've only met you a couple of times before. I don't even really know you. And yet here you are, offering me more money than I have ever seen, just to stay in competition with you."

"I don't see you as competition. I see you like me, at around the same age. You have the same drive and desire. It's a strange business, Al. Most people don't understand it. They think it's a lark—that you get to fish all summer, hunt all fall, play poker and drink all night, and never have to wear a tie. Us owners, we know what malarkey that is. No CEO of any business on Wall Street can even begin to understand the unique stresses and strains of this job. You have to be everything to everyone all the time."

Al nodded his head in agreement. "Ain't that the truth!"

"You're more than chief cook and bottle washer. You're also a tinker, tailor, soldier, and sailor. There's no such thing as a job description. You do anything and everything that needs to be done. Not many men can hack it. But you, Al, I know you can make it. You're not afraid of work and not afraid of risk. I respect that, and

I believe you should be given every chance to succeed. So when Jimmy Adams radioed me this morning and told me of your dilemma, I knew that I had to do something."

"I don't know what to say—"

"Say thank you." Barney slowly rolled over and got up on his knees. Al offered him a hand up.

"No, gotta do it myself." He struggled to his feet then brushed off his pants.

"Come on down to the lodge," said Al. "The least I can do is offer you a cup of coffee."

"Well now, I'd love nothing better than to visit a little longer, but I have to get back. I like to greet my guests at dinner."

"I understand. I like to do the same thing." Al walked Barney back to the dock, untied the Cub, and with a wave, pushed him off. As Barney taxied away, a familiar boat pulled up.

It was Bill Pire, the fisherman who had purchased gas that morning.

"Bill!" greeted Al. "Back for more gas already?"

"Not this time," smiled Bill. "We barely used any gas today because the fish were just where you said they would be. We never caught so many big ones in our lives!"

"Glad to hear it. So what is it then that brings you back to my humble little camp?"

"Camping! It's just not as much fun as we thought it would be. After a day of reeling in all those fish, you kinda just want to sit back and relax, not get a fire going and have to cook for yourself. So the guys and I talked it over and well . . . we were hoping that maybe . . . if you had room . . . we could book in tomorrow? For a few days?"

Al couldn't believe what he was hearing. This would certainly help straighten out his budget! He didn't even pretend to look at his bookings book. "We'd be glad to have you." Al paused a moment, then added, "Hungry? You come on down to the lodge. We can rustle up something for you to eat. Wait till you sample my cook's home cooking. You'll be glad you're staying here!"

"That's mighty hospitable of you," answered Bill. "I'd love to."

The card room was already full of jovial well-wishers when the two men entered a few minutes later.

"'bout time you made it to your own party!" exclaimed Albert. He cracked open a bottle of Hudson Bay Scotch and threw the cap into the trash. "We won't be needing that anymore!"

He poured liberal amounts of the golden liquid into each glass and handed them around.

"What, you told everyone it was my birthday?" cried a surprised Al, as Albert handed both him and Bill a drink.

Albert grinned. "Course. You don't think we'd let the day go by without a little celebrating, did you?"

"Of course he didn't!" The Colonel sauntered up, his bland face ruddy from indulging in a little pre-party cheer. "Mr. Reid has a lot to celebrate, the least which is not this amazing place! I have never experienced fishing like this ever before."

"Really? I thought your day had been disappointing!"

"Quite the contrary, Mr. Reid. I was just a little tired from reeling in over one hundred walleye by noon, just fishing off that rock! You can be sure we'll be rebooking with you for next year. Especially since it looks like you'll have a septic system." The Colonel winked at Al. "Yes, I've been watching its er . . . progress, and I believe you are now on the right track!"

Al downed his drink in one gulp. Even a leaky old boat and botched septic tank couldn't deter guests from loving this place.

"Al's here!" shouted Helen, peering in from the kitchen. "We can get this birthday party started! Come on, Lori. Girls! Come join us for a toast before dinner."

Elsie nodded to Agnes. "You go with Helen. I'll bring Lori in in a minute . . . She has a little surprise for her dad."

Elsie retrieved Al's birthday cake from the shelf, where it had been hidden behind a large bag of noodles.

"Okay, Lori. I'll light it, and you carry it in."

"Me?" The little girl's eyes widened. "Take it out in front of everyone?"

"Now don't you worry, I'm right behind ya."

Helen watched as Lori timidly entered the card room. She began, "Happy birthday to you," in her clear soprano voice, and everyone else joined in.

Lori set the cake down on the card table in front of her father. "What? What's this?"

Elsie was beaming. "Lori made you a cake all by herself."

"She did what?"

"She said she could 'do it on her own.'"

"I can't believe it. You did this all by yourself? For me?" He gave the little girl a big hug. "It's the best cake I've ever seen."

For a moment, Lori seemed to forget everyone was looking at her. "Make a wish, Daddy!" she said proudly.

"I don't have to. It already came true!" He took a big breath and blew out the candles.

Everyone gushed over the little cake.

"Best cake I've ever seen."

"Do you think there'll be enough for me?"

Phil cried, "I want an end piece!"

The cake was cut into minute pieces so that everyone could have a bite.

Elsie grinned at Helen. "I can't think of a better way to use four eggs, can you?"

"Four!" Then, "Certainly not, Elsie. Certainly not."

"Open your presents, Dad!" insisted Phil.

"Presents! I wasn't expecting any presents! This party is all I need. And a good shot of scotch! Can somebody fill me up?" Al held out his empty glass, which was promptly refilled. He began to open his gifts, which, for lack of wrapping paper, were all wrapped in tinfoil. The first one was from Agnes and James. It was a beautiful pair of moccasins made from the softest of moose leather. They were lined with fleece, trimmed in rabbit fur, and decorated with intricate beading.

"They're beautiful! You made these by hand? For me?" Al was awestruck.

"Yep."

"Looks like a perfect fit. How'd you know my foot size?"

"Traced your wet footprint onto a piece of paper. Off the floor in the staff room. When it was raining a couple of weeks ago." It was a long speech for Agnes to recite in front of guests.

"I remember that! My rubber boots were leaking, and my feet were soaking wet! I thought you were worried about me taking off my boots and messing up your clean floor! Well you couldn't have given me a better present. After a day in Kodiak boots, it'll feel mighty fine to slip these on. Thank you."

Agnes positively beamed.

There was a new shirt from Helen that she had brought with her from the city and Lori's picture of the family. Phil gave him a decorative bottle, which he had made by gluing various-shaped macaroni to an empty scotch bottle, then covering it with aluminum paint. Al was thrilled with each and every gift.

"Sorry we didn't get to Eaton's to buy you a present, Al," joked Albert as he handed him a package.

Al opened it and held up something that looked like a furry animal.

"What the hell is it? It won't bite, will it?"

Everyone laughed.

"It's a shapka," said Albert.

"A shapka. That explains everything."

"A shapka! A Russian fur hat. Remember that Count that was up here bear hunting this spring? Well he gave this to me. But I figure you'll make more use of it. Happy birthday, Al!"

"Oh, God. I remember it now. I thought he was *wearing* a bear on his head!" Everyone laughed. "Gee, thanks, Albert. This'll come in handy on these balmy summer nights!"

"It's not for now! It's for winter when we come up here to cut ice. You damn near froze your ears last year."

"That I did."

"Besides, a bear hat is a sign of prosperity," added Elsie.

"Then it will come in very handy!" Al plopped the hat onto his head and pulled it down past his eyebrows. "I feel richer already!"

And he did. Al looked around at all of his friends, mingling together in this room, in his camp, paid for with his sweat, his determination, and his vision. They were laughing, enjoying themselves, having a good time. This was prosperity. This was what it was all about. Al was invigorated—he would figure out a way to make it all work out.

Al never used Barney's cheque. That gesture, along with so many other gestures and comments from friends and family that day, gave him the confidence to "do it on his own."

Lori stroked the shiny black fur before returning the shapka to its nail. It reminded her of another story involving "bear parts"—parts not quite so furry and soft. It had taken place the following year. She removed a youth's blue baseball cap from the wall—

1966

P hil loved to meet the boats at night. At 5:00 p.m. on the dot, he was on the dock, pacing and fiddling with his cowboy hat, waiting for the guests to return from their day of fishing. He was too young to guide, but he wasn't too young to help. He unloaded the fishing rods and tackle out of the boats. Then he helped unload the fish—sometimes they were so large he had to use the wheelbarrow. The fish and the guests were then all steered to a sunny, picturesque spot on the shoreline, just perfect for those brag shots. First the fish was hooked onto a scale and weighed; then, they were laid out on the grass and measured tip to tail. Finally the fish would be hung on display.

There was a wooden sign, maybe six feet long, that read *Reid's Stork Lake Camp*, spelled out in twigs bent into letters. Underneath this lettering were two dozen hooks. Each group of guests would hang their fish on the hooks and take turns having their picture taken in front of it. It was a rare day when every hook wasn't filled with at least a few of the scaly monster tails reaching right down to the ground. When the last of the weighing and measuring and picture-taking had been done, the guests returned to their cabins to wash up and drum up more fish stories to tell over dinner. Phil would then again help the guides move their fish, this time picking them out of the grass and transporting them to the fish house, where they would be filleted and iced.

However, on this hot July evening, Phil was late. He had been piling kindling and had just about finished when the whole stack fell over. By the time he'd fixed it, the sun was sending its last burning rays of the day, and the boast session was over. There was no one left in front of the Stork Lake sign except James and his guests' fish.

"I'll finish picking your fish up for you, James," Phil said, hurrying to the spot. "Please?"

"Okay, but not the muskie. It's Roger's, and it's much too heavy for you. I'll take it."

"Sure thing."

"Thanks." James flashed Phil a dazzling smile, then unhooked the huge muskie and carried it to the icehouse.

Phil grabbed the wheelbarrow and started throwing some northern pike into it. He was almost finished when his sister came along.

"Can I help?" asked Lori.

"If you want to."

Lori carefully picked up a walleye by its gills. "This is so slimy and rough!"

"Do you even know what kind of fish your holding?" asked Phil.

"Of course. It's a walleye. I know it is because it has big glowing eyes." She threw it in the wheelbarrow. "The ones with long noses and spots are northerns. And muskies are always really big fish with little stripes. Like the one Roger's guy got."

"They don't *have* to be big. I've got a muskie, and it's not big at all."

"The ones the guests bring in are *always* big."

"They're big 'cause catchin' the big ones is harder. You couldn't catch one 'cause you're still too little. And you're also too little to ring the gong!" Phil threw the last fish in the wheelbarrow. "Which

I'm gonna do tonight!" Quickly he ran the wheelbarrow down to the fish house, dumped the fish off, then raced back down the path toward the lodge.

Once he had hit the large sawblade gong with a hammer several times, Phil disappeared into the kitchen to retrieve a small package out of the new refrigerator. He stood outside the door, looking out for "the guys"—Ricky, Danny, Joe, and Roger. He had impatiently waited all day for them to finish guiding and get back to camp so he could show them his surprise.

He didn't have to wait long. The four boys rounded the lodge corner and headed toward Phil. As they walked toward him, Joe reached into his pocket and pulled out a pack of Player's and a chrome Zippo lighter he had received as a gift from a guest the week before. Joe held the lighter up until the end of the cigarette ignited, took a deep drag, exhaled a ring of smoke, then tucked the pack and lighter back into his pocket.

Ricky was first to reach the outdoor washstand. He pulled off his cap, turned on the taps and filled up the chipped enamel wash bowl, then grabbed a bar of soap and started scrubbing his face and hands. Behind him, the other three boys joked and laughed with each other.

"Hi, guys!" Phil said. "How was fishing today? Roger, I saw your guest's muskie! It's humungous! How much did it weigh?"

Roger gave his small pal a lopsided grin. "Weighed in at over thirty-two pounds."

"Wow! Thirty-two pounds! That's huge! I bet you caught it over at Knuckle Buster."

Roger laughed. "Nope, Two Marker. He was sunnin' himself in them weeds."

"Caught him on a Johnson's silver spoon, right?"

"Mepps #5. Best bait for this time of year."

"How long did it take to reel it in? Ten minutes?"

"Closer to twenty, I'd say. Bill Pire is as a good a muskie fisherman as they come, but that fish kept chargin' under the boat."

Ricky lifted the wash basin and tossed the water onto the grass, narrowly missing Danny. Danny gave him a kick and a grin.

"Next!" Ricky called.

Danny stepped up to the stand and turned on the taps.

"I got a muskie today, too," said Phil, as nonchalantly as he could.

Roger stared at him in disbelief. "Did not."

"Did too."

"Where'd you get it?"

"On the dock."

"Now I know you's lyin!"

"I'm not lying! I was cleaning the dead minnows out of the minnow tank. I had just scooped out a bunch when a muskie jumped up after them and landed on the dock."

"No muskie's gonna go after minnows. Musta been a perch or something."

"It wasn't no perch! It was a muskie!" With that, Phil pulled the plastic bread bag he had been holding behind his back and dumped a fish about six inches long into his hand. The boys all gathered close to take a look. Sure enough, the miniature fish had all the telltale signs of a true muskie: a missile-shaped body, pointy tail fins, and a duck-like snout.

"I'll be damned! A baby muskie!" Joe roughed up Phil's wheat-coloured hair. "The baby caught a baby!"

Phil was crushed. It wasn't the response he had envisioned. He desperately wanted to be one of the guys. Even though the boys tried to include him in their activities as much as possible, he still felt too young to quite fit in. He had hoped his little muskie would help, but apparently, it just reminded them of the age difference.

"Heh, at least he got a muskie today, Joe," said Ricky.

"Yeah," said Roger. "You didn't even raise one for old Maury."

Joe threw his cigarette on the ground and crushed it out with his boot. "Well let's see how well you do tomorrow when you don't have Bill Pire as a guest. I hear you'll be guiding those couple of guys that have never seen a lake before. I mean, they brought golf clubs to a fishing camp!"

"Well I think your muskie is pretty cool, Phil," Danny said kindly. "Maybe your dad will have it mounted for you."

"You think? I better get it back in the freezer then!" Phil ran to preserve his trophy while the rest of the boys went into the lodge for dinner.

***

Elsie really needed to pee. The guides were already filing in for dinner, so if she didn't go soon, it would be too busy for her to leave. Yet she still hesitated.

A bear had been nosing around the camp for several weeks, figuring he had hit the mother lode with the 'sup hole stop.' The sup hole was a pit dug deep into the ground where all kitchen waste was disposed of, including dishwater and table scraps. A tight wooden lid was securely bolted on top to keep whatever animals may happen by out of it. However, this bear would simply rip the whole top off as easily as if he were peeling back the lid on a can of sardines. He then would dive right into the pit, wallowing in a sea of grease, half-eaten buns, and bones, gorging until he could barely crawl back out again.

The sup hole was a ways from the kitchen, hidden by a clump of trees, and right behind the outhouse. Thus Elsie's dilemma—the proximity of this bear bait sup hole to the biffy. If the bear decided to ramble by for a snack while she was using the facilities, her bad leg, coupled with a not inconsiderable belly, would not make for a quick getaway. She took a deep breath and approached Agnes, who had just finished setting up the guide table for dinner.

"I hate to ask, but will you come to the biffy with me? I can't see past them trees far enough to see if there's a bear hiding in 'em."

"Sure," said Agnes.

Tentatively the two women set out on their trek, keeping a lookout for anything furry and black moving in the bush. All was clear.

Elsie stepped into the small shack. Agnes, looking like a sentry, arms crossed, stood a couple of yards away, staring out toward the lake. Hearing a rustle, she froze, tilting her head toward the sup hole to hear better.

Nothing. Relaxing a bit, she turned her head back toward the biffy. There stood the bear, right beside the outhouse door!

"Elsie?" whispered Agnes loudly.

"What?"

"There's a bear."

"Where?"

"Right beside you!"

"Oh, for God's sake!"

Elsie flung open the biffy door, and in the fastest hibble-hobble you ever did see, raced toward the lodge. Her pace wasn't the least bit impeded by the fact her undies were still around her ankles. Even Agnes had a hard time keeping up behind her. In no time flat, she reached the door.

"A bear! There's a bear behind me!" shouted Elsie.

Joe threw open the door, and Elsie and Agnes burst through. The four boys ran toward the sup hole, but the bear was already gone. They returned a moment later, howling.

"That was the funniest thing I've ever seen!" cried Joe.

Elsie, with her undies once more pulled up, answered in defence, "I'd like to see what you'd do with a bear that close!"

"You wouldn't find me runnin' from no bear!" snickered Roger. "Especially not before I pulled my drawers up!"

"You boys! Stop!" Red-faced, Elsie disappeared back into the kitchen.

The boys were still laughing when Albert strutted in. "What's going on?" he asked as he sat down at his usual spot at the head of the table.

"You should have seen Ma—boy, did she put on a show!"

The boys recited what they had just witnessed. Albert, however, was not as amused.

"That bear's getting braver! I tried firing off warning shots several times now, but he still takes his sweet time haulin' himself out of that sup hole before strolling off like a Sunday walk in the park. Next thing you know, he'll be sittin' right at this table eating with us!"

Agnes, still slightly white-faced, came in with a tray of soup and set brimming bowls in front of each guide. As Albert dipped his spoon into his soup, he said, "I'm afraid we can't have him around the camp any longer. It's getting too dangerous. All we need is a guest to come across him, and we'll be in deep trouble. He'll have to be shot tonight—once everyone is in their cabins."

"Can I come with you, Dad?" pleaded Roger.

"Yeah, come on," said Joe.

"Us too!" chimed in Ricky and Danny.

"You can come if you stay out of the way."

"I can come too?" asked Phil in an excited voice.

"No, Phil. You're too young." Ricky dismissed Phil with a shake of his head. "Your mom would never go for it."

"Sure she would."

"No way."

"Well I bet my dad will let me!"

Albert slowly wiped his mouth with his napkin. "Ask your parents. If they say okay, it's okay with me."

***

Phil came flying into the cabin later that evening, swinging the door wide open.

"Mom, Dad, can I—"

"Where have you been? It's late." Helen had already changed out of her shift and into an iridescent orange caftan trimmed with gold braiding, better suited for a kasbah than a cabin. She was sitting on the sofa, brushing her hairpiece. Having given up on fancy hairstyles after the mole incident the first year there, she now simply pinned on these curls.

"You know that I've been with the guys, fishing off the dock," answered Phil impatiently. "They're going to shoot the bear tonight! Albert says I can go with them!"

Helen gasped. "You're *not* going to do any such thing." She turned toward her husband, who was sitting in the big armchair with a pyjama-clad Lori in his lap, gently filing her nails.

"Al, tell him he can't go."

"You can't go," said Al.

Phil turned to his dad. "You're just saying that because Mom told you to. Pleeaase, Dad—I want to go. Roger and Joe are going and—"

"I don't care if Roger and Joe are going. You're not. You're a lot younger than they are," Helen retorted.

"Mom!"

"Do as your mom says, Phil."

Helen was adamant. "That's the end of it, Philip. Now wash up and get to bed. I'll be in to tuck you in in a minute."

Downhearted, he shuffled to his room.

"You better get to bed too, pussycat."

"Yes, Daddy." Lori gave her dad a hug, slid off his lap, and disappeared after Phil.

"Poor little guy," commented Al. "He wants to be one of the boys so bad."

Helen's eyes widened. "Al, he can't go off bear hunting in the middle of the night! He's nine!"

"I know! Still, it's hard for him always being just young enough to be left on the outside all the time."

"I can stand him being left out a while longer!" retorted Helen. "That will all come soon enough."

***

Bang! Phil was abruptly awakened by a sharp crackle. "A gunshot! They shot the bear!" He squeezed his eyes shut in disappointment. Why did the other guys have all the fun? When would he ever be old enough to join in?

The next morning, Phil raced to dress and get down to the staff room. He wanted to hear all about the bear hunt. For once, the boys were at breakfast early.

Phil barrelled in the door. "I heard the shot. Just one, right? Did you get him?"

"You bet!" exclaimed Danny with a flip of his brown bangs.

Joe continued, "I spotted him first, coming out of the bush by the biffy. That old bear was waddling up to that sup hole, brave as can be. Didn't even stop when he saw us. He sure didn't know what was comin'!"

"Yeah, then Dad just popped him," piped up Roger. "He stumbled, tried to walk a few steps, then just dropped."

"Did you use a shotgun? Did you shoot him in the head?" Phil was very interested in the details—the gorier, the better.

"Nope. Albert used a high-powered rifle and shot him just behind the shoulders. It was too dark for a crack shot to the head. A shot to the shoulder collapses the lungs and heart, and they die pretty quick." Ricky sounded expert on the subject, although Phil was pretty sure this had been his first bear hunting expedition.

"Good thing too, because a shotgun would have shattered the skull, and that would have ruined it," Joe said. He pulled out his cigarettes and Zippo lighter. "We was up at dawn carving that bear up. I got the skull. Once it's boiled, it'll make a great trophy."

"You're gonna keep the bear's head?" Phil was impressed.

"Sure am! It's on ice in the fish house."

"Where's the rest of the bear? Is he still by the outhouse?"

The boys looked at one another. "Ah, well, we couldn't leave him lying around for the guests to see, so we had to get rid of him."

"Where is he then?"

"Well, Albert tied a rope around his back legs, then we all dragged him to the shore, dumped him into the fish gut boat, and trolled out to the middle of the bay just around the corner. Then we weighed him down with stones and sunk him in the middle of the bay, behind that there little island."

Danny said, "Should be a great walleye hole in a couple of weeks."

"Huh?" Phil was confused.

"The walleye will be attracted to the bear carcass, silly. I know where I'm taking my guests to fish a couple of weeks from now!" Danny laughed. "We'll have to mark it on the map. Call it Bear Carcass Reef!"

"So I don't get to see the dead bear?" Phil was truly heartbroken.

Joe took pity on the young boy. "It's okay, sport. I'll show you my skull. You can even help me boil it."

"And look what Danny and I got." Roger reached into his pocket and pulled out a handful of bear claws.

Phil was awestruck. "Ever cool!"

"They're worth money, you know. There's a medicine man in Bloodvein that still uses them in some of his potions. Either that or he wears them on a necklace during powwows—I'm not too sure which."

"What about you, Ricky? Did you keep anything?" asked Phil.

The boys looked at each other. "Yeah, sport, he kept something," said Joe as he giggled. "He got the swizzle stick."

Phil looked confused. "I don't get it. What part is that?"

"Oh, for God's sake! You boys." Elsie, who had been listening to their chatter, now stood behind them, hands on her ample hips, shaking her head. "You cut off his head, cut off his claws, and cut off his pecker! It's bad luck to dishonour a black bear in such a way."

"Cut off his pecker?" Phil was horrified.

"Bad luck?" Roger said, with skepticism in his voice. "Ma, cut it out. You and your superstitions!"

"I'd have thought it was good luck," added Ricky. "You don't have to be scared to go the biffy anymore!" There was laughter around the table.

"You'll see. You boys still have a lot to learn 'bout these things. You've bought yourself a barrel full of troubles."

"Aawh Elsie, what could possibly happen?" asked Joe. "Is that bear gonna haunt us now?"

Danny mopped up the rest of his egg with a piece of toast and popped it in his mouth.

"We should get going, Ricky," he said with his mouth full.

"What are you guys up to today?" asked Phil.

"We have to go to South Lake and get a boatload of gravel for making cement. Geez, I hope we're not building another septic tank. That one last year was a heck of a lot of trouble—I can't believe we actually finished it."

"Shovelling gravel? Doesn't sound like much fun. Glad I'm guiding." Joe looked at his watch. "I better get going. I want to go over my boat once more before Maury gets down to the dock, and he's always there at the stroke of eight, exactly."

***

Maury Weisman was a very tall, very stout man in his fifties, with a bulbous bald head, a pointed nose, and a fleshy face. Joe knew that Maury was obsessive-compulsive, and he insisted his boat be *very* clean, with not so much as a leaf or a speck of dirt to be seen. He was also loud, obnoxious, demanding, and impossible to please. Yet every guide wanted him in his boat. Why? Because he was the biggest tipper any of them had ever come across.

Every year, Maury came up for ten days for two reasons, and two reasons only: big fish and big shore lunches. He had a voracious appetite for both. On this trip, he brought his sixteen-year-old nephew, Micah, with him. It was not an act of kindness or even an act of charity. He simply needed a fishing partner, and no one else would come with him. Poor Micah didn't even like to fish. He was miserable most of every day.

Joe just had enough time to get down to the dock and check out his boat before Maury waddled up, his bulk almost totally obscuring the skinny lad behind him.

"Morning, Maury!" Joe jumped up to help him with his gear.

Maury mumbled a half-hearted greeting.

"Sleep well?" asked Joe, trying to be as pleasant as possible.

"Would have slept better if I'd caught a muskie yesterday!"

"I understand, sir," said Joe, piling the rods and tackle box into the boat. "But we'll get one today."

"I hope so, Joe. I hope so!" boomed Maury. "We don't want a repeat of yesterday. I was less than pleased with the spot we were at. Too many damn boats passing by. I don't like being even within hearing distance of another boat . . . disrupts the fish too much."

"We're off to North Lake. It's a long ways off, about a forty-minute ride, but it will be worth it. We're guaranteed to catch something big there, I promise you. Won't be any other boats around neither. I checked this morning, and all the guides are staying at this end of the lake."

"All right then. No, I don't need any help." Maury waved Joe's outstretched hand away and, with a great deal of grunting and wheezing, heaved himself into the boat. As he sunk into his seat, the boat also sunk several inches into the water.

Maury cast his beady eyes around. "Where's that nephew of mine? Micah?"

"Yes, Uncle Maury, I'm here," said Micah glumly, still standing on the dock.

"Why aren't you in this boat yet? I want to get going."

"Yes, Uncle Maury." The youth stepped into the bow of the boat, barely causing a flutter.

"Now let's get at 'em!" roared Maury.

It was policy to always fish for shore lunch before fishing for sport. At least then you knew you would eat. They spent an hour jigging for walleye. Normally four nice-sized fish were enough for three people. Seeing how Maury had devoured three fish himself the day before, Joe decided to keep six of the largest they could catch. When the last walleye was unhooked and slipped into the sack, Joe washed his hands off in the lake, wiped them off on his jeans, then proclaimed, "There, now we can get down to muskie fishing!"

After a short ride, Joe pulled the boat up beside a reef that barely broke the surface of the water. "We'll try here," he said.

Maury hooked on a yellowbird globe while Micah disinterestedly selected a beaten-up mud puppy. Maury cast and reeled in with a great deal of precision and skill; Micah cast half-heartedly, then absently wound in. It was clear Micah was not enjoying himself.

From the time they pulled up to the reef, Maury never let up on the poor kid. "You don't know how to cast. You don't know how to fish. What good are you, anyways?" or "What kind of fishing partner are you? You don't put anything into it! Don't you know fishing is work? You're lazy boy, lazy. You gotta put your arm into it!"

Grimacing, Micah raised his arm, swept the rod forward, and released the bail. The mud puppy landed with a splash a few feet in front of him.

"Not like that! Do I have to show you *again*?" Maury furiously wound his line in till his yellow globe was floating beside the boat then waited impatiently while Micah slowly retrieved his line. The mud puppy gurgled through the water. *Blump, blump, blump.*

Joe, who intently watched every move, saw a long, dark shadow just under the surface of the water tracking Micah's line. "There's a muskie behind your bait, Micah," he said quietly.

"What?" exclaimed Maury. He peered over the edge of the boat. "My God! It's gotta be thirty-five pounds!"

The kid's eyes grew big, his arms frozen in terror.

"Don't you know what to do?" barked Maury. "Make an eight!"

Micah obviously had no idea what an eight was. He still just sat there, staring at the gigantic fish looming around his bait. Suddenly it glided under the boat.

Clump! The muskie reappeared on the opposite side and swallowed Maury's floating yellow globe, taking off like a torpedo.

"My God!" Face flushed, Maury swung his bulk around and grabbed his rod just in time. The boat rocked. Joe desperately hoped Maury wouldn't fall into the water as he would never be able to fish him out.

The fish stripped line off his reel with whining speed. Maury loosened the drag and let him run until—sudden stillness. Maury set his bail and started hauling it in. He pulled and reeled, pulled and reeled. His large cheeks wobbled as he continued to pull and reel his line. Finally after fifteen minutes of battle, he raised the tired muskie up alongside the boat.

Joe stood up, ready for it, net in hand. *Maury has got his muskie!*

He slid the net under the belly and triumphantly scooped the muskie headfirst up out of the water. The muskie promptly slid right through the net, spit out the yellow globe, and without even a ripple, disappeared into the depths of the lake.

Joe stood there transfixed, holding the net, which now sported a large hole at the bottom.

"I . . . I don't understand. I've used this net lots of times."

Maury glared at him. "Apparently you've used it *too* many times."

Micah, meanwhile, barely squashed a smirk.

Shore lunch is going to have to be the highlight of the day, thought Joe as he absently pulled the boat up onto the rocks at one of the shore lunch spots. With the loss of a trophy fish, he was going to make sure it was spectacular. He'd get a nice hot fire going, then be extra careful filleting the walleye so that Maury wouldn't find a single bone in his meal.

Joe chopped some wood into kindling and carefully arranged it in the firepit. He then placed the grate on top and pulled out his Zippo. *Flick. Flick.* Nothing. He gave it a shake and tried again. Still nothing.

He checked the shore lunch box. The girls always stuck a pack of matches in there—except today. He checked the boat. He always carried a spare pack in the boat. They were not there.

Maury and Micah were sitting at the picnic table. Micah was sullenly holding a fresh spool of fishing line while Maury wound it onto his muskie reel.

"Excuse me, do either of you have a light?"

Maury looked up. "No. Why?"

"My lighter doesn't seem to be working."

"Don't you have any matches?"

"I always carry extra matches, only . . . I can't seem to find them."

Forty minutes away from the camp and no other boat in the whole area. They had cold beans and bread for lunch.

Joe felt awful as he packed up the remains of their meagre lunch. Nothing like this had ever happened to him before. He was going to have to get these guys some really big fish this afternoon to make up for the morning's calamity. He was still hungry and needed a smoke real bad.

"Joe?"

He turned around. "Yeah, Maury?"

"Our boat has floated away."

The three of them stood with their mouths open as they watched their boat bob in the lake with the seagulls, the aluminum hull blending in splendidly with the sparkling silver water.

Even Maury appeared to be at a loss for words. "What are we going to do now?"

There was only one thing Joe could do. He quickly pulled off his boots and socks, jumped in the lake, and swam after the boat.

***

Meanwhile, Roger and his two guests had stopped in Beaver Bay for their shore lunch.

Paul and Craig were two of the most unlikely fishermen Roger had ever seen. Total wilderness novices, they were both from New York, and from their appearance, he knew they had never fished before. The two men were dressed in city slicker wilderness wear: khaki pants with razor-sharp creases, contrived plaid shirts, baseball caps that had never seen a head before, and hiking boots that had never seen a hike. The cork handles on their fishing rods still had the plastic on them, and their reels were shiny and scratch-free. They had no fishing skills whatsoever, but Roger had guided them through the basics, so they had—in a short time, with grace and good humour—managed to tackle themselves a nice feed of walleye. Thrilled with their morning's action, they now walked excitedly around the tiny island, pointing in fascination at various rocks and plants while Roger started the fire and began filleting the fish.

"What type of plant is this?" asked Craig.

"That there's bedstraw." Roger wasn't sure it was, but he wasn't going to admit it.

"I think I saw some drawings on a rock back there. Do you think they were done by Indians?"

"Might be." Roger secretly believed they had been done by some fishermen's kids.

"What's this?" Paul asked, pointing to a fresh pile on the ground.

"Just signs of a bear," answered Roger.

"You mean bear manure?"

"Bear shit, yeah." *How could they be so naive?*

"Oh my goodness, there are bears?"

"Oh, Paul," said Craig. "Can you imagine if we saw one?"

"I've got to make sure my camera is ready!" cried Paul, diving into his bag.

Roger finished filleting the fish and started peeling potatoes while Craig and Paul circled the tiny island, looking for photo ops. They returned a few minutes later.

"I think we heard a bear back up there in the bush, Roger."

"Probably just a squirrel." *These guys want to see a bear so bad, they are hearing things. Too bad they hadn't been on the hunt last night!*

"Sounds bigger than a squirrel. I mean . . . I'm no expert, but it sounded like something heavy stepping on branches."

Roger continued to slice potatoes. "Sound travels in the bush. Besides, a bear ain't nothing to worry about."

A few minutes later, Craig tapped Roger on the shoulder. "Ah, Roger?" he whispered.

"Yeh?"

"What should we do now? The bear's at the table."

"What do you mean, it's at the table?" Roger turned around and looked, and there was the bear, standing at the picnic table, nose deep in their shore lunch box.

Paul pulled out his camera and snapped a couple of pictures of the bear deftly unwrapping some bread and stuffing it into his mouth. "Are these bears tame?" he asked. No one answered. "Roger? ROGER? Where'd you go?"

"There he is!" exclaimed Craig, pointing to the water.

Roger had sprinted to the safety of his boat and was already several yards from the shore.

***

Danny and Ricky towed a second boat, the fish gut boat, behind them to South Lake. This garbage boat, usually filled with fish entrails, would today be filled with gravel.

About a half-hour later, they reached their destination: an escarpment close to the shore. They wasted no time grabbing their shovels and digging in. The work was not easy. The loose gravel on the escarpment made it difficult to maintain a good footing. The hot sun beat down, heating up the gravel and searing their skin. The boys stripped off their sweat-sodden shirts and continued shovelling.

After a couple of hours, Danny straightened out. "Man, this is hard work! My back's killing me. That's got to be enough gravel. Al said to fill it here." Danny pointed to an area halfway up the side of the boat.

"Yeah, but if we fill it fuller, we won't have to come back and do this again tomorrow," said Ricky.

"Good thinking!" agreed Danny.

They continued to fill the boat, shovelful after shovelful until they had filled it right to the gunnel.

"There . . . can't squeeze any more in now!" said Danny, his bland, honest face dripping.

Ricky was pleased. "Wow, man, Al's gonna be so happy. He expected we'd just get part of a boatload today. Instead we got a full boatload!"

They threw the shovels on top of the pile.

Danny stared at the boat. "Sure is low, though." The top of the boat was no more than eight inches out of the water.

Ricky sloughed it off. "It'll be okay . . . as long as we go slow."

With a great deal of effort, they pushed off and started for home, Ricky at the helm.

After about ten minutes, Danny spun in his seat to face the stern. Beyond Ricky's shoulder, the second boat seemed to be lower in the water.

"Ricky!" Danny shouted over the hum of the outboard. "Does that boat look lower in the water to you?"

Ricky glanced behind him. "Nay, it's just the wake that makes it look that way."

"Well go slower then."

"If I go any slower, we won't get home till dark!"

The boys continued across the lake.

After a few more minutes, Danny checked the trailing boat again. He could barely make it out above the water.

"It's sinking!" cried Danny.

"It can't," answered Rick. But slowly, it did. And as it did, it started to take their boat down with it.

"My God, we're going to sink too!" Danny was now frantic.

"What do we do?"

"Pull over to shore!"

"We'll never make it to shore! There's only one thing we can do." Ricky turned off the motor, unsheathed his fillet knife, and cut the line.

The boys watched as the second boat sunk completely out of sight.

Danny's voice was small. "Oh crap, we're in trouble now."

***

Around five o'clock, Rick and Danny met up with Roger and Joe in front of the store.

Danny said glumly, "Man, did we have a bad day! Did you hear we sunk a boat to the bottom of the lake?"

"It's all over camp. Was Al mad?"

"He will be when we tell him."

"You haven't told him yet?"

"I'm in no hurry to inform Al that we worked all day yet still came back without any gravel *and* without his boat!"

Roger shook his head. "I wouldn't put it off too long . . . the longer you wait, the madder he'll be."

"Like you're so brave, Roger," scoffed Ricky. "We heard you were so scared of a little black bear that you took off in your boat and left your guests on shore with it!"

Roger's eyes dropped to the ground. "Don't know what came over me. Just took a look at that bear and had to get away."

"So your poor city slickers scared the bear off for you!"

"Yeah, but not before he stole all our fish. We had to make do with beans and fries. Their first shore lunch ever, and it's bloody beans and fries!"

"Geez and I thought we had a bad day, but you screwed up even worse! By the sounds of it, you'll be demoted from guiding and be back on grass cutting detail tomorrow!"

"Okay!" exclaimed Roger. "Knock it off. God, I need a cigarette. Joe, give me one."

Joe looked crestfallen. "Don't got none. Forgot to take 'em out of my pocket before I jumped in the lake."

Danny and Ricky turned their attention to Joe. "Okay, we gotta hear this! Why'd you jump in the lake?"

Joe recounted the events of his day.

"And to top it off, we didn't even get a nibble all afternoon! We couldn't raise one crummy fish."

Danny's eyes glazed over. "Wow. That's like . . . freaky."

Joe exploded. "Do you know Maury Weisman has asked for a different guide tomorrow? I've *never* had an unhappy guest before!"

Roger scratched his head. "How could we all have had such bad luck today?"

The other three boys were silent.

"You guys know why. You's just not saying!" Joe pulled a fistful of bear claws out of his jean pocket. "These damn things are cursed! Just like Elsie said!"

"You think?" Danny looked confused.

"Of course I think! The boat we used to ditch the bear ends up at the bottom of the lake like a watery grave? A bear scares the bejesus out of Roger. What are the odds of Roger running into a bear today? It's like the bloody thing *was* reincarnated!"

"It does seem strange that so many things could go wrong spontaneously—"

"Of course it's strange!" Joe continued. "And this was just the first day! Can you imagine what could happen tomorrow?"

"No use taking chances. I can't have another day like today." Ricky looked miserable and more than a little scared.

"Me neither," added Roger. All at once, the boys didn't look so confident or so grown up.

"If we don't get this fixed up, it could be catastrophic. We could have drowned today!" cried Danny.

"Okay, okay," agreed Rick. "Roger, let's find out from your mom what we have to do to stop the curse."

Danny patted Joe on the back. "It'll be okay. We'll get this fixed up. Come on. I'll buy you a pack of smokes first."

"I need a lighter, too. Lost my Zippo when I jumped in the lake."

***

Elsie was frying ham slices when the boys slunk in.

"Hey! How was your day?"

"Ma, you gotta help us!"

Elsie whipped around, her eyebrows raised in concern. "What's wrong?"

"We've been cursed all day! You said we was gonna be cursed, and we were."

"I never said you would be cursed. I said a dishonoured bear was bad luck."

"Same thing! Elsie, you gotta help us make it stop! Please!" cried Danny.

"Hmmm," she mused. "You have to give something back, something personal, to show you are sorry. Hair would be good. You have to take your hair and burn it, along with the claws and that there pecker. And the skull."

"Sounds like voodoo."

"You asked me. If you want to straighten out your spot in the universe, yous'll do it."

***

After dinner, when Ricky and Danny and Joe retired to their cabin, Roger did not join them. Instead he restlessly walked the length of the camp, unsure what to do. He felt sick. He didn't want to cut his hair! He turned off the path and walked to the end of the dock, where he whipped off his cap and gazed down into the lake. The still waters reflected a face framed with thick, luxurious locks. Back in Kenora, his hair was a real babe magnet. Girls were always telling him how much they loved his curls. There had to be another way! After all, nothing that bad had really happened to him, except perhaps a momentary lapse of guts. Maybe he just had to burn the claws. That should do it! Relieved to have made his decision, Roger headed back to his cabin. He'd tell the guys they could do what they wanted, but he wasn't going to cut one lock off his head!

Helen was also slowly heading back to her cabin after a long day of work. As she passed Roger, she gave him a tired smile, then reached up and pulled the bundle of curls off her head. Roger gasped. He had never seen—or even heard of—a hairpiece and had no idea how Helen could possibly pull off her hair. His eyes opened even wider than they had that afternoon when he had seen the bear at the picnic table.

"Holy cripes!" He took off faster than a wildfire in a dry forest.

***

"Roger?" called Helen, but he didn't stop. *What was wrong with him? Had he seen something? Another bear?* Helen whipped her head around. Nothing but trees.

Still she decided it might be prudent to walk just a little faster herself. She took off in a trot.

Her pace didn't slow till she reached her cabin. Inside, she breathed a sigh of relief and checked on Lori, who was already asleep in her bed. She slipped out of her clothes and into her caftan, then started to comb out her hairpiece.

Buzz, buzz. A couple of annoying mosquitoes circled her head. One thing Helen would not tolerate was incessant insects humming around her head. She grabbed the mosquito fogger and furiously pumped the handle. Over and over, she took aim and fired until the air was blue and syrupy, and every last bug had dropped dead.

There! That's better, she thought, as she sunk to the sofa in satisfaction. She wished all the camp nuisances could be controlled so easily. This business with the bear had been most disconcerting; she didn't like bears nearby, yet she didn't like people running around during the night shooting at things. She was just glad it was over; maybe now everything could return to normal.

Just then, Phil flung open the door and entered the cabin like a whirlwind.

"Night, Mom!" he yelled as he flew by her.

"Shut the door! I just fogged the place!" shouted Helen, but he had already run to his room without even bothering to take off his jacket and cap.

"Honestly, that child!" Helen rose and closed the door. Everyone seemed spooked tonight.

***

The next morning, the breakfast table was unusually quiet. The boys, who usually joked and laughed through their meal, silently spooned cereal into their mouths, neither talking nor looking at each other. The boyish grins that usually lit up the room were missing, except for Phil, who was smiling from ear to ear. Al strode into the staff room.

"Morning, crew. How's everyone today?" Al glanced around the table, frowning. "Why do you boys have your caps on at the table? Where's your manners?"

Still they didn't answer. Instead they stared intently into their bowls of oatmeal.

Al walked up behind Phil and pulled his cowboy hat off. There was only a shadow where his hair used to be—he was totally bald!

Flabbergasted, Al turned and barked, "Boys, caps off. NOW."

Slowly they removed their caps. Four bare exposed skulls gave them the appearance of a clutch of newly hatched baby birds. A hush fell over the table. It was apparent no one knew quite what to say—that is until James spoke up.

"Looks like you've all been scalped."

The table broke up in laughter.

Al ran a hand over his own crew cut. "Never thought I'd see the day when my hair would be longer than yours."

Ricky pleaded to his uncle. "It was that damn curse, Al!"

"What are you talking about?"

"The curse of the bear! Elsie said by taking the claws, we dishonoured the bear, and she was right! All sorts of things went wrong yesterday!"

"Tell me about it! I lost a boat, I have no gravel to make cement today, and I have a valued guest who is *very* unhappy. And you say *you* had a bad day! I didn't even keep any bear claws! You don't know what a bad day is!"

The boys looked totally miserable.

"So is someone going to explain how shaving your heads makes everything right?"

Roger finally spoke up. "Ma said we took something from the bear, so we had to give something back, like our hair. So last night, we's all got together, shaved our heads, then headed to the firepit at The Point and burned all the bear parts along with the hair."

Al couldn't believe what he was hearing. This took Elsie's superstitions to a whole new level.

"You really believe this stuff?"

"Didn't feel like taking any more chances."

"Elsie!" shouted Al.

Elsie hobbled in around the corner, took one look at the boys, and started to cackle. "Oh, for God's sake! What have you done now?"

"What do you mean, what have we done?" cried Roger. "You told us we had to give our hair to break the curse. Now Ma, don't be telling us you was lying!"

"I wasn't lying. But I didn't tell you to shave your head. For God's sake, you only had to burn one curl!" she exclaimed.

The boys whooped. "Now you tell us!"

Al looked back at Phil. "And why are you bald? You weren't even there when they cut up that bear!"

Phil beamed. "I wanted to be one of the guys, and now I am!"

Lori replaced Phil's hat on the wall. For whatever reason, the boys' luck did change after they performed Elsie's bizarre ritual, and they were able to enjoy the rest of the summer without any undue misfortune. It was amazing. Elsie's superstitions almost always came true. Like when she forecast the arrival of "someone important." Lori reached for the tan Panama hat—

1967

Jimmy Adams watched through the large picture window of his dockside office at O.C.A. as two smartly dressed men climbed out of a rental car. Immediately recognizing one of them, he wondered why this unlikely fisherman was in this neck of the woods. He pulled the toothpick from his lips, adjusted his aviator sunglasses, then casually strolled onto the dock to find out.

Within twenty minutes, he had loaded the men and their luggage onto a Cessna bound for Stork Lake. And in true Jimmy fashion, he decided *not* to radio ahead and tell Al and Helen who would be arriving at their camp. After all, what would be the fun in that?

***

"Look, there's that weasel!" cried Agnes.

A furry head peered up from a small hole in the floor, then silently stole up and into the slop pail, his long, bushy tail hanging over the side. He was a handsome specimen; his sleek body was covered with a lustrous coat, and there was a small patch of brilliant white at his throat, just under his pointed chin.

"I bet you're wondering what's on the menu today," laughed Elsie. "Well, you's got your choice of sausage or bacon for your 'take out.'"

Elsie, Helen, and Agnes watched as he dove down into the pail and rummaged through goodies before finally popping back up with a sausage link. His tiny but fearless eyes now stared up at them as if to say, "What are you looking at?" He posed for them a moment longer before taking his prize and slowly slinking back into the floorboards.

"What a brave little fellow." Helen laughed, leaning back into the table.

Clunk! A butcher knife slid off the edge and landed on the floor.

"Unexpected company coming," said Elsie. "And by the size of the knife, I'd say someone very important."

Helen knew that every piece of spilled cutlery meant something to Elsie. A fallen spoon foretold an unexpected lady visitor while forks were equated with men. Knives were reserved for influential people: policemen, lawyers, clergy. The bigger the knife, the more important the visitor. Since Elsie's predictions were pretty much always right, Helen wasn't the least bit surprised when, a short time later, she heard the roar of an unscheduled plane.

"I'll go see who it is," said Helen, brushing a stray wisp of hair away from her forehead. "And find out how many extra potatoes we need to put in the pot. I hope these unexpected people aren't too important, Elsie. I haven't had a chance to wash my hair in days!"

Helen exited the lodge and started down the path. As she rounded the last cabin, the bright morning sun struck her in the eyes, making it difficult to see—she could just make out two men chatting to Al. Who were they? Helen shaded her eyes and scanned the dock. One of them looked familiar. She took a few more steps, then stopped and squinted. *Why, it looked like . . . No, it couldn't be! Could it?* The man was the right age, about mid-forties. True, he was a little heavier, but he still had that dazzling smile—

She shook her head. There was no way Gordon MacRae, the star of so many of her favourite musicals—the star of her very *favourite* musical of all time—was right here on the dock of her little camp. She had been thinking about music a lot lately; it was the thing she missed the most up here. And she had been singing "Face to Face" just a couple of days ago. Maybe she was just seeing things—maybe she was just *wishing* things! Her pace quickened until she was right smack in front of him.

"Helen." Al turned to his wife. "These gentlemen are here to fish for a few days. This is Gordon MacRae and his friend Stu Tauber."

"Hello, Helen," said the deep baritone voice of countless well-known songs.

She was, really and truly, face-to-face with Gordon MacRae! Helen was speechless, for a moment, anyway. Then her babble set in.

"Hello! Hi! Oh my! I'm sooo happy to meet you! I *love* your movies. I know all your songs. I listen to them all the time, only not here because we don't have a record player. Well we do, but not here, at the camp. I hope that's not a problem? I mean, will you want to listen to records?"

"No, not at all!" boomed Gordon, who seemed to have understood Helen's gabble perfectly. "We're actually looking forward to some solitude! We just want to get away from it all for a bit, you know, to relax and catch a few fish. That man at the float base, what is his name . . . Jimmy? Well he recommended your place here. He promised it wouldn't be 'full, fussy, fancy, or fished out,' which is exactly what we're looking for."

"Yes, that's us! We're not full, and we're not fancy at all! And no one's going to fuss over you! I mean, not that they shouldn't, it's just we know now you don't want it."

"So let's not fuss then, Helen," interjected Al, "and instead find these gentlemen a cabin so they can get out on the lake and do what they've come to do, and that's fish."

"Of course! Of course! I'm sorry. You'll want to get settled in right away! I'm afraid it'll have to be one of the older cabins, won't it, Al?" She didn't wait for his reply. "Our two newest cabins are already in use."

"Doesn't matter the least bit to us." Gordon smiled.

"Cabin 2 is free. It's right beside the lake—"

"Then that's the one we'll take. I can't imagine waking up to this view in the morning!" Gordon swept his hand in the direction of the lake, shimmering in the early morning sun. "It's like a stage setting. It's so perfect!"

"All right then! It's not far. Al! Grab their bags and bring them up right away."

"Yes, dear," said Al mockingly as he picked up their bags. He often helped with guest luggage but was not usually ordered to by his wife as if he were a bellboy at the Hilton.

Unperturbed, she continued, "I'll come in with you and make sure everything is in order, then you can let me know if there is anything else you need. Please, just follow me." As the little group set off up the hill toward the cabin, Helen thought she would pee her pants. Gordon MacRae and some other man were here!

***

"Elsie! Agnes!" Helen yelled into the kitchen a few minutes later. "Where are yooou?"

She found them in the pantry, where in front of its warm eastern window, Elsie was kneading up her own personal concoction: Red River bread, which was an innovative way to use up the morning's leftover Red River cereal. This bread was everyone's favourite: crusty on the outside and freckled with flax, cracked wheat, and rye on the inside. Agnes stood beside her, stuffing freshly baked jumbo-sized spiced raisin cookies into apothecary jars.

"You will never believe who the unexpected company is! It's Gordon MacRae!"

Both Elsie and Agnes's faces were blank.

"You know! He played Curly McLain? The guy with that gorgeous voice? He sang 'Surrey with the Fringe on Top' from the musical *Oklahoma*?"

Agnes shrugged her shoulders.

Elsie looked confused. "I don't think I seen that one."

Their nonchalance did nothing to take the wind out of Helen's sails. "Well he's a famous star, and he's staying here! Now let me think. Agnes, you'll have to set two extra spots at one of the guest tables for supper tonight." To Elsie, she asked, "Do we have enough meat out for two more people?"

"I haven't taken the meat out yet."

"We really should decide this the night before. Don't we have a prime rib? That should be good enough for a movie star. If we take it out now and pop it in the oven sooner, it should be done in time for supper."

"Sounds good."

"What about soup? What kind of soup were we going to have?"

Elsie waddled into the kitchen and peered into a pot bubbling on the stove. "Hmmm . . . I think it's turning out to be 'refrigerator soup.'"

Refrigerator soup could mean anything because it was a combination of everything. Leftovers were never thrown out; food was too precious, too expensive to fly in to be wasted. When the fridge filled up with leftover rice, noodles, vegetables, and meat, Elsie would throw them all together and somehow always end up with something out of this world.

"That'll be okay." Helen already was on to the next thought. "What shall we have with the roast?"

"Potatoes in their jackets?"

"Good idea. We'll use real butter and some of the chives from the garden. Too bad we don't have any sour cream. If I had known Gordon MacRae was coming, I would have ordered some in special. Lori, where's Lori? Looori!"

"I'm in here, Mom."

Lori was playing in the staff dining room with her new toy poodle, Chezy. Chezy was a small ball of white fluff with a tiny baby doll face, two big black saucers for eyes, and a button nose. Even though she barely weighed a few pounds, she fearlessly barreled at any opponent as if she was a hundred-pound Rottweiler. She took great joy in chasing mice and squirrels, barking gleefully until they ran away. The larger the animal, the higher-pitched the bark. Ducks and rabbits incurred a midrange bark. Bears earned almost a shriek.

It was a cool morning, so Chezy had on a rust-coloured sweater, which was actually an old sweater of Lori's with the sleeves cut off.

Helen peered around the corner. "Lori, put that dog down. I swear she doesn't know she has legs . . . then take a pail and fetch about ten potatoes, baking size. Gordon MacRae is here for dinner tonight!"

Lori's blank stare told Helen that she too had no idea who Gordon McCrae was; however, she obligingly did as she was told. She gently lowered Chezy to the ground, and the little dog promptly scooted behind the wood stove, the warmest place in the kitchen. Lori slipped out the door and skipped along the stone path to the root house a few yards away. The little cellar had been cut into the side of the hill, its small door and straw-covered roof just barely poking out of the grassy expanse.

Lori opened the door and stepped into the cool hut. A bare bulb, hanging from the ceiling, barely lit the house enough to see the walls lined with shelves holding margarine, crates of eggs, and cans of juice and beans. She dug into a burlap sack of potatoes, pulled out ten decent-sized ones, then ran back to the kitchen, along with her father, who had just arrived.

Helen met them at the door. "Is Gordon still here? Do they need anything before they go out on the lake? Maybe something to eat? Elsie could whip up—"

"They've gone fishing already. I loaned them some rods and reels. Funny thing, they didn't bring any fishing gear with them. I also loaned them some rain gear—"

"Not used rain gear!"

"What's wrong with used? It keeps out the rain just as good."

"It's just that I'm sure he's used to having the best of everything. He probably shops at Saks." Helen sighed. "Can you imagine shopping there? Dior, Yves St. Laurent, Givenchy. Saks carries them all. I hear the designer's fall fashions are really something this year. The belted wool coat is back in style, you know."

Elsie seemed to be more interested in the store name than the current styles. "Sacks . . . never heard of it. Clever though, naming it after bags."

"Not sacks, S-A-K-S."

"Well imagine that! That don't make no sense at all."

Helen crooked her brow. "I guess . . ." She turned back to her husband. "Who've they got for a guide?"

"Uncle Pete."

"Oh no!"

"What do you mean? He's a real card! They'll get a kick out of him."

"I know. It's just I wish someone more . . . experienced had been available, like Roger or Peepsight."

"Uncle Pete'll be fine. He hasn't got lost for weeks and has hit most every reef, so he knows where they all are now." Seeing his wife's distraught face, he explained, "I'm joking! He's a great guide, and his guests have been bringing in some pretty decent fish."

"All right," sighed Helen. "Oh, Al, this is the most exciting thing that has happened since we got this place! Maybe if they have a really good time, they'll come back again! And bring some of their Hollywood friends! We really have to make sure everything is perfect. I should change their towels! And I noticed a cobweb in their bathroom—" Helen flew out the door, singing "Oh What a Beautiful Morning" in her clear soprano voice.

Al scratched his head. "Don't see what all the fuss is about."

"Anything that makes a wife happy, that's a good thing," replied Elsie. "When momma's happy, *everyone's* happy."

"Everyone won't be happy if she forgets there are still other guests in camp. I better remind her she has to clean *all* the guest cabins," said Al jokingly as he left. They both knew that as excited as Helen was about Gordon MacRae, she was almost as thrilled to have Twin Disc back in camp.

Since enjoying the distinction of becoming Helen's first customers, the Twin Disc party had remained Stork Lake's most steadfast and lucrative account. They came up several times every year, never finding anything to complain about. They always found the fishing and hunting exceptional, the accommodations better and better—and of course, they loved the staff.

Instead of Jack Yetter, this trip was led by one of their top moneymen, Bill Shurts. He was a silver-haired, slim man with a smooth, rosy complexion and a ready smile. Easy to please, his group asked only one thing—that they be allowed to bring up their favourite American canned beer to enjoy in the boat while they were fishing. Al happily complied with this small request.

***

Helen's excitement about Gordon MacRae had in no way dulled when, later, the staff all sat down to lunch.

"I loved him in musical *By the Light of the Silvery Moon*. He was in it with Doris Day. You *must* know who she is."

"Ah!" cackled Elsie, "The girl with the freckles. Yea, I know her! She's wonderful."

"The lady has freckles like me, Mommy?" asked Lori, who was sitting beside Agnes, munching on a grilled cheese sandwich.

"Yes. And you know who she is, Lori. She's in your favourite show, *Please Don't Eat the Daisies*."

"Oh her, I love her. But I don't think she has freckles, Mommy. She looks all smooth like you. She doesn't look like me." The little girl rubbed her speckled nose. "I wish I didn't have any."

"Well, she does. You just can't see them on TV. And Doris Day loves her freckles, and you should love yours, too," retorted Helen.

"She does? And this man knows her? Then I like him, too." Lori beamed, showing off her two missing front teeth.

"Well I've seen Doris Day movies, but not the one you're talking about," said Elsie.

"It was famous! And he's famous! Al, tell them how famous he is!" insisted Helen, perturbed that no one here knew who Gordon MacRae was.

"Oh, he is famous," answered Al, stirring his tea. "Don't know any of his songs, though. I'm more of a John Wayne man myself."

"John Wayne! Now there's a star!" exclaimed Albert.

"Oh, I like him," swooned Agnes, scratching the left palm of her hand.

"You've been scratching that palm all day," said Elsie.

"Yep. I'll be able to order that new sweater set from the Eaton's catalogue."

Helen was often confused by these sudden turns in conversation. "What does an itchy palm have to do with that?"

"It means she's going to come into some unexpected money," explained Elsie.

"Shouldn't you wait till you actually get the money before you order it?" Helen asked Agnes. "What if your itchy palm is just an itchy palm? Then you will have bought something you can't afford."

Agnes and Elsie both looked surprised. "An itchy palm is never just an itchy palm," said Elsie.

Helen just shook her head. "Of course not. I should know better." She rose from the table and started to stack dishes. Lori seemed to take this as her cue to escape. She quietly slid off the bench and headed for the door.

"Hold on there, missy!"

Lori stopped dead in her tracks.

"You either stay here with me or go to our cabin and stay there. I don't want to have to go looking for you! I have no time to hunt for you today. I just want to get these dishes done quickly so I can do something with my hair before supper. I don't want Gordon MacRae to see me like this!"

"I'll stay in the cabin," replied Lori.

***

Disappointed that her adventures had been curtailed, Lori slowly sauntered up to their cabin on the hill, Chezy trotting at her heels.

Once inside, she glanced down at the little dog. "What should we do, Chezy?" The little dog's prompt reply was to hop up onto Helen's bed for a little after-lunch nap.

"Lot of fun you are." Lori trudged to her room, flung open the large window, rested her elbows on the broad sill, and stared out at the forest. She could be picking tiny Johnny-jump-ups or toadflax. She could be squeezing the sweet-smelling golden buttons of tansy or popping the pods of touch-me-nots. She could be hunting for baby bunnies, trying to catch minnows, climbing in her mansion, or climbing trees. She could even be with Philip, helping Albert saw wood for the new building! There was so much she could be doing outside, if only she wasn't stuck in here!

She looked around her room. There was not much to see. There was her bed, which she made up every morning, being careful that the stripes on the bedspread were nice and straight and that the heavy Hudson Bay blanket was neatly folded at the foot. The room was too tiny for a dresser; instead, her clothes were kept in a wooden cubicle, skirted with a heavy rosebud-patterned material. A rod strung along one wall was where her mother hung her clothes.

What was there to do in here? She had very few toys at the camp. There was never enough room on the plane to bring much with her. There were a few books piled beside her bed and a puzzle or two. But she had read all the books *and* finished all the puzzles. There was a sand bucket and shovel in the corner, but she would have to go outside to play with them.

She spotted her red plastic Barbie case lying on the floor.

"I know. I'll play Barbies!"

She grabbed the case, opened it up, and took out a couple of Barbies. She had heard her mom say this morning something about belted wool coats being in style this year. Her Barbies had no wool coats. Maybe if she dressed her doll up and did her hair, she would look like Doris Day, the Doris Day without the freckles.

Lori thought about Chezy sleeping on her mom's bed, still wearing that old sweater of hers for a coat. If her mom could make a sweater for Chezy out of something, maybe she could make a belted coat for her Barbie out of something. But what? The blanket at the foot of her bed was wool—and it was such a pretty colour green—it would match Barbie's go-go dress perfectly!

She found a pair of scissors in her mom's sewing box and then carefully cut a piece off the Hudson Bay blanket and tried to fashion a coat out of it. It didn't work out too well—the material was too thick and stiff to wrap around Barbie properly. It looked nothing like a coat, and the string she used for a belt looked like—well, string. She was so desolate over her deficient dressmaking skills that she did not even hear her mother come into her room.

"Lori, have you seen . . . What's that?" Her mother was staring at the doll wrapped in a square of green wool, the exact size and colour of the missing corner of the blanket.

Lori could not say a peep.

"Did you cut this blanket?"

Tears stung her eyelids. *What had she been thinking? Why had she been so stupid?* She braced for the torrent she knew was about to come.

It never did. Instead, Helen sat on the edge of the bed and gave Lori a big hug. The little girl could not have been more surprised than if her mother had cut up the blanket herself.

"It's okay," comforted her mom. "I remember when I was about your age, I cut up one of my mom's blankets to make a coat for my doll, too. I never seemed to have enough clothes for her. Was that why you did it?"

Lori silently bobbed her head up and down.

Helen stroked the doll's silky golden head. "Listen, next week we won't be so busy. I'll get my sewing machine out, and we'll make your doll a nice coat. How's that?"

"Could we make her a new dress, too?"

"Of course. Okay, then. Dry your tears, and help me find my rollers. I like the style of your Barbie's hair. I'm going to try to make my hair look like that!"

***

"He'll be in for supper any minute. How's my hair?" Helen asked Elsie, turning her head side to side. "Does it look okay?"

"Eh?"

"My hair. I tried to curl it, but when I went to put my hair dryer on, Albert started using the table saw, so I had to shut it off. You'd think by now those men of ours would have figured out how to run more than a couple of electrical appliances at a time—"

"I'm sure it's fine," Elsie answered absently. She was busy filling breadbaskets with her fresh, warm rolls, still glistening with melted butter on the top. When all the baskets were full, she bagged up the rest of the buns and the dozen loaves of bread she had made that day. She stacked them all neatly on the table beside the jars of cookies. That task accomplished, she turned her attention back to supper. She opened the wood stove door and poked her head in.

"Oh oh."

"What do you mean oh oh?" Helen's voice held an edge of panic. "We can't have any oh oh's tonight, Elsie!"

"Nothing, nothing." She quickly closed the oven door. "It's just—I think I'll put another log in the stove."

"I hope Twin Disc comes on time tonight. I don't want the meat to get overdone. And I hope they don't fill up on those Kringles." Helen started to worry again. Kringles were a couple of pound ovals of hand-rolled and filled Danish pastry made only in Racine, Wisconsin. Along with beer, the Twin Disc party always brought up boxes of them to munch on while they were fishing.

"Oh they'll eat," laughed Elsie. "They's always bring their appetites."

Sometime later, when the dinner gong was rung, no one appeared for dinner.

"I know Twin Disc is always late. But where are Gordon and his friend? I wonder if they know they're supposed to come when we ring the gong? Should I go up and get them?" Helen started to worry again.

"They'll come when they come," said Elsie giving the soup another stir.

"Yup," agreed Agnes, who was sitting on the kitchen stool, reading a magazine.

"I hope they enjoyed their day. And I hope Uncle Pete got them a lot of fish. I just can't get over that they are here. Oh, Elsie, I wish you had seen *Carousel*. That scene with him and Shirley Jones—" She began to sing "If I loved You."

Gordon, who had just quietly walked in the door, crept up behind Helen and joined in for the next few lines.

"*Oh my!*" exclaimed Helen. She thought she would faint. She had sung with Gordon MacRae!

"You have a beautiful voice, Helen!"

"Oh, go on."

"You do! I think I'll take you back to Hollywood with me."

Helen giggled like a schoolgirl. "I don't think my husband would approve."

"Drat husbands anyways. Husbands always seem to have the best girls! Honestly, doll, you have an amazing voice!"

"You think so?" Helen giggled again. "That is the greatest compliment anyone has ever paid me."

Just then, Gordon's friend, Stu, walked in and joined them.

"Good evening, Mr. Tauber!" Helen finally remembered his name. "How was your day?"

"Please call me Stu. It was amazing. I caught my first muskie, a thirty-eight pounder!"

"And I caught more fish than I could even lie about!" boasted Gordon. "It was in a place no one had ever fished in before. I suggested we name the spot 'Gord's Goldmine' but finally agreed to name it 'Pete's Hole.' Not as catchy, but I suppose Pete does deserve *some* credit since he was the one who found it. He's a great fellow—had us in stitches all day. That man could do stand-up comedy!"

"He is a card, isn't he?" Helen breathed a sigh of relief. They liked Uncle Pete! "I'm *so* glad you had a good day." She was gushing but couldn't help it. "And I hope your evening is just as good. We're having prime rib for supper. I hope that's okay with you, gentlemen."

"You mean we get supper, too? I thought that with all that food at shore lunch, you only served one huge meal a day around here!" Stu said as he laughed.

"No kidding!" said Gordon. "I can't remember ever eating so much. My God, that fish! And those fries! But don't worry, I'll find a way to squeeze in another meal! And, yes, we love prime rib!" Gordon inhaled deeply. "The smells whiffing out of this kitchen are heavenly. When did you say we eat?"

Bill Shurts and his crew entered the dining room shortly after, and all the guests sat down to dinner. Elsie's refrigerator soup was a success. So was her salad. Now it was time for the main course. Elsie started slicing up the roast.

"Do you think it's done enough?" she asked Helen anxiously. Used to preparing cheaper cuts, Elsie believed every piece of meat needed to be cooked until you needed a chainsaw to cut it. It had taken Helen years to get her to cook beef rare. However, this seemed beyond rare—it was blue.

Helen barely glanced at it. "It'll be fine. They won't mind. I know Bill and his people like their meat real rare. Most Americans do."

Indeed, the Twin Disc party gobbled up platterful after platterful of the blood-red beef—they loved it. In fact, there was only one person in the whole dining room that did not: Gordon. He motioned Helen over to the table.

"Love, will you come here a moment?"

"Yes, sir, what can I do for you?"

"Do you hear that?"

"Hear what?"

"My meat. I think I'm detecting a heartbeat."

"You would like a piece a little more well done?"

"Not well done. Just cooked till it's dead, deary." His tone and bright smile took the sting out of the words. Still, Helen wished she could crawl under the floorboards.

"No problem. I'll be right back." With a smile pasted on her lips, Helen took his plate and headed for the kitchen, where she knew there was not one piece of beef cooked to medium.

"Elsie! Elsie! Gordon wants his roast done more!" She was almost in a panic.

Elsie was far too polite to say, "I told you so." Instead she said, "Is that so?"

"Yes, that's so. What should we do? Throw it in the frying pan?"

"We can't do that. It'll get hard and brown. Just blot the blood off it then—it'll look more done, and he'll never know the difference."

He didn't. Gordon strode into the kitchen after supper, patting his stomach. "You sure know the way to your guests' hearts! That was the juiciest, best-tasting prime rib I have ever had! And the warm homemade buns! Why I barely had room for apple pie, and that would have been a shame to miss. It was better than Mom used to make!"

"Oh? Glad you liked it," said Elsie simply.

"Liked it? I loved it! I think I'll take you back home to cook for me! Or do you have a husband, too?"

"Oh y-yes," stuttered Elsie. "I got one of those."

"Drat!" he groaned to Helen. "I told you husbands get all the good ones! Well if there are no single women around here, I may as well go for a dip in the lake, though I'm so full I'll probably drown." Suddenly his eyes grew wide. "My God, there's a mink in your kitchen!"

The weasel had arrived for his supper. Scavenging around, he found a prime rib bone with a good bit of meat still on it. He grabbed his prize and tried to shove it down the hole in the floor, but it was too big. The critter pulled and prodded, oblivious to his audience, intent on his task.

"Oh, that's not a mink. It's a weasel," said Elsie.

"A weasel? Isn't he dangerous?"

"Don't think so. He hasn't attacked any of us, anyways."

Just then, someone opened the door, and Chezy flew in and took off after the weasel, barking like crazy, totally unaware the weasel could easily have enjoyed her for dinner if he so chose. But he didn't. Maybe he did not like the shrill of the poodle's bark bullets on his tiny but very sensitive ears. Whatever the reason, he slunk away, minus the bone. Chezy ran up, picked up the bone, and scurried behind the wood stove with her prize.

Gordon howled. "Now I've seen everything!"

***

The next morning, Elsie stood in the middle of the pantry, staring at the empty table in disbelief. Every cookie, every loaf of bread, every bun was gone. Not a bag was left, not even a crumb. In front of the table, the screen window was torn right open; it had obviously been the point of entry and getaway for the thief.

"Albert! Albeeeert!"

Albert came running in from the staff dining room, where he had been enjoying his morning coffee and cigarette.

"All my baking's missing! It was here last night when I left! Something broke in and took it during the night. Can you believe it? Right through the window! It took everything out right through the window."

Albert stepped outside and around to the outside of the window. "Bear tracks here." He grinned at Elsie through the hole where the screen had been. "Even bears can't resist my wife's baking."

Elsie laughed, taking it all in stride. She then stepped back into the kitchen, put on her apron, and set the water on the cookstove for oatmeal. "It was supposed to be French toast this morning. I guess with no bread, it'll have to be pancakes."

***

Baked goods were not the only thing missing that morning. Bill Shurts approached Al after breakfast. "I hate to have to mention this to you, Al, but we left a case of beer out on our porch last night. This morning, there was no sign of it. Did someone by chance move it?"

"I wouldn't think so unless someone thought it was the camp's by mistake. Geez, I'm so sorry, Bill! I'll ask around then check down at the store and see if someone accidentally moved it there. I can assure you it's got to be some sort of misunderstanding. My guys know they'd be thrown out of camp if they touched it."

"Oh, I'm not accusing anyone of stealing it! I know no one here would do that!" reassured Bill. "It really doesn't matter—we have more than enough. It's just curious, is all."

"It sure is. Believe me. I'll get this cleared up." Al's tone was quiet but had a steel edge to it.

***

Helen, too, was trying to get something cleared up once and for all. As they stacked up the breakfast dishes, she made one last attempt to explain to Elsie who Gordon MacRae was.

"He was in *Moonlight Bay*. Doris Day was in that one, too. Have you heard of it?"

"Can't says I have."

"You've *got* to know who he is! He was also in *The Best Things in Life are Free*."

"Was it on TV?"

"No! He's not on TV. He does movies," explained Helen patiently. "His wife's on TV, though."

"He's married? I thought he was a single man, what with all that talk about husbands having all the good women."

"Nah, he's just kidding around. He has a lovely, talented wife."

"Really? What's she been on?"

"Have you ever watched the new *Honeymooners* with Jackie Gleason?"

"Oh yeah, lots of times. Albert loves that show!"

"Well, Sheila MacRae is the new Alice."

"I like her! Her husband, eh? I guess he must be something to be married to a big star like her."

Helen gave up. There was no way culture was going to make it to this backwoods; no, this was *Green Acres*, and she was Lisa Douglas, transplanted from the real world of stores and music and theatre to the surreal world of animals acting like people, life-changing decisions made on the itches and aches of body parts, and a generator that worked only with a limited number of electrical appliances.

***

The boats had all come in for the night, and most of the guests were in their cabins, washing up for dinner. Lori heard Gordon whistling as he came down the hill. It wasn't a warm day, but he had taken to having a bath in the lake, no matter what the weather. He stood on the shore in his swim trunks, a bar of soap in one hand and a towel in the other.

Lori was making sand cookies on the dock. She collected beer caps that washed up on the beach, filled them with wet sand, then unmolded them onto her "cookie sheet" dock. The sweater-clad Chezy was with her, sniffing and pawing at the sand cookies as if they were real.

"Hi, sweetheart!" Gordon called out. Lori waved back.

"That's a fine guard dog you've got there," he said, pointing to Chezy.

Just at that moment, Chezy spotted a loon leisurely paddling near the shore. Always the boss, she barked at it as if to say, "You bet I'm a guard dog! And this intruder is not welcome at my camp!"

The loon continued its course, unaffected by the barked orders. Chezy edged nearer to the end of the dock.

Splash!

"Chezy! Chezy!" cried Lori. She ran to the edge of the dock. Chezy looked shocked as she surfaced and valiantly tried to dog paddle, but the wool sweater sucked up water like a sponge. After a moment, she started to sink. Lori reached down as far as she could, but her arms were not long enough to reach the little dog.

Just as Chezy's cotton-top head started to go under, an arm reached down and hauled the dog out of the water by her sweater. It was Gordon, down on his bare knees on the dock.

"Chezy!" Lori hugged the little dog, wet sweater and all. Her eyes glowed as she looked at Gordon. "Thank you for saving my dog."

Gordon laughed. "You're welcome, sweetie. Wouldn't want to see her become muskie bait."

***

Later, when the guests were all in the lodge eating supper, the bear made his appearance, carrying a package of Kringles in his mouth. He casually climbed down the hill from the guest cabins, took a seat on the roof of the root cellar, opened the box, pulled one out, and took a big bite.

"The bear!" cried Elsie, who had just happened to look out the kitchen window at that moment.

Instantly, every guest was out of his seat, peering through the windows.

"Hey," cried Bill Shurts. "He's eating our Kringles! Where'd he get those?"

"Apparently from our cabin," chuckled one of his fishing mates. "He's been busy since we came down to dinner!"

The kitchen was not the only place the bear had decided to break into.

Gordon opened the screen door to get a better look. Out flew a now-dry Chezy, a fluffy projectile fearlessly exploding toward the enemy. She raced toward the bear, barking her "bear bark"—a real high-pitched howler.

Elsie, from the protection of the kitchen, shouted for her to come back, but Chezy ignored her. The bear, however, did not. He picked up his Kringle box and ambled off into the forest. For the second time in as many days, Chezy had defended the kitchen against predators. She turned around and proudly trotted back to the kitchen.

Gordon turned to Elsie. "A bonsai dog wards off a pastry-eating bear. What, is this all part of the entertainment? It's better than any TV show!"

Elsie, meanwhile, had collapsed with laughter. "Imagine that! Musta enjoyed my baking so much that he went nosing around for more. The thief!"

***

Albert suddenly realized the bear was stealing more than baked goods, but he would have to wait until dark to prove it. He sought out Al to relay his plan.

Bill had been puzzled when, after dinner, Al had asked him to leave beer on the stoop one more time.

"I'll reimburse you double if it goes missing. It's worth it to me to prove to you none of my guides are thieves."

"I'm not worried about being reimbursed, Al. And I know no one here's a thief, except that bear. Wait . . . you don't think—?"

"Let's just see," answered Al.

So Bill left a case of beer out on the porch as promised, and later, after the sun had set, Albert and Al crept to a neighbouring cabin to keep watch. They did not have to wait long.

"Albert, look at this!" Al could not believe his eyes.

What a sight it was—the bear walking on hind legs carrying off a case of beer!

"Let's follow him and see where he takes it!"

They snuck out of the cabin just as Gordon and Stu passed by, out on an evening stroll.

"Where you going all covert-like? Sneaking out on those gorgeous wives of yours?"

Albert put a finger to his lips. "We're following that bear over there. Look." He made a motion. The outline of the bear and the beer was clearly visible against the indigo sky.

"I don't believe it." Gordon was astounded. "What's he going to do with that?"

"Why don't you come with us and find out?" offered Al. "We'll probably have to trample through some bush."

Gordon looked down at his shiny dress shoes, the only pair he had brought with him. "What the hell! Let's find out where this big boy is going. Looks like it's going to be some party! Come on, Stu."

The furry burglar leisurely continued through the bush, apparently unconcerned with the four men tailing him. After a few minutes, they came upon a small clearing not far from the garbage dump. The bear stopped there, among a circle of empty beer cans, bread bags, and Kringle boxes. He squatted down in his own pantry, ripped open the case of beer, grabbed a can, punctured it with his teeth, and sucked the whole thing down. He then dropped the can and started on a fresh one. One by one, he swilled down the suds until every last one was gone. Wobbly from his drinking binge, the bear tried to get up but failed. After a few attempts, he gave up, plopped down, and went to sleep.

Gordon shook his head. "Well, I'll be damned! In my heyday, I couldn't down 'em as fast!"

"Think we should shoot him?" asked Albert.

"Nah," said Al. "It seems rather unsporting to shoot him while he's drunk."

***

Later the next day, Gordon rapped on the door of the house cabin.

"Gordon!" Helen swung open the door. "Come in!"

"I just popped by to say thank you and goodbye. We have to leave today."

Helen put on her brightest smile. "We'll be sorry to see you go. I hope you enjoyed yourself. It must have seemed awfully back woodsy to you."

"Are you kidding? You could bottle this air and sell it! The fishing was amazing, the food was fantastic, and the company exceptional. And the entertainment! Thieving weasels, beer-guzzling bears, and attack poodles wearing turtlenecks. This was just what I needed. I'll never forget this holiday. Here . . ." He reached into his pocket, pulled out a bill, and stuffed it into Helen's hand. "Give this to the girls in the kitchen. They are truly living dolls."

Helen looked down. A hundred dollars! No one ever left the girls that much! Agnes's itchy palm had come true!

"I'll never forget it, either. You just made the year for me!" Helen paused for a moment. "I hate to ask, you must get so tired of it, but do you think you could give us your autograph?"

"Honey, I would autograph that drunken bear's rump if it made you happy."

Helen called out, "Looori! Where are yooou? Come quick!"

Lori peered around the corner.

"Run and get something special, something you plan to keep always. I know, your Barbie case. Gordon MacRae is going to autograph it for you!" Helen did not believe in paper autographs; they were too flimsy. If she was going to get an autograph, she was going to get it on something substantial. She herself was going to have him sign her cosmetic case. That way, every day, when she put on her face, she would be reminded of being *Face to Face* with Gordon MacRae.

Lori returned from her bedroom carrying her red Barbie carrying case. Inside on the lid, he wrote, *To sweet Lori, Love Gordon MacRae.*

"Thank you, Mr. Gordon. And thank you again for saving my puppy." Lori flashed him one of her toothless grins.

"Think nothing of it, doll." He patted the little girl on the head.

After he signed the cases, Gordon looked up at the hats on the wall.

"What an interesting collection. Where did they all come from?"

"They all belong to people who have been here, both as guests and staff," said Helen. "Some people come back year after year, and their hat is here, waiting for them. Others just leave their hat as something for us to remember them by."

Gordon removed the Panama hat from his head and handed it to Helen. "For your wall. I wouldn't want you to forget me."

Lori replaced the Panama hat on the wall. Entertainment didn't have to come in a glitzy package. As Gordon MacRae had found out, sometimes it came in a furry, four-legged one. Lori next removed a worn Stetson from the wall. Adventure, too, came in many different packages—

1968

To the staff and guests, they were Frank and Kay. To Lori and Phil, they were just Nana and Gup. They were Al's parents, and everyone was thrilled to have them at Stork Lake.

For the past hour, Gup and Lori had sat on the stoop of the work shed, facing the lake. Here, the morning sun was brightest, burning away any shadows that might be cast on their work.

Lori loved to watch Gup work with wood. Even with several fingers missing their top joints on both hands (the unfortunate results of not one but two incidents with a circular saw), his remaining fingers were still nimble enough to carve a piece of diamond willow into nothing less than a sculpture.

Gup spent hours looking for just the right piece of wood. He would tramp deep into the bush, into the bog where the mosquitoes were worst. Here, where the willow stands were dense and their growth very slow, was where he found the best specimens— dead, deformed pieces of drab grey wood with barely discernable diamond-shaped blisters. He knew that under this ugly disguise would be a diamond in the rough.

Gup gripped the stick of wood with his two good fingers on his left hand. Holding a simple fillet knife with his *other* three good fingers on his right hand, he peeled away the grey bark, revealing the satiny sapwood underneath. Then using a gouge, he etched out the hollows, slowly, one layer at a time, until deep, ruby-coloured diamonds emerged.

"What's it going to be?" asked Lori.

"I don't know yet," replied Gup. "I let the wood decide. As I peel away each layer, it becomes clearer. By the time I reach the heartwood, I know the piece. I know every twist, every line, every scar. Then I can tell you what it will be. Sometimes a base for a lamp, sometimes a candlestick, or maybe another leg for a chair, or a spindle for the stairs. It's a tough hardwood. You can make just about anything out of it, and it will stand up to the test of time."

Lori peered up at her grandfather's face. Like the stick he now worked on, life had worked lines and scars into his face. However, just like the willow, this worn shell housed a tough inner core that kept him strong in spirit and young at heart.

At sixty-seven, Frank was still slim and wiry with a head of thick bristly grey hair. He, too, had run his own fishing camp at War Eagle Lake near Kenora for many years. Understanding the pull of the outdoors, Frank had not hesitated to loan his son the ten thousand dollars he needed to purchase the camp four years before. He knew a man had to follow his dreams. He also knew his son was just as tough and determined as he was, and he would make it work.

Frank had sold the War Eagle Camp some years before, and Kay, his wife, had retired this past winter from Eaton's, where she had worked forty-seven years in the button department. When Al asked if they would like to work at Stork Lake for the summer, they jumped at the chance. They had been dying to see this place that had consumed their son's time for the past few years and were tickled pink to be part of it, to still be needed.

And needed they were. Frank was an excellent carpenter; he helped Albert fix sloping floors, crooked doors, and broken screens.

He had painstakingly constructed and fine-finished the polished pine counter in the new office building, which now stood proudly along the lakeshore. Fishing experience of over sixty years made him an expert guide— and an exceptional yarn spinner. The guests loved him. Meanwhile, Kay was a welcome addition in the kitchen; she was great at flipping eggs, so Al no longer had to cook for the guests in the morning. She baked fabulous desserts, cleaned cabins till they sparkled, and with almost fifty years under her belt as a sales clerk, she too could chinwag with the best, from postmen to presidents. Even Agnes had an easy time chatting with her.

"Can I do some carving?" Lori asked Gup.

"Why not?" He handed her the wood and the knife.

"Be careful now and take your time. Don't try to take off too much at once."

Lori held the knife tightly then vertically cut at the grey bark. It was difficult, but she managed to take off a slice, exposing the pale wood underneath.

"Look, Gup, I did it!"

"You sure did. Now do some more." Time passed agreeably, the grey head bent next to the small blonde one, carefully coaching and coaxing the small fingers to bring the wood to life.

"Now, Frank, don't be telling me you gave that knife to a seven-year-old. What, you want her fingers to look like yours?" Arms folded, Kay stood over them, trying to look stern without succeeding. This time together with her son and his family was a gift, and both she and Frank were careful not to squander any of it.

"Nana, look! I did some carving!" Lori held up the stick.

Kay bent down and carefully inspected Lori's handiwork. "And a very good job you've done of it, too—" She paused a moment. "I have another job I think you might be good at. It's just about lunchtime. I thought you might like to ring the gong today."

"Do you think I'm big enough to do it?" Lori asked.

"Well now, let me see." Kay pushed her rhinestone-studded glasses up the bridge of her nose, took a closer look at the little girl, then straightened back up again. "Yes, I believe you're just the right size for the job."

"Yeah!" Lori jumped up. "I got to carve my first piece of wood, *and* I get to ring the gong! Wait till I tell Phil!" As she skipped away, she glanced back. "See you at lunch, Gup!"

"I'll be listening for the gong!" Frank gave a contented sigh, then smiled up at Kay. "You would think watching our granddaughter growing up would make me feel old, but it doesn't. In fact, it makes me feel young again!"

***

"They're here!" Helen's voice rang through the lodge. "Al! They're here!"

"I heard you. Gawd! The fishermen in North Lake heard you!"

Al, who had been fixing a leak under the kitchen sink, put down his wrench, then got up and brushed off his knees. He would not admit it, but he was just as excited about the arrival of the Cessna as his wife was. The plane arriving this early August morning held some very special guests: Ray and Eunice Rubin.

The Rubins had started as customers in 1964 but had quickly become close friends. At first glance, Ray appeared pleasantly ordinary, even a little quiet and conservative. In fact, he was a brilliant, cultured man with a sharp sense of humour, a big heart, and a small ego. Eunice was a bubbly, bright-eyed, All-American sweetheart who loved playing games and collected everything 'Snoopy.'

Their arrival at the camp meant a week of fun, and even a little downtime for Helen and Al, as they would often fish and dine with their friends. Lori and Phil also loved having them there. Eunice and Ray loved kids and tried to include the two children in their activities, which were not limited to fishing by any means. Eunice always brought with her a wide range of games and puzzles, hammocks and horseshoes, and crazy trinkets and novelties. There would be something for everyone.

As Helen and Al headed out the door, Kay called out. "I'm coming, too . . . I've heard so much about these people, I feel like I should be greeting them like friends!"

"Don't worry," answered Al. "In about two minutes, they will be!"

By the time they reached the dock, the group had swelled to six; Frank, Lori, and Phil had joined them.

The door of the plane swung open, and Eunice's vivacious face peered out.

"Eunice!" shrieked Helen.

"Helen!" squealed Eunice. "Al! Everyone! Hello! Wow, what a greeting committee! You must have been expecting someone important, and it's just us!"

The pilot jumped out his door, with Ray, who had been sitting in the co-pilot seat, hopping out right behind him.

"Ray! How the hell you been?" Al gave his friend a smack on the back.

"Great, now that I'm here!"

"I have that effect on people, don't I?" joked Helen. "We've missed you guys!" She threw her arms around Ray and gave him a kiss on the cheek.

Meanwhile, Eunice bent over the doorway, holding a white bundle.

"Okay, Eunnie, what have you brought this time?" inquired Al.

Smiling, she handed the bundle down to him. There, looking up with big blue eyes, was the Rubin's eleven-month-old daughter, Renee.

"Ahhh! A new little fisherman!"

Eunice's face lit up, and there was mass commotion as everyone exchanged hugs and greetings.

"What a darling little girl! Look at that smile! She looks just like you, Eunice!"

"Funny, I thought she looked just like Ray!"

"My goodness, Phil, have you grown!"

"Lori! Love the new haircut!"

"You must be Al's parents. He's told us all about you."

"All good, I hope." Frank smiled. He took an instant liking to this couple.

So did Kay. She took her turn holding Renee. "Oh, what a wee pet. How did she like the plane?"

"Slept like, well, a baby. Of course, this girl's racked up the miles. She's already been to London and Sweden."

Ray sucked in a lungful of fresh Ontario air, his alert eyes darting around, missing nothing. "God it's good to be back! I've been looking forward to this all year."

"Me too!" said Al. "Maybe I'll get out fishing for a change."

As they chattered, Frank, Al, and Phil unloaded the plane. There was bag after bag, box after box. It was hard to believe they had stuffed so much baggage onto the small Cessna.

"Just how long are you staying, Eunice? The rest of the summer?"

Eunice giggled. "I wish!"

"We better call a few more guides to help us carry all this to your cabin. Otherwise, you won't be settled before shore lunch," joked Al.

"We can't miss that!" cried Eunice. "Ray, help the boys with the bags. We have to get out fishing!" She turned to Helen. "You're all coming for shore lunch?"

"Of course! It's the only time my husband takes me out to dine!" quipped Helen.

***

It was a perfect day—bright and sunny with a slight breeze and not a rain cloud in sight. James and the Rubins headed out fishing in one boat while Phil, Lori, and Frank jumped into another. Helen and Al would not take time off to fish, but they would join them at the designated spot for lunch. Kay begged off, not wanting to leave Elsie and Agnes alone with all the work.

As always, Phil wanted to drive the boat. He grabbed the throttle, and the boat blasted off from the dock like a rocket, almost blowing Gup's Stetson off his head. Lori crept up to the little seat right in the bow. This was her favourite spot. The boat bounced better up there, spraying water in her face. The lake mates headed to Gup's "secret spot"—a quiet, sunny little bay with a deep reef right in the middle.

Once there, Phil and Gup traded places so Phil could fish. Gup liked to back troll; he turned the motor off and slowly paddled up and down the reef. Phil expertly baited his line with a bright yellow jig from his tackle box and in no time flat had his line in the water. Lori also had her own tackle box, a rather battered old one of her dad's. She opened it up and took out a pretty pink jig with a feathery tail.

Phil sounded flabbergasted. "The fish have been biting on yellow, not pink! You can't use pink just because you like it! You have to use something like yellow."

"I want to use pink."

Gup glanced over. "Let her use pink."

Lori carefully placed the lure on her leader, then reached her hand into the minnow bucket and pulled one out. The little minnow seemed to know the jig was up and opened his mouth for her. She threaded the hook in through the mouth and out through the gill, released the bail, and—with a plop—her line dropped straight down into the water. Once it hit bottom, she rhythmically began jerking the rod up and down, bouncing the lure on the bottom. Not a minute later, there was a nibble. With a snap, Lori set the hook and reeled it in. Once it was in the boat, she unhooked the walleye, and with a secret little smile, held it up for Gup to see.

"It's a keeper."

She had caught the first fish of the day—on a pink jig!

Phil caught the next one. In no time at all, they landed seven two-to-three pounders.

"That should be enough to feed us and your mom and dad, too," said Gup, as he stuffed the last flipping walleye into the gunnysack. "We won't worry about the Rubins. James will make sure they catch enough to eat!"

Phil returned to the motor, and they headed for Lunch Bay, aptly named because it was located in a sheltered bay with a shore lunch spot on it. James and the Rubins were already there. Ray was helping James gather wood while Eunice stood there, pretty as a picture in her strapless polka dot top and black pedal pushers, holding a bunch of waxy yellow water lilies and smiling ear to ear.

"Ahoy there, fellow fishermen!" she called. "Come on ashore!"

Phil landed the boat, and Frank jumped out to pull it up on the rocks.

"What a day!" Eunice's voice crackled. "We came across this gorgeous bay with all these waterlilies . . . I couldn't resist picking some for our lunch table."

"You mean you couldn't resist getting James to pick some for our table." Ray had come up behind his wife. "Poor guy got wet up to his shoulder then had to clear ten pounds of lily pads off the propeller before we could take off again."

"Did Renee enjoy her boat ride?" asked Lori, joining Eunice on the shore.

"She sure did! In fact, we can't get her out of the boat. Look!"

With all the fishing gear removed, the Rubins' boat was now a playpen for Renee. She crawled around the bottom of it in her sunbonnet, dragging her stuffed Snoopy dog. With her white socks and pants attracting every bit of dirt on the bottom, she looked quite like her toy dog—white with black blotches.

Lori opened up the lunch box, unpacked a red-checkered tablecloth, and spread it on the picnic table, smoothing any creases.

"Oh, how lovely!" said Eunice. "Hang on." She grabbed the water lilies, now slurping up water in a 7up bottle, and set them on the picnic table.

"There!" she announced in her quivering voice, which just added to her charm. "Atmosphere is everything. And this restaurant has it all."

"You hoo! We're heeerrre!"

Helen's high-pitched voice was audible even over the drone of their outboard. Everyone on shore turned around as Helen and Al roared up in their boat. There was no mistaking who it was—only Helen would wear a psychedelic bandana and a theatrical wool cape to a shore lunch. The humongous designer sunglasses only added to her dramatic appearance.

"You sure know how to make an entrance," said Ray, giving Helen a hand out of the boat, no easy task since her arms were restricted in the folds of her cape.

"You bet. It's not every day I escape out of the kitchen for a few hours!"

"Welcome to Stork Lake's kiosk!" giggled Eunice. "On the menu today . . . fresh walleye!"

"I can hardly wait," groaned Helen as she flung off her cape. "I live at a fishing camp all summer, and the only time I get a feed of fish is when you guys come!" Helen turned back to Al. "Al, hurry up and unload our boat. We've been here two minutes already, and Eunice and I still don't have a drink!"

"Yes, ma'am!" Al pulled out his "special" lunchbox, loaded with iced martini glasses, vodka, fresh lemons, and a shaker. He set up his bar on a flat rock, then placed the lemons on a stump, where he carefully carved lemon twists for their martinis using an axe.

Eunice watched intently. "Such finesse!"

Ray agreed. "The master himself making it look easy! Though couldn't you find a bigger hatchet or maybe a chainsaw to cut those lemons with?"

Drinks distributed, Al and Ray sat on a rock and discussed the weighty subject of vodka versus gin martinis. Eunice scooped Renee out of her boat playpen, set her in her toddler seat, then pulled out the lunch specially prepared for her by Elsie. Helen stood beside them, peeling potatoes.

"What do you think of Billie Jean's win at Wimbledon?" asked Eunice as she fed Renee. "I know you enjoy watching and playing tennis as much as I do!"

Helen took a swig of her martini. "Amazing. What's more amazing is that I didn't even hear about it until last week! I asked every new guest that arrived, but no one seemed to know the results until I finally hit upon a tennis fan. I swear it would be faster to get news by carrier pigeon!"

"How about carrier seagull? You have enough of them around here!" Since the boats arrived, at least two dozen of the white birds had converged just offshore. They bobbed there like buoys in the water, patiently waiting for handouts.

While the adults chatted, Lori explored the island. She climbed on the moss-covered granite rocks, skipped some stones, searched for schools of minnows. She meandered along the shore until she circled back around to the spot where Phil stood, watching Frank and James clean fish.

"Can I try now?" asked Phil.

"Okay, Phil, just as I showed you," commanded Gup.

He imitated the motions as best he could, then held up his version for inspection. It definitely had less flesh and more bones. Phil's art of filleting was not yet perfected.

"I'm not eating that mangled one!" cried Lori.

"There's nothing wrong with it," complained Phil. "Besides, it's better than you could do. You can't even fillet a fish yet!"

"I can still help."

She grabbed the glistening entrails, head, and tails and threw them into a washtub. She carefully washed each fillet in the lake and handed them to James, who dunked the silvery meat in a pan of evaporated milk, then into a bag of seasoned flour and cornflake crumbs.

Meanwhile, Eunice had returned Renee to her playpen and had started taking pictures. She always took lots of pictures. *Snap. Snap. Snap.* The day was recorded in detail for future playback.

"Renee! Look up at Mommy! No, don't chew the dog's ear . . . You had enough lunch! Lori, stand beside Phil. Now pose with your grandpa. Ray, look at those pans . . . Oh my goodness, I gotta get a picture of this gourmet meal in progress. Helen, stand beside the fire. You too, Al. We have to have both our hosts in the picture. James, look up—wow, that smile of yours is brighter than my flash!"

The frying pans were now *hot*; the fries were dumped in one, the onions in another. A few minutes later, the fish was added to a third pan. Everyone now stood around, staring at the bubbling pans.

"You'd think none of us had eaten for a week. Why are we all watching?" asked Helen.

"Because the anticipation makes it taste even better!" answered Ray.

In a matter of a couple of minutes, the fish was done to a crisp golden brown. The feast was spread out buffet style, and everyone dug in.

"Oooh, look at all the goodies! Tomorrow we diet!" squealed Eunice.

"Nothing like fresh walleye! The best taste on earth!" Ray grabbed his third slice of Elsie's homemade bread and ladled on a thick coating of Nabob raspberry jam. "Though this bread and jam is a serious rival." He sighed. "It just doesn't get any better than this!"

Everyone ate until they could not take one more bite—that is until Elsie's homemade cookies were pulled out. Everyone had room for them. Phil took a fistful while James poured out cups of coffee from the pot boiling over the fire. He walked over and handed Helen hers.

"For you, Boss Lady."

"Thanks, James." Helen took a sip, then made a face. "That'll put hair on your chest." The coffee—affectionately called swamp water—looked like tar.

Phil and Lori grabbed their pop cans and their rods and headed to the shore for a little post-lunch fishing. Renee fell sound asleep in her playpen while the adults kicked back and relaxed. The shore lunch and martinis had filled up every empty space inside them, leaving no room for activity. Eunice spread a blanket on the rocks for Helen and her to sit on; Ray lay straight out on the cleared picnic table, unable to move. Frank and Al sat on upturned logs.

"You've had a busy year," said Ray to Al. "I am impressed with the new store. It sure has a lot more room."

"Isn't she a beaut? The problem is I can't seem to fill it up! I've ordered more of everything—more fishing gear, more confections, more beer—and the place still looks empty. I thought next we'd order up clothing to sell. You know, some T-shirts and caps made up with our logo on them, something for the guests to take home with them."

"That's a great idea. You could perhaps also look into jackets. I bet even the guides would be interested in those."

"Yeah, now you've got my wheels turning!" said Al.

"And you've finished that cabin you started last summer, and you're building another one beside it?"

"You bet. Albert has the old mill just smoking."

"Things are really progressing."

"That's the idea! Next we have plans for a new fish house and a new laundry room so the girls can do the wash indoors. It's a bugger in the early spring and late fall to do laundry on that stand. Their hands freeze up."

"I can imagine. I've been up here fishing in October a couple of times. It gets so cold I've seen my line freeze on the ferrules as I cast. Speaking of freezing . . . What's this I hear about you starting another camp up in the Arctic? Aren't you busy enough here?"

"Oh, I got my hands full here all right, but I can't pass up this opportunity. Ray, the lake has never been fished! I caught at least sixty lake trout every day, not one of them under twenty pounds, and a lot of 'em weighing in near fifty! Would have caught even more, but it takes so damn long to bring in those bloody Arctic fish!"

"No kidding!"

Eunice took a bottle of suntan lotion out of her bag and began slathering it on her arms. "That sounds like your kind of place, doesn't it, Ray?"

"It sure does."

Frank interjected. "Tell him where the lake is, Al."

"Henik Lake is 850 miles north of Winnipeg. There are no other camps for hundreds of miles. Mine will be the only one." You could see the fire in Al's eyes.

"That's pretty far up there."

"It sure is . . . so far up that during the summer, the sun never sets. You can fish at midnight if you wanted!"

"Twenty-four-hour fishing!" Ray's eyes, too, began to smoulder. There was nothing he liked to do better than fish.

"And it's not just the fishing. The land . . . it has its own special beauty. Some people say it's just tundra, that it's barren, but somehow it gets under your skin. It's addicting."

"Or maybe it's just the adventure that's addicting to you."

"Maybe. It *is* one hell of an adventure."

"So when do you start building?"

"Next year. We'll get started on the landing strip. The following year we'll get the buildings up. We'll be open for business in '71."

"I guess Albert won't be able to construct the cabins for you."

Al laughed. "No chance. The only trees I've seen there were at the far south end of the lake, and they weren't any thicker than my arm. No, we'll have to haul in pre-fab buildings."

"How about you, Frank?" asked Ray. "Are you going to go up there?"

"Hell, I'm going to guide up there!" Frank's eyes were also alight. You could see where Al got his spirit, his thirst for adventure, the drive to seek out the biggest fish, the most remote areas. It was his father who had instilled in him the capacity to follow your dreams.

"So, Al, how are you going to run both places?" asked Ray.

"Summer's only six weeks long up there. With Albert's help, Helen can take care of things here for that long."

"You wouldn't be going up there, Helen?" asked Eunice.

Helen looked at Al. "Not a chance. I prefer to be closer to a town than two hundred miles! And you know me, I don't like flying at the best of times, and it takes seven hours to get there in the Goose. No, I couldn't do it. I've had some bad experiences on that plane. The last time I flew in one, it was supposed to be a ten-minute flight from Red Lake. It ended up taking over two hours because they had engine trouble and had to land on a deserted lake. I was *not* impressed. If a plane can get into trouble in ten minutes during perfect weather, can you imagine what could happen in seven hours? In the middle of the Arctic?" Helen shuddered.

Al argued, "If you had to go up to the Arctic, you wouldn't have to take a Goose. The landing strip will be finished by then, so you'd fly up right from Winnipeg in a nice, comfortable DC-3."

"You won't be taking that toy plane you have sitting at camp?" asked Eunice. "I've never seen anything so cute!"

"So you like my new little Piper Cub, Eunnie!"

"I love it! It must be fun to fly."

"It's a blast."

"Anyone flown with you yet, Al?" asked Ray.

Frank spoke up. "I was his first passenger . . . flew all the way from Winnipeg with him this spring. The ink wasn't even dry on his pilot's licence."

"Brave man!" said Eunice.

"Phil and Lori have both gone with me. My mother has even flown with me. Helen won't step foot in it," complained Al.

"Why? Don't you trust Al as a pilot?" asked Ray.

Helen answered, "I'm sure he's a very good pilot. I just don't care for planes in general, and that one, well, our canoe had more of a fuselage than that thing! I worry every time he takes off."

"There isn't a safer plane in the sky. It buzzes like a mosquito at a trail-blazing 75 miles per hour. That means that with a good headwind, a duck could fly faster. And if something happens to your engines, it just floats down to earth like a leaf. It's almost impossible to crash— I don't know why you worry." Al glanced at his watch. "Well, I guess we better get a move on. I'd love to sit and shoot the breeze all day, but I've got a cabin to finish. Poor Albert can't do it all himself."

The dirty dishes were packed up, the fire doused. James and Frank spread the leftover beans, corn, and even onions out on the rocks, then everyone climbed into their respective boats and pushed off. This was what the shore-trolling seagulls had been waiting for. Immediately they took off in flight. Like a scene out of the movie *The Birds*, they swooped down en masse, devouring the smorgasbord. When they were done, not one bean, not one French fry was left.

Ever since lunch, Lori had been trying to think up something special to do for the Rubins. They were always so nice; this year they had brought her this fun towel set you could play checkers on. An idea came to her while Ray was enjoying his bread and jam. If he liked raspberry jam so much, just imagine how much he would like fresh raspberry pie, especially her grandmother's! Nobody, not even Elsie, could make as good a pie as Nana. So just as they were about to shove off and head for home, Lori turned to Gup.

"Do you think we could go raspberry picking? Just for a while?"

"I don't see why not." The only thing Frank liked better than diamond willow picking was berry picking, especially with his two grandkids. "I know just the spot, too. I'll have to drive there, though. There's a reef close to shore that's not marked, and it's pretty tricky to find. I sort of have to feel my way through."

"Heck, a bucket of berries is worth not getting to drive!" Phil took the middle seat, and off they went. After a ten-minute ride, the sandbar came into view. Frank cruised closer. Mesmerized by the hundreds of raspberry bushes, he did not pay close enough attention to where he was going.

Clunk! The boat stopped dead.

"I think we found the reef."

Peering over the edge of the boat, Lori could clearly make out the jagged edges suspended just under the water. Frank tilted the outboard out of the water and inspected the prop. "Bent like a bloody banana."

Phil had helped Albert with enough bottom ends to know what this meant. "Guess we aren't going anywhere fast, are we Gup? What do we do now?"

Frank scratched his forehead. "Let me think . . . Wait, I think I hear a boat coming." They all listened. Sure enough, they heard another outboard heading toward them. A moment later, the Rubins' boat appeared from behind an island.

Frank shouted, "Wave them down!"

All three of them jumped out of their seats and began to wave at the boat with both hands. As they zoomed past, Eunice, Ray, and James all merrily waved back. Then they were gone.

"Now what?" Phil turned to his grandfather. This was Gup. He was a bushman. No mere crumpled prop would stop him.

Frank adjusted his Stetson. "We could wait until supper when they would miss us. Your dad will send out a search party, and besides everyone being worried sick, that would just be too embarrassing. I've spent my whole life in the woods, boating and fishing. I would never live it down if the whole camp found out I got us stuck on a rock!" He stared at the north shore for a moment, then traced the shoreline with one of his stubby fingers, following it as it curved around the bay. "There's only one thing to do. We paddle."

"All the way home?" Phil sounded astounded. Fishing boats tended to paddle about as quickly as a barge in the water.

"Not all the way home. Just to the shore." Frank grabbed the paddle and dug deep into the water, urging the boat along.

"But the berries are the other way!" said Lori.

"I know, honey, but they're on an island. We have to paddle to the mainland side."

Slowly the boat inched to the shore. It was only about fifty yards, but the wind and the waves worked against them, pushing in the opposite direction. Finally, after what seemed like forever, rocks crunched on the bottom of the boat. They had landed.

Frank awkwardly climbed out onto the slippery wet rocks and pulled the boat up further on shore.

"Now what, Gup?" asked Phil. "Do we just wait here till someone else comes?"

"You two will wait. I'll be back in an hour."

"*What?*"

"I'm walking back. I know this north shoreline is part of the mainland that eventually leads back to the camp. It won't take me more than an hour or so to reach the camp by foot. I'll get your dad to bring me back and help us free the boat so we can get home. We could all be back by dinner, and no one would have to worry. More importantly, no one else would have to find out."

"You can't walk all the way back! It's too far! What if you get lost?"

"It's not far, and I won't get lost," harrumphed Gup. "I've been in the bush my whole life and never been lost yet."

"Can't we come with you?"

"Yeah, Gup, can't we?" To Lori, it sounded like fun. She had never explored this particular bush before. Maybe they would find an old trapper's cabin—or a cave!

"You're wearing sandals. You won't be able to walk through the bush. Besides, it's faster if I go myself. Now, Phil, you're in charge till I get back."

"Okay, Gup," said Phil, sounding disappointed.

"Will we go raspberry picking when you get back?" Lori looked at him earnestly. Somehow, this afternoon had to be salvaged.

"Sorry, sweetie, it'll be too late. We'll have to go another day." Lori was as disappointed as Phil—no exploring *and* no raspberry pie!

***

It was a couple of miles of hard hiking—Frank crawled over felled trees, prickly bushes, and sharp rocks. He was already tired from all the exertion he had put into his paddling. At a part along the bay where his feet sank into the spongy bog, he noticed some of the most magnificent specimens of diamond willow he had ever seen. "Figures," he groaned to himself. He plodded on, his legs feeling like lead weights.

Finally, Frank made it back to camp. He crept up the hill and headed to where he knew Al would be, working on the new cabin. Sure enough, there he was with Albert, banging a stud into place.

"Al!" he shouted up to him.

Al turned around.

"Can I talk to you a minute?"

Al put the hammer down and walked to the edge of the building to where his father stood. "What is it?"

"I need a lift," said Frank.

Puzzled, Al asked, "Where do you need a lift to?"

"My boat."

***

The next morning, Ray, Al, and Frank headed down to the beach, where Al kept his new plane.

Ray watched as Al filled up the nose tank with aviator gas then filled up the extra wing tank, which he had just installed a few days before.

"I assume an extra tankful of gas makes the plane heavier. Doesn't that affect your lift-off distance?" he asked.

"Can't lift off at all if you don't have fuel," Al answered. "And it's a long way between gas stations around here."

"That's all too true." Ray inspected the new configuration. "I assume this hose here runs from one tank to the other?"

"Yep. When the fuel gauge shows I'm getting low on gas, I just open the tap, and the gas flows from the wing tank into the nose tank."

"And this increases your range to what?"

"I'd say over 425 miles. I could fly to your house in Minneapolis!"

"Not today, I hope," quipped Ray. "I was hoping to fish with you this afternoon!"

"Not a chance! I wouldn't miss that! No, I'm just flying to Red Lake to pick up a few supplies. I'll be back in about an hour."

Frank pulled his hat down. "I can tell by the breeze on my brim that the wind has picked up. Sure you're still okay to take off?"

Al glanced at the flag fluttering on the flagpole that acted as his windsock. "Doesn't look too bad. It's a crosswind, but if I lift off in front of the island, it should shelter me a bit. Don't worry about me, Dad. I won't hit any rocks!"

Ray and Al both chuckled. Frank's hopes of keeping his little adventure the day before quiet had not quite panned out. By supper, the story was circulated throughout the camp, and Frank had had to take a lot of ribbing from the guides about how the great outdoorsman was beaten by a rock.

"You know best."

Frank and Ray untied the plane, pushed it to the water, then held the tail in place while Al stood on the float of the canvas plane and hand-propped the Cub until it came to life. Its purr was not unlike that of a real bear cub's pulsing hum. Al hopped into the cockpit, and he was off, taxiing toward the two islands in front of the camp.

The plane listed slightly to the right, the heavier side where the wing tank was. As he passed the point and entered less sheltered water, the wind picked up. The little plane was blown off course; the waves sloshing over the floats were higher than they looked from the shore. Then suddenly, a large gust hurled it toward one of the islands.

***

"Doesn't look good," said Frank, concerned. "I knew it was too windy."

"He's going to be blown right into the trees!" said Ray, worried.

They watched as the plane veered perilously toward the island. At the last moment, Al managed to steer it away.

"That was too damn close," said Frank.

The words were barely out of his mouth when another breath of wind caught the plane, lifting the lighter wing and causing the downwind heavier wing to dip into the water. Spray from the waves washed over the propeller. Almost instantly, the little Cub began tipping over. It continued to roll, almost in slow motion, the engine acting like a lead weight, pulling it over. Suddenly there was no more purring—only silence.

"Oh my God," breathed Ray. "Can Al get out?"

"I'm not waiting to find out." Frank, still sore from his workout the day before, stiffly ran to his boat while Ray watched helplessly on the shore as the cockpit slipped closer to the water. Just as it was about to be completely submerged, the door opened, and Al popped out. He quickly scampered onto the bottom of the pontoon, the only part of the plane now sticking out of the water.

By this time, Albert had arrived on the scene.

"What the hell happened?"

In disbelief, Ray answered, "Al flipped his plane and didn't even get his feet wet!"

"Plane's gonna be a little soggy, though," commented Albert calmly.

* * *

Slightly dazed, Al did not notice at first the boat that pulled up beside him. Finally, glancing down, he saw the top of his dad's Stetson.

Without batting an eye, Frank turned his face up to him. "Need a lift?"

Al could not believe it—now they were even—two "great outdoorsmen" beaten by the elements.

As he jumped into the boat, Frank asked, "You hurt?"

"Just my pride," said Al, sitting down.

As they motored back to shore, Al looked back at his submerged Cub. "It's going to be a bitch hauling her back to camp."

"That's not going to be the hardest part," replied Frank. "The hardest part's going to be telling Helen!" Frank was right; while it took an hour for Albert and Al to tow the plane the short distance back to shore, it took over an hour for Kay and Eunice to convince Helen that Al should ever fly again.

Once the plane hit the shallows, Albert pulled the cigarette out of his mouth and flicked it into the water. "Okay. Now let's drain her."

"We can't, Albert," exclaimed Al. "We'll split the fuselage."

"We can. You know I don't like the word *can't*."

They tied one end of a rope on the tail and the other end high up in the birch tree on the shore. With a block and tackle, they hoisted the plane up by the tail, inch by inch. It was a painstakingly slow job because if the water rushed out too fast, it would indeed split the canvas skin. When all the water, gas, and oil had dripped out, leaving dark puddles on the sand—and a whole day had passed—they finally lowered it back upright onto its floats. Now Albert could survey the damage. "Well we'll have to get to work on the engine first." He opened the cowling. He took the carburetor apart and took the mags off.

"Gotta get these dried out."

"That'll take days," lamented Al.

"No, it won't." Albert picked them up and trotted down to the kitchen.

"Elsie, what've you got in the oven?"

"Ham."

"Well pull it out. You'll have to cook it on top."

Elsie did not even ask why. She pulled out the ham, and Albert stuck the mags in. "Let me know when they're dry."

He returned to the plane; Al was busy taking all the oil out of the crankcase and flushing it out. Albert pulled the plugs.

"That's all we can do for now," said Albert. "We have to wait for her to dry out."

***

After dinner the next evening, Ray, Frank, Al, and Albert made their way down to the plane. Al refilled the gas and oil while Albert replaced the now bone-dry mags and installed new plugs. He did a final inspection of the engine then replaced the cowling. Next he checked out the cockpit. The seats were still damp, but everything else looked okay.

"Fire her up," ordered Albert.

Al grabbed a prop blade and pulled. The Cub coughed and then sputtered to life. Albert and Al both stood on the float and listened carefully as she began to purr. Albert nodded his head. "Sounds okay."

"It looks okay and sounds okay," yelled Al over the hum. "Only one way to tell if it flies okay."

Ray shouted back. "Did I hear right? You're going to take it up? Before it's checked out by a mechanic?"

Al nodded to Albert. "My mechanic did check it out."

Al trusted Albert's judgement, and Ray trusted Al's. There was nothing further to say. "All right, then. I'll push you off." Albert jumped down, and Al started to climb into the cockpit.

"Wait a minute!" called out Frank. "Why should you have all the fun? I'm coming with you."

They took off. The Cub lifted off and flew, at first just above the water, then finally, higher and higher. Around the lake they fluttered until Al was sure everything was in order.

"Well, I'll be damned," said Ray in amazement.

"She's pretty forgiving, ain't she?" Albert gave a short, sharp laugh. "There are advantages to simplicity."

"You've got that right!" agreed Ray. "You know," he added, "I don't know why Al and Frank think they have to go all the way up to the Arctic for adventure. They seem to have more than enough escapades right here!"

***

"How was it?" Albert asked after they had landed.

"Better than before!"

"Okay then, let's get a drink."

The men headed for the lodge, where the women were waiting for them in the card room, Helen having bitten every hangnail she had.

"Thank goodness the test run is over!" cried Helen. "I feel nauseous . . . I should have taken a Gravol."

Al looked over at Frank. "We were the ones in the plane, and she's the one that's airsick!"

"Don't make fun, Frank," cautioned Kay. "Sometimes it's harder being the one left on the ground. We'll be remembering this little episode for some time to come!"

"That reminds me, Al. I snapped some photos of you yesterday, dragging your plane back into shore by boat. I'll send them to you . . . for posterity," announced Eunice.

"Gee, thanks, Eunnie . . . like I'm going to want to remember that!"

Albert pulled out a bottle of Hudson Bay Scotch, opened the bottle, and threw away the cap. "We won't be needing that anymore."

After he had poured them each out a good shot, Ray raised his glass into the air. "A toast to the Piper Cub . . . May its simplicity and elemental design keep it tumbling across the sky."

Lori lovingly replaced Gup's Stetson. The Piper Cub was a hard plane to damage and easy to fix, not unlike some people she had met. Lori picked up a fishing hat covered in lures—

1969

Every muskie fishermen lucky enough to have James as a guide agreed: he provided the hunt of a lifetime. Instinctively, he knew the secret hot spots; he knew where this predator prowled, he knew how to stalk them, and he knew how to entice them into biting your line. Best of all, he knew how to boat this fearsome, fickle fish. Rewards for battles won varied; appreciative guests leaving with trophies would leave James big tips, boundless praise, and very rarely, even though it was strictly forbidden, a bottle of booze.

***

One such bottle, a forty ouncer of Jack Daniel's whiskey, had lain hidden under his bed for several weeks now. James was determined not to touch it until his vacation, when he would then take it into town with him and have a good night's "howl" with friends while Agnes visited her folks. He had no intention of drinking it while he was at Stork Lake. Not only would it be against the camp rules to drink it, but it would be against Agnes's rules—she forbade James to drink while he was working. So the bottle lay under the bed, wrapped in an old flannel jacket.

At first, it was easy, leaving the bottle under the bed. James loved guiding, loved the thrill of the hunt. In this element, he did not need to drink to get a rush. James did not have much of an education. He had not done well in school and had dropped out in eighth grade. Classrooms were too confining, the work too confounding. But guiding—guiding, he excelled at. He *understood* fish and fishing. In the boat with his guests, he was the boss, the hero, the warrior. In the boat, guests sought out his wisdom, took his advice, and treated him with respect. But today, James did not feel like a hero or a warrior. He felt like a failure.

John Royalty had been James's guest all week. He was a stocky, strong man from Texas with bulky arms and thick wrists that made him a powerful, tireless caster. He was a seasoned fisherman who possessed the three attributes needed for success: knowledge, patience, and feel. Yet, all week, John had been shut out. Sure, he had caught the odd northern, but he had not even caught a shadow of a muskie.

While this would be disappointing to many guests, James knew this was devastating to John. He was not at Stork Lake for comradery with his friends or to enjoy the sunshine and the great outdoors. He was not even here to enjoy the fresh walleye at shore lunch. He was here to acquire a trophy muskie, his reward of the day's hunt, a badge for his battle with nature and his supremacy. John had come to Stork for three consecutive years now, and every time, James had chased one down for him. With a perfect 3-0 record, John didn't only hope for a muskie this trip; he *expected* one. For the past five days, the hunt had been on—with no luck. Now it was down to the wire, and John had only one day left.

Until this day, James knew his record had been perfect. He never failed to at least sight a muskie for his guests. They might not always boat one, but they always had the excitement of *seeing* one. James was proud of this record; he honestly enjoyed seeing his guests happy. This first-time failure consumed him.

After another muskie-less day, without even the flip of a tail to offer hope of success, James was miserable. His beaming smile was decidedly absent. At supper, after crunching a handful of soda crackers into his chicken soup and swirling them with a spoon into oblivion, he gave up trying to eat. He stood up and left the dining room, slamming the door behind him. Outside, he took a deep breath. He adjusted his cap, rubbed his chin, then took a plug of snuff out of the can in his pocket and pressed it between his gums and cheek. Restless, he wandered down to the shore and stared out over the lake. It was a lovely evening, the warm evening breeze gently running its fingers along the surface of the water and causing little ripples to sparkle and peak. James thought of all the fish lazily swimming just below, many of them grandpa muskies of gigantic proportions. If there were so many, why couldn't he find one?

James shook his head and turned away. No, he was not going to think about muskies anymore tonight. He did not want to think about his disappointed guest. He did not want to think he had only one day left. He wanted to burn these thoughts out of his head, at least for tonight. Tonight, he wanted to forget. Tomorrow— tomorrow he would worry about it. He headed to his cabin.

***

The next morning, Agnes crept into the kitchen, eyes downcast. "That James!"

"What?" asked Elsie.

"Last night, he drank that bottle he put away. You know, he's still drunk! He won't be able to work today."

"Uh oh. The camp's plum full. Frank and even Albert and Al have to guide today. With James out of commission, they'll still be one guide short. Does Al know?"

"Not yet." Agnes's answer was almost a whisper.

"Make the coffee," said Elsie. "I'll tell Albert. *He* can break it to Al."

***

There was only one person left in camp that could run a motor and take fish off hooks. Al found him filling up the lawn mower.

"Phil?"

"Yes, Dad?"

"You've been promoted to guide. Get boat #13 ready. You're taking out the Gardners."

"Really? Honest? I get to go guiding?"

"Yep. Now go."

Phil instantly dropped the gas can and ran off to get his jacket and gear. He was ready for this! He knew the lake, and he was an expert at running a boat. He knew how to make a fire and fillet a fish. He had waited for five years to be a guide. *Finally*, this was his chance. Wait until Roger heard he got to be a guide younger than he did! Maybe the youngest guide ever! He grabbed his tackle box and his fishing pole. This was going to be a great day!

The euphoria lasted until he reached the dock. That was when he realized the enormity of the situation. Eight hours in a boat with two guests who not only expected to catch fish, but lots of them. Eight hours of making conversation with two adults. Shore lunch! My God, what if he burnt the fish? What if he forgot something important, like matches for a fire or pliers to remove a stubborn hook from a fish mouth? What if they didn't catch any fish, and they got angry at him? What if they wanted to go muskie fishing! He wasn't sure he could help land one of those! What if they thought he was too young and *laughed* at him? No, he couldn't be, wouldn't be, laughed at. Tears flowing from his eyes, Phil ran back to the office and burst through the door.

"Dad! I can't do this! Please don't make me go! I'll cut grass . . . I'll cut grass all day, every day and never complain about it again. Just please, please don't make me go guiding!"

"Guiding?!" Helen had just walked in.

Al threw her a piercing stare, then walked from behind the counter and put a hand on his son's shoulder.

"Phil, you can do this. I wouldn't ask you if you couldn't do it."

"But . . . but what if I mess up?" asked Phil, tears still streaming.

"What makes you think you will mess up? You could guide in your sleep. You've guided Gup, right?" Phil nodded. "You've guided me, your mom, your sister. It's the same thing, just different people.

And you've known these guests for years. The Gardners are a nice couple. I've talked to them, and they understand it's your first real day of guiding, and they're excited about it! And you won't be alone. Roger promised to stick with you all day. Where he takes his guests to fish, you'll fish in the same spots. And you'll have shore lunch together."

"I . . . I guess." Phil rubbed his eyes.

"This is your lake! You've grown up here. You know it much better than they do. I promise you. It'll be all right. Now get back down to the dock and wait for the Gardners."

Phil hung his head low to hide his tears and slowly walked back down to the dock.

Helen, who had been standing behind her husband and had witnessed her son's meltdown, grabbed her stomach as if someone had punched her in the gut. "Al, he's only twelve! Do you really think he should be out guiding?"

"What? You'd rather take the Gardners out for the day?" quipped Al. Helen's eyes grew large. She didn't even know how to start an outboard motor.

"For Pete's sake, Helen, the kid can handle a day tagging along with Roger. Now, I don't have time to discuss this any longer. I have to get out guiding myself." He strode out the door.

***

One after another, the boats roared out, one of the last being Roger's, Phil following him as close as he could without running right over him. Al finally was able to turn his attention to his own guest for the day.

John Royalty was already in the boat. He had loaded his own gear and was sitting in the middle seat, rearranging his colourful fringe of muskie lures hanging from a string running along the gunnel.

"John!"

"Morning, Al!" John hung the last bait and closed his tackle box. "Have you seen James? Usually he's already in the boat when I get down here, but I haven't seen hide nor hair of him this morning."

"James isn't feeling well this morning."

"That's too bad! Nothing serious, I hope?"

"Nothing he won't get over in a day or so. I'll be taking you out instead."

"The boss man himself! This should be quite a day. Now I know I'll get that muskie!"

"How can you be sure about that?"

"Pride, Al, pride! You're too proud to come in empty-handed. What would your staff think?"

Al decided not to answer. Instead he untied the boat and jumped in. As he did, the hanging lures jingled.

"You know, you shouldn't hang your baits like that. I've seen guys get tangled in their own hooks. I've even had to cut a few out of hands."

"Don't worry, I'm careful. Besides, I can't waste time rummaging around in my box. I need the convenience of quick changes. This gives me more time with my line in the water."

"It's your call." Al sat down at the motor. "So, we ready to go? You got everything? Where's your hat? It's going to be brutally hot on the water today."

"Don't need one. Sun doesn't bother me. I grew up in Texas. Besides, I can't stand the feel of them. It's like some big foreign object holding onto the top of my head. It just doesn't feel right."

"I just don't want you to get sunstroke."

"Don't worry about that! Just worry about me getting my muskie! Gawd, Al. Hats, baits . . . James doesn't lecture me like this." John laughed.

Al turned and started the motor. He was not going to argue with a paying customer, even when the sun shone off John's shiny forehead and the lures started to dance as the boat bounced away from the dock.

***

Lori had had a terrible night. She had lain awake for hours, tossing and turning in her little cardboard room, thrashing around in her sheets. Even Chezy grew irritated with her and had jumped off her bed to find a more peaceful place to sleep. Exhausted, Lori finally fell into a deep sleep in the early hours of the morning but rose late, still tired. She pulled on a pair of shorts and a T-shirt, then peered into her brother's room. His bed was empty. A glance out the front window showed all the boats had already left for the day. She had not even heard them leave.

Lori raced down the hill to the lodge. Elsie was the only one left in the kitchen.

"Hi, Elsie! Any breakfast left?"

"There's some bacon and toast on top of the stove."

Lori grabbed a plate and started munching.

"You hear 'bout your brother?" asked Elsie as she crumbled a large package of hamburger into a sizzling cast-iron pan.

"No, what?"

"Went guiding."

"No!"

"Yep."

"I can't believe it! He must have been so excited! He's been wanting to guide forever. The lucky crumb! Geez, I sleep in one morning and miss all the excitement! How come he went out?"

Elsie grabbed a spatula and started turning the meat. "Oh, James got into a bottle last night, I guess." Not wanting to dwell on the subject, Elsie continued. "If you're finished your breakfast, I think your mom wants you to help Agnes clean cabins. She's a little tired this morning. I guess James kept her up late."

"She's not the only one beat this morning. I had a lousy sleep, too." Lori stuffed the last piece of bacon in her mouth then headed up the hill to the guest cabins. She enjoyed working with Agnes— the calm, quiet little woman was always sweet to her.

***

When it came to fishing, Al knew that John was all business. He didn't like wasting time going after walleye for his shore lunch. In fact, he didn't like even stopping for shore lunch. When you were in a boat with John, you fished for muskies and muskies only, for eight hours straight. And while John may not have cared about lunch, his guides did, so Elsie would pack sandwiches for them to eat right in the boat.

Al drove for about fifteen minutes before slowing down at Hell's Pass, a shallow, weedy area close to the channel where muskies were known to sunbathe while waiting for their supper to swim by.

"What should I try on my line first?" asked John, slipping off his jacket.

Al surveyed the kaleidoscope of shiny lures circling the inside of the boat and pointed to a red-and-white spoon. "Try that daredevil."

John attached the bait to his leader and headed up to the bow of the boat. He stood, legs slightly spread to keep his balance, and thrust the lure into the lake. He let the bait settle a moment, then reeled in with rhythmic motions designed to resemble a struggling fish. John's biceps bulged as he jerked his rod, his face intense, perspiration already gleaming on his forehead. Just as the bait broke the water, Al noticed a long, dark log just below the surface tailing it. John's teasing motions had worked. A muskie had followed the bait up.

"There's a muskie!" yelled Al. "Get your bait back in the water!" He could already envision John bringing the monster in. This day had just gotten a whole lot better!

John quickly drew his flex-tipped rod over his head, and cast. The heavy, scalpel-sharp lure snapped behind him and buried itself right into the back of his own head.

With a surprised look on his face, John looked back at Al. "Damn, I think I missed."

Muskie forgotten, Al sprang into action. He cut the motor and immediately took his fillet knife and cut the bait free from the fishing rod.

"Sit down, John. Let me see the damage."

John obligingly sat down in his seat. Al bent over and took a good look at John's head. He had plenty of experience removing hooks from various body parts: legs, arms, fingers, and even heads. But this one was deep, real deep. The hook was buried up to the shank.

"Can you get it out of my head?" John was trying to stay calm.

"I can't do anything about it here. We'll have to get back to camp."

"I can't believe I did this!" exclaimed John. "Now I'm going to miss some muskie fishing time!"

That's the least of your problems, thought Al, starting the motor.

***

Helen was the first to hear the boat approach the dock. Boats only came back to camp during the day for three reasons: weather, repairs, or health. Since it wasn't the first, she dearly prayed it was the second. However, her hopes were dashed when Al opened the screen door, and he escorted John into the staffroom.

"Oh my God." Helen thought she was going to be sick.

"What's the matter?" Elsie trotted in, took one look at John, and then pulled out a dining bench. "You better have a seat," she said calmly.

"I feel so silly," said John. "Fished all my life. Nothing like this has ever happened to me before."

Helen covered her mouth with her hand. "It's really stuck in there!"

Al shot his wife a warning glance. "Why don't you run down to the office and radio for a plane? John's going to have to get some medical attention. Damn, what a time for my Cub to be in town for inspection! I could have flown him into Red Lake myself."

Helen usually avoided using the radio phone at all costs—the party lines, the buttons to press and release, the connections, they all confused her. Still it was better than staying here; she was feeling quite squeamish looking at that hook dangling down the side of John's head.

"I'll try," she said, relieved to make her escape.

"Well, John, I don't know if there's much I can do until the plane gets here. Maybe I should just help you to your cabin, and you can lay down for a bit . . ."

"Gawd no, Al!" interjected John. "I don't want this thing in my head that long! I want you to get it out! I don't care what you have to do!"

"I don't think I should touch it—"

John begged, "Please, just get it out. I can't stand this thing flopping around on my head."

"Maybe we could just bandage it up for you."

"No! I want it out! Please, Al. I don't care how you do it. Just get it out of my head."

"It's your call. Let me look at it again." Upon closer inspection, Al said, "The hook is too large to be backed out and too deep to be pushed through. I'll have to cut it out."

Al looked up at Elsie. "Can you get the first aid kit and a fresh pack of razors? And some towels—"

"Certainly."

"Oh, and can you dig up some wire cutters?"

Elsie did not bat an eye. "There's some in Albert's toolbox here."

A few minutes later, she was back with the necessities. Al laid everything out on the table. Using the wire cutters, he snipped the hook free from the rest of the bait.

"Ah . . . better already," sighed John.

"I wouldn't say that. We haven't done the hard part yet!"

"Bad news. The radio's out. Al, *what are you doing*?" Helen had arrived back with Kay in tow and noticed the staff dining room now looked like an operating room.

"What do you mean the radio's out? Are you sure you did it right?"

"Kay helped me. We couldn't get through. There was nothing but static. Again, what are you *doing*?"

"What does it look like? Getting the hook out."

Helen caught her breath. "Oh my God! You're not going to try to *cut* it out?"

Kay stepped in and said, "Elsie, maybe Helen can help you in the kitchen now. I'll stay here and help Al."

"Yes, Helen," said Elsie, catching on. "You can help me with"— she thought a moment—"the chili. Why don't you come taste it and see what it needs? I might not have put enough chili powder in."

"Yes, okay. I suppose I could do that. Unless, Al, you need me?"

"We'll be fine without you," answered Al dryly.

Grateful for another excuse to leave the staff room, Helen followed Elsie back into the kitchen.

***

One problem solved, Al turned back to John's head, grabbed a bottle of antiseptic, and poured it over his head. The liquid ran down John's forehead and into his eyes, but he sat still as a statue.

"Still okay?" asked Al. John had not spoken for a few minutes.

"Fine. Keep going."

"Maybe we should freeze it before you cut," suggested Kay. She disappeared for a moment and returned with a block of ice wrapped in a tea towel. Al held the pack to John's head for a minute or two and then tapped the area. "Can you feel this?"

"Kinda."

"Good enough." Al took a new razor blade out of its pack and slowly carved around the hook. John's head started to bleed like a stuck pig, dripping all over the dining room floor.

"Sorry for the mess," apologized John.

"My gosh, don't worry about that!" exclaimed Kay.

Al stopped. "Don't know if I should keep going . . . It's pretty deep."

"I don't care. Please, Al, cut. Just get it out."

"Okay. Wasn't planning on performing any trepanning today, but here goes—" Al raised the razor and cut deeper into the scalp.

John gurgled and took a deep breath.

Kay left again, returning a few moments later.

"I have something for the pain."

"It really doesn't hurt that much. It's just seeing all this blood—"

"Something to calm you down, then." Kay placed a bottle of scotch on the table.

"Oh, thank the Lord. Pour me out a couple of fingers, will you?"

Kay obliged. John grabbed the glass and tossed back the contents. "That's good. Another would be better."

Kay refilled his glass a couple more times before Al was finally able to release the hook from John's scalp, but it was still bleeding badly.

Al rummaged around the first aid box, pulled out a box of gauze, and inspected it. "This isn't thick enough to stop the bleeding. I need some kind of pressure bandage, something to sop up the blood. Can you find something, Mom?"

Kay paused for a moment. "I'll be right back." She disappeared out the door yet again.

"How you feeling, John? Do you feel faint?" Al was starting to worry about the copious amounts of blood he was losing.

"Fine, just fine, Al!" By now, John was a little relaxed and just a little tipsy.

When Kay returned, she was holding several Kotex pads. Al looked up at her but said nothing to John. He covered the cut with a Kotex pad, bound it to his head with roller bandages, and secured the whole thing with adhesive tape.

"How's that feel?"

"Like some big foreign object holding onto the top of my head, but a helluva lot better than something dangling off it!"

"Good. Now you're still going to have to go to Red Lake as soon as I can get through on the radio. You're going to need a couple of stitches. In the meantime, I'm going to help you back to your cabin so you can lie down. That'll help the bleeding to stop."

"I think I will lie down for a bit." Unsteadily, he rose to his feet. The scotch had done its job.

As Al helped John out the door, Lori entered. She looked at the bandaged man, the blood-soaked gauze, the puddle of blood congealing on the table and spattered on the floor.

"Okay, what did I miss this time?"

***

"I wonder how Phil's doing on his first day of guiding?" said Al after settling John in his cabin and finally sitting down with the girls for some lunch. "Hope he's having a better day than me!"

"Don't give me anything more to worry about!" exclaimed Helen. "I'm a basket case as it is." She glanced at her watch. "Five more hours till he gets back in. And I don't know how many hours till poor John gets out. You weren't able to get through on the phone yet, were you?"

"Not yet. If this keeps up, John won't be getting out until morning when his scheduled plane comes to pick him up."

"Gawd," grumbled Helen. "Do you think he'll be okay until then?"

"Ask him yourself," said Al, pointing to the door.

"John!" Kay dropped her sandwich and sprung to her feet. "You didn't have to get up! We were going to bring your lunch up to you."

"Don't want any lunch. I want to go fishing. I've had enough of this laying around."

"You can't go back out!" said Helen.

"I feel fine. Besides, look—" John banged the bandages on his head. The bloody bandages had dried and hardened like Plaster of Paris.

"Look at that. Should have put it on before I got the hook in there!"

"For God's sake!" cried Elsie. "It looks like he's wearing a helmet!"

John turned to Al and pleaded, "Please, Al. I'm an accountant. I make a good living, but it's not very exciting. I *need* these few days up here every year. I need to go fishing."

Al thought for a moment. "Right then. Just let me gather up my gear, and I'll meet you at the boat."

"Great!" John disappeared out the door.

Helen gasped. "You're not really going to take him back out fishing, are you?"

Al wiped his mouth with his napkin and stood up. "Of course I am."

"Al, what if he passes out because of blood loss? We'll have a lawsuit on our hands!"

"It's his choice. No one's making him go."

"I don't understand. Why would he take the chance?"

"He told me he needs to. That's good enough for me."

"Fishing is a want, not a need! No one *needs* to go fishing."

"All these years in the business, and you still don't get it. Fishing *is* a need because it's whatever *you* need it to be. Some guys like to keep it simple. They have a couple of baits and one rod. They sit in the boat and relax. They don't care if they ever catch a fish. Other guys, well, they like it more complex. They have a different rod for each species. They have a tackle box the size of a coffin, filled with every colour and every shape of bait known to man. They study the wind direction, lake depth, water temperature, and barometric pressure. Some guys keep charts on how many each guy in their party catches and who catches the biggest fish and bet heavily on the results. Other guys can't even tell you how many they caught that day. Fishing can be relaxing or exciting, philosophical or mindless, basic or high-tech. How you fish changes as you change, but one thing that never changes is the need to fish."

Several heads around the table nodded in agreement. This crew knew fishing was more than about fish. Only Helen still looked baffled.

"Look, we'll go out for just a couple of hours. By that time, maybe we'll be able to get through on the radio."

Helen took a gulp of coffee as she watched her husband walk out the door, then turned to Kay. "It never fails to amaze me how passionate fishermen are about their sport. If they are half as passionate in their work, it's no wonder they are so successful and can afford yearly trips up here. It is important to give everything you do your all, even fishing!"

"Too true," said Kay, "And John's perseverance might just get him his muskie after all!"

However, it was not to be. A couple of hours later, Al and John came back in, still muskie-less. It looked like John's perfect record was going to be blown. Al finally got through on the radio and ordered a plane in. A short while later, a Cessna arrived.

As John's plane blazed away, Al headed to the Stork Lake sign, where the guests were just finishing having their pictures taken with the day's haul.

"Who caught all these?" Al stared in amazement at the mass of northerns lying on the ground. "Roger?"

Roger grinned. "Nope. Your son."

"You gotta be kidding me."

"Dad! Dad! I've been looking for you." Phil ran up to his father, his face the colour of a beet, burnt crisp from a day on the lake. "Did you see all the northerns we caught today? And we caught enough walleye for shore lunch in, like, fifteen minutes! And we caught a lot more, only we let them all go. The Gardners are such cool people. They gave me pop all day, and chocolate bars, and Harry, he even helped me start the fire at shore lunch . . . though I could have done it all by myself. And I didn't hit any reefs or rocks or anything! It was the coolest day ever! I can hardly wait for tomorrow!"

"Well, James will be back on the job tomorrow. You won't have to go out."

Phil looked dejected. "But Dad, I have to go out! They're my guests! Besides, Harry says he's gonna give me a big tip. I've never gotten a tip before!"

"We'll see. Now why don't you find Gup, and he'll help you gut and gill these fish."

"I don't need any help, Dad! Gup's the one that showed me how to gut and gill! I can do it myself!"

"Still, just have Gup watch you. I don't need any more accidents today."

As Phil ran off to find his grandfather, Roger pulled a pack of cigarettes out of his jacket pocket and lit one. "So, Al, your son's first day out, and he did good. No mishaps and lots of fish. Better than one guide I know . . . His guest caught nothing but himself!"

There were no secrets in this small town.

Al shook his head and laughed. "You cheeky bugger, you." How could he live it down— that the only accident of the day was in the camp owner's boat.

***

Lori rang the gong for dinner, then slipped back inside to finish putting the coffee and tea on the guides' table. As she did, Phil ran in.

"You didn't even come down to see all the fish I got my guests on my first day as a guide!" he cried. "What kind of sister are you?"

"I just woke up a few minutes ago! I was so tired, but my room was too hot to sleep in, so I snuck down to the icehouse and fell asleep in there. It was so nice and dark and quiet and cool that I didn't even hear the boats come in. Drat, I've missed everything today! You know I woulda come down to see."

"Well, I caught tons anyways. I mean, my guests did. I think I did even better than Roger. Someday I'm gonna be top guide!"

The rest of the guides filed in. The talk around the table was jovial, with the odd comment about the "big fish" Al's guest hooked that day. However, no one mentioned James's "day off" or the fact that he was not at supper. Even Al, who had sat down to eat with them, did not say anything. He did not expect the subject to be brought up ever again. It wasn't their way.

Al didn't have a chance to sit there long. He had only taken two spoonfuls of his chili when they heard the buzz of an airplane.

"Why can't I ever get through a meal?" complained Al, leaving his bowl of chili to get cold.

He arrived at the dock just in time to see John Royalty step off the plane. His Kotex bandage had been replaced with a small white wrap.

John flashed Al a Texas-sized grin. "Al! I'm back!"

"I can see that. Should you be?"

"Doctor says I'm right as rain. They stuck in a few stitches, cleaned me up, and here I am. Let's go fishing."

"I don't know—"

"I paid for today, and I want to go fishing. It's my last chance. I'm going home in the morning. Look, I even bought a hat when I was in town." John pulled a fishing hat out of his pocket and placed it on his head. "I won't get hooked again!"

"Okay, John, but we'd better get going. It'll be dark soon."

"I'll take him."

James stood there. His eyes were a little bloodshot, but they had a determined gleam to them, a look that said he was there to redeem himself.

Al gave a small nod to James.

"Then let's get going!" exclaimed John.

So for the third time that day, John headed out fishing.

***

Hours passed. The topaz sun smouldered away and dropped behind the islands, leaving the day dusted in grey ashes. Supper came and went; the dishes were dried, the tea towels hung up to dry. Staff and guests alike made their way to their respective cabins. The camp grew quiet. And still, James and John weren't back.

Most of the lights in the cabins had been extinguished, the result of a long day of fresh air, food, and relaxation. The only light still shining on the hill came from the house cabin, where Helen waited like a mother hen for the last boat to come in.

Al, too, was still awake—not because *he* was worried about James and John, but because *Helen* was. A napped-out Lori also was still awake. She sat in front of the large picture window, watching her mom do her petit point. Every so often, her mom would pause, needle still, and listen for the sounds of an outboard motor.

"I'm worried, Al. All I can hear is the generator. Do you think something's happened?"

"Of course not."

"But they're not in yet, and it's dark."

"James knows his way home blindfolded," replied Al.

"I hope John's all right. He shouldn't have gone back out on the lake."

"He'll be okay."

"Wonder if they had motor trouble?"

"Then James'll paddle home."

"He couldn't paddle all the way home! Maybe we should send someone out—"

"Out where?" chirped Lori. "Where would they look? It's a big lake."

Helen looked stricken, and her needle paused midair. For a moment, she was still. Then she started to stitch again. "You should go to bed. Even your brother is asleep already."

"I'm not missing anything more today!"

"Why, you think something's happened?" Helen's circle of worry started all over again.

Finally they heard a faint hum in the distance.

"Is that a boat?" Helen listened a moment longer. "It is! They're home. Thank God, now I can relax!"

A few minutes later, there was a tap at the door. A gleeful John stood there.

"I hope I'm not disturbing you folks," he said. "I noticed your light was still on."

"Not at all!" boomed Al.

"I just wanted you to know I got my muskie!"

"You caught a muskie?"

"I caught it all right! You know, I got so damned excited, I pulled my bait right out of the water again. Christ, I thought I was going to get another hook in my bloody head! This time, though, that muskie jumped after it. He landed right in the boat and got tangled in all those lures hanging there! James was actually giddy. He laughed and said, 'Look who's impaled now!'"

"I'm so happy for you."

"As happy as I am, you should see James. Looks like both our records are intact! I gotta tell you, I cast a treble hook into my own skull, bled like a stuck pig, had to have my head sliced open with a razor and stitched up, and yet this was the best trip of my life. It had real challenge to it."

Al was glowing. Apparently John and James weren't the only ones thrilled that they had finally boated their prey.

"I want to give you this." John held up the brand-new fishing hat. He had studded it with a colourful array of lures from the boat, including the red daredevil. "Hang it on the wall. I'll be needing it next year!"

Henry David Thoreau once said, "Many men go fishing all of their lives without knowing that it is not fish they are after." Lori hung the hat fringed in lures back on its nail and took down a small red baseball cap. It reminded her of another Thoreau quote: "The squirrel that you kill in jest dies in earnest."

1970

Kay stood on the stool in the pantry, reaching up into the rafters for a case of soda crackers. She lifted it up easily, too easily.

"Uh oh."

"What's the matter?" Elsie stood just below her, kneading a large lump of bread dough.

"Feels pretty light, even for crackers." Kay stepped down, set the still-sealed box on the table, and ripped open the flaps. Both women looked inside. It was full of empty wrappers: the only telltale sign of the thief was a small hole gnawed in the bottom corner.

"Those darned squirrels!" exclaimed Elsie. "Last week, it was cereal they got into." She lifted a floury hand to her brow. "No way to keep them out, neither. Doesn't matter how high we keep them boxes. They scamper straight up them log walls just like that . . . *bop, bop, bop.*"

"They'll have to be shot," said Kay matter-of-factly.

"Yep," agreed Elsie. "I'll tell Albert at dinner. I'll also have to tell Helen to order more crackers. Will we have enough until the plane comes in on Tuesday?"

"Not a chance."

Elsie returned to her bread dough. "Then I better make more buns."

***

Lori had a friend this summer.

Lawrence was James and Agnes's son. Until now, he had spent summers with his grandmother. However, she had died this last winter, so Al told the loyal couple to bring their boy to Stork Lake with them.

"Have to start training the new generation of guides now."

James had laughed.

They decided not to live in one of the staff cabins but instead in a tent on the tiny island that floated just about fifty feet from the shore, right near the lodge. Most years, the water was low enough that you could wade across, but Agnes did not like the water, so the family paddled a canoe back and forth.

Lawrence's parents affectionately called him Makoons, which in Ojibwa meant *little bear*. He was a year older than Lori but much smaller. Agnes, as neat as a pin herself, kept him scrubbed and—for a very active boy—remarkably tidy. His shirts were tucked in, his laces tied, his glossy black locks always neatly combed under his small, clean baseball cap. His outgoing personality, impish smile, and hearty laugh mimicked his father's.

In the morning, Agnes brought Lawrence with her to work. He was well behaved, doing as his parents asked without question or dalliance. He stayed clear of Helen and Al and out of sight of all the guests. In fact, the only one who noticed he was around was Lori.

He attached himself to her like a barnacle, and she loved having him around. Not only did she finally have someone to play with, but for once, she was not the smallest or the youngest at the camp. Phil was always taunting her, telling her she was too little to drive the tractor or tend the store. She always felt small and insignificant around him because she did not know or understand as much. Now here was someone smaller than her, who knew less about camp life than she did. Here was someone who let her pick out the games and who listened to her wealth of wisdom.

The two children spent their days fishing off the dock, climbing trees, and playing hide-and-seek—no small feat since there were hundreds of places to hide. They explored the paths crisscrossing the bush, skipped stones, and taught Chezy tricks. They smashed mushrooms with sticks, raced pine beetles and snails, and picked and ate raspberries until their lips, tongues, and fingers were bright red.

One of their favourite activities was searching for new animals. Lori escorted Lawrence down to the marshy point where the Canadian flag proudly flew on its pole. There, where the reeds reached up to meet the mint, both tadpoles and frogs hid in droves. They scooped minnows out of the shallows by the docks and dug for freshwater clams. They chased chipmunks and jackrabbits. They searched the tall grass for woodchuck holes and the forests for martens. They scanned the back bay by the lodge for beavers and the adjoining marsh for muskrats.

On rainy days, they headed to the card room to inspect the "inside animals." "See how the hair grows up instead of down on a moose's muzzle?" asked Lori. The pair stood in front of a gigantic moose head that looked like it had just crashed through the wall.

"Whoa."

"This deer has what you'd call 'a good rack.' See, it has ten nice long points on its antlers."

"Wow."

"See the bear rug lying there by the hearth? It was shot in the summer."

"How'd you know?" asked Lawrence.

"By its coat. It's not as thick as it would be if it were shot in the fall or winter."

"Ohhh."

"When I was little, I used to think these fish were toys," said Lori. The kids stood in front of the mounted fish. So many mounted fish—their glass eyes watching, their scales gleaming in the sunlight.

One by one, they inspected each motionless creature in this log room zoo: the stuffed grey owl about to take flight, the strutting stuffed loon, the mallard's webbed foot made into an ashtray. With each animal, Lori repeated a story she had heard her father recount endless times to the guests. Neither child found anything strange about these still lifes at odds with the real life teeming outside. They were simply symbols of death imitating life.

When they grew tired of their post-mortem, the kids played cards. Lawrence had never played cards before that summer, so they sat at the poker table, and Lori showed him how to shuffle and deal. She taught him War and Fish first, and then Crazy Eights and Gin. As he caught on, he became a worthy opponent, one she was bent on beating.

Their rivalry continued to outdoor games, where Lori quickly found out she was not only bigger but stronger. And so, almost every day, she insisted on competitions of strength: arm wrestling, running, climbing, jumping.

"Race you to the lake!"

Lori would always win.

"Let's see who can climb higher in the woodpile!"

Lori always did.

"Bet I can jump further than you."

And she did. "See, I told you I could jump further! I bet I could jump almost as far as that squirrel." Lori pointed to a squirrel bounding easily from tree to tree. He never contradicted or condemned Lori's boastful accomplishments. It was not his way.

Lawrence always disappeared with his mother after the lunch dishes were done and would not return until the next morning. He had to help his mom with chores in the afternoon and evenings he spent with his dad on the island. So Lori spent her lazy afternoons napping or swimming and evenings helping in the lodge—setting tables, serving supper to the guides, clearing dishes, and washing up. If work was finished early enough, there would be a boat ride with Nana and Gup before bed to cool off. And so one day melted into another in such a rhythm that Lori had little conception of how much time was passing.

"When are you leaving?" asked Lawrence one day.

"Leaving for where?"

"You know, your other home. The one you're at when you're not here. How much more time you got?"

The question startled Lori. How much time did she have left before she had to return to Winnipeg? Was the summer almost gone? Was it going to end soon? Dates meant little up here; it was hard to keep track. She ran to the kitchen to look at the calendar, where each day that had passed by was crossed off in big red *X*'s. She was relieved that it was only the nineteenth of July.

"It's okay, Makoons," she said to the little boy, who had followed her in. "We still have weeks and weeks to play. Come on. Let's go outside and see who can lift the heaviest rock."

***

Bang!

Lori looked up. The sound came from right outside the kitchen. She knew what it meant: no more empty cracker boxes.

She dashed off outside, just in time to see Albert walking away, rifle in hand. Phil was walking on the roof; he had been told to retrieve the squirrel's body.

"Got him!" Phil agilely scampered down the log ends, squirrel in hand.

"What are you going to do with him?" asked Lori.

"Throw him in the garbage, of course." Phil looked at his sister as if she were crazy.

"Can I have him?"

"What are you going to do with a dead squirrel? You can't keep him. He's just going to rot away and get full of maggots and bugs."

"I want him."

Phil shrugged. "Fine."

Lori held her hands out, and Phil dropped the squirrel into them. "I don't care what you do with him now." He walked off.

Lori looked down at the lifeless little body. She was used to dead animals. They were all around her. The mounts in the lodge, the fish brought in nightly and hung proudly on hooks for all to see. She was the first one to rip the wings off a mayfly or cut a leech in half to see if both sides would live. However, this was different. This was no fish or bug. This was no cold, lifeless statue. This wasn't even like the bear they had shot for stealing bread and buns. He had been big and dangerous. No, this animal was small and defenceless. And it was still warm.

She sadly stroked the bright red pelt with her fingers. This might have been the squirrel that had sat on top of the woodpile, tail aloft, scolding her. This might have been the squirrel that she had watched leap tree to tree. This squirrel had been alive. She could not bear the thought his body would end up at the garbage dump, full of maggots and flies.

"Makoons!" Lori called out to Lawrence as he appeared from around the corner.

"What?"

"They killed the squirrel that was eating the crackers."

"Oh."

"I think we should have a funeral for him."

Lawrence shrugged. "Okay."

The children grabbed a shovel and searched for a cemetery site. They found one under the shady birch beside the house cabin.

"This is a good place for a grave. Dig here," ordered Lori.

Obligingly, Lawrence dug the shovel into the grass. It was hard work, but he persevered. After a few minutes, he had made a shallow hole. They dropped to their knees and buried the little body in the shallow grave. When it was done, they knelt there for a moment, heads bowed, in silent thought.

Gup happened to walk past as they laid the little squirrel to rest.

"Hey, kids." They looked up. "Come with me!"

They followed him into the workshop. Lori loved it here. Every inch of every wall had hanging on it some sort of tool: hammers and saws, wrenches and screwdrivers, chisels and planes, drills and bits. There were dozens of glass jars filled with every sized screw and nail—everything you needed to build something out of nothing. In the corner was a box of scrap lumber, odds and ends from different projects. Gup rummaged through the box until he found two thin pieces of wood. He selected a chisel off the wall and very carefully filed out a groove in a piece of wood.

"What are you making?"

"You'll see."

He then took another piece of wood and fit it lengthwise into the groove. The finished product was a small cross. He held it out to the kids. "For your squirrel."

"Oh, Gup, thank you!!"

Lori and Lawrence ran and placed it on the grave. Lori looked down at the little cross standing in the freshly dug ground, and somehow it made her feel a little better.

After a few minutes, Lawrence asked, "What should we do now?"

"Let's go to my swing." They headed back down to the long path until it reached the hill. Here, Gup and Ray Rubin had constructed the swing just a few weeks before. They had fastened a beam between two large poplar trees. From this beam, hemp ropes connected to the wooden seat. It was an amazing swing, with a grand sweeping arc that gave you the sensation of flying, far more fun than the pokey little swings in the schoolyard back in Winnipeg. Lori sat in the seat and began to slightly rock back and forth, her feet dragging the ground. Lawrence sat on a stump nearby.

"Want to see who can swing the highest?"

"Nah."

"How come?"

"Because you always swing the highest."

"Maybe you will this time."

"You just swing. Then I'll just swing. Okay?"

For once, Lori agreed. "Okay." Just as she was about to push off, a small image caught the corner of her eye. She stopped and watched in amazement as a baby squirrel slowly crawled toward her then edged timidly onto the top of her white runner.

In a whispery voice, Lori exclaimed, "Look at that!" Gingerly, she reached down and picked him up.

"There's more!" From behind the stump, they could see three more small bundles moving about. They both sat there, staring at the tiny red fur balls with fluffy tails, their baby faces mostly taken up with big black innocent eyes. "Where do you think the mother is?"

"You don't think—"

Lori immediately thought of the little cross under the birch tree. She was horrified. "We shot their mom! They don't have a mother!"

Lawrence shook his head. "Poor babies."

"We'll have to be their parents."

Lori looked down at the sweet little faces. "It's okay. You're safe now. We won't let anything hurt you."

"What do we do with them now?" asked Lawrence.

"We need a box."

"They could climb out of the box."

"You're right. We need some sort of cage. Let's look in the workshop." The kids carried the squirrels down to the workshop.

They looked around. "What about this?" asked Lawrence.

Hanging from a nail on the back wall were a couple of minnow traps. They were made of wire mesh, just the right size to keep the little squirrels in. Gently they transferred the squirrels to their new home. The babies huddled together at the bottom for a moment then began climbing the wire sides.

"I think they like it! They're playing."

"I think so too," agreed Lori. "But they need some sort of bed."

"I know!" said Lawrence. "Those wood shavings at the new cabin! They're soft, and there are lots of them, so we can change them every day for when, you know, they poop and stuff."

"Good idea! Take a box and go get some. I'll stay with the squirrels."

A few minutes later, Lawrence was back with the shavings, and the kids filled the bottom of the cage.

Content with their sanctuary, Lori's next concern was food, and she knew just who to ask about it.

They found Agnes hanging laundry, her wide, colourful skirt billowing in the breeze.

"Agnes, you have to help us!" cried Lori. "The squirrel Albert killed had babies, and now they have no one but us!"

"Let me see," said Agnes in her soft voice. She slowly knelt and took one of the babies out. "Oh, he's sweet!" She gently tickled under his chin. The baby responded by opening his mouth. "He has some teeth already, so he's weaned. That's a good thing. They are almost ready to be on their own. You just need to help them a bit longer . . . you know, make sure they have food to eat and water to drink."

"What do they eat? Nuts? Don't squirrels love nuts?" asked Lori.

"Nuts and sunflower seeds. I think I saw some in the store. Also cut up vegetables, like lettuce and broccoli. And fruit. There are some apples in the root cellar." Agnes stroked a set of tiny soft ears. "They can't stay in this tiny cage, though. They need room to run and play. And they need to be played with."

"Don't worry! We'll give them lots of love and attention! We'll get them some food right now, then find Gup and ask him to build them a big cage." Lori stared at Agnes's placid face. "How do you know so much about squirrels?"

"I don't know about squirrels. I know about kids." She glanced up at her son and, with a small smile, lovingly reached up and tugged on the brim of his cap. "They're nature's gift to us."

***

Agnes watched the two children run off with their precious cargo and then slowly headed back to the washstand. Standing over the tub of hot water suddenly made her feel hot— too hot. She wiped the perspiration bubbling on her upper lip with the back of her hand and slipped off her sweater. Just as she was about to run the next set of sheets through the rollers, a pain shot through her like fire, and she felt like she was going to pass out. Gasping, she bent over, clutching her abdomen. *The pain is getting worse*, she thought. Still she straightened up and carried on until all the laundry was done.

***

"And that's that," said Helen the next morning, bringing the last few plates in from the guest dining room. "I better go wake Lori before I finish these dishes, though I wish I could just crawl back into bed with her. I'm so tired this morning. I had the worst sleep last night. I had this dream. It wasn't even a nightmare, but it woke me then kept me up the rest of the night. It gave me this . . . I don't know how to describe it . . . this uneasy, awful feeling, worse than if it had been a nightmare."

"What was the dream?" asked Elsie as she scraped Red River cereal from the bottom of a pot.

"I dreamed about a bed. I was trying to smooth the covers. I kept running my hands over it, but I couldn't get rid of the wrinkles. The more I tried, the more agitated I got. Gad, now I have to go make up about ten real beds. Hope I don't have the same problem! Elsie, what's the matter?"

Elsie had dropped the pot she was holding and now stood there, her eyes and mouth wide open. "Oh *no*! That's no good!"

"What's no good? Elsie, what are you talking about?"

"Dreaming about tryin' to fix up a bed is *terrible*. That's a foreboding dream. It means somethin' bad is gonna happen!"

Helen gasped. "Like what?"

"My ma used to say that fixin' up a bed in a dream meant someone soon be fixin' up a resting place in this world, and I don't mean for sleeping!"

"You don't mean . . . like a *grave*?"

"That's what I mean. Shh!" Elsie pointed out the window. "I see Lori got herself up and is coming around the corner."

A moment later, the bright-eyed little girl skipped into the room.

"Morning! Isn't it a beautiful day? I couldn't sleep any longer. I was so excited to see how my baby squirrels were doing. The new pen that Gup made last night is perfect! You should see it, Elsie. It's made of wire and has a tarp on the top. We filled it with pinecones and sticks and leaves for them to play with, and branches for them to climb on, so you know, they learn how to be squirrels. Makoons is there now, waiting for me to bring something for their breakfast. Can I have some lettuce?"

Still rattled, Helen began filling the sink. Intently squeezing out some soap into the water, she said, "You need to eat something yourself first."

"Oh, all right." Lori began rummaging through the mini-box cereals on the shelf. "Why is it that we get cases and cases of variety packs and still have no variety? There's, like, one Fruit Loops per case. The rest are always crummy, like Bran Flakes. They must think everyone here is old and constipated."

"Just pick one!" ordered Helen.

"Sheesh! Okay." Lori grabbed a box. "I'm gonna go eat outside with my squirrels. Maybe they'll like cornflakes more than I do."

***

After lunch, Lori returned to the solace of her cabin and lay in the warm sunshine on the stoop. It had been a strange meal with her mother still in a bad mood, Elsie acting jumpy, and Agnes talking less than usual and eating nothing at all. Only her grandmother and Lawrence seemed nonplussed. She had been glad when it was finally over and was trying to think up ways to burn up the afternoon when a shadow momentarily blocked her sunbeam. She looked up to find Lawrence towering over her.

"Want to do something?"

"How come you didn't go home with your mom?" Agnes always took Lawrence back to the island after lunch.

He shrugged. "She said I could stay."

"Heh, then we can go for a swim!"

Lori jumped up and disappeared into her cabin, where she quickly changed into her bathing suit, grabbed a towel, and headed back out. Lawrence still sat on the stoop, fully dressed.

"For Pete's sake, you can't swim like that. Take off your shirt and shoes," ordered Lori.

"I can swim in my shirt," Lawrence replied stubbornly.

"Well at least take your shoes off. And your cap!"

Lawrence reluctantly removed his shoes, plucked the hat off his head, and threw them down on the stoop. The kids headed down to the lake. The normally pristine beach was littered with piles of decaying fish flies that had washed up on the shore, creating an offensive odour.

"Ugh!" Lori turned up her nose. "I'm not walking through all that mush!" With that, she ran to the end of the dock and jumped in.

Lawrence hesitated. He had never learned to swim, so usually, he just waded in the shallows. However, the shallows were full of stinky fish flies, so he walked to the end of the dock where Lori was splashing around and tentatively dipped his foot in the water.

"Is it deep? Can you touch bottom?" he asked.

"I can't, and if I can't, you won't be able to. Why?"

"Just asking"

"Why don't you jump in?"

"I . . . don't think so."

"What, you chicken?"

"No—"

"I dare you to!"

"I don't want to."

"Yes you do. You're just being a baby."

Goaded, Lawrence finally jumped in—and promptly sunk, his entire head disappearing under the water. Kicking furiously, he managed to just rise to the surface. Then he screamed out in panic, reaching out to Lori, who was right beside him. He grabbed onto the top of her head and pushed down, using her as a buoy to keep his own head above water. Lori's head plunged under the surface, and down she went, her nose and mouth filling with water. Not until her feet touched the bottom was she able to push off and bounce back up to the top. Her head broke the surface, and she took a gasp, only to be instantly submerged by a still squealing Lawrence again. Lori tried swatting him away, but his legs thrashed about the water like eggbeaters, kicking her arms and stomach. She was dunked again and again until she could no longer break free and rise up to catch her breath. In sheer panic, Lori flailed around but could no longer reach the surface. *I need air*. But there was none.

Her brain said *breath*. She almost relented and was about to take in lungfuls of water when suddenly the pressure on her head slackened, and she bobbed back up to the top. Lawrence had finally grabbed the edge of the dock and hauled himself up. Lori slowly followed. They both lay dripping on the dock, gasping for breath.

"You almost drowned me!" heaved Lawrence.

"*You* almost drowned *me!*"

"Why'd you dare me to go in?"

"Because you should know how to swim, for pity's sake! You live on an island!"

Lawrence sat up and shook his head. Droplets sprayed off his hair. "I don't like the water. And so what if I live on an island? My dad doesn't swim. My mom doesn't swim. And I don't have to swim!"

"Okay, okay."

***

"What in the world is going on?" shouted Helen from the shore. With purpose, she strutted onto the dock and up to the children. "All I hear is yelling. Lawrence, your clothes are wet. Did you fall in? Did you hurt yourself?" After what Elsie had said this morning, she was spooked.

Lawrence immediately muted, dropping his eyes to the dock.

Lori piped up, "He's not hurt."

"Then why were you yelling?"

"Makoons almost drowned me."

"What do you mean, he almost drowned you?" Helen thought her heart would stop.

"Well I dared him to jump in the water, but when he did, he sunk. He used me like a life preserver to keep his head above water. I couldn't catch my breath. My nose was full of water. I think I almost *died*."

"My goodness, you children have to be more careful! You never dare someone who can't swim to jump in the lake, and you never try to save someone who is drowning. They can drag you down."

"I wasn't *trying* to save him!"

"The point is, you could have both drowned!" Helen's angry tone disguised the absolute fear she was experiencing. Elsie's premonition had almost come true! "Agnes will be fit to be tied when she hears what happened. I won't blame her if she doesn't let Lawrence spend afternoons here anymore. Lori, you're coming to the cabin with me. Lawrence, go find Peepsight and ask him to take you home."

Lawrence did not need to be told twice. He jumped up and raced off the dock, not even stopping to retrieve his cap or shoes from Lori's stoop.

***

The Twin Disc party was in camp, and it was their watuni night. Watunis were a concoction of Jack Yetter's own invention. They were martinis made with scotch instead of vermouth, and they packed quite a punch. It usually meant a prolonged cocktail hour and a late-night supper. The clock struck ten before the last dish was dried.

"You girls have had quite the day. I feel bad keeping you all here so late. I know we're not the easiest guys to deal with. Can I show our appreciation by offering you a drink?" Yetter stood there, a cigar hanging out of his mouth and a full pitcher in his hand.

Helen placed her hands on her hips. "Just what the doctor ordered! Agnes, grab some glasses. We're all going to have a drink!"

***

Lori had been banished to her cabin after her supper. Usually, Helen insisted Lori meet the guests, an act that petrified her. Nothing was worse than being shown off like a trophy muskie, especially to all these scary, smart, rich people. Unlike when she was with Lawrence, these people somehow made her feel inferior and small, with nothing notable to say. Tonight, however, was different. Unsettled from her afternoon's experience, she would have gladly stayed at the lodge with her mom and dad. Her brother was off somewhere, and the feeling of being alone wrapped around her like the suffocating water had earlier. Maybe she would go have a peep and see if they were about ready to pack it in for the night.

Clad only in a long, flannel nightie, Lori slowly crept barefoot down the hill, a pitch-black pathway punctuated only by the light emanating from the occasional cabin. She was just nearing the lodge when the door opened. Lori quickly hid behind a tree, not wanting to be detected. Albert and Al came out, half carrying, half dragging

Agnes. She had one arm around each of their necks, and her head hung back, eyes closed. Out of her mouth came low guttural moans like Lori had never heard before. *What was wrong with Agnes? She couldn't be drunk?* The two men dragged the tiny figure toward the canoe resting on the shore. They gently lay her on the bottom of the canoe, and Albert climbed in and slowly paddled toward the island. Al turned to head back to the lodge, and Lori, afraid of being discovered out alone in the dark, turned and fled back to her cabin.

***

The sun was just peeking above the horizon the next morning when Albert sat alone with his coffee and cigarette in the staff dining room. He coughed a few times, took a drag of his cigarette, and then a long slug of coffee. As he did so, the screen door screeched open and James slowly entered. Albert lowered his cup and immediately noticed the look of terror on his face.

"What is it, James? What's wrong? Where's Agnes?"

"Please come. She . . . she won't get up."

Albert jumped out of his seat, and together they headed over to the island.

Solemnly, Albert approached the tent. He took a deep breath, opened the flap, and peered in. Agnes lay on the ground, a very solemn Lawrence standing over her.

"Agnes?" Albert called out. "Agnes?"

She was lying on her side, one arm stretched above her head, still fully clothed. Her eyes were closed, her parchment cheeks drained of colour.

"*Agnes!*"

Carefully, Albert rolled her over onto her back. As he did so, her arm that had been stretched over her head stood straight up in the air, her index finger pointing directly at Albert. His blood ran cold.

Twenty minutes later, Albert returned to the kitchen. In a grave voice, he reported to the three anxious, waiting faces, "Agnes is dead."

"Oh, for God's sake!" exclaimed Elsie.

"Oh no!" Helen dropped down into a chair. "I can't believe it! This is awful!"

"How?" Kay now, too, dropped to a seat in shock.

"Can't tell. All I knows is rigor mortis has already set in. I better let Al know right away. We'll have to call the RCMP." Albert disappeared out the door.

Helen was in shock. "No, no, *no*! This is my fault!"

Kay tried to console her. "Helen, it's not your fault. We all thought that because Agnes didn't usually drink that she was staggering and moaning last night because of the watunis. And even if we had known she was sick . . . if she was . . . there's nothing we could have done that time of night. No one could have seen this coming."

"Yes, we could. My dream told us!"

"That's just a coincidence!" said Kay.

"It's not a coincidence . . . It's destiny," said Elsie sadly.

***

Lori heard the arrival of the turboprop. *Oh no. That plane always means something important is about to happen, and usually it's not good.*

She quickly ran down to the kitchen, which was eerily quiet. The guides should have been eating breakfast, and there wasn't one in sight. Elsie was at the table with her mom, who was crying, while Kay and her dad quietly talked to two burly RCMP officers.

Kay, seeing the white-faced little girl, excused herself and went to her.

"Nana, what's going on?"

Kay held out her hand. "Come on, Lori. Let's go back to your cabin, and I will explain it all to you."

Sometime later, two boats pulled up to the shore. Albert, James, and Lawrence got out of one while two officers exited the other. It was eerily quiet on the dock as they lifted the shrouded body out of the boat and onto the plane. Lori sat motionless on the stoop of her cabin, watching—watching Lawrence stand on the dock, his hair tousled, his face emotionless, tearless. James, hat in hand, head down, remained stoic, the anguish of his spirit showing only in the dragged-down corners of his eyes and mouth. One of the officers motioned to them, and they joined Agnes on the plane for one last time.

As the plane taxied away, Lori did not think she would ever feel as awful as she did at this moment. Someone she had known all her life, someone who had accepted her and treated her as well as any daughter, was dead. She picked up Lawrence's red cap, which still lay on the stoop beside his shoes from the day before, then looked over at the baby squirrels in the pen beside her. Like them, he now had no mom. She could not think of anything worse happening. It was just too much to take.

Who will take care of Makoons now? Lori whispered to herself.

An autopsy showed Agnes had died of a burst appendix. James returned to work a week later—without Lawrence, who went to live with an aunt. Lori, too, raised her adoptive furry family until the squirrels were big enough to be released back into the wild.

She returned the small cap to its hook and picked up a yellow rubber rain hat. Yes, there was nothing worse than a child losing a mom—

1971

The first thing most people say after they greet you is, "And what about this weather?" It is a polite question, usually asked only to keep the conversation moving. But at a fishing resort, it's not just small talk. The weather is everything. It decides if guests will be able to fly into camp—and when they'd be able to fly out. It decides if the fish will be biting anything and everything or if they'd be hiding, coaxed out only by great skill or great luck. It also decides if surface reefs will be exposed or hidden, discovered only by the bottom of a motor. On bright, sunny days, everyone was happy, guests and staff alike. On rainy days, spirits dipped, with no diversions like television within watching distance to change the channel on your mood.

That summer, it rained almost every day. Planes couldn't get in, and planes couldn't get out. It was impossible to get anything dry. The sheets hung limp on the lines for days. The waterlogged firewood produced steam but very little fire. The paths dissolved into slick clay slides. The waterlogged ground was riddled with puddles. Worst of all, the fish seemed to have disappeared into the depths of the lake.

***

One evening as they were finishing off their dessert, the guides were discussing this absence of fish. It was beginning to be a serious problem—even just getting enough walleye for shore lunch was a challenge.

Albert pushed back his pie plate, retrieved a cigarette out of the pocket of his green work shirt, lit it, and took a deep drag, exhaling through his nostrils. "Has anyone tried Bear Carcass? There's usually fish there."

Eyes around the table dropped. No one said anything.

"Well?" continued Albert. "Has anyone?"

Finally, Peepsight spoke up. "Not this year."

"Why not?"

"There's an eddy." Peepsight made a circular motion with his hand. "Beside the island. Wasn't there before." Several heads nodded in agreement.

"So? I seen it. It ain't dangerous. I seen eddies swirling down a sink drain bigger 'en that one," said Albert.

There was more silence. Suddenly James stood up, grabbed his hat, and trudged out, quickly followed by Peepsight and the rest of the Native guides.

"Guess I know how to clear a room." Albert tapped his cigarette on the edge of the ashtray, then turned his sights to the two lanky teens on his right. "Either of you know what has them all spooked?"

"I don't know." Al's nephew Grant fidgeted uncomfortably in his seat. "I really haven't been here long enough to get to know any of them—"

"You do so know!" contradicted Jack. Grant's plain-speaking best friend certainly was not about to hide any delicious details. "They say an eddy means the island is haunted! Probably because James' wife died there."

Grant stroked his chin. "No, they don't say *who* haunts it—they just say *she* haunts it."

168

"Well who else would it be?" argued Jack. "The dead bear that was dumped there?"

"Heh, it could be the bear!" piped up Roger. "I NEVER fished at Bear Carcass . . . even before Agnes died. There was no way I was going near that place after all that . . . stuff happened. I nearly got scalped 'cause of that bear!"

"If they just got spooked this year, it ain't because of the bear," said Albert. "More than likely, Jack is right, and they think Agnes is haunting the island. They don't say her name because, to them, that'd be taboo. I guess the island is taboo, too. Even James has been back there only once, and that was to pick up his stuff. He moved into one of the staff cabins right after. Been married to Elsie for forty years. I know no amount of common sense will overcome superstition."

"Common sense certainly can overcome superstition." Lori and Kay had overheard their conversation as they dished out their own supper. They now both came and sat down at the table, with plates in hand.

"That island is not haunted, not by Agnes, and not by any old bear." Kay spread a napkin on her lap and picked up her fork.

"What, Kay? You don't believe in ghosts?" said Roger.

"Not in ghosts, and certainly not in ghost bears."

Roger shook his head. "You may find out differently. I did. Except my ghost bear took the form of a real bear."

***

Lori, however, was not so sure. The image of a haunted island was thrilling and terrifying at the same time. What would it be like? Was there really a ghost? The thought piqued her curiosity. Maybe seeing some spirits would pick up her own sagging spirits.

This summer had been hard enough without Agnes's calming presence. Then two weeks ago, Lori's mom, dad, brother, and grandfather had all left to work at Al's Arctic camp on Henik Lake. Lori was curious about this new camp, now open for its second season. She would even have sacrificed a week or two at Stork Lake to go see it. However, her mother was adamant.

"No, Lori, you have to stay here with Nana Kay. Even with Elsie's daughter Alice here to help out while I am gone, they are still going to need an extra pair of hands. Besides, I'm going to be too busy organizing the kitchen at the new camp to watch you."

"But, Mom! I don't need watching."

"Of course you do. I can barely keep track of you here."

"Keep track of me? How can you lose me at the Arctic camp when there are only six buildings and zero places to get lost? There isn't even any forest. The nearest tree is like a hundred miles away!"

"There are different dangers up there. The lake is so cold that if you fall in, you'll freeze to death."

"Why would I fall in?"

"The bug population rivals the Amazon's."

"Bugs don't bug me!"

"There's bog everywhere. It sucks you in like quicksand."

"How does everyone else walk around without being swallowed up?"

"Don't get smart with me. I said *no*, and that's the end of it."

So, Lori moved in with Nana. The bullpen, as it was called, was a dark, one-room cabin with two small windows, one electric light bulb dangling from the ceiling, and no bathroom. She had just unpacked her clothes and cut-outs and settled Chezy by the pot-bellied stove when Nana popped her head in.

"The plane's leaving. Better come say goodbye."

As Lori watched her family taxi away in the *Norseman*, its low rumble the saddest sounding of any plane, she felt angry, rejected, and deprived all at the same time. Her mother could be so, so *selfish*. It was just so typical—always thinking of herself. Didn't she think that maybe her daughter would like a new adventure in a new place? And why did her brother get to go? He was going to get to see ptarmigan and caribou. He was going to get to fish for grayling and char. And she was stuck here, with not even a black bear around camp to amuse her. Obviously the crummy weather had even them hiding out.

Still, the first week had ended up being fun. That afternoon, after her family left, Kay donned a blue one-piece bathing suit and a bathing cap covered with brightly coloured flower petals.

"Let's go swimming."

"In the rain?" Lori had never swam in the rain before. Her mother was always too worried about lightning.

"It's more fun in the rain!"

And it was. The water was warm—warmer than the air, and the tingle of raindrops mixed with the waves. Time after time, they jumped on the back of grey muscled waves and rode them back into shore. When they grew tired, they flipped over onto their backs and floated on top of them instead.

Other afternoons, they trampled through the forest. Her grandmother threw on an oversized raincoat, rubber boots, and a broad-rimmed rain hat and off they went, searching for berries and flowers and animals. Lori loved the smell of the damp bush, the soggy moss beneath her feet, the diamond drops clinging to tree branches and hanging onto the green leaves. During these excursions, her grandmother told her stories: stories of Scotland and how she had trudged about in the rain and the fog there. It made Lori feel like she, too, was a pioneer.

In the evenings, after work, they'd build a fire in the pot-bellied stove. Then Lori would patiently wait for her grandmother to take down the two tin boxes on the shelf above her bed. One tin box had roses painted on the top and an assortment of buttons inside that Nana had collected when she worked in the button department in Eaton's. Kay had changed just about every button on every piece of clothing she owned, and Lori now, too, loved to rummage around in these buttons, selecting unusual ones for her grandmother to sew onto her own sweaters and blouses. The other tin box had a picture of Queen Elizabeth painted on the top and hid chocolate cherries. Every night, Nana took it off the shelf and treated each of them to one delectable chocolate. They then played cards until bedtime, unless it was Sunday. Up here, Lori rarely even knew what day of the week it was, and Sunday certainly wasn't any different than any other day. You got up at the same time, did the same amount of work, and went to bed at the same time.

"Why can't we play cards on Sunday?" Lori would ask.

"I don't play cards on Sunday. My mother taught me you never gamble on the Sabbath."

"But we're not playing for money."

"Doesn't matter." Though Nana Kay would have done anything for her granddaughter, in this, she was firm. Instead they would sit quietly together and sew buttons or write letters to friends and family back in the city.

Slowly, however, even the thrill of staying with Nana in the bullpen diminished. The hostile weather not only continued, but it grew worse. The wind shifted around to the north, dropping the temperature and bringing in a pall of clouds that halted over the lake and ladled out a never-ending stream of wind and rain. The sky's ceiling kept dropping lower and lower until it hovered just above the trees. It closed in all around them, creating a gloomy barrier from the rest of the world. Afternoon swims and even hikes were now out of the question.

To make matters worse, "her" baby ducklings were disappearing. A couple of weeks ago, a mother mallard had proudly escorted her brood of a dozen tiny balls of fluff among the shallows where they could feed. Lori was thrilled this new family had settled so near the camp where she could so easily observe them. However, since then, the ducklings' numbers had decreased—11 to 9, then 8, then 7. In the dangerous natural world, they were a delicacy, snapped up in the jaws of northerns and muskies. Every day, Lori looked out at the reeds by the flag pole and watched the mother bravely lead her dwindling pack around the other side of the point. Life out there seemed precarious at best.

I can't swim, I can't hike, and I have to watch my ducklings disappear. Why couldn't I be in the Arctic, too? Lori thought. *There I could run across a caribou. Maybe I could even have a caribou calf for a pet! But no, I'm stuck here. Phil is going to have so many more exciting stories to tell when he gets back!*

Lori's spirits gradually slumped, at least until she found out Agnes might haunt the island. The Arctic didn't have a haunted island, not that Lori knew of, anyways. When her brother returned with all his stories of adventure, she could boast that she had walked on the haunted island. She would go tomorrow.

Whuff.

Lori, who had just settled under her covers with Chezy, popped back up. "What was that?"

"Probably just a tree branch rubbing against the screen," said Kay calmly, sitting on the edge of her bed, rubbing lotion on her hands. "That wind is miserable tonight."

Lori simmered back down under her covers.

Whuff. Whuff. WHUFF.

Lori shot back up. "Nana? Did you hear *that*?"

Kay, shaking her head in affirmation, rose and pulled on her dressing gown.

Suddenly a black silhouette appeared in the window, backlit by the moon. It raised its foreleg and scratched its claws across the screen. *Sree. Sree.*

"There's a bear at the window!" Lori whispered loudly. "Or do you think it's the *ghost bear*?"

"I don't think ghost bears have fur, and I don't think real bears have fingers under their paws," Kay whispered back. She reached under her bed, pulled out a shotgun, and headed for the door. In a loud voice, she said, "I can take care of any type of bear." Then with a wink at Lori, she flung open the door and cocked the gun.

All Lori could see were the backsides of Grant and Jack, fleeing the scene.

"Nana, you could have shot them!" cried Lori.

"Not a chance, sweetheart. The gun wasn't even loaded. I knew it was them." She laughed as she stooped down to retrieve the bear rug. "Did those boys actually think they could scare me into thinking they were a real bear?"

"How did you know it wasn't?"

"The alarm system didn't go off," smiled Kay, pointing to Chezy, who was still sound asleep under the covers.

***

There may be no ghost bear, but Lori still wasn't sure if the island was haunted by another type of ghost. She waited until just before lunch the next day, then snuck over to the reedy shoreline closest to the island, glancing back to make sure no one was watching where she was going. She wasn't sure why she didn't want anyone to know—she hadn't been *forbidden* to go there; it just seemed verboten. She could just make out a slash of white canvas between the feathery framework of firs. It didn't look so scary. She slipped off her sodden shoes and rolled up her pedal pushers past her knees, exposing her toothpick legs. Gingerly she took a step in the water, scanning it for eddies. With the wind finally calm and the rain easing to a drizzle, the pearly grey lake was still, barely a ripple disturbing the surface. Looking rather like the leggy blue heron who suspiciously watched her from the safety of his sandbar, Lori waded deeper and deeper till the water crept up past her knees. She was more than halfway there when she saw the eddy, a circle of swirling water in the otherwise motionless depths. How had she missed it from the shore?

She couldn't turn back now. She splashed on through the last few yards, breathing a sigh of relief when her toes finally touched land. Slowly she picked her way over the sharp stones, cursing herself for not bringing her shoes. She rounded a clump of pines, pushed back the branches—and there it was—the tent.

She took a step forward. *Snap!* A tree branch cracked under her feet. *Lori, get a grip*, she told herself sternly. Slowly she tiptoed forward. There was a firepit in front of the tent, still covered with a rusted grate, and some kindling piled up against a poplar tree. Higher up on the tree, some pictures had been carved into the bark. She squinted, trying to make it out, then realized the small round ears and furry bodies were that of bears—a papa bear, a momma bear, and a little bear. Makoons.

She could imagine Lawrence here in the evening when the sun was long in the sky, sitting beside the smoky fire, waiting for his mom to return from work. With his dad fishing on the shore, she imagined Lawrence sneaking his dad's filet knife to carve a version of himself and his family on the tree, not realizing it would become his mother's epitaph. Had his mom had a chance to see the carving?

Had he done it weeks, days, hours before that last awful night? That night when she had stood in the darkness, watching Albert and her dad drag an agonized Agnes to the canoe. It was too terrible to think about. Lori turned back to the tent.

It was still daylight, but a feeling of darkness draped over the island. The air was motionless, yet the tent softly billowed, moving like it had a life of its own. Funny, all through the hollowing winter months and the spring thaw, the tent had remained standing, like a shroud over the ground where Agnes had died. Eyes big, she crept a little closer and peered inside.

The tent was completely empty except for one thing—a worn black-leather Bible hung stock-still from a rope tied to the roof of the tent. Lori took a step into the tent, and as she did so, the Bible began to swing like a pendulum. Back and forth, back and forth, slowly at first, then faster and faster. Her breath caught in her throat. A sudden chill hung in the air—a foreboding. Abruptly, a crisp sepulchral wind sprung up from nowhere and, with a shrill cry, tore at the fluttering canvas. The whole tent quivered on its poles. The wind ripped at the trees, sending the leaves shuddering. What was that wailing sound? It sounded almost like a child crying!

A sudden flash of lightning, then a great crackle of thunder ripped the sky apart, opening up the heavens. With a harsh croak, the blue heron suddenly stretched out its massive wings and quickly took off as if in terror.

She'd had enough. Lori bolted in an uncontrollable panic. She stumbled out of the tent, and as she did so, a pale face appeared like a spectre from among the bushes, too watered down to make out. Was the face Agnes's? The hair stood up on the nape of her neck. She didn't think so, but she didn't want to hang around to find out. Lori ran back to the shore, stepping on razor-sharp weeds that pierced the tender insoles of her feet. Boughs grabbed at her clothing, and raindrops pelted her skin. She slipped on the wet rocks, and down she went, skinning her palms and her knees on the sharp stones, a large black patch growing on her pedal pushers.

She got up and struck out into the lake. Mud sucked at her toes. She dared not look over at the sinister eddy. Raindrops punctured the surface of the grey lake. The wind whistled behind her—calling her. She had to get away. The short trip through the waves seemed to take forever.

Finally she reached camp. Breathing heavily, she bent down to retrieve her shoes. From the corner of her eye, she could see a dark silhouette. Slowly it moved closer and closer. Lori jumped up, startled, pinpricks in the tips of her fingers. It was James, hidden inside a slicker, with the hood pulled up over his head. What was he doing stealing around in this weather? Why wasn't he out guiding? Had he seen her over on the island? His face gave away nothing. He was looking past her, out onto the lake, over to the island. Did he wonder why she was snooping around there? Was he thinking about his wife?

Leaving her shoes in the grass, she dashed headlong for the safety of the lodge with its glowing lights in the windows and the woodsmoke in the stack.

Lori stumbled into the kitchen, startling Elsie and Kay. Kay looked at her granddaughter's white face. "My Lord, look at you! You look like you've seen a ghost! What's wrong?"

"I . . . I was startled by the lightning."

"Startled right out of your shoes, by the looks of it. Goodness gracious, child, your feet are bare!"

Kay came closer and saw her mud-caked knees and palms, not quite hiding the angry red abrasions.

"What happened?"

"I just fell on some rocks."

"Poor wee pet! You have to be careful . . . everything is so slick, what with all this rain. Let me get a wash basin, and I'll get you fixed up."

Even as her grandmother gently sponged off her knees, the feeling of strangeness continued. Lori couldn't throw it off. What had the swinging Bible meant? Was it a sign? What about the face? It hadn't looked like Agnes, and yet, whose face would it be? God, how she wished she could ask Elsie! But she couldn't— she couldn't let anyone know she had been to the island. Suddenly there was an eerie wail.

Elsie peered out the window toward the tent. "They's cryin'," she said.

Lori's eyes bulged out of their sockets. "Who's crying?"

"Them loons there, flyin' over the lake. They're cryin' while they're flyin'. That means someone's lost."

Lost? Could it mean a *lost soul*? A lost soul wandering around a haunted island?

"Nothing lost but our good weather!" said Kay matter-of-factly. "We best get ready for lunch. I have a premonition of my own—it's going to be a full house!"

Heavy rain during the day meant no shore lunch for the guests, which in turn meant everyone came into camp to eat their fried fish. As each guide entered the kitchen to drop off a pile of hard-found filets for Elsie to cook, the floor became wetter and wetter until there was an intersecting trail of damp footprints criss-crossing the linoleum. Lori, who had been drafted to help, grabbed a pile of bread and butter plates to set on the tables. Still distracted and shaky, she slipped on the wet floor, and the dishes went shooting out of her hands.

Only one dish survived— the rest lay in shatters. Lori's breath caught in her throat. "Oh noooo!"

Kay quickly strode over to reassure her. "It's okay, sweetheart. I'll help you clean it up." She bent down and began picking up the larger pieces.

Lori felt her bottom lip quiver. "But Nana, you don't understand! One broken dish means you have to warn your family that something bad might happen to one of them. I've broken a *bunch*, and I can't warn any of them because they're not here!"

"Goodness. I think this foul weather is making everyone even more superstitious than normal, if that's possible," said Kay, straightening back up. "The only thing this pile of broken dishes means is that they can't fall any further. Now why don't you run and get the broom? Let's get this cleaned up before the guests arrive."

They had just finished sweeping up the last fragments when Albert strode in the door.

"Good news, Lori! Your dad just phoned. He said your mom whipped that Arctic camp kitchen into shape in no time at all.

Said there was nothing left for her to do, so she's coming back to 'civilization.' She left Henik Lake this morning and will be here tonight."

"Now isn't that a pleasant surprise," said Kay. "See, Lori, the day is brightening. We'll move your things back up to the house cabin after supper."

Lori cracked her first smile of the day. Her mom was coming home! As much as she loved staying with her grandmother, she really did miss her mom. And if she couldn't go to the Arctic, at least she could complain to her mom about it.

"Yeah!" said Lori. Then a realization hit her. "Oh, but Nana, Gup's still up there. Won't you be scared in the bullpen alone? Maybe you should come stay with my mom and me."

"Scared of what?" Kay looked truly puzzled. "I can't think of anything here that would scare me. I'll be just fine where I am. Besides," Kay gave a little wink. "I got my shotgun."

A shotgun won't help against a ghost, thought Lori.

After lunch, Lori returned to the bullpen to pack up her things. She was stuffing shirts into a duffel bag when Nana entered. Raindrops spattered across the shoulders of her rain coat, and dripped off the brim of her rain hat. Slowly she sat down at the table where they played cards. "Come sit with me a minute."

Lori could tell by the look on her face it wasn't good news.

"This bad weather was supposed to break up today, and it did, for a bit. That's why your mom's plane left Henik Lake this morning. But then another storm came along, and the plane ran into it. Your mom's pilot radioed Jimmy Adams at O.C.A. and told him they were going to fly around the storm front. That was hours ago. They haven't heard from them since, and they didn't show up at their projected stop for gas. Now they aren't sure where the plane is, and no one has been able to contact the plane."

"You mean my mom is lost?"

"They're not lost . . . It's just that they should have been at God's Lake by now, but the Goose never checked in—"

"She's in a Goose?" interrupted Lori. "She's had plane trouble in a Goose before! Remember when she went shopping to Red

Lake and promised to bring back ice cream? And her plane broke down, and they had to land somewhere, and by the time they found them and picked them up in another plane, all the ice cream had melted? And she's in a Goose again?"

Lori knew she was rambling but couldn't help it. Her mom was lost—in the Arctic. The Arctic was big and empty. How would they find her?

"I wouldn't worry." Kay stroked the little girl's hair. "I'm sure they're okay. 'Don't borrow trouble,' my mother always said. I just wanted you to know why your mom probably won't be here by tonight. You'll have to spend another night with me, I'm afraid."

Lori was terrified, but she didn't dare show it. Everyone around here always seemed so stoic, except her mother, who was not here because she was lost in the Arctic. She sat silently beside her grandmother, listening to the steady downpour outside. Like nails on a blackboard, the relentless wind snagged the branches of a nearby birch tree and rubbed them up and down the edges of the roof. A fly, having taken refuge on the inside, buzzed near the window.

Tunk. Tunk. Tunk tunk. It continued to batter the blurred glass until Lori couldn't stand it anymore. She jumped up, grabbed a fly swatter, and viciously squished it against the pane.

"Why don't you come to the kitchen with me? I was thinking of making scones. You could help. It'll take your mind off all this for a while. I bet by the time they're made, we will've heard news about your mom's plane."

They returned to the kitchen, quiet now that everyone else had left for the afternoon. Lori sat on the stool and watched her grandmother mix the batter, roll it out, then cut it into squares. She picked up the first square and expertly flipped it from hand to hand, coating it with flour. Then *plop!* Onto the griddle it went. She waited a couple of minutes, took a spatula, and flipped it on the other side.

"Want to try?"

Lori picked up a piece of the dough and began sifting it from hand to hand. Nana was right; it did make her feel a little better, like things were normal and going to be okay.

Once the scones were made, it was time to test them. Kay split one open and spread on a thick layer of butter. As Lori bit into the warm, snowy scone, she caught a glimpse of something white fluttering in the wind over on the island—it was the tent. She had never been able to see the tent from this window before. Then it occurred to her. She had gone to the island—she had disturbed the spirits, made them angry by trampling over the sacred ground. The guides were right; you didn't mess with this stuff. She had brought down their wrath—she had caused her mother's plane to get lost. It was her fault! And the face—the face hadn't been Agnes's. It had been her mother's! It was the face of her mother's spirit!

Planes, they crashed. Her dad had flipped his plane. And every year, you heard about someone you knew crashing. Sometimes they made it out unscathed, and sometimes they didn't make it out at all. The Arctic was a long way away, a long way for a Goose.

And mothers—they could die. Hadn't Lawrence lost his?

Lori placed the rest of her scone back down on her plate. The lump in her throat made it impossible to swallow. Here she was, cozy by the wood stove, eating scones with Nana. Where was her mom? Was she cold, hungry? Was she with a planeful of strangers? Was she scared? Was she *hurt*?

"Is there something wrong with your scone, pet?"

"No, Nana, I'm just not hungry." Lori didn't think she would ever be hungry again.

The afternoon passed. Supper came and went. Still there was no word on her mom's plane.

Albert came walking slowly into the kitchen. "Just had a call from Jimmy at O.C.A."

Lori looked expectantly at him.

"They haven't heard from the Goose yet. They probably ran low on fuel circling that storm and had to do a forced landing somewhere."

"Then why haven't they radioed to let anyone know where they are?" asked Elsie.

Albert shrugged. "Weather's bad. Like our radio phone, sometimes the plane's radio can't get through. The radio waves bounce off the cloud banks."

Or they could have crashed and burned, and there was no radio left, thought Lori. Those were the words no one was willing to utter.

"I'm sure they found somewhere to spend the night," said Kay calmly. She glanced down at Lori. "You look tired. Why don't you grab Chezy and go get ready for bed? I'll just finish these last few dishes and then be right there, okay?"

"Okay." Lori laid down her tea towel, picked up her jacket and the little dog, and trudged down the muddy path. To her left, the lake was a monochrome picture—black islands, grey sky, charcoal water, white froth. The only dots of colour were momma duck and the brown bundles following her. She counted—only six ducklings left. Another baby gone. She stared at the angry grey lake, the wind ripping white caps off its surface.

Inside the bullpen, she pulled the curtains shut to close out the grey, then wandered around the room. Nana had a picture of her family pinned up beside the mirror. It had been taken their first year at Stork; they were all sitting on the bearskin rug on the floor in front of the fireplace in the card room. Everyone looked so happy: her clad in a red leotard, held by her mother in a wool sweater that looked like a fuzzy animal, her brother and father both grinning ear to ear. It had been taken before this stupid Arctic camp had taken her family away. Her mother away.

***

The bullpen was muzzled in darkness when Kay came in some time later. Thinking Lori was already asleep, she quietly pulled off her jacket and rain hat and shook them out. Kay stirred the fire's embers and added a birch log. The fire leapt to life, exposing Chezy's big black eyes staring up at her from beside the wood stove. There was no way the little dog would be here if Lori was asleep in her bed; she always curled up beside her.

"Lori?" Kay snapped on the light bulb above her head, illuminating the shivering figure sitting silently on top of her bed.

"What are you doing in the dark? And in the cold? Goodness's sake, you still have your wet clothes on!" Kay grabbed a towel off the hook on the wall. "Get out of those clothes and into a nice cuddly nighty. The fire should have this place toasty in a minute."

Lori silently obeyed her grandmother.

"Up into bed now." Kay stuffed Chezy under the covers like a hot water bottle, then pulled the flannel sheets and Hudson Bay blanket up to her nose.

"Good then. How about you try to go to sleep?"

***

Sleep? How could she sleep when her mother was missing? How could she sleep?

However, she did eventually drop off—and dropped into a nightmare. She was sitting in the bullpen, eating scones. Agnes came in from the rain wearing her grandmother's rain hat and told her that her mother's plane had arrived. Lori ran outside, excited that her mother was safe. She watched the Goose flutter down from the sky—down, down. Only it didn't land on the water. It touched down then plummeted below the waves until it disappeared from sight, just like the baby ducks. She screamed for someone to come, to go save her mother, but Agnes just came up beside her and put a hand on her shoulder.

"It's too late . . . They've all drowned."

A Bible hung from the tree by the shore. It started to swing wildly. Her mother was fish food now, just like the bear carcass. She could hear the crunching. It was too much. Then her mother's face appeared on the surface of the lake—the same watery face she had seen on the island.

The face! The face *had* been her mother's! She was dead!

With a gasp, she woke, drenched in night sweat, with a heart beating so fast it felt like it would jump out of her chest. She bolted straight up in her bed, a cry escaping from her lips.

Kay quickly came and sat on the edge of Lori's bed, tenderly brushing her forehead. "Shh, now, it's going to be okay. Did you have a bad dream?"

"It wasn't a bad dream . . . It was a premonition!"

"Now why in the world would you say that?"

Lori sobbed. "Elsie says every dream means something. She says dreams are a door to the spirit world!"

"Stuff and nonsense!"

"Nana, it's true. The dream was telling me it's my fault mom is missing, maybe even dead!" Lori started to sob harder.

"That's impossible! You didn't create the weather!"

"Nana, you don't understand! I went to the island! I disturbed Agnes's resting place."

"There, there now, you did no such thing. Agnes's resting place is in a grave in her hometown a hundred miles from here. That tent is just a tent, and that island is just an island."

"But it had a Bible hanging from the ceiling, and it started swinging—"

"Of course it started swinging. It was hanging, wasn't it? Hanging things swing."

"I saw my mother's face. It was blurry and wet."

"You *think* you saw your mother's face. Honey, it was just your imagination!"

"But the island! It felt *haunted*."

"What you felt was fear from all the ghost stories everybody's passing around. Honestly, what this place needs is a good dose of Scottish common sense! The unknown is a scary place for most people. People don't understand why Agnes passed in such a tragic way, and it scares them. You don't know where your mom is and that scares you."

"That's easy for you to say . . . Nothing scares you. You're not even afraid to stay alone."

"Oh, I've been scared plenty. But then I tell myself that fear can only live if I let it. Now, the best thing you can do for your mom right now is to get some sleep. After all, when she gets home tomorrow, she's going to want to hear about everything you have been up to for the last two weeks, like swimming in the rain, tramping in the bush, baking scones—" Kay's voice grew further away as Lori slowly dropped off to sleep. The last thing she thought was that Nana had said "when" her mother got home tomorrow, not "if."

***

Lori woke to blackness, caught up in the depths of her bedcovers. She heaved the blankets off her tousled head and opened her eyes. The cabin was empty—Nana Kay was already off to work. Lori jumped out of bed and peeked out the window. It was still grey, but the clouds had lifted, and the rain had stopped. As she pulled on her clothes, she heard a plane. Quickly, she ran out to the dock.

"Is it my mom?" she asked Albert, who was standing there, squinting up at the circling plane.

"Don't know yet."

As she stood there, big-eyed, she felt a hand on her shoulder. It was her grandmother. They watched as the plane flew lower and lower. Lori held her breath as it hit the water just in front of the islands, water spraying up over the windows—and it stayed above the water! The Goose taxied to the dock at an agonizingly slow pace. Was it her mother's plane? It had to be her mother's plane!

Just then, the sun finally burned a hole through the heavy clouds. The hatch opened, and a head popped out, a head of blonde hair gleaming in the sunshine.

"There's your mother!" cried Nana Kay, and Lori's eyes filled with joyful tears.

Lori slowly replaced the rain hat on to the wall. Her grandmother had taught her how to overcome her fears by facing them head-on and standing them down. Lori stared at an empty nail on the wall. The next year would have no such guidance—

1972

Come the first of June of every year, all Lori could think of was getting back up to Stork Lake. Her mother would make her annual trip down to the school to visit Mr. Dotten, the principal. The children would have to leave school a few weeks early, she would explain. The camp needed her, and she could not leave without the children. And every year, Mr. Dotten would smile and give them his blessing. He had been an active outdoorsman before polio took his legs away and firmly believed the education Lori and Phil received in the wilds of Ontario was just as valuable as what they learned in the classroom.

After much organizing, arranging, and packing, the family would finally be on their way. The anticipation and the excitement built during the hour-long plane ride. As Lori looked down at the shimmering lakes and miles and miles of forest, she would wonder: *Did the camp look different? Was the new building finished? How much had the trees grown? Who would be up there? Did Eddie make it back? How about Roger?* Barely able to contain herself as they taxied up to the dock, she would peer through the scratched back window of the old Beaver or Beechcraft to see who was standing on the dock waiting for them to arrive. There was Peepsight! There was James! And there was her dad! Her heart would beat with excitement at the thought of seeing him after over a month apart.

The camp changed bit by bit—new buildings, new equipment, indoor plumbing! And the people changed bit by bit, too. Silent Tommy got his first pair of false teeth—he still did not say much, but he smiled a whole lot more. Albert was a little greyer, Elsie a little rounder. Everyone was just a little older.

There were also staff changes. While almost everyone returned year after year—the food was good, Al was a fair boss, any staff member running short of cash during the winter were given an advance—there were always a few new faces, a few old faces missing. Some of the guys married and moved on or wanted to try guiding on different waters. Perhaps their education was finished, and they had now started their "city" career. Sometimes they just didn't make it through the winter. Sandy Redskye had died two years before of diabetes, and Joe Loon drowned when he slipped off a rock into the cold lake waters that spring. He had been a guide and a trapper for over forty years but had never learned to swim.

This year, there were two more missing. Nana Kay had died in January. With her passing, Gup had decided to hang up his cowboy hat and move out to the coast. It was a heart-wrenching loss. The strong-yet-gentle-souled couple had been dearly loved and respected by all the family, the staff, and any of the guests privileged to have known them. However, it was Lori who felt their absence the keenest. While new help could be hired to make pies or guide guests, you couldn't replace grandparents.

As Lori had packed up her books and clothes in preparation for the summer, she had wondered what she would do without Nana and Gup. She loved her parents, but it was her grandparents who had the time to teach her birdcalls, to insist she had just the right amount of freckles. They never reprimanded her for sinking into the shadows when new people came along that made her feel awkward and tongue-tied. They were her confidence boosters, her companions, her confidantes. Who would make her feel secure in her changing world?

At eleven, she was suffering that awkward tween stage of life. Her body didn't quite fit any longer—tall and lanky, and she had yet to grow into her arms, legs, or nose.

Inwardly she was also going through a perplexing stage. Friends at school were starting to dream about what they wanted to be. They talked about wanting to be teachers or nurses or secretaries. Lori wouldn't even consider any of these occupations. She had to find a job that still allowed her to come to Stork—there was no way she was going to spend summers in the city. Besides, she wanted adventure! Hence, her dilemma. What type of work would give her everything she wanted?

Having someone to chum with at camp posed another problem. She was too young to hang out with the staff, yet not young enough to still be content with just trees and animals for friends. Her grandparents could always be counted on for a game of crib, a swim, or an evening of fishing. Just who would fill this incredibly deep void?

Not her father or brother—they would both be leaving for the Arctic camp soon. And not her mother—she was always so busy, and besides, she didn't like to do anything outdoors, which is just where Lori wanted to spend most of her time. So she wondered, just what was this summer without her grandparents going to be like?

***

Exactly twenty minutes after Lori's plane arrived at Stork Lake for that summer, she had already hugged her dad, received a pinch on the cheek from Albert, and a "My, you've grown!" and a handful of chocolate chip cookies from Elsie. Now she was roaming the grounds, checking old haunts, and searching for alterations. There was a new building on the hill, a pile of dirt where an outhouse used to be. Sadly the proud old poplar by the water was gone. Lori prayed her favourite old spruce had made it through the year and dashed back over to the bay by the kitchen to see.

Just before she reached the heirloom conifer, she stopped short. Staring intently up into its arching branches was a statuesque woman about her mother's age. Sudden shyness overtook her. She was about to creep away when the woman turned and dropped warm brown eyes on her.

"Hello," she said in a voice as soft and melodic as the wind.

"Hello," said Lori, frozen by the bright white smile pinned between high polished cheekbones. While the woman's beautiful features were classically Cree, her style was not. Instead of the flowing skirts many Native women around these parts still preferred, she wore modern polyester pants with a bright printed shirt, and her gleaming black hair was carefully coifed into the latest style.

"Want to see something?" she asked Lori.

Buoyed by her friendliness, Lori took a step closer to the woman.

"What is it . . . some kinda bird?"

"Nope, it's a baby bear."

Lori's heart started to beat faster. She stepped beside the woman and looked up. Huddled in the heart of the conifer and hanging on for dear life was a tiny, furry figure.

Shyness forgotten, Lori exclaimed, "Oh, he's *so* cute! I wish I could see him better, but the boughs are hiding him."

"I wonder if we could coax him down lower." The woman pursed her lips and made a sound between a purr and a cry. The cub didn't move.

She shook her head. "So much for my mother bear impersonation. Hmmm . . . maybe he needs a bribe to be brave."

"Here!" Lori cried. "I have cookies! All kids love cookies."

Lori held her handful up toward the tree. Still the furry bum didn't move.

"He can't see them. We have to get them closer. I'll be right back." With a couple of long strides, she reached the old washstand, grabbed a corn broom, and came back with it.

"I found an elevator!" She held the broad side up to Lori, who placed her cookies on the broom. Then slowly, she raised the broom up toward the bear. Almost immediately, a small face bent down, nose twitching. Tentatively he lowered himself, one paw at a time until he was low enough to—with an awkward swipe—grab a cookie. They watched in companionable silence while the little guy munched away.

"Now what trouble are you two getting into already?" asked Al, who had just happened by and witnessed the whole show. "Don't you know you should never feed a bear, even a baby one? It encourages them to come around more. Next thing you know, he'll be crawling in your bedroom window. Or worse yet, his mother will!"

Lori and the woman looked at each other and cracked up laughing. So started a lifetime friendship.

***

The woman's name was Alma, and she had taken on Nana Kay's duties at the camp. Like her grandmother, she was unflappable, outgoing, and loved waiting on the guests. She had a great sense of humour, and fits of laughter could often be heard outside the kitchen window as Elsie, Alma, and Helen found the comical in the most absurd of situations.

What Lori liked best about Alma was that she loved to spend time with her. Alma's own five children were all almost grown, so she too had a space in her heart, which Lori was happy to fill. After the lunch dishes were done, Alma often spent a couple of hours with Lori. Sometimes she sat on the dock sun drying her hair in big fat rollers while Lori splashed around. Other times they headed into the bush, where Lori would usher Alma through the maze of pathways. One afternoon, they found a fallen birch tree, struck down in its prime by a flash of lightning.

"Birchbark makes good paper. But never strip bark off a live tree. You might kill it." Alma took the filet knife she had brought with her and sliced through a section of bark, gently peeling back the silvery skin. She handed it to Lori.

"Here, you can write to your grandpa on it."

"Thanks, Alma. That's exactly what I'm going to do!"

Alma wasn't Lori's only new friend that summer. Alma's fun-loving husband also insisted on adopting her as a surrogate daughter. Andy was short, shorter than his wife, and skinny as a rake, with an angular bony face burnt to an aged patina. His wide, wisecracking mouth worked overtime, delivering a bounty of observations and opinions. His body was no less active—when he wasn't working, he was fishing. When he wasn't fishing, he was building something. From scrap wood, he made Alma a clothes rack, a table, and a stool. By the time the last dish was dried, most guides were already settling into their cabins for the night. Not Andy. Even after a full day on the water, he would once again climb into his boat and take Alma and Lori for a ride to cool off.

One night, as they approached the dock, they heard Andy shout out, "Come on, girls. Your carriage awaits!"

"Oh, look—" cooed Alma.

"Wow!" Lori ran and flung herself into Andy's boat, then promptly started to twirl in one of the new fibreglass swivel seats.

"I love these!" exclaimed Lori. "Where'd they come from?"

"Cassa brought them up," said Andy, helping Alma into the boat.

Alma tested it out for a moment, then chuckled. "I feel like I'm on a throne!"

"Cushy, ain't they? Never seen a company like Cassa. They're so good to their people. You know, they take those possum-bellied tackle boxes they make and fill them plum full of every bait known to man and then give each of their customers one to use while they're here. They supply them with rods and reels, too, the best you can buy. At the end of the trip, we pack it all up and store it in the old laundry room for the next group. Cassa sends people up so often in the summer, they don't bother ever taking any of their equipment back with them."

"Do you think they'll leave the seats here, too?" asked Lori eagerly.

Andy nodded as he untied the bow. "Not only are they going to leave them, they're giving 'em to your dad as a present. Just wish guides could have 'em, too. Hey, I know!" Andy gave Lori a broad grin. "Why don't you run the boat tonight so's I can relax in one of these newfangled seats."

"Can't. Don't know how," replied Lori.

"You mean you don't know how to run an outboard yet?"

Lori shrugged. "No one's ever shown me."

"Well we'll fix that right now. Into the driver's seat with you, Miss Reid!"

Lori stepped into the stern of the boat and sat on the cushion. Andy jumped in, sat down with a flourish, and turned to Lori.

"Okay, make sure the gear on the side is in neutral, the choke out. Got it? Now turn the throttle to start and pull the cord."

Lori gave it a few quick pulls, and the engine roared to life.

"Great," Andy shouted over the blare of the motor. "Choke in, gear in forward, and slowly twist the throttle, just a bit."

Lori blasted away from the dock like a rocket, heading straight for The Point.

"Slow down! Turn right. Turn right!"

Turn what right, the throttle or the boat? The more she turned right, the faster she went, and the further left the boat veered.

They ended up beached on the beach.

"That was a gas!" laughed Alma.

Andy straightened his cap. "That was pretty good," he said with a straight face. "Let's try again."

Lori eventually got the hang of it, and they drove down Rice Creek, aptly named for the wild rice that grew there. They motored through the creek until they hit a dead end: the beaver dam.

It was of superb construction, completely obstructing the waterway, making any normal means of passage impossible. Every spring, Albert and Al would blast it with dynamite in the hopes of using the creek as passage up to Rice Lake. It never worked. It would only take the industrious northern engineer a matter of days to rebuild it better than ever.

"I wonder what's on the other side?"

Andy looked at her. "You've never been past the dam?"

"How? Portage around it?"

"You could. But jumping is easier. Not easy, but easier."

"Can we?"

"You bet we can. But you better let me drive. You get in this seat and hold on!"

Lori and Andy switched places. Then with the outboard at full throttle, they charged forward. There was a loud bang, a moment of lift-off, and then a bumpy landing on the other side. Lori giggled at the thrill of it.

Alma giggled. "Almost as much fun as you beaching us, eh?"

They continued down the silent creek. There was an eerie beauty about the place, the creek sharply twisting and turning, the evening mist rising off the water. They slowly snaked through the thick weed beds, swathing a trail behind them. Suddenly in front of them was Rice Lake Falls.

Andy cut the motor. Pristine waters spilled over the granite edge, the cascading water winding and bubbling. As it washed over the boulders, the sound washed over her, not a pounding or drumming as it may have been in the spring, but more of a shimmering voice of nature. Lori sat mesmerized by the constant, soothing rustle, the billowing water frothing and foaming. A moose stood unperturbed in the shallows, munching on a bunch of waterlilies.

"Let's get closer to him," said Alma.

"Yeah!" agreed Lori.

Andy shook his head. "Not a good idea. Moose sometimes take it in their head to charge a boat. They can run on the bottom of the lake just like they was runnin' through the bush. And boy, can they cause damage!"

They watched the majestic animal for a few moments longer. Finally, Andy said, "Time to get back. Don't want to have to navigate the creek in the dark. We'd probably end up on the shoulders of that there moose!"

***

Late the next afternoon, when the thermometer still read over ninety degrees, Lori wished she could be standing under the cool, gurgling falls she had seen the night before. Instead she was helping set up for supper in a kitchen that felt more like a pressure cooker.

"I'm too hot!" moaned Lori, tearing up lettuce and throwing it into a bowl.

"You go cool off by the lake," offered Alma. "I'll finish up here."

"Really? Thanks, Alma!" The offer was too good to even pretend to put up a fight. Lori quickly whipped around, ready to flee before her mother came in and found her absconding from her duties. As she did so, her hip caught the handle of a butcher knife. It spun around and landed on the floor.

"Oops. That mean someone famous is coming, Elsie? Maybe Gordon MacRae coming back?" joked Lori, bending down to pick the knife up.

Elsie gazed up from her soup. "Not this time. That knife there's got rivets, like brass buttons on a uniform. Means the law is coming."

Long as they're not coming to bring me back to this kitchen! thought Lori as she scooted out the door.

Free at last! She had run all the way down to the shore, where she now watched the boats return to camp for the evening.

Oh, to have been on the lake all afternoon! thought Lori enviously. The dazzling sun overhead, the cool blue water underneath, the wind blowing away the heat bubbling up under your skin. Yes, that was just what a body should have been doing on a day like today. She did not envy Alma or Elsie or even her mother their jobs. As confused as she was about what she wanted to do with her life, she was sure she didn't want to have to sweat it out in a hot kitchen forever.

Just then, Andy's boat roared up to the dock. *Great, someone to hang out with till dinner,* thought Lori.

***

"You can fillet faster than all the other guides," said Lori a little while later as she watched Andy deftly slice through the translucent flesh of a walleye.

"That's because I used to work in a fish factory," replied Andy.

"I've watched it done millions of times, but I've never filleted a fish myself."

"You mean to tell me your grandpa taught you how to carve them sticks, but he never taught you how to carve up a fish?"

Lori shrugged. "I guess we were too busy doing other things." She looked up at Andy with hopeful eyes. "Do you think you could teach me?"

"Look who you're talkin' to! Course I can. In fact, not only will I teach you how to fillet, I'll teach you how to gut and gill, too. Got a whitefish that my guests will be wanting to bake."

"Gut and gill? Yippee! What if I mess up, though?" asked Lori, taking the thin knife in her hand.

"You won't. And even if they aren't perfect, I'll cook 'em and eat 'em myself!"

"But your guests . . . they're leaving tomorrow! If I mess up, they won't have enough fish to take home."

"Don't you worry about that. There's a few extra walleye kicking around this place."

A half-hour later, Lori stared at her handiwork, now neatly packaged and labelled. She had done good, if she did say so herself. She had only mutilated one fish.

"That was cool! Guides get to do far more fun stuff than the kitchen staff."

Andy tilted his cap. "Ah, so that's why you got me to teach you how to run a boat and fillet fish . . . You want my job!"

Surprised, Lori asked, "What, be a guide? There are no girl guides. I mean, other than the kind that sells cookies door to door."

"Doesn't mean *you* couldn't be one."

"I guess not."

"You'd rather be tramping around, exploring outside than indoors anyways. And look, here you are filleting fish instead of slicing bread. Do what you want in life. Now my apprentice, how about getting those filets of yours on ice?"

Lori picked up the packages and headed to the brand-new chest freezer.

"I don't know if I could ever be a guide . . . stuck in a boat all day with two adult strangers? I wouldn't know what to say! But you are right about one thing, Andy. I *will* do something exciting!" And with that, she flung open the lid.

"A few extra walleye kicking around? This freezer's crammed almost to the top with fish! Why is there so much?"

"Oh, you know, them guests always want the biggest walleyes to take back home with them," said Andy as he cleaned fish guts off the wooden filet table. "They may have caught their limit of fish the first day, but the next day they catch some that are bigger and want to take those home instead. So you keep them. The bigger the fish, the bigger your tip."

Lori knew this was not right. There were rules—fish and game rules, set out by the province as to how much fish a camp could have at any given time. She heard these rules often enough from her father. Ignore the rules, and you would have trouble with the game wardens.

A tingle went down her spine as she closed the freezer door. Elsie had mentioned the law, and Elsie was never wrong.

"I should tell my dad. Elsie could make fish chowder or fish balls . . . or . . . something to use up the extras."

"Now don't you worry your little head about this," replied Andy. "Cassa's leaving tomorrow, then I promise you us guides will get this freezer cleaned out. We don't want no trouble, neither."

"Okay." Lori felt relieved. She trusted Andy—she knew he would never lie to her.

It had been a busy morning. Planes flying in, planes flying out. Finally it was quiet. The gong had sounded, and everyone left in camp had headed into the lodge for lunch. Everyone but Lori. She took this time to steal down to the dock, to be alone. The little village was silent, and she could enjoy the beauty around her without the serenity interspersed with hammering, sawing, and drilling. Lori dropped down beside the minnow tank and lazily scooped up dead minnows with her net, throwing the carnage to the two northerns circling the tank like sharks.

Out of the corner of her eye, she saw something move between the islands in front of her. The silent profile of a turbo Otter appeared. Funny, she had thought there would be no more planes today. Then it hit her. She could *see* it, but she couldn't *hear* it. This was not guests arriving—regular O.C.A. planes did not shut off their engines and glide into camp.

Like a flash, she was up and running. She didn't stop until she reached the lodge, bursting into the staff room where everyone was eating.

Breathless, she exclaimed, "Game wardens just landed!"

Al instantly shot out of his seat, and so did Albert. There was a rush for the door.

"You stall them at the dock," he said to Albert. "I'll head to the freezer."

Lori sunk down onto one of the benches and prayed the freezer had been emptied by now.

***

Al found maybe twelve fillets—six fish in total—scattered on the bottom, well within the camp's legal limit. Confident there was no problem, he headed down to the dock—confident that is until he saw Albert circled by six uniformed wardens. Usually there were only two. They held their arms stiffly at their sides, sunglasses fastened over deadpan expressions. Al arranged his face so it was as emotionless as theirs. He had a bad feeling in the pit of his stomach, but there was no way he was going to reveal it. He scanned the group with his hard silver eyes.

"Gentlemen. Good afternoon," he said briskly.

A large man stepped up. "Afternoon, Mr. Reid." Behind hidden eyes and a drooping moustache, he looked familiar—Al had met him before.

"Mr. Gordon, isn't it?"

"Yes, sir," he said abruptly.

"What can I do for you?"

"Just a routine check."

"Fine. I'll walk you to the freezer."

"We're not interested in the freezer today, Mr. Reid. We're interested in some tackle."

"Tackle? You want to look in my store?"

"No, Mr. Reid, your store*room*. We would like you to take us to where you have stored a company called Cassa's fishing equipment."

Now Al was confused. How did the game wardens know Cassa left their equipment here? And what was wrong with that? There was nothing illegal about leaving your tackle at the camp where you fished—nothing Al knew about, anyways. However, from the look on these men's faces, something was definitely wrong.

"Follow me." Al turned and led the men down the path to the old laundry room and opened the cupboards. Mr. Gordon took one look, then nodded to his team. Immediately they began emptying the shelves, removing every rod, reel, and tackle box.

"What the—?"

"Mr. Reid, we are confiscating this tackle. Once we are done here, you will accompany us back to the dock, where you will remove every seat from every boat currently in the camp."

"Now just a minute! You're taking tackle purchased legally by good customers of mine and now want to take my boat seats, too? Well, I know there ain't no damn regulation saying you can't have a seat in a boat."

"True."

"So what makes you think you can take them?"

"Because they were purchased by Cassa."

Cassa's tackle. Cassa's seats. Had Cassa sent them?

Al argued, "Yes, Cassa brought them to the camp . . . and gave them to us to keep. The tackle is theirs, but they wanted to leave it here. We didn't steal anything!"

"We are not accusing you of theft."

"Then what's going on? I want some answers!"

"Mr. Reid, are you aware that the Cassa group left your camp this morning with three hundred walleye . . . two hundred and forty walleye over their legal limit?"

Al was in shock. Never, under any circumstances, did he ever allow any guest to leave the camp with more than their legal limit.

"There has to be some mistake—"

"There is no mistake, sir. We intercepted them at the Kenora Airport just as they were about to take off and leave the province. A thorough search of the aircraft and its contents showed the suspect party in question to be in illegal possession of two hundred and forty walleye."

"But we only loaded ten boxes of fish onto the planes with Cassa this morning. I counted them myself."

"Yes, Mr. Reid, but each box had thirty walleye in it."

Al stood there, speechless.

"Under the Ontario Fishery Regulations, we are within our rights to confiscate all the property of anyone who contravenes these regulations. We have even confiscated Cassa's private plane. Now we are here to take all their tackle and their seats."

"But they gave the seats to us!" Al finally found his voice.

"Do you have a receipt, a bill, something to prove a transfer of ownership took place?"

"No."

"Then, Mr. Reid, we are taking the seats."

***

"You know, they fined my dad, too? Three thousand dollars!" exclaimed Lori to Alma the next afternoon. The two were lounging on the dock, Alma flipping through an old *Popular Science Magazine* while Lori wrote to Gup on her birchbark paper.

Alma grimaced. "I can't even imagine being fined that much. It's more money than I make all summer!"

"It couldn't have been an accident that the wardens knew to search the plane," Alma said. "I mean, they even knew about the tackle and the seats. I don't think anyone from Cassa would have voluntarily told them where all their stuff was! So how did they know?"

"Jimmy Adams from O.C.A. found out how it happened," Lori said. "He said soon as he heard about the bust, he went snooping. You know how the wardens found out? It was those guides that flew out for their holiday!"

"*No!*"

"Yep. They got off the plane in Kenora and immediately went to the bar and started to brag how they had made a bunch of money in a couple of days, just on tips. 'Course no one believed them, so the guides told them about Cassa's seats, the tackle, and the extra fish. They even told them Cassa was leaving that afternoon in their own private jet."

"That still doesn't explain how the game wardens found out. I can't believe the guides would have told the wardens," said Alma.

"They didn't. Someone else did. Dad thinks they must have made someone in the bar jealous of all their tips, so they went and snitched to the game wardens. You know, I sorta see why the guides did what they did. They did it for tips. But the guys from Cassa, they have money. They could buy all the fresh walleye they want. Why would they do something like this?"

"The gift of a lift."

"What are you talking about?"

"It's not about the fish . . . it's about the game," replied Alma. "You don't get to the top of them large companies without gumption. You have to take a lot of chances. Some people get addicted to that feeling. It's like a rush. The more money you have, the harder it can be to get that rush."

"So stealing a hundred pounds of fish is *fun*? Geez, I get a rush just fishing for it."

"And I get enough of a rush just eating it!" Alma laughed. "So is your dad still mad at the guides?"

"He forgives fast. And I doubt there will be a repeat offence after the balling out they got!"

Lori thought about how supper the night before had been terse with Al's steely eyes freezing the guides to their seats while Albert's torrent of French curses lashed their eyes sheepishly to the ground.

"I'm upset with myself, Alma. I could have prevented this if I had only spoken up."

"It's not your place to worry about these things. You're a kid."

"Still—" Lori's head jerked up. "Uh oh."

"What's the matter?"

"Hear that? A plane's coming. We're not expecting any planes today, are we?"

"I don't think so," said Alma slowly.

Lori squinted into the sun, just making out a small plane fluttering down between the islands, then heaved a sigh of relief.

"Thank goodness. It's just Barney Lamm. Probably coming to see if there's anything he can do to help."

As the Piper Cub chugged to the dock, Al strode onto the dock to meet it. When it got close enough, he grabbed the strut and peered inside.

"Oh, for Pete's sake!" He laughed.

The pilot's door flung open, and a head appeared. It wasn't Barney; it was Sherry, his seventeen-year-old daughter.

"Sherry! To what do we owe this pleasure?" asked Al.

"Just doing my cross-country, Mr. Reid. I'm hoping by the end of the summer to have my pilot's licence."

"Well judging by your landing and the way you taxied up to my dock without as much as nudging it, I'd say you'll have no problem getting it. Can I offer you a drink? A pop or iced tea?"

"Thanks but this is just a short stop. I want to stick as close as I can to the ETA on my flight plan. I had to perform one take-off and landing en route, and I chose your place to do it. I better shove off now."

"Good seeing you, Sherry. Good luck with your cross-country, and I'll be watching for you in the sky come fall!"

Al slammed the door shut and pushed the little plane off. As it puttered away, he turned to Lori and Alma, who had both sat transfixed during the whole exchange. Neither of them had ever seen a woman bush pilot before—never mind one as young and pretty as Sherry.

"Imagine that," he said. "She'll probably end up flying our guests in for us someday!"

Alma looked down at Lori. "You could do that, too, you know. When you're old enough."

"You could," said her dad. "You've taken the stick on my Cub a few times. You liked it, didn't you?"

"I loved it!" Lori remembered the rush she had felt—the freedom of floating above the clouds, the excitement of going with the wind. But until this moment, she had never dreamed of getting her pilot's licence. In total wonder, Lori replied, "I could, couldn't I? Imagine that!" Quickly she turned back to her birchbark paper and frantically started writing. "Know what, Gup? I'm going to be a pilot!"

Cassa came back the next year and for many years after that. They paid Al's fine for him and brought replacement seats for all the boats, and when they left, they always had just their limit of fish with them—

Lori's eyes next fixated on the sequined green beret hanging next to the empty nail. As she removed it from its hook, she mused that the guests of Stork Lake were sometimes quirky, often entertaining, and seldom boring—

1973

"Lori, you will have to pack up your things. Dad has rented out our cabin for the next few weeks."

This was not unusual. At least once or twice each summer, the house cabin would be rented out—the opportunity to make extra money was too good to pass up.

Lori, who had been brushing Chezy on the cabin stoop, looked up, squinting into the bright sunlight that backlit her mother.

"Where are we going to stay?" In past years, they had either moved into the bullpen with her grandparents or into an empty guide cabin. This year, both were already full of staff.

"In a tent."

"Not on the island!" exclaimed Lori, clasping her hands to her cheeks in horror. Though the tent where Agnes had died had finally blown away in the wind, the memories had not.

"Of course not!" Helen shuddered. "No, Dad's pitched a tent just across the path from the bullpen. We'll probably have to stay there for a few weeks, at least."

The threat of ghosts as bed buddies gone, the prospect of new digs immediately appealed to Lori's sense of adventure.

"Wow . . . that's going to be"—Lori searched for a word big enough to express her excitement—"stupendous!"

"Stupid would be more like it," said Helen as she began her packing. "A tent of all places! Where are we all going to sleep? Where will I hang my dresses? And just where will I plug in my hair dryer?"

Helen needn't have worried. The tent was large, high enough to stand up in, and roomy enough for four army cots, a hamster cage, a poodle, a pot-bellied stove, and a fully-stocked bar—everything that was important. Al had strung an electric line from the bullpen, so there was even a light hanging from the ceiling with a plug for Helen's hair dryer. Helen's dresses hung from a pole holding up the roof of the tent. An empty Smirnoff Vodka carton beside Lori's bed served double duty as a container to store clothes and as a night table to hold her books and silver-domed Love's Baby Soft hand cream.

At first, Lori found living in a tent fun. When the large blue flaps of the tent were open, the lake breeze rustled through, keeping it much cooler than their stuffy cabin during the hot afternoons. When the temperature dipped in the evening, the flaps were shut tight, and Al would get the pot-bellied stove stoked up, making it all warm and cozy.

At night, once her mom had donned her dad's pyjamas and work socks and pumped the tent full of DEET until it resembled the inside of a cloud, they would all crawl into their respective sleeping bags, and the conversation would begin. Phil joked about his guests' first attempts at casting that landed him a couple of trees and a lot of rocks but no fish. Her mom laughingly told them they had run out of ham at supper, so Elsie worked her magic, and by the time she was done, not one guest noticed their ham was out of a can and not out of the oven. And her dad bragged how the booking sheet was filling up—if it stayed this busy, they would have to spend the rest of the summer in the tent!

Eventually, one by one, they would drop off to sleep. The days were long and full, and sleep was a welcome respite. Lori would pull the covers up to her nose and squeeze Chezy a little tighter, warm and content.

However, the novelty of her new housing soon wore off. It wasn't much fun being demoted to an outside biffy, with its sickening sweet smell of air freshener, flies buzzing on the screen above the door, and the limp toilet paper.

The tent itself also became problematic. The walls were thin, to say the least—anyone walking down the path beside it could hear every cough, every sneeze, and every fart. And not only could they hear you—at night, they could see you! Or at least the shadow of you, which was annoying when you were trying to change into your 'jamas at night. She also couldn't stay up and read; as soon as her dad said lights out, the one lightbulb was snapped out, and that was it. Lori missed the privacy of her own little cardboard room. Worst of all, both her parents snored!

***

Oh how I hate to get up in the morning,
Oh how I hate to get out of bed!
When I hear the bugle boy
BO BO BO BO BO BO BO,
You got to get up, you got to get up,
You got to get up in the morning!

Her mom's daytime soprano song was very different from her nighttime chainsaw sonata. To Lori, still huddled in her sleeping bag cocoon, the sound was no less grating. The delicious liquid notes bounced off the canvas walls and flowed down to Lori's ears, where they drowned out her dreams, and she burst back to the surface of consciousness. How could anyone be so annoyingly perky first thing in the morning? Slowly she poked her nose out of her sleeping bag—

Her mother had whipped back the flaps of the tent, allowing the bright rays of sunshine to flood in, stabbing Lori in the eyes like knives. The fire was long out, and there was a chill in the air. She would have liked to stay huddled in her cozy little bed till the temperature crept up a bit—it was, after all, still only 7:30. However, her mother—who had already completed several hours of kitchen work—was making far too much noise, humming as she folded clothes and smoothed out the empty beds.

"Just because we have to sleep in an overgrown bread bag doesn't mean it has to be crumby," she told Lori one morning.

"Don't you want to get up? You're sleeping this beautiful day away!"

"Like that could *ever* happen around here," grumbled Lori. She grabbed her clothes from the box beside her and tucked them under Chezy, then lay her head back down on the pillow.

"What are you doing *now*?" asked Helen, fluffing Phil's pillow. He had vacated the tent an hour before to go guiding.

"I'm warming my clothes up."

"Oh, for Pete's sake, just get up! Once you start moving, you'll be warm. Besides, Alma will need your help. There are seven cabins to clean today." Helen grabbed a broom and started sweeping the tarp floor.

"All right! All right!" Lori awkwardly dressed under the covers and dragged a brush through her hair. She grabbed her sneakers and knelt down to peer into her hamster cage stationed near the tent doorway. It was still empty. Sandy, the hamster, had escaped three days before. A thorough search of the tent turned up no living creature—no living creature that fit Sandy's description. She had slipped out into the wild beyond. Outside, Lori had searched for the little critter for hours: under every leaf, in every tree nook, beside every stone all around the whole tent. She had alerted all the guides to keep a lookout, just in case the teeth marks in their soap or the scurrying sounds under their beds were not from just some run-of-the-mill mouse. She even left trails of food heading back toward the tent and the cage door open, all to no avail.

Helen glanced over at Lori. "You shouldn't get your hopes up. There are all sorts of predators out there. Your gerbil probably didn't last a day, I'm sorry to say."

"Sandy is a hamster, not a gerbil, and don't say things like that!" She rose and stormed out of the tent, acting outraged but knowing in the sinking pit of her stomach that her mother was probably right.

***

Alma placed the last mug on its hook, folded her tea towel, then turned to Lori, who was eating her breakfast beside the wood stove.

"Ready to go?" she asked as she pulled on her sweater.

"Sure am!" Lori crammed her toast into her mouth. Once up and awake, she actually enjoyed her chores; they made her feel, well, like she *belonged* and wasn't just underfoot all the time. Usually she puttered away the morning in the kitchen with Elsie since they now had Gladys—a large, quiet woman with a beaming smile—to help Alma tidy the cabins. Today, however, the camp was so full that an extra pair of hands was welcome.

Outside, the bright sunshine had not yet taken the tang out of the air or the smudge from their breath. Lori rubbed the goosebumps from her arms as they climbed the hill and crossed the grassy slope, still damp with clinging dew. After a quick stop in the laundry room to stock up with linens, they headed out.

"Where first, Alma?"

"Let's see . . . Gladys says she's doing Cabin 4 and 7."

"Ah shucks. I was kinda hoping we could do Green Giants' cabins. They always have cool stuff like those little capsules that change into Jolly Green Giants."

"We can switch with her tomorrow. I want to see what crazy stuff they brought up this year, too. Last year, I got to keep some of their pillowcases. You know, the ones that said, *The Jolly Green Giant Slept Here*. Andy gets a real kick out of them." Alma paused. "How about we start at Cabin 3?"

"We could, but"—Lori pointed—"Eddie's still at the dock."

Alma squinted. Sure enough, there sat Eddie in the back of his boat, which was still tied up, patiently tossing a line into the water and slowly winding it back up. All the rest of the boats had been gone for ages.

"He's probably trying to get enough fish for shore lunch. By the time the Boshes get out, it will be time to cook it, not catch it!" Lori laughed.

It was no surprise the inhabitants of Cabin 3 were still in camp; the Boshes rarely left on time. A diminutive, middle-aged couple from Chicago, they were good customers who had been coming up twice a year, every year since the very first season. They rarely complained, tipped generously, and always took time to enjoy every nuance of the trip, may it be lingering over coffee in the morning or admiring a sunset at night.

"Maybe we should just skip this cabin and go to the next," said Lori.

"No, they might be almost ready to leave. If so, then we won't have to backtrack." Alma shifted her load of towels to one arm then banged on the door.

"Just a minute—"

Janet Boshes came to the door, dressed in a pink yoga outfit.

"Oh, you're here to tidy up already? Can you come back? Can you make up a different cabin first? I have to finish my yoga before we go fishing."

Before either of them could reply, Janet continued, "You see, I have to do my yoga. I always eat too much here. I say, just give me one piece of toast. I can only eat one piece of toast. But then, Alma, you bring my breakfast, and you always bring me two. I tell you, 'Take one back.' And you say, 'It's okay, just leave it on your plate.' How can I leave it on my plate? That's wasteful. So I eat it. And then what happens? The next morning you bring me two pieces again. So I have to do my yoga."

"No problem," said Alma. "We just thought if you were almost ready to get out and fish—"

"Yes, yes," interjected Janet. "And we will get out there soon. I love to fish. Fishing is good. But not if it's rushed. Not if you get tied up in knots. No, for me, you have a nice breakfast, one piece of toast. You do a little yoga to get your body and spirit moving, then you fish. To me. . . well to me it's philosophical."

"Philosophical." Janet's husband, Maxi, schlepped up to the doorway, still in his slippers. "It's not philosophical. It's fishing. You put a bait on and you catch a fish. That is if we can ever get out there."

"Maxi, what are you talking about?" Janet waved her tiny, expressive hands in the air. "No one is more ruminative about fishing than you. If you fish on the right side of the boat, you use one bait. If you fish on the left side of the boat, you use a different bait. If we troll forward, you change your bait. If we troll backward, you change your bait again. Put a bait on, take it off, put a bait on, take it off. You spend more time putting baits on, taking baits off . . . It's amazing your line is ever in the water long enough to catch a fish."

"At least I try different baits," said Max, raking his fingers through his wispy grey hair. "You, you don't use anything but Mepps. Mepps, Mepps, Mepps. You put a Mepps on in the morning, and you put a Mepps on at night. That's all you got in your tacklebox, every size Mepps that's ever been made."

Janet shrugged. "So? Mepps works for me. Something works, you don't change it. See, it's philosophical."

Maxi shook his head. "She calls it philosophical. I call it mindless. You fish mindlessly. You don't have to think about it if all you're going to use is Mepps. Where's the challenge?"

"I don't want fishing to be challenging." Janet turned toward the girls. "Didn't I just tell him I want it to be philosophical? Maxi, he never listens. Have you noticed that? Men never listen."

"Men never listen? Maybe so, but at least we notice when we are keeping someone from their work. You're holding these girls up with all your talk about philosophical fishing."

"You've been talking, too, Maxi. You've been talking, too. I'm sorry to keep you girls. We'll be out soon."

"It's no problem, Mrs. Boshes," reiterated Alma. "We'll just move on to the next cabin."

"Thank you. You're such dears. Such nice people here, aren't they, Maxi?"

"Yes, yes, nice people. Now let them go already."

***

"It's freezing in here!" complained Lori. "And I thought it was cold in my tent!"

"I can't work in this. My hands will freeze to the toilet," Alma joked. "I'll get a fire going lickety-split."

She opened the lid of the pot-bellied stove and lowered a flame onto the paper inside. After a moment or two, a little flame began to lick the wood. Alma added another log and shut the lid.

They were in Cabin 2, where two fathers and two sons had been staying. Now it was empty, and no one could be happier, although the circumstances of their quick departure were dreadful.

Lori thought about what a nightmare the two boys had been. On egg morning, they wanted French toast, and on pancake morning, they wanted eggs. They didn't want fish for lunch, so Elsie packed them sandwiches, which they tossed to the seagulls in favour of chips and chocolate bars.

At supper, the boys had gleefully sung the ballad "On Top of Spaghetti" as they rolled their meatballs along the table and onto the floor. They then proceeded to race between the tables, ducking and hiding behind the other guests. The two fathers, who were as nice as punch, didn't seem to notice their disruptive behaviour. When Helen had subtly commented on their conduct, one father had replied, "Yes, isn't it amazing how they still have so much energy left at the end of the day?"

Alma had confided to Lori they had spied on her in the shower and locked their guide Tommy in the lunchroom "for fun." Poor old Tommy wouldn't yell out for the life of him, so he was in there for over an hour before Andy finally caught sight of him through the window and let him out.

They had chased poor Chezy up and down the shore with a fishnet until they caught her in it, then swung the petrified poodle in the air, chanting "Fresh muskie bait!"

Finally this past evening, the boys had caught a bunch of the fat green frogs that lived in the marshy grass at the point. They then proceeded to shove lit cherry bomb firecrackers down their throats and throw them high in the air to watch them "pop." This was the last straw for Albert. Lori watched as he angrily marched up to them, then suddenly one of the boys—attempting to elude him—stepped on a ground wasp nest hidden in the reeds.

"His screams musta been heard all the way to the lodge. There were hundreds of wasps attacking him. Albert grabbed the kid and dragged him into the lake, dunking him under the water. He finally got the wasps off the kid, but not before they had stung him from the top of his head right down to the tips of the toes hanging out of his sandals," Lori told Alma. "I almost felt sorry for the heathen. I can't imagine the pain that kid went through. I remember when I ran into a hornet, and he stung me on the knee five or six times. I yelled like a banshee."

"His face was so swollen, I was scared he wasn't going to be able to breathe," continued Alma. "It's a good thing it didn't happen any later. It was already almost too dark for your dad to fly them out."

At a fly-in camp, the cloak of darkness cut you off from the rest of the world; you were all alone until daybreak, when planes could again take to the sky. Even Al's newer, larger Cessna 206 that had replaced his Piper Cub that spring could not land or take off on water at night. Luckily there had been just enough light left to fly them into Red Lake—a town ten minutes away—where the boy could receive medical attention. A phone call from Al later that night eased all their minds; he was okay. They all stayed in town overnight, and Al had returned early this morning, minus the two fathers and two sons.

"They were leaving for home today anyways," said Lori. "We're supposed to just pack up their bags to be sent out on the plane later."

"Okay, but first, let's strip the beds so your mom can get started on the washing."

As Alma pulled back the covers, a frog lunged out at her.

"Aghh!" Two more green projectiles leapt up from the bed.

"What the—!"

Lori threw back the covers of the next bed. Several more frogs sprung out.

"Guess those kids didn't pop all their frogs after all. They saved some to stuff in their dads' beds!"

Frantically they chased the creatures between beds and under tables. Catching them wasn't easy—just as you were about to wrap your hands around one, they'd leap away. Lori pounced at several before finally catching one by its leg.

"Gotcha!" The frog dangled from her fist like an elastic band. "One down, a gazillion to go."

One by one, they rounded up the critters and placed them outside until there were no more bulging eyes bouncing along the floor.

"Do you think we got them all out?" asked Lori.

Alma grinned. "I sure hope so. I'd hate the next set of guests to find some in their shoes!"

The cabin was now frog-free, so they finished cleaning and packed up the guests' belongings. As Lori shoved a pair of sneakers into one of the kid's duffel bags, she caught sight of an unopened box of firecrackers.

"Guess the boys will continue their reign of terror back home. Lord, I don't know what my mom would have done if I acted up the way they did. What would you have done to your kids, Alma?"

"Do? I wouldn't hurt frogs."

"I know *you* wouldn't. I mean, how would you stop your kids from hurting frogs?"

"That's how. I wouldn't hurt frogs."

Seeing Lori's confusion, Alma continued, "And . . . he stepped in a wasp nest and got stung really bad."

Then suddenly, she remembered something Alma had told her earlier. Natives didn't believe in interfering with their children's choices, good or bad. Behaviour was structured through example, and nature took care of the rest.

***

"Do you think the Boshes have left yet?" asked Alma.

"They're just leaving now. Look, there's Mrs. Boshes heading for the boat."

You couldn't miss her: the tiny figure was topped with an emerald green beret entirely covered in large, disk-shaped sequins, not unlike you would see adorning the head of a gypsy. The sequins quivered as she strode down the hill, shimmering in the dazzling morning sun.

"My goodness," exclaimed Alma. "What kind of a fisherman wears a hat like that?"

"Don't make fun. She's catching all the big fish!"

"I can see why . . . the fish purposely swim to her because they think *she* is a tasty frog!"

The girls backtracked to Cabin 3 where Janet had already made up the beds. The bathroom was almost spotless as well. Lori cleaned the sink, toilet, and bathtub—the only bathtub in camp. Every other cabin only had a shower, which most of the fishermen preferred. Janet, however, liked to soak in the tub after a day of fishing, so the Boshes always requested this particular cabin for that reason.

It wasn't the Boshes's only request. Every year, on the last day of their trip, Maxi would pull Al aside, take a large wad of bills out of his pocket, and pay his tab in cash. He would then peel off a couple more bills and hand them to Al.

"This is to reserve the same week next year. We'd also like the same guide, Eddie. He knows how we fish. He knows where to place my tackle box and to save only two walleye for lunch. We only eat two fish, so why save more? The other guides, though, always save three. And I want to reserve the same table in the dining room. Janet likes that table. She likes that it has a nice view of the lake. It's right beside the fireplace there, so it's warm on those chilly mornings. To me, a table's a table, but to Janet, the table is important, so I want to book the table, too." Al was always happy to oblige such good customers.

Lori finished the bathroom by wiping down the floor. The towels had not even needed replacing—they were neatly folded on the rack, with a note on them that read, "Don't take the towels. We only used them once. What's the point of washing them? We're clean people."

Lori scrunched up her face and inspected the towels more closely. This year, Maxi had brought a box of towels with him from the hotel he owned on the south side of Chicago—towels he said were too worn to be used in the rooms any longer.

As he handed them to Al, he'd said, "Why throw them out? They make perfectly good rags. People, they buy rags. I don't understand it. These here, you can use them to wipe out boats."

After Maxi left, Al had opened the box and found stacks of spotless white towels in better condition than the ones now stacked in his own laundry room.

Lori chuckled. The towels hanging on the rack were the very same ones Maxi had brought as rags.

***

"It's warming up," said Alma, tugging off her sweater as they walked toward Cabin 5. Suddenly they heard a muffled voice calling out.

They stopped and looked at each other in amazement.

"Did you hear that?"

They both listened again.

"Help!"

"It's coming from the duplex, but I don't know which side," said Lori. Cabin 5 and 6 were housed in one building.

They heard the plea again. "Help! Help!"

"It's coming from Cabin 5 . . . the Solomon cabin!"

What they found when they opened the door was Dr. Solomon's four-year-old son sitting on the toilet. Dr. Solomon was nowhere in sight.

With big eyes and bare feet dangling, the little boy looked up at them. "Pleeeasee . . . somebody come wipe my bummy!"

***

Every place has one guest who is so obnoxious that you just wish they would not come. One that, every year—despite Machiavellian efforts to the contrary—appeared on your doorstep. At Stork Lake, this one guest was Dr. Solomon.

"Mr. Reid, it's me! Dr. Solomon!" His loud voice, with its thick Austrian accent, could be heard by anyone in the same room as the telephone. "I'll be flying my plane up on Friday for a few days of fishing. And of course, I'll be wanting Roger as my guide."

Al would try his hardest to dissuade him.

"I'm sorry, Mr. Solomon, we're full."

"I'll stay in the laundry room."

"The fishing has been terrible."

"My horoscope says it will be great."

"We're renovating . . . the kitchen . . . it's not functional right now."

"I'll eat shore breakfast, shore lunch, shore supper. Roger won't mind cooking."

"Roger's booked with some other guests."

"Switch them to someone else."

"I can't do that."

"What a kidder you are. See you Friday!"

Al would shudder as he hung up the phone.

"Damn!" he said to himself. "I'd rather have an empty camp than have that man here! He has no respect for my guides and doesn't know how to take no for an answer. Well, I better call Jimmy Adams and tell him to warn his pilots that Dr. Solomon will be in the sky on Friday." Not only was Dr. Solomon obnoxious, but he was a terrible pilot.

Usually Dr. Solomon came alone (who would come with him?) but this year, he brought his son with him—the young boy who was now stuck on the toilet.

"My goodness, Paul!" cried Alma, racing over to help the youngster with his dilemma. "Where's your dad?"

"Gone fishing."

"And he left you here!"

"He said I'd scare away the fish."

Alma pulled the boy's pants up.

"Is he coming back for you?"

Paul shrugged. "He said Mrs. Reid would take care of me."

"As if I said I would take care of his son for him! Like I have nothing else to do all day. I explicitly told him I could not take care of Paul, and I explicitly told him I could not do his laundry today, and he *still* dumped his child on me, and he *still* dumped a pile of dirty clothes in with my sheets. My Lord, he only arrived yesterday! What did he do, bring his dirty laundry with him?"

Alma had called Helen over to see the surprise Dr. Solomon had left for them. She now stood in the middle of the cabin while Lori amused Paul outside.

"I can't watch him—he's bound to get into something when I'm outside hanging sheets. And you have too many cabins left to do to have him tailing you the rest of the morning. Al will just have to watch him. He's the one who always *lets* that . . . that man come here every year."

Helen huffed as she shot out the door. "Come on, Paul, have I got a playmate for you!"

Alma and Lori finished Dr. Solomon's cabin and moved on to Cabin 6, where Barney Lamm was staying. Barney's own lodge, Ball Lake, was not open this year. A paper mill upstream from his place had spewed its mercury poisoning into the waters for so long that the fish had become contaminated, and he had felt obligated to shut down. The tragedy, however, hadn't ended there. Barney was arguing against a government that refused to believe the truth of the situation and battling for compensation for his million-dollar resort. So far, he was losing on both fronts.

Knowing Barney's own little piece of heaven in Ontario was no longer open to him, Al offered him respite at Stork Lake. Though not nearly as glamorous or luxurious as Ball Lake, Barney still gladly accepted the invitation. Nothing could make you forget your woes faster than a muskie on the line—except maybe Barney's fishing partner and roomie, Jimmy Robinson.

Clark Gable, Bing Crosby, Jack Dempsey, Ernest Hemingway, Barron Hilton—just a few of the famous who fought to hang out with Jimmy. These big names did not impress him; only big game could do that. As the only man to be inducted into six outdoor halls of fame, Jimmy was an accomplished sportsman in his own right, wielding rifle and rod with equal ease. His first weapon of choice, however, was his pen; as a writer with *Sports Afield* for almost fifty years, he continued to be one of the world's most famous hunting and fishing writers.

Of course, you would never guess any of this by looking at him. Jimmy was now around seventy-five and looked eerily like Alfred

Hitchcock in a baseball cap and checkered shirt—a checkered shirt spattered with tobacco juice down the front of it. His nervous eye made it look like he was constantly winking at you—or maybe he really was winking. With Jimmy, it was impossible to know for sure. He was a card *and* a card shark, having beaten Gary Cooper, Will Rogers, and Babe Ruth at gin rummy. Cards were not his only gambling passion; he also loved to play the ponies and was a regular at the Santa Anita track. During these visits to Las Vegas, Jimmy had a gratis suite at the Tropicana, courtesy of his friend, Deil Gustafson. Fact be known, Jimmy had gratis suites all over the world—this cabin being one of them. It was the only type of accommodation the loveable mooch accepted.

As the girls began to tidy up, Lori asked, "Andy's guiding Barney and Jimmy, isn't he?"

"Yep. And he loves it! He says you can believe the yarn those two spin. He thinks maybe *he* should be paid to spend the day with them!"

"They would be great guys to guide. Not only do they have amazing experiences, but they also understand what a hard job guiding really is."

"Not like Dr. Solomon," continued Alma. "Jimmy told me this morning that he rapped on this here wall last night and asked Jimmy if he could 'have' Andy today. Imagine wanting to switch guides like they were trading cards."

"I wonder why?"

"He saw all the fish Jimmy and Barney brought last night and thought it was Peepsight's fault that he hadn't caught as many. But it was Dr. Solomon's own fault he didn't catch much yesterday— he insisted on changing fishing spots every couple of minutes. Peepsight said they spent more time motoring around than they did fishing. Anyways, Jimmy wasn't impressed. He told Dr. Solomon to quit treating his guide like he was nothing but a draft horse."

"He would. He knows they are also a chef, babysitter, psychiatrist, historian, and clairvoyant!"

Alma grunted as she attempted to move a large box off the unmade bed. "I wish I was clairvoyant—then I'd know why this box was so heavy." She peeked inside and pulled out a book, *The Life and Times of Jimmy Robinson* by Jimmy Robinson.

"It's full of more books? Geez, I'll have to warn my dad. Yesterday, Jimmy handed out a free copy to almost every guest, then gave my dad a bill for all of them. Dad just laughed when he paid him and said, 'So Jimmy, that's how you sell so many books!' He gave me an autographed one, too. Then he asked if I'd learn to shoot yet. He knew Annie Oakley, you know."

"Really?"

"Yep. He was the one who got her to fire her last shot ever at some big trap shoot. She was sixty-five and still broke 97 out of 100. One of the first stories he ever wrote was about her. He's no slouch of a shot himself. He's won a bunch of awards. He said if we got the skeet thrower out tonight, he'd give me some pointers. I can't wait!'"

Alma looked at the tobacco juice and pistachio shells all over the floor. "For someone that is supposed to be such a good shot, he sure can't aim his spit!"

***

Jimmy and Barney's cabin completed, Lori turned to Alma. "Just one left . . . Cabin 1. My family's cabin when we're not living in a tent. For the rest of this season, anyways. Next year, we'll be living there." Lori gestured with her chin to the skeleton of the new lodge they were now just passing.

"How do they know where everything goes?" wondered Alma. "Everything fits together so perfectly, like a puzzle."

"What do you mean?"

"Well they start with a pile of parts that look nothing like a building . . . logs and boards. And from that pile, they make a lodge. How do they know where to put what log? And what in the world holds up the ceiling?"

Lori thought about the straggly line of cabins perched on top of the hill, adorning it like a crown. She had watched each being built yet had never really thought about where the ingenuity came from. Her father, with no architecture degree, designed every building;

Albert built every building without having an engineer's degree, and the guides, with no building experience, helped wire and plumb, saw and nail them together.

During the day, when it was hot, Albert milled the lumber because the sawmill was under a canopy of trees. Then in the evening, after it had cooled a bit, he constructed the lodge. He and Al and a handful of guides worked until dark every night. Albert was driven. The sawmill was running full steam. Logs were cut, limbed, peeled, dragged back to camp, where they would bob in the water tied together until it was time for them to be milled. It was a daunting task to select, cut, and mill the over two hundred logs needed for the two-thousand-square-foot building. Not only logs for the walls had to be milled, but for the support beams and trusses as well. Footings had been poured, the floor nailed in place. Then, every board, every log was lifted into place with nothing more than ropes and sweat. Each day, the walls grew higher, the rooms started to take form.

It really did give Lori a new appreciation for what the men could do.

"It is kinda amazing, isn't it?" said Lori.

"And big!"

"It's big, all right. But do you want to hear about something bigger? Tex Witherspoon, the guy staying here—" By now, the girls had entered the house cabin. "Well, my dad said he just finished building a new home, and the master bedroom is the size of the whole new lodge!"

Alma shook her head. "I don't think I'd like my bedroom to be that big. I would lose poor little Andy in there!"

"You could lose more than Andy . . . apparently the house is about 20,000 square feet in total."

"No!"

"Yep. And it has two swimming pools, a bowling alley, a movie theatre and sixteen bathrooms! That's a lot to clean."

"I'm sure they have someone do it for them," said Alma. "How does someone make enough money to build a house like that?"

"Tex Witherspoon owns two hundred Pamida stores."

Alma whistled. "And yet he and his three boys are so nice, so down to earth. Wait, isn't he the tall, lanky guy holding the huge muskie on the front of Stork Lake's brochure?"

"That's him. He's been coming up for years. Funny, with such a huge, beautiful home, they like staying in our tiny log cabin."

"Maybe they like the coziness, for a change."

"You know, you could be right. I think I will miss this place for the same reason. In the new lodge, everyone in my family will have their own new big bedroom, but there is no room where we can gather together, just the four of us. There's nowhere to chat, no place for family time. The one good thing about not having doors on the bedrooms is that we talk to each other."

She gazed up at the wall. "And I'll certainly miss the hats! When I was little, I used to put them on and pretend to be the person who would fit the hat."

"Did you ever try on Mrs. Boshes's green beret?"

"Yep."

"And pretend to be what?"

"Some exotic French woman who travels all over Europe." She got a dreamy, far away look in her eye, imagining all the wonders out there to see. "I'd love to go to Europe someday. See the Eiffel Tower, visit my relatives in Scotland, swim in the Mediterranean. But it would have to be spring before camp opens. I *never* want to miss a summer here!"

"Loooori! Where are yoooou? Lori!" For the second time that day, Helen bellowed Lori out of her dreams.

A small smile appeared on Alma's lips. "I think she is the only person that can be heard everywhere from anywhere. You better go. I'll finish up here."

Lori found her mother at the entrance to the tent.

"What is it?"

"Your gerbil's back."

Lori peered into the tent. There was Sandy, in her cage, happily munching on her food.

"Who found her?" exclaimed Lori excitedly.

"I think it found its own way home. Look." Right there, beside Sandy's cage, was a hole chewed in the tent, just the right size for a hamster to squeeze through. Probably finding life on the outside just a little too rough, Sandy must have gnawed her way back into civilization and escaped back into her cage.

Lori replaced the green beret on the wall. She had grown up on a concoction of commendable, industrious, and occasionally misguided and contrary guest behaviours. Too bad she had felt it took a "concoction of another colour" to be brave enough to change her own behaviour. Lori lifted a ridiculously large, bright orange, floppy hat off the wall—

1974

Time had been kind to Helen. Ten years had painted her blonde hair just a shade darker, sculpted her figure just a little fuller, and stamped her lovely complexion with just the odd character line. Time had also been to her kind in another way: it had coloured Helen with contentment for the camp. Certainly there were always things that could be improved. Some of the cabins needed redecorating, and she dearly wished to burn the last unsightly outhouse to the ground. All in all, though, she was pleased with how things had turned out. She was especially pleased with the new lodge.

The striking, rich brown structure looked majestic against its backdrop of emerald green forest. Inside the lodge was no less spectacular: satiny gold log walls stretched up toward the two-story cathedral ceiling, where several massive wagon-wheel–shaped chandeliers shone down on the great hall. Large picture windows dominated the room, presenting a magnificent view of the shimmering lake, craggy shores, and fiery sunsets. At one end, a dining area comfortably sat thirty-five guests at honey-toned fir tables and chairs. At the other end, several poker tables and overstuffed sofas created a cozy sitting area. The piece de resistance was the centre beam: it was a full-scale tree, twenty feet high and complete with limbs, each painstakingly polished and varnished by Albert to a smooth, glossy finish. Several smaller trees acted as coat racks, and matching knotty pine branches acted as balusters for the stairway reaching to the second floor.

The new stainless-steel kitchen was no less impressive. The large commercial dishwasher in the corner hissed and gurgled its way through mounds of dishes, saving hours of time and leaving every piece of the white dinnerware sparkling clean. There was row upon row of shelving, holding every conceivable pot and pan, every size bowl, every possible gadget. There were two glass door refrigerators and a large griddle. Even with all this modern equipment, the room still looked empty; the old wooden table with the hole in the middle still looked lost in the centre of it.

"Elsie!" Helen gasped when she saw it for the first time, about a month after it was finished. "This kitchen's huge!"

"That's true . . . I do a lot more travelling!" Elsie said, followed by a cackle.

"How do you like it?"

"Oh, it's good," she said in her typical understated way. "But I miss my wood stove."

Helen glanced over at the gleaming new six-burner gas stove. "Why on earth would you miss that beast?"

"The bread is never as good now! The crusts just ain't as crusty. And I don't think Al likes the bread as much either."

"Why would you say that?"

Elsie leaned closer and lowered her voice to a whisper. "I'll tell you a secret. See that there big new freezer? It has ten loaves of bought'n bread in it. Your husband ordered it."

"No, Elsie! You cheating now?" Helen joked.

Elsie blushed. "Not yet. I told Al I'd only use it in a pinch!"

Helen liked the fact her own room was right off the kitchen and had large windows facing the guest cabins. This meant she could keep track of what was going on both inside and outside the lodge. Lori and Phil had rooms off the storage area, and Elsie and Albert had their own suite at the back of the lodge. Gone were the days when Elsie would have to brave bears at the outdoor biffy.

The lodge was only one of many improvements. There were also new boats, new motors, new docks. There was a new generator and a new tractor. Much to Helen's relief, there was even a new pilot to fly Al's Cessna—the call letters *CUL* painted on the side of it now had an additional meaning. It truly was "see you, Al" every time the plane took off.

These big changes also meant a bigger staff—more guides, more camp hands, more kitchen help. Helen was finally free of hanging sheets and waiting on tables. Now she had the time to tend to details and the money to carry them out. She planned more elaborate menus, whipped up curtains, moved furniture. She categorized the large storage room adjacent to the kitchen, lining up the boxes, cans, and bottles in neat rows. She even re-organized the chaotic kitchen so well that for weeks Elsie couldn't find anything.

Yes, Helen was pleased—the camp had finally caught up to Al's dreams. Everything was just about right. Now if she could just do something about Lori —

***

"My, you've grown, yous look like Olive Oyl!"

Lori knew Elsie did not mean to be derogatory; it was her plain and simple way of saying Lori had become quite tall. However, Lori took it to mean giant, skinny, and gangly because that was how she felt. Added to the picture, her fine blonde hair clung to her head like a skull cap and did nothing to flatter her face that was already challenged with a row of railroad tracks on her teeth and a crop of zits on her cheek. Her brother did nothing to dissuade her from this image she had of herself.

At seventeen, Phil was six feet tall, with broad shoulders and long, shiny blond hair. He was handsome, vivacious, personable, and popular with both staff and guests. Mature in many ways, he still was not above teasing his little sister.

"You're sooo ugleeee!" he'd taunt as Lori stood in front of her mirror, trying to unglue her hair from her head.

"Shut up! Gawd . . . I hate you! Can't you just leave me alone?"

"I can't because you're sooo ugleeee!" Lori would take a swipe at him, which he'd easily dodge.

"Missed me!"

"Oh, grow up, you skuzz bucket!"

"I am. It's you that's still in your awkward stage. That's why you're . . . sooooo ugleee!"

These brother/sister love fests did little for Lori's fragile ego, especially with her new interest in boys. It was a cruel act of nature that she looked her very worst at the exact time she wanted to look her best. Even crueller was the fact that she had never been shyer.

She could communicate with Andy, confide in Alma, or kid around with Albert. What she could not do was talk with strangers. Their words entered her head and shuffled her thoughts like a deck of cards, her brain heartlessly stalling any reply until some ten minutes after the conversation was over. Talking to good-looking, male teenage strangers was even worse; her palms became clammy, her legs rubbery, and any words that managed to dribble out of her frozen mouth were as lame as her limbs. However, for the life of her, she could not make her mother understand. She knew her mom saw her shyness as something that could be cured by coercion.

One area where she did have confidence was in her work. Used to the rhythm of the camp, she was organized and energized, speeding from one task to another, knowing what to do without being told. Under Elsie's expert tutelage, she had even learned to cook; her feather-light cakes were quite improved from the one she had made for her father's birthday when she was four.

Lori decided this was the year to join the Stork Lake workforce as a full-time, seven-day-a-week paid employee. She could contribute to the camp while collecting a salary—money she could spend on makeup to hide her face and clothes to hide her body. It was a win-win situation. So she approached her mother with the idea.

"Okay," responded Helen agreeably. "You're old enough to wait on the guests now anyways. It'll be good for you. Get you out of your shell a bit."

"Absolutely not!"

"Why?"

"Because."

"Because is not an answer."

"Because that's not what I had in mind. I was thinking kitchen duty, maybe serve the guides. I don't mind waiting on them. I know them all."

"Serving soup is serving soup, whether it be to Charlie or to Mr. Smith."

"It's not the same thing. The guests, they want *to talk*."

"So they talk, they don't bite! Maybe if you tried socializing more, it would get easier."

"It doesn't get easier. They know so much more about everything. Anything I say sounds stupid. If I have to wait on guests, I won't work at all!"

Lori felt her mother's disappointment. She knew the camp business was all about "the talk." It wasn't like at an ordinary resort, where you might catch a glimpse of your guests as they bobbed in and out. Except when they were on the lake, guests here were confined to the few acres of land that comprised the resort. There was nowhere else to eat, sleep, or play. The only smoky bar, the only gambling casino, the only steak joint around were right here — you were the only game in this town. That meant the customers had time to get to know you, and Helen and Al made sure they made time to get to know them, and the best way to get to know them was by talking.

After a day on the water, the guests gathered in the new lodge, drinks in hand. Helen would sweep in and, with a great smile, break the ice. She knew instantly how to make everyone feel welcome and at ease—and very, very special. She knew whom she could kid with, who couldn't take a joke. She knew how to compliment, and she knew how to handle a complaint. No one was immune to

Helen's charm—from the German Count to the accountant from St. Germain. She would get them all talking, and of course, the talk would soon turn to fishing because the only thing better than catching a big fish was exchanging stories and telling tales about it. This is where Al came in.

Al was the master of this story time. He would move from table to table, hearing the reports about the "one that got away," the fabulous shore lunch, the glorious day on the lake. Then everyone would sit at attention as he came up with a related story, always pertinent to their own experience. As avid a listener as a story weaver, it was this time at the end of the day that made this camp special, kept guests coming back year after year. Al never failed to thrill and entertain.

Once the fish stories were weighed, measured, and tallied, the personal stories took over. Helen and Al learned which schools their guests' kids went to, who was up for a promotion, who had just had a gallbladder operation, who had retired. And the guests learned about them. They knew when Elsie had her first great-grandchild, where Alma spent her winters. This personal touch made them much beloved among their guests and was the reason so many of them ended up as close personal friends.

Phil had easily learned the art of the talk. He was already a bloody great glad-hander, enthusiastically greeting every new pair of boots that stepped off a plane. In no time at all, customers knew he would be graduating from high school next year, that he had a girlfriend named Linda in Winnipeg, and that he had caught three muskies for his guests the week before. Everyone also knew he was the owner's son, but only the closest of guest friends knew there was "a Lori." Without the family gift of gab, she remained hidden, invisible. However, from the way her mom was acting lately, Lori felt she was soon to change this situation, and she didn't like it one bit.

***

"Wow, they sure plowed through the Morning Dawns!" said Helen upon entering the kitchen, holding up an empty pitcher.

Morning Dawns were a concoction of brandy, vodka, orange juice, and pineapple juice, served to special guests at breakfast. "Even with all the teenagers in camp who don't drink, I think we'll still need a double batch tomorrow morning. Speaking of teenagers, did you see when the Asmussen's daughter walked in for breakfast? I thought the Cooper boys' eyes were going to pop out of their heads!"

Lori shoved the tray of dirty dishes into the washer and slammed the door down with such vengeance that both Elsie and Helen were startled.

Though Lori had only caught a glimpse of seventeen-year-old Sue Asmussen dining with her family the night before, she already hated her. She hated her because she was petite and curvy. She hated her because she had perfect hair, perfect skin, and perfect teeth. Most of all, she hated her because her mother kept talking about her—how cute she was, how outgoing she was. She probably wished Sue was her daughter!

"Maybe you should leave Gladys to finish there," said Helen, "and come clear tables. I don't want all my new dishes broken."

"Fine." Lori stomped into the now empty dining room and began gathering up glasses and cups onto a tray. Still distracted, she did not hear Mrs. Cooper, a large woman with brassy hair and bright red lips, walk in.

"Excuse me, miss . . . it *is* miss, isn't it?" she grunted, sizing Lori up and down, chins shaking. "So hard to tell nowadays! You girls and boys all dress the same. It's a shame the way girls unsex themselves. Is it old fashion for a girl to look like a girl?" She didn't wait for Lori to answer but raised her voice another notch or two. "Couldn't be! There's that lovely young girl sitting at our table, what's her name . . . Sue? Now, *she* looks like a girl." The woman did not appear to notice Lori's dismayed silence. With red-tipped talons, she held out a water jug. "Anyways could you fill my thermos with drinking water?"

"Drinking water?" Lori asked timidly.

"Yes, drink-ing wa-ter," the woman annunciated each word this time as if she were talking to an imbecile. "I don't care to drink lake water while I'm out fishing. I want drinking water."

"The drinking water *is* lake water," replied Lori.

"What's that? Speak up, miss. I can't even hear you. You're quiet as a mouse!"

That did it. "Drinking water *instead* of lake water, yes, okay," said Lori, much louder this time. With that, she marched into the kitchen, filled up the thermos with tap water—which, of course, was just lake water. She then returned to the dining room and gave it to the woman.

"Here you go, Mrs. Cooper. Special drinking water."

What a horrible woman, thought Lori. She picked up her tray and dragged her feet back into the kitchen.

"For goodness sake, pick up your feet when you walk," said Helen, sounding annoyed. "I know it's those jeans. Why you wear them so long is beyond me. They make you shuffle your feet, and they end up all ragged on the bottom."

"It's not my jeans. I just don't feel like picking up my feet, okay?" Why was everyone picking on her today? "I'm just feeling kinda . . . depressed."

"Depressed . . . I hate that word. There's no such thing," responded Helen with impatience in her tone. "Maybe if you dressed a little neater and got out into the dining room and met some new people, you wouldn't feel so sorry for yourself."

Meet new people, like that boiled crab of a woman who just thought she was a boy? Yeah, that was going to make her feel better! And how come she had to have the only parents in the whole world that didn't believe you could ever be depressed? She had never seen either of her parents even feel sorry for themselves. How did you deal with people like that? They weren't even human!

"In fact, I think you should help me take the hors d'oeuvres out to the guests tonight."

"But I have to serve the guides," objected Lori.

"Alma can do that." Helen's tone was final. "And wear a decent pair of pants!"

***

At suppertime, Phil filed into the staff room with the rest of the guides. He was just about to sit down on one of the benches when he spotted his sister sitting slumped at the wooden table in the middle of the kitchen, plating crackers with slices of cheese. He walked right up to her and peered closely at her face.

"What happened to you? You look like a pumpkin!" He burst out laughing. "God, even your hands are as orange as that cheese! What in God's name did you do?"

"It's Mom's fault," spat out Lori. "She wants me out in the dining room with her tonight. I hate these forced entries, showing me off like I'm some sort of specimen under glass."

"You do look like a specimen. Of what, I'm not sure."

"Shut up! Anyways I hate when people find out who I am. I'd rather be an anonymous mute than a tongue-tied Reid. Everyone compares me to her or to you, and I always come up lacking."

"But not in colour—"

"Will you stop?"

"Okay, so how'd you end up orange?"

"I thought that if I could make myself look a little better, you know, not so anemic, that I might feel better, and then maybe I'd be able to talk easier. So I decided to try the Coppertone QT that one of the guests left in their cabin. On the label, it said it would give you a tan in three to five hours without the sun."

"You should have used the sun."

"You can't get a tan in one afternoon. Maybe a burn but not a tan."

"You would have looked better with a burn."

"Now, now," consoled Elsie from her corner beside the stove. "It's not so bad."

"Elsie's right," chortled Phil as he sauntered back into the staff room. "At least no one will notice your zits now!"

***

Lori turned away, her cheeks already too bright for Phil to notice she was blushing. She wished she could crawl under the table and hide. There was no way in the world she was going out in that dining room now.

"I thought I told you to wear something presentable tonight?" Helen had swept into the room and immediately zoned in on Lori, taking in her ragged jeans and T-shirt.

Didn't her mother have eyes? "I didn't bother getting dressed up because I'm not going out there," said Lori.

Helen grabbed a bowl of walleye ceviche out of the fridge. "Of course you are."

Was her mother a monster? Was she purposely trying to humiliate her? Didn't she care how embarrassed she would be to have everyone see her looking like this?

"Now bring that cheese and let's go," Helen ordered and headed into the dining room, Lori grudgingly trailing behind.

"Hello! And how is everyone tonight?" Helen's musical voice carried over the buzz of guests already gathering for cocktail hour. She orbited around the room, offering jovial greetings, small delicacies, and, of course, introductions. "Have you met my daughter? This is my daughter, Lori. Lori, come meet the Asmussens. Lori, you know the Gardners."

The maze of faces, each holding a tinkling tumbler and engaged in lively conversation, reminded Lori of the congregation of sparrows that gathered in their leafy bird condo outside her bedroom window, chirping and gabbing about their day.

"And Lori, these are Mrs. Cooper's sons."

Two good-looking teenage boys politely turned to Lori, who promptly turned to mush.

"Nice to meet you, miss," said one of the boys in a soft southern drawl.

"Likewise." As soon as the word was out of her mouth, she regretted it. It sounded flip and uncaring, and that was not the way she felt—after all, unlike his mother, at least *he* had realized she was a girl! *And* he was so darned cute! How could she make it up? Should she start again and say hi? Or ask how their day of fishing went? If they'd like a piece of cheese? She was still debating what to say when Sue strolled into the lodge. She wore fashionable clogs on her tiny feet, her toenails tipped with polish that matched her lips. A crisp, white peasant blouse and hip-hugging jeans showed she had curves in all the right places.

"There's Sue! Let's see what she caught today!" The two boys took off across the room, leaving Lori standing there, still holding up the plate of cheese.

I know what she caught . . . the two of you, she thought to herself.

"We should go over and say hi to Sue, too. You haven't met her yet, have you, Lori?" questioned Helen.

Let that girl see her looking like this? And let the Cooper brothers see a side-by-side comparison of them—one girl glowing and the other positively fluorescent? That was too much. The wagon-wheel chandelier above her head started to spin. Lori couldn't breathe; she had to escape.

"I have to . . . go."

Over her mother's stern don't-you-dare-leave look, Lori dropped her cheese plate on the closest table and quickly slipped out to hide behind the hot, steamy dishwasher, where her tears mixed with the orange sweat streaming down her face.

***

"What are we going to do with Lori?"

The workday was finally at an end. Even the most diehard of poker players had retired to their beds for the night, and Al wanted nothing more than to retire to his, if only his wife would let him. He ran a hand through his hair, which now was liberally sprinkled with well-deserved silver.

"What do you mean?"

Helen finished rolling the last pin curl into her hair and secured it with a bobby pin. "I brought her out into the dining room, and she was there all of two minutes before she scurried back to her corner! She won't wait on the guests, won't talk." Helen stalled for a moment. "You know . . . you and I are meeting up with the Coopers for shore lunch tomorrow. Why don't we ask the Asmussens to join us, and we'll take Phil and Lori along. It'll be nice to get all three families together. The Cooper boys are great kids, and Sue is such a sweet girl. I'm sure the kids will all get along great. And it will be good for Lori. Get her out of her shell a bit."

"If you like." Al was much too tired to argue.

"I just don't understand her sometimes," continued Helen, pulling down the covers on her bed. "She climbs trees and woodpiles, drives boats and tractors and planes. There isn't a bug or an animal that can send her running, yet she's terrified of walking into the dining room. How can someone be so fearless and yet so shy?"

Al looked over at his charming wife, who could comfortably step into any room yet was scared to step onto any plane. How could someone be so fearful and yet not shy? As he snapped out the light, he wondered how Helen could not see that she and her daughter were simply mirror images of one another.

***

"Now, Lori, you'll be ready to go at 11:30, won't you?" asked Helen as she packed special goodies for their shore lunch.

"Do I have to be?"

"Yes, you have to learn to be sociable if you don't want to end up a hermit! I told Phil to take you to shore lunch in his boat. We will all meet up there. Elsie, are there any more lemons?"

"I already told the girls to pack you some in the shore lunch box," replied Elsie.

"That's for the fish. I need one for the martinis. Which reminds me, I better find Al and make sure he is bringing his portable bar."

While Helen fluttered off, Lori miserably finished stocking the fridge with the fresh milk and cream that had arrived that morning. How could her parents torture her this way? Didn't they realize what they were doing to her? It felt like the Jackson Five were dancing on her solar plexus. She rubbed her stomach for a moment, trying to relieve the knot she knew would not untangle until after the dreaded shore lunch. There would be no escaping this time; she would have to endure hours of torment, stuck on an island with Sue and her ogling suitors.

Just how did people figure out what to talk about? She thought about her brief experience in the dining room the night before—there certainly had been no shortage of conversation. Come to think of it—there had been no shortage of cocktails, either. In fact, everyone had a drink in their hand. It seemed tongues easily trudged along a track greased with whiskey or gin or—she caught sight of the pitcher of Morning Dawns on the top shelf of the glass-door fridge. More than half of the eye-opener was still left from this morning. Maybe that was the answer. A little sip of something before shore lunch just might make it easier to transfer words from her brain to her lips.

Lori waited until Elsie's head was buried in the freezer before she grabbed a glass off the shelf, took the pitcher of Morning Dawns out of the fridge, and quietly carried them to her bedroom.

The first sip was horrible. This was the celebrated cocktail? The elixir everyone enjoyed? It certainly did not taste the way it sounded—and certainly didn't seem to merit the merriment it inspired. She took another gulp and forced the volatile liquid down her gullet. After a few gulps, it didn't taste as bad. She drained the glass and refilled it.

She started to feel lightheaded and giggly. Wow, this stuff really worked! She could even talk to the Queen right now! Lori glanced at the clock. What time did she have to go again? Maybe she should get ready just in case it was soon. She picked up her lip gloss and smeared it on, almost keeping it on her lips. Then she brushed a strand of hair back behind her ear and took a good look at herself in her mirror.

That old Mrs. Cooper doesn't know what she is talking about. I do look like a girl!

Somehow the brandy-fueled mixture made her feel more feminine, like she could bat her eyes and flirt with the best of them. *I'll show her sons there's more than one girl around here!*

Unfortunately her walk did not match her newfound finesse. Slowly and clumsily, she descended the steps of the lodge. How come there were so many stairs today? As she finally reached the bottom, Alma poked her head out of the doorway of the storeroom.

"Could you take those last few sheets off the line before you go?"

"No sweat!" Lori noticed that her voice sounded strange—like it was far away. "I sound funny!" She giggled.

The laundry proved more challenging than the stairs. She tumbled into the line of sheets, pulling them to the ground with her. "I'm a mummy!" she said, giggling some more. This was so much fun!

∗∗∗

"I love days like this, Al," said Helen contentedly as she threw her woollen cape over her shoulders. "A reprieve from work for a few hours while we enjoy shore lunch with family and friends. And lovely weather to boot! Not a raincloud in sight and almost no wind. My bones won't get rattled on the boat ride over to Bird Shit Island."

"It'll be a great afternoon," agreed Al.

"Now you have everything, don't you? Did you remember the cooler?"

"Yes."

"The bar, the tablecloth?"

"Yes, Helen, I have everything. This isn't my first shore lunch. Now, are you coming?"

"I have to get my hat. You go on ahead," said Helen, adding a pair of large sunglasses to her ensemble.

Helen's hat resided on the wall in the house cabin. It was a broad-rimmed, floppy, braided hat in a particularly gauche fluorescent orange, a veritable garden of flowers growing out the side of it. She had bought it as a lark on a trip to Mexico some years before and wore it to every shore lunch, more as a conversation piece than a hat since it was impossible to keep on her head while flying around in a boat and was an actual hazard to all while fishing. Trying it on, she tilted her head side to side, this way and that before the mirror, before deciding on just the right tilt for the proper comic effect.

Perfect! she thought and flounced out the door.

∗∗∗

"Looori, where are yooou? It's time to go!"

Her mother's high-pitched voice pierced through Lori's foggy brain. "Go? Oh yeah, the shore lunch!" Lori unwrapped herself from the sheets, then slowly got up and started down the hill. Only her feet didn't seem to want to listen. She tried putting one foot in front of the other, but they ended up wandering off to the side somewhere. By the time she manoeuvred to the dock, her mom and dad had already left.

"Quit goofing around and get in the boat," said Phil impatiently. "We're going to be late."

Lori stumbled into her seat, and they took off.

By the time they arrived at Bird Shit Island, Lori didn't feel so good. Despite the wind whipping boat ride, her face was hot and both her belly and brain felt like they were still rolling on the waves even after they arrived. Unsteadily she tried to stand, only to have the ground spin away from her. She flopped awkwardly back down in her seat.

"Lori? Lori? What's the matter? You don't look well. Are you sick?" Helen approached the boat, concerned. "Phil, help your sister out. What's the matter? Is it your stomach? Let me feel your head."

Blearily, Lori gazed about her. She was vaguely aware of the mirage of people walking about but unable to focus on anyone in particular until she saw the ridiculously bright orange hat hover over her.

"Hey, your hat's the same colour as my face," quipped Lori.

"What the . . .why . . . you smell like booze!" cried Helen.

"I . . . want . . . I'm tired."

And with that, Lori slid down to the bottom of the boat and passed out.

Lori replaced her mother's hat on the wall. Once she sobered up, she had feared her parents would be so angry for embarrassing them in front of their friends that they would never forgive her. But to her surprise, there was no retribution. In fact, they never even mentioned the incident, and her mother never again forced her to socialize with the guests.

Next, Lori picked up a hat that looked like something you would wear on safari. By the next summer, Lori was not only ready to socialize, but she was on the hunt—

1975

"I know who you are."

With arms crossed over his chest, the boy standing on the dock above her struck the proud pose of an Ojibwa chieftain. His were strikingly classic features: a reddish-brown complexion, high chiselled cheekbones, hawk nose, and a distinctive jawline. Warm brown eyes shone below a head of sleek, shoulder-length black hair, neatly kept in place by a blue bandana. It was the generous mouth held in an impish grin, however, that she recognized—that smile had always lit up his whole face.

"And I know who you are."

Lori sat on the dock and dangled her feet in the water, and she tossed back her golden head. Her long, feathery fishhook earrings danced in the wind, framing her delicate face yet untouched by the sun this early in June.

"No one told me you'd be here this summer."

"And no one told me you were coming here today."

"You look different but the same."

"You look the same but kinda different."

"You're not going to try to drown me again, are you?"

"You're not gonna compete with me in everything again, are you?"

"I might! Oh, I missed you!" Lori grinned with delight as Lawrence held out a hand to help her up.

"So when did you get here?" inquired Lawrence as they padded down the dock.

"About an hour ago. How about you?"

"Couple weeks ago."

"That long ago? And I thought I got out of school early! My mom always takes us out a few weeks ahead."

"I don't go to school no more. My dad thought it was time I became a muskie guide."

"Oh, yeah, you must be an old man of fifteen. Almost too old to become a guide, aren't you, Makoons?" kidded Lori.

"I sorta don't go by that name anymore."

Lori could have bitten her tongue. She knew that was the name Agnes had called him. "I never had the chance to say sorry to you for what happened to your mom—"

"It's okay."

She wanted to tell him she had gone to their island and had seen his carving of the three bears, but she wasn't sure if what she had done was taboo. She wasn't even sure if the island was still off-limits since the tent had long ago been torn down by the elements and spirited off into the wind.

"Not working today?" Lawrence looked hopeful.

"I was going to, but the first day back here, I always just like to enjoy. What about you?"

"I was cleaning lunch spots with Dennis and Jeremy, but I'm finished now."

"Dennis and Jeremy?"

"The two new pale faces working here."

"Oh? How old?"

"They're old . . . like 18! But cool. You'll like them. So what do you want to do?"

"Visit all our special places! Come on. I'll race you down the beach!"

They jumped off the dock. Just like in the old days, they took off down the sand, each footprint leaving the passage of time further and further behind.

***

Later that evening, Lori slipped out of her Adidas's and waded in the cool shallows of the lake. The sun, still firmly pinned between the two islands, was just beginning to melt into the horizon. She glanced at her watch.

Nine o'clock—at least another hour of daylight. What in the world was she going to do for the rest of the night?

After spending the day crawling over rocks, climbing trees, and skipping stones with Lawrence, she had chowed down on Elsie's famous stewed chicken with the kitchen staff while catching up on camp gossip. Alma had then shooed her out the door. She had insisted Lori enjoy her first night at Stork out in the fresh air instead of elbow-deep in a sink full of dirty dishes. So she had donned a pair of shorts and a cherry scratch-and-sniff shirt and set off for a run. Her nostrils and lungs immediately filled with the rich earthy smell of the bush as she entered the maze of paths that crossed through the forest. Pinecones crunched under her feet as she ran past the sawmill, up to the smouldering dump, then through the lacy canopy of young poplars to the "hardware store," a place where junk was stored until it magically became crucial spare parts. At a fork in the path where a fallen birch lay naked, its bark skin long ago stripped for notepaper, she veered left, a route that led out of the brush. Once back out in the open, she passed the old brown wooden outhouse, flew along the stretch of green grass and sweet-smelling clover that rolled out to meet the lake, and finished up at the water's edge. It was a good half-hour run, but *still* she hadn't used up all her teenage energy.

"So are you dog tired from running around in the bush like a blue-arsed fly?" Lawrence had approached on silent feet and now stood in front of her, grasping a dirty white ball in both hands.

"I'm on the track team at school . . . just want to keep my stamina up. And no, I'm not the least bit tired. Why?"

"Jeremy, Dennis, and me are playing volleyball and could use you to even up the teams."

Lori reached up behind her head and tightened her ponytail. If Lawrence had asked her to play volleyball with two new guides last summer, her answer would have been no. However, over the past year, her shyness had been buried under a coat of makeup and crazy clothing—masquerading as a confident, quirky teenager had turned her into one.

Lori hopped up onto the dock and picked up her shoes. Armed with new courage and an old friend, she found herself anticipating the meeting of the latest additions to the camp.

"Lead on," she declared.

***

Dennis scratched the scruffy beard speckling his chin. "Hmmm, let's see . . . Here's another one. Why doesn't a chicken wear pants?"

"I know I'm going to regret asking, but here goes . . . why?" asked Jeremy.

"Because his pecker is on his head."

"Okay, enough with the dumb jokes," grimaced Lori, swatting Dennis with the end of her long braid.

"I wish I brought my guitar. I could have entertained us instead," said Lawrence.

"I don't think so," Dennis said seriously. "There's something wrong with it."

"No, there isn't. I was playing it last night."

"Yeah, and it was moaning . . . sounded like it needed an aspirin."

It was a cool, cloudy evening. The four friends sat on stumps around a smoky bonfire, bundled in blue Stork Lake bomber jackets, listening to Dennis's slightly crude jokes and illicit limericks.

For the past few weeks, Lori had found herself often heading down the hill after work at night to hang out with them. She had always been comfortable around Lawrence, and just like the old days, he continued to good-naturedly act as a measurement for Lori's achievements. This ease of fellowship extended to Jeremy and Dennis, who, while treating her with respect, never made her feel like the dreaded "boss's daughter."

With tawny blond bangs flopping in his eyes, Dennis reminded Lori of a big, happy-go-lucky St. Bernard. Although he was hired as a guide, it was quickly found that this was a waste of his talent—he had an amazing mechanical aptitude. Now he worked with Albert, inhaling diesel and tweaking the machines that were the pulse and the life of the camp.

Jeremy had a wealth of experience on the water. The consummate guide, his ebony eyes literally burned with lust every time he talked about fishing. And growing up in the bush, he knew about wildlife. In his soft-spoken voice, he enriched nights with his love and knowledge of wildlife; he would explain why the eagle overhead built his nest so high; why the loons "danced" on the water; that the tracks on the shore belonged to a moose and her calf.

They played horseshoes and badminton and "Volleyfoot," a game they had made up. They lowered the volleyball net to about three feet then volleyed the ball back and forth by kicking it with their feet. Afterward they would take a late-night dip until their bones were chilled enough to warrant heading back up to the lodge for a pot of steaming coffee, or, like tonight, head to the point to warm up by the fire.

"Should we put another log on?" asked Lawrence. He pulled a tin of Copenhagen snuff from his jean jacket pocket and cracked it open.

"It's getting late. Let it go out. What's your fascination with that stuff?" asked Lori curiously, pointing to the glinting snuff can in his hand.

"I don't know. My dad chews it, so I chew it."

"Can I try some?"

"Wouldn't you rather try a cigarette? Dennis could give you one."

"I've tried a cigarette. I haven't tried snuff. Please?"

"Okay," said Lawrence, holding the tin out to her.

Lori removed a sizeable plug and stuffed it into her mouth. She swished it over her tongue, between her teeth, chewed a bit, then swallowed the whole swampy mess. The snuff slid down her throat, shredding it as it descended.

"Agh! How can you stomach that stuff!"

"Don't tell me gutted the chew? Are you nuts?" said Lawrence incredulously.

Jeremy and Dennis both stopped talking and looked over at her white face and bulging eyes.

"Uh oh," said Jeremy slowly.

Immediately Lori realized something intensely violent had just happened to her body. The nicotine buzzed her brain, her heart pounded, and her head felt like it had lifted off her shoulders. Her entire body suddenly broke into a cold sweat.

"I . . . feel . . . sick—" she said, her face contorted.

Eyes watering, she stumbled to her feet and over to a small bush and vomited.

Jeremy was behind her, patting her shoulder. "You okay, sport?"

"Oh, God," whimpered Lori, wiping her mouth. "That bloody putrid concoction wasn't any better the second time round."

"Here, come sit back down before you fall down." Jeremy led Lori back to her stump, where she crumbled on top of it.

"Have some of my 7up," said Lawrence. "I've seen guys swallow snuff juice, but man, the whole thing? That's hard core."

Lori took a long guzzle from the pop can. Her throat still burned, and she was incredibly lightheaded and horribly embarrassed. "Why would anyone chew that stuff?"

"You don't really chew it," said Lawrence. "You place a pinch in your lower lip or between your teeth and cheek. When it's dry, you spit it out."

"You could have told me!"

"You didn't ask."

Dennis, who had quietly been watching the whole fiasco, suddenly piped up;

"There was a young lassie named Lori
Who once she chewed snuff was quite sorry

It spewed out her nose
She threw up on her toes
And it took away her pride and her glory."

"That's the stupidest limerick I've ever heard, Dennis," groaned Lori.

Lawrence gave her a lopsided grin. "I thought it was clever." Suddenly a bright streak lit up the sky. "Uh oh. It's going to storm. That's why the mosquitoes are so bad. Let's douse the fire and move indoors. We could go to my cabin and play some Euchre."

Lori stood up. "I can't play Euchre with you."

"How about Mexican Poker or Cheat?"

"No, you don't get it. I can't play any card game with you guys. My mom would have a heart attack if she found me in your cabin."

"I live in a one-room cabin with my dad, for Pete's sake," said Lawrence. "What better chaperone could there be than James? He's like your own dad."

Still feeling slightly dizzy, Lori rose back to her feet. "Wouldn't matter if there were ten chaperones . . . my mom still would crucify me. Thanks for the offer, but I think I'll go home and shower. I want to wash the stench of snuff off of me. See you all in the morning." Lori set off up the hill.

***

Helen was on her way to the kitchen when she spotted James leaving the staff showers. She let out a long wolf whistle. "Look at you, James! Got a hot date?"

James had emerged a new man. His shiny, still damp hair was neatly combed off his forehead, and he had scraped a razor over his chin, smoothing off the odd hair that managed to grow there. He was even wearing a red-checkered shirt, still freshly creased—and crumpled—from the package.

"You bet, Boss Lady!" He grinned. "Fritzi's coming today."

"Of course!" said Helen as she opened the kitchen door. "I should have known you'd doll yourself up for her. Well you look very handsome, so handsome in fact you better watch it . . . her husband might get jealous!"

James let out one of his big, hearty laughs. Truth be told, he did have a bit of a crush on Fritzi Flanagan, but then it would be hard for any man with a love of fishing or hunting not to love her because Fritzi excelled at both.

＊＊＊

Inside, Helen found Elsie standing in front of the stove frying up donuts.

"For Doc?"

"Yep, don't know why he likes my donuts so much . . . they ain't my best dish. They're always a little dry. But he says they're perfect for dunking, so I always make sure there's a fresh batch 'specially for him."

"Everyone likes doing special things for the Flanagans. I guess because they're special people. They've certainly always been good to us when we've gone to visit them in Fond du Lac." Helen's eyes darted around the room, missing nothing. "Isn't the meat out for tonight?"

Elsie lifted a golden brown donut out of the pot with a slotted spoon and laid it on a rack. "Not yet."

"We really should always get the meat out the night before so it can defrost."

"We could do that."

Helen opened the freezer and rummaged around inside. "So what can we defrost in a hurry? Can't be a roast."

"I was thinking meatloaf for the boys and maybe steak for the guests."

"We can't have steak. Tommy Kawa's coming in today."

"Oh?" Apparently the name meant nothing to Elsie.

"He owns Johnny's Cafe . . . you know, the one I told you about . . . the steakhouse in Omaha. He serves the best steak in the Midwest."

"Oh, for God's sake."

Helen thought a moment. "How about breaded pork cutlets? They'll defrost quick."

"But the Applebaums are here. They don't eat pork."

"Oh, for Pete's sake." Helen thought a moment. "Well, then, we have no choice. We'll have to tell them it's veal."

Elsie didn't miss a step. "Okay. And we can have noodles with the *veal*. And beets. Thems add a bit of colour to the plate." Helen knew that Elsie wasn't the least bit intimidated to serve her food to someone who owned a world-class restaurant. In her own quiet way, she knew what she had to offer would stand up. It was Elsie's food as much as the fishing that kept guests coming back.

"And for dessert?"

"Cake. For Doc and Fritzi."

"Oh my Lord, their wedding anniversary! Good thing you said something. I had forgotten all about it. You know, you have an amazing memory. You remember guests' birthdays, anniversaries, and even their dietary requirements. How do you remember all these details?"

"The little recipe cards in my head have faces and dates beside 'em."

"Do any of those recipe cards tell you where I put the streamers and fancy candles? I'll have to decorate the dining room."

"They're in a box in the storeroom behind the wax paper."

Helen retrieved the box and brought it back into the kitchen. As she slid the box onto the wooden table, one of Elsie's freshly made loaves of bread rolled upside down.

"Uh oh," said Elsie in a low voice.

"No. Elsie, don't even say it! I know you think an upside-down bread loaf is bad luck, but that was an accident."

"Don't matter. Last time you done it accidentally, you almost chopped your fingers off cutting kindling."

"Well, I'm not cutting any kindling today." Helen nervously righted the loaf of bread and picked the box of decorations back up. "I don't think I'll do the decorating after all. Maybe I'll just clean the storeroom instead. You know how Doc likes to go in there and read the French side of the canned goods. Calls it his French lesson. Lori can decorate when she's finished cleaning the cabins. Suddenly the thought of getting on a ladder to hang streamers isn't so appealing."

"It don't work that way," murmured Elsie. "That bad luck's brewed now and could catch up with anybody around here—"

***

"Lawrence! You free this afternoon?" Lori had just finished decorating the dining room for the Flanagans and was on the prowl until dinner.

"I have some time. What were you thinking of?"

"Taking the canoe out."

"It's kind of windy—"

"Fiddlesticks! What's a few waves? How can you become a guide if you're still scared of the water?"

"I'm not scared!" Lawrence declared with false bravado. He still couldn't swim very well, and the winds *were* stirring up the lake.

"Good, then if you're feeling brave, you get the canoe. I'll get the paddles."

They had paddled only as far as the end of the dock when Lori reached up and grabbed onto one of the boat anchors.

"Stop! I have a better idea. Want to try gunwale tipping?"

"What's that?"

"We both stand on the gunwale, one at the stern, and one at the bow, facing each other, and rock the canoe. The person who stays standing the longest wins. It'll be fun in these whitecaps . . . way more challenging."

"I don't know . . . doesn't sound like much fun to me—"

"I dare you."

"You really haven't changed much since you were nine, have you? Everything still has to be a competition."

"Of course."

"Okay, then. I accept your stupid dare."

"Wait . . . you *can* swim now, right?"

"I can keep my head above water."

They pulled off their shoes and socks and threw them on the dock. Lori crawled up on the rim like a cat, unperturbed by the rocking and rolling. Lawrence, however, looked like he did not find it as easy. Crouching low, he unsteadily curled his toes around the gunwales of the small aluminum canoe and slowly started to rise. He wasn't even in an upright position before—

Splash. He went tumbling into the lake.

"It's flippin' co-cold!!" he sputtered, surfacing. "I'm not playing this game anymore!" He pulled his soaking frame back up onto the dock and flopped onto his back. He felt around in his pocket. "Darn it . . . I lost my snuff."

Still rocking on the gunwale, Lori smirked. "That's what happens when you can't stay on your feet. Too bad you don't have the superior coordination of a girl."

That goaded Lawrence into action. "Oh man, you're going in, too." He got up, water dripping off his nose and grabbed a paddle. He gave her enough of a nudge with it to send her plunging into the lake, too.

Lori disappeared for a moment, then her head popped up and bobbed on the surface. "Ouch," she cried. "I think I banged my shoulder on the canoe when I fell in."

"Serves you right for laughing at me. Hey, see if you can find my snuff can."

"I don't want to find that disgusting stuff!" But she obligingly stood on the bottom of the lake, the water almost to her neck, feeling around in the muck with her feet. After a few minutes, she gave up. "I think you're going to have to buy a new can, Lawrence. I can't feel anything down here but the odd log and a lot of seaweed. And it's no use diving for it. I can't see a thing because I've turned up the bottom too much. Geez, I probably turned up ten million leeches." Lori shuddered. "Agh, I'm probably covered in them."

Grabbing the edge of the canoe, Lori led it back to shore. As she reached the beach, she placed her right foot on the dry sand, then stopped and stared.

"What is it? You really pick up a bloodsucker?" Lawrence made his way over to see.

A thin red line had appeared from the base of Lori's big toenail all the way to her ankle. As they stared at it in fascination, the red line slowly became thicker, blood oozing. It dripped down the sides of her foot and spilled onto the sand.

Lori looked up at Lawrence's horrified face. "I think I need some Mercurochrome."

"Mercurochrome's not gonna fix that," moaned Lawrence.

***

It took a plane ride into Red Lake and fourteen stitches to fix it.

"If you were more careful, these terrible things wouldn't happen to you." Helen propped a pillow under Lori's foot. She had almost passed out watching the tired-looking doctor at the Red Lake Clinic sew it up. Now, several hours later, they were back at the camp, and Helen still felt shaken.

"More careful? How was I supposed to know there was a broken pop bottle in the water? It was half-buried in the mud."

"How about the not one but *two* nails you buried into the bottom of your foot last year that also required a trip to Red Lake for medical attention? Who walks around a fishing camp with no shoes on?"

"I'm a Pisces . . . Pisces have trouble with their feet."

"Oh, Lord. I don't need any more mumbo jumbo right now. How's your shoulder?"

"My shoulder is fine, just a bit of a bruise. But my foot is killing me now that the freezing has worn off." Lori sighed as she caught sight of the grotesque red, swollen gash laced up with black sutures, painted yellow with iodine just before the doctor wrapped it up with gauze. "You realize I'm marred for life. My foot looks like it belongs to Frankenstein's monster."

Helen shook a couple of 222s out of the bottle and handed them to Lori along with a glass of water. "Take these. Your foot will heal fine. There will barely be a scar . . . that is, if you don't break open your stitches. Please, for one night, just stay put! No tramping down the hill to hang out with those boys. Just stay here and rest. Of all days for you to do this, what with the Flanagans in camp and the party tonight. It's already after five, and I have to fix my hair. Alma will bring you some supper later."

***

How am I supposed to stay put? Lori thought to herself after her mother left. *I spent the morning making wedding bells out of Javex bottles, hanging streamers, and arranging wild roses on the tables for the Flanagans' supper party. I even made boutonnieres for them out of tissue paper. I want to at least see Fritzi and Doc and wish them Happy Anniversary . . . besides, there's gonna be cake!* Gingerly, Lori lifted her foot off the pillow and set it on the floor.

Gosh it hurts! But it's gonna hurt whether I'm in bed or not, so let's see what pants are gonna hide this darn bandage—

***

The Flanagans' celebration party was in full swing by the time Helen finally entered the dining room.

"Oh my gosh, Helen. Al told us all about Lori's accident." The slim, dark-haired woman who approached her could not be called beautiful; her face was too angular, her jaw too strong. Yet there was something dynamically appealing about her. "How is she doing? Is she going to be able to join us? I want to thank her for doing such a lovely job of decorating and making us these lovely boutonnieres." Fritzi feathered the large, gauche paper flower adorning her designer wool suit.

"I'm afraid not. She's resting tonight. She'll be fine by tomorrow, I'm sure, though she won't be wearing a shoe anytime soon."

"I can sympathize. While I've never cut my foot open like that, I have bunions the size of rutabagas. It was all I could do today to get my shoes on."

"I don't know why you don't have those turnips removed." Fritzi's husband Doc joined them, handing them each a Manhattan of his own special recipe.

"I would never do that. My bunions tell me what the weather's going to be like." Fritzi took a sip of her drink, savoured it a moment, then swallowed agreeably.

"Lord, you've been around Elsie too long," said Doc.

"And you've been in the sun too long, Papa. Your face is red, and your makeup is running." She turned to Helen. "My adorable, red-haired, freckled Irish husband has taken to using my foundation as sunblock, with dubious results."

"For God's sake, woman, why don't you buy a better brand of makeup?" he said, rubbing his streaky cheek.

"Why don't you just buy a better hat? I told you to run down to the store and purchase one of those Stork Lake caps."

"And not wear my lucky one? I don't think so."

"That white 'pith' helmet of yours is better suited to hunting elephants than hunting muskies, and it hasn't brought you any luck yet."

"Has too. When you start waving your rod around, casting all over the place, my head is protected."

"You're joking. I never wave my rod around."

"I have the scars to prove it. Cheeky woman . . . I don't know how I've put up with you for thirty years," he said, giving his cherished wife an adoring look.

"Happy Anniversary, Papa," said Fritzi, planting a kiss on his sunburnt, makeup-streaked cheek.

Just then, Lori appeared at the party, wearing thick black eyeliner, a shocking pink sweater, and white bell-bottom jeans. She had tied a silk paisley scarf over her hair and hung a huge cross crafted from springs and copper wire around her neck. Two sponge mops doubled as crutches.

Helen's eyebrows shot up, but before she could say anything, Fritzi motioned her over.

"Lori, it's lovely to see you!"

"Hi, Fritzi! Hello, Doc! Happy Anniversary! How are you?"

"I'm fine, but what's this about you?" asked Doc. "I hear I'm not good enough . . . You're flying out to see other doctors now. Though it's just as well. Us otolaryngologists would faint if we had to sew someone up like a Thanksgiving turkey!"

"I'd say she looks more like a peacock," said Helen. "Last year, I couldn't get her out of her ragged jeans, and this year she looks like a gypsy."

"Nana told me never to dress down, dumb down, or dip down to anyone else's level, ever," said Lori defiantly, carefully lowering herself into a seat.

"God, I loved that woman. She might have been a sensible Scot, but that didn't stop her from wearing crystal beads with her Kodiak boots!" exclaimed Fritzi, who also owned her own style. "I have one more for you, Lori . . . never fuddy-duddy down."

"Something *no one* would accuse you of doing, my darling," interjected Doc.

"What does that mean?" inquired Lori.

"Grow up, grow old because people expect it of you or think you should. Your grandmother certainly didn't. I remember one year, when your cousin Grant and his friend Jack . . . which reminds me, I saw Jack on the dock and invited him up to the party tonight . . . love that kid, he has spunk. Anyways he and Grant thought they'd play a prank on Kay. They took that old bearskin from the card room, draped it over them, then marched over to the bullpen where Kay and Lori were staying. They started grunting and scratching at the window with the bear's claws, thinking they were going to scare this poor old woman. Well Kay knew it was them, but instead of just calling them on it, she came out the door blazing a shotgun. The boys almost peed their pants, thinking they were going to get blasted."

Lori howled. "I remember that night!"

"So never fuddy-duddy down. You can be responsible but keep the fun."

"She's got the fun part nailed. Now if she'd just learn to be responsible," sighed Helen.

***

After every scrap of Elsie's meal had been devoured, Lori excused herself and left the adults to party on. She was back lying in bed reading *The Money Changers* when she heard a "Psssst!" from outside. Upon investigation, she found Dennis, Jeremy, and Lawrence's grinning faces below her open window.

"Come on out! We have something to show you," Lawrence whispered.

"What is it?"

"Just come to the back door."

"Okay, but it better be good. My foot's killing me."

Lori grabbed her "crutches" and hobbled out the back door to where the boys were waiting.

"I don't see anything," she said, confused.

"You have to come to the old lodge to see it," replied Jeremy.

"I can't get down those steep steps with my mops!"

"You don't have to. We'll chair ride you." With that, Dennis and Jeremy linked hands, scooped her up, and carried her down the hill.

When the old lodge was abandoned in favour of the new one, it had been divided into several sections. The dining rooms were sectioned off and made into additional staff quarters. The old kitchen now housed the shore lunch boxes, and the card room had been turned into a storage room—until now. Upon entering, Lori discovered it had been transformed into a rec room.

"Surprise!" cried the boys in unison. The rolls of carpet, fishing nets, toilets, and boxes of miscellaneous spare parts had magically disappeared. The floor was swept and most of the cobwebs removed. Centre stage was the ping-pong table, brought in from outdoors, and a card table where PeepSight, James, Eddie, and Charlie were playing poker.

"What the—"

"And look—" said Dennis, with a mock salute. In the corner, hanging from the beams, was a plush, swinging bamboo chair. "We made a throne, just for you."

"And you guys told me you were all too tired to do anything last night!"

"We were renovating," said Jeremy. "We asked your dad if we could have this space for a staff recreation room. It's no one's cabin, and there are tons of old people around, so your mom should approve."

"You did this for me?" she asked incredulously.

"Sure," answered Dennis. "This way, we can see your funny face even when it rains. Now let's help you up into your throne—"

***

The anniversary party was still in full swing. Al continued pouring cocktails while Helen took turns dancing with Tommy Kawa and his fishing partners. Fritzi, Doc, and Jack, however, were bantering about fishing.

"You've got to use twenty-pound test," insisted Doc.

"Like I'd come to you for piscatorial advice—"

"Piscatorial? Now there's a fictional word if I ever heard one!"

"It pertains to fishing, a fact you would know if you were a true fisherman."

"Now I have to be a Scrabble champion to fish?"

"No, but a little eye-hand coordination wouldn't hurt. Maybe then you wouldn't snarl your line every second cast and catch nothing but lake cabbage because you don't reel in fast enough. Poor James—"

"Nothing but lake cabbage! Listen, woman, who caught lunch for us today?"

"Anyone can catch a walleye in this lake! When's the last time you caught a muskie? And who won the fishing derby today?"

"What kind of a world is it turning out to be when the women are out-fishing the men?" Jack flashed a cheeky grin. Part of his charm was that he was never above baiting a battle.

Fritzi laughed as she took a menthol Virginia Slim out of its package with a hand embellished by a deep orange fire opal ring, vivacious and radiant like her.

"Like the slogan says, we've come a long way, baby." She slipped the cigarette between her lips.

Jack gave a toss of his brown bangs. "At least men are still braver."

"Oh, you think so?" An amused smile lit up Fritzi's face. She turned to Doc. "What do you think, Papa?"

Doc shook his head. "I'm not touching that one."

Fritzi turned back to the younger man. "How are they braver?"

"Well for one thing, we're more daring."

"More likely to take a dare, you mean?"

"Sure, I mean, you can't back down. For a man, that would be cowardly. It's acceptable for a woman."

By now, everyone in the room had stopped what they were doing and were listening.

"So if someone dared you to, say dump me in the lake, you would do it because it would be cowardly to back down?"

"I would have no problem doing it." Jack scanned her lean figure. "Fancy suit and all."

Fritzi did not hesitate for a moment. "I dare you."

Jack glanced over at Doc, who shrugged and replied, "Heh, she's her own woman. Be my guest."

***

Even from the new rec room, Lori and the boys could hear the commotion on the dock. She hopped off her throne. "I want to see what's going on! Let's go."

They arrived in time just to see Jack at the end of the dock, Fritzi in his arms, and the rest of the entourage watching from the shore.

"If I'm going in, so are you," warned Fritzi.

"No problem." With that, Jack jumped into the water.

"My God! Fritzi!" screamed Helen.

Two heads appeared out of the black water. Laughing, Fritzi gave her head a shake, her opal ring flashing in the moonlight. "My boutonniere is ruined . . . and my cigarette went out!" She turned to the head bobbing beside her. "I've got to say this to you, you do have guts!"

Jack spit out a mouthful of water. "Happy Anniversary, Fritzi!"

Lori hobbled over to where her mother was standing on the dock.

"For God's sake, Lori, what are you doing down here?"

"What am I doing down here? Hey, I'm not the one rinsing out my clothes while still wearing them."

Helen looked slightly sheepish. "We're just having a bit of fun is all."

"Admit it, Mom. You guys are just proving you'll never fuddy-duddy down, aren't ya?"

Lori returned the pith helmet to the wall. She had learned that being grown-up didn't mean you had to grow old—not that she had been in any danger of either. She removed a straw hat from the wall—

1976

Two crows entered into a loud conversation outside Lori's bedroom window.

Caw caw.

Caw caw caw.

Back and forth they went. This steady vocalization seemed to have no end. Lori rubbed her eyes, squinted at the clock, then quickly jumped out of bed. She had finally learned that the faster you arose, the less it hurt. Clad only in her red pyjamas, she waded over to her window through the sea of cast-off clothing and threw back the curtain to expose the grand light show of sunrise—the deep cobalt blues of dawn blending into magenta, then tangerine, and finally warming into the full gold of daylight. Every sunrise was different, a never-ending melody where the lyrics kept changing. Lori loved this daily melodramatic birth; it filled her with renewed hope and anticipation.

"What's going to happen today, I wonder?" Lori turned to the rumpled pile sleeping in the next bed. "Hey, Muckakee, time to get up." She slowly picked her way through the debris back to her side of the room and began searching the floor for something to wear.

"Have you seen my whatchamacallit?" she said to the still lifeless form.

A mound of black hair appeared from beneath its covers. "They're beside the thingamajig, Sunisquoi," was the muffled reply.

Lori picked up a piece of wood and tossed it aside.

"No, they're not."

A hand shot out and pulled the covers a little lower to expose the sleepy face of a young woman. "Maybe the whatzit's on top of it."

Lori plucked up several sweaters and found the jeans she was looking for. "You're right. Here they are!"

This summer, Lori shared her work and her bedroom with Liz. The nineteen-year-old from Red Lake fit into the position of friend, roommate, and co-worker like a custom-made moccasin. Unlike her friendship with Lawrence—who this year had decided to stay at his job in the city—this was more like a sisterhood. The two girls had even come up with their own language—a blend of "Stork Lake" and Aboriginal that only the two of them could understand. Only the two of them could understand the inner workings of their bedroom, either—how they could ever find anything among the dirty plates, dried flowers, empty makeup bottles, stacks of magazines, and pop cans. They even had a large collection of stones, their version of pet rocks, which they argued had more personality than the ones sold in novelty stores. Liz had given each rock a nickname. She had given Lori a nickname, too: Sunisquoi because of her lifelong fascination and horror with the bloodsucker. In return, Lori called her Muckakee, meaning frog, since she blinked every time she swallowed.

Liz finally sat up, stretched her arms above her head, then inhaled deeply. "Hmm . . . I smell bacon!"

"Which means Elsie has already started making breakfast! We better get a move on."

The girls quickly dug for the rest of their clothes, got dressed, and emerged from their lair.

"Morning, Albert!" greeted Lori as she began setting up the tables. Albert nodded and tried to smile through his cough. "Oh yeah, morning to you, too, Phil," she kidded.

Albert was always the first one up and at the table, followed quickly by Phil. The two of them would sit there, working on the dregs of yesterday's coffee while a fresh pot was being brewed. Albert always sat at the head of the table, his coffee cup and ashtray in front of him. As soon as he lit his first cigarette, he would start coughing. He had always coughed, but lately it was much worse. He'd cough and cough—all the air exiting out, nothing coming back in, his face purple. Albert would then wheeze a bit, shake his head, and eventually some air would get through. He'd take another drag of his cigarette, his colouring would return to normal, and then he and Phil would talk.

***

After Phil had graduated from high school, Al had sat down with his son.

"So what do you want to do now?"

"Run the camp, of course!"

"What about university?"

"I don't need university. You never went to university, and you've done okay."

"It's different now—"

"Maybe for some jobs but not for me. Is university going to teach me where the fish are hiding? How to keep staff in camp when the Red River Ex is going on? My education is taking place right here, right now. No book can teach you how to run a camp. Only you and Albert can do that."

"It's a hard life," said his dad.

"I don't care. It's all I've ever wanted to do."

"All right," conceded Al. "But if you think you are just going to step into management, you've got another thing coming. There will be no shortcuts. You're going to earn your way, learning every facet of this business from the ground up. You've still got a lot to learn. You can start by apprenticing under Albert."

"But I've been working under Albert all my life! What more can he teach me?"

Al shook his head. "If you ever *think* you know it all, then you don't. You will never have a greater teacher than Albert. You watch him and take time to ask questions. If you ever know even one-tenth of what he knows, then maybe, someday, you'll be ready to run the place."

So now, every morning, Phil met up with Albert in this classroom in the bush. They would spend the few minutes they had alone discussing the day before the rest of the guides came in for breakfast. However, these morning meetings had not yet taught Phil the most important lesson Albert was trying to teach.

***

"Geez, I'm wiped this morning," said Kris in his high, squeaky voice. He pulled off his Jughead hat, exposing a thatch of untameable, frizzy brown hair. It was now 6:30 a.m., and the rest of the guides were coming in for breakfast. "I don't know how you get up so damn early after a late night of cards."

"It's the bacon," answered Phil. "I know if I come in early, I can steal an extra five or six pieces while Elsie's frying it up."

"That'll do it," agreed Kris as he slid into the seat next to Phil and poured himself a cup of coffee. "Bacon's important, being one of our main food groups."

He wasn't kidding; Phil and Kris had decided that summer that breakfast was going to be the only meal they would eat. The rest of the day, they would live on Hot Rods and Heineken.

Phil figured that if he were truly going to learn from the ground up, he would have to return to the bottom, so he moved out of his ivory tower up on the hill and back down to the staff quarters, which had no bathrooms and no running water. Here, like Lori, he had to share accommodations for the first time with his bunkmate, Kris. Also, like Lori and Liz, Phil and his new roomie quickly became great friends. Kris hailed from Kenora and was about the same age as Phil. He was a collected soul who was enjoying spending his summer at Stork, even though he had yet to make any money—his store tab was always larger than his paycheque. That didn't matter. Life here was great. They raced the Ski-Doo down the grassy slope, barely staying out of the drink. They shot clay pigeons in the backfield and cast lines off the dock. And because of their Hot Rod and Heineken diet, they never had to eat a vegetable.

Opening the door to Phil and Kris's cabin was like opening a photo album into the past. It was a messy vision in sepia: the logs here were old, darkened to a mahogany, and bare yellow light bulbs washed the cabins in a golden glow. The room was, if possible, even messier than the girls'; unmade beds were crumpled with greying sheets, dead flies stuck to cardboard traps hanging from the ceiling. Pin-ups adorned the walls, old beer bottles littered the tables, cigarette butts overflowed in the ashtrays. None of this mattered— for the first time, they were on their own, and it felt great. The boys grew beards and grew brave but had yet to grow up.

***

Over breakfast, Albert studied the men around the table, then lifted a heavily calloused finger, stained yellow with nicotine. Pointing, he barked, "You, you, you, and you and you . . . with me today."

The "chosen" knew what that meant. When Albert was in "shantyman drive," he was wont to engage in any diversions. It would mean a day in the bush of work—hard, nonstop work—harvesting trees. Albert did all the falling, limbing, and bucking, which meant he cut the trees down, limbed them, and cut them into saw length. All he asked the guys to do was peel them. The trick was you had to keep up with him, and it would take all five men to do it.

Albert stood up. "Charlie and Peepsight, take one boat. Phil and Kris, take another. Eddie, you're with me." He pointed to his watch. "All you, be at the cutting site in exactly half an hour." With those parting words, he left, the three older men immediately following behind. If they hurried, they might just make the thirty-minute deadline.

***

Phil, however, leaned back in his chair, his arms crossed behind his head. "Geez, I've been up since the crack of dawn. I need another cup of coffee before I can go work my ass off. Elsie! Is there any bacon left over?"

Kris lit another cigarette. "So what do you think . . . Trans Am or Camaro?"

By the time the two boys finished their bacon and their car debate and finally moseyed on down to the dock, Albert and the others had already left.

The morning was cool and clear, each log cabin sending off a stream of sweet-smelling smoke. A thick mist hovered over the clear mirror lake, shrouding the islands in a mystical veil.

Phil and Kris stood and chatted on the dock, watching the fog burn off the lake by the fingers of the sun and the islands reappear as if by magic. One by one, the boats and planes all left until there was only Phil and Kris left.

"Well, think we should go to the worksite?" asked Phil.

"Okay, but I'm driving the boat. I don't trust your driving."

"What do you mean? I'm a great driver. You ate my dust in our drag race on the lake last night!"

"You *were* beating me until you threw your arms up in victory and forgot to steer. Lucky thing that log you hit slowed you down, or your boat would have ended up in the fish house."

"Yeah, okay, you can drive," conceded Phil. "I don't want to get to work too fast anyways."

***

With all the guests gone fishing, the day really began. The calm was over—you could hear the tractor, the chain saws, the outboards, the lawn mowers, the clothes washer, the dishwasher. The girls scrubbed, rubbed, swept, lathered, mopped, and brushed their way through the morning. Finally it was time for a coffee break. Lori grabbed her book and a cup of coffee and sat down. Jeremy and Dennis soon joined her.

"How come you guys got out of Albert's log detail?" asked Lori.

"I'm the only one besides Albert who can keep the tractor running," quipped Dennis, stirring a spoon briskly around in his mug.

"And I was supposed to be guiding Dr. Solomon, but he hasn't shown up yet. Maybe this time he really did get lost flying up here," said Jeremy.

"Dr. Solomon? Poor you!" Lori took a sip of her coffee.

"Oh, I have no problem with him. I just pretend I don't speak English, so I don't have to do anything he asks."

"Good one!" Lori laughed then sat up as Liz approached. "What happened to you? I thought you were right behind me."

"I just had to change my shirt."

"You had one speck on it."

"One speck too many. You *know* I can't handle that. My OCD kicks in."

"OCD? Girl, have you seen our room?"

Liz shrugged. "It is what it is."

"So, did you find out?" she questioned Lori.

"Sure did."

"What are you guys talking about?" asked Jeremy.

"She woke me up in the middle of the night because she had a nightmare," complained Liz, pushing her glasses back up the bridge of her nose. "Me, I'm in the middle of a *groovy* dream, ya know? I was with this cool dude, and we were just about kiss, so I close my eyes, and when I open them, what do I see? Not my handsome stud, but some white *iskwew* hanging over me!"

"Well it was scary at the time," Lori shuddered. "I was surrounded by dead people. Ugh! I was trying to walk around their bodies, but there was so many of them . . . all in different stages of decay. It really freaked me out. I want to know what it all meant, so I looked it up in here." She pointed to the dream interpretation book she was holding.

"You don't really believe this stuff, do you?" asked Dennis, amazed.

"Of course I do . . . I've grown up with Elsie, haven't I?"

"Of course she does," reiterated Liz. "You should see the rest of the books she has. Palmistry, witchcraft, astrology, numerology . . . it's quite a scene. What did the dream mean?"

Lori flipped through the pages. "It says here that dreaming about dead people is good luck."

Dennis shook his head. "You guys are nuts."

"I've had loads of dream interpretations come true! Just last week, I dreamed I was picking rhubarb—"

"Who the hell dreams of a rhubarb plant?"

"I do! Anyways the book said that meant 'pleasant entertainment would occupy my time for a while.' Right after that, Liz's mother sent her a bunch of beads, and one of the guests left me three Moody Blues cassettes, so for the past week, Liz and I have been listening to new music while beading cool earrings and headbands."

"That's just coincidence. Moms send stuff all the time, and guests leave stuff all the time."

Jeremy stroked his face. "Wait a minute. Why don't we put it to the test? How about we play poker tonight? It's the old guys' turn to use the rec room though. We'd have to play at our cabin."

Lori hesitated for a moment and then proclaimed, "You're on!"

"But . . . the Happy Hooker Kebogawbo—"

"What's the Happy Hooker?" asked Dennis.

"Helen," replied Liz.

"Helen's called the Happy Hooker?" Dennis was incredulous.

"Because she's hooking rugs, silly! Get your mind out of the gutter! I've given nicknames to everyone here. Given names are far too generic."

Fascinated, Dennis asked, "Really? What are some of the other nicknames?"

"Al's the Great White Chief. That's self-explanatory. And, Phil is Weeble, 'cause no matter how drunk he is, he wobbles, but he don't fall down!"

"Can we get back to the poker game?" questioned Jeremy. "So what is it about your mom, Lori?"

"It's just that my mom still freaks out when we come to your cabin after work. God, you'd think we were downing mickeys or smoking up, the way she freaks out about it. She's actually forbidden us to visit you guys unless we are in the rec room. Poor Liz. She gets in trouble, too, even though she's nineteen and should be able to do what she wants. It's like she casts her net out, and everyone within swimming distance of me gets caught. It's not fair. God, I can hardly wait until I'm eighteen, then she won't be able to tell me who to see and when to come home! I'll do as I like! Three more years. It seems so far away."

"No problem," said Jeremy. "We'll just play another night."

Lori gazed around the table at Dennis, Jeremy, and Liz. They never treated her like she was a little girl. Why couldn't her mother do that?

***

Kris and Phil finally arrived at the job site but didn't feel much like working. It was turning into a beautiful day with a gentle breeze blowing off the lake—much too nice a day to break a sweat. So while Albert and Eddie and Charlie and Peepsight cut, scraped, peeled, and dragged tree after tree, the boys told jokes and fooled around; Kris lit his sixth cigarette, Phil packed his second plug of chewing tobacco. They pushed each other into the soft moss, arm-wrestled, and sat on rocks and watched the water and morning drift by.

Finally, Kris looked at his watch. "Oh my God . . . it's 11:30 already!"

"Really!" exclaimed Phil. "Well then, it's time for lunch."

After chewing on a box of Hot Rods and guzzling a six-pack of Coke, the boys settled under the speckled canopy of spruce.

"God, it's hot," said Kris. "A Heineken would taste great just about now."

"Sure would," lamented Phil. "If only we didn't have to work today."

The two boys continued to chat about girls, eight-track tapes, and beer until the constant hum of chainsaws and axes in the background lulled them to sleep.

***

After lunch, Lori and Liz headed back to their room.

"I hope you two are planning to clean up that pigsty of a bedroom!" called Helen after them.

The girls groaned. After washing endless dishes, scrubbing floors, making beds, and folding laundry, who wanted to clean their own room? The couple hours off in the afternoon was for fun, not more spit and polishing.

"I guess we should pick up a little," said Liz.

But after ten minutes of half-hearted cleaning, the room didn't look any different.

"I give up," sighed Lori. "It's a gorgeous day, and we're wasting it inside. "Do you want to take a canoe out? There might be a nice breeze between the islands."

"Nah, feeling too lazy."

"Just head to the dock, have a swim to cool off, then chill?"

"Better."

"Okay, I'll grab some towels and my sketchbook, and we'll blow this joint!"

There wasn't a cloud in the robin's egg blue sky, and it was now so hot the invisible cicada bugs were shrilling. They strolled down to the lake, Lori bareheaded so that her golden hair would turn lighter and her face darker, while Liz wore a wide-brimmed straw hat so that her dark hair would stay darker and her face lighter.

After a refreshing dip, the girls plunked down in the seats of one of the docked boats to dry off.

"You're adorned." Lori picked a couple of fish flies off Liz's modest swim attire, which consisted of a T-shirt and cut-off blue jean shorts.

"They don't eat, you know. They don't have a mouth. That's why they only live a couple of days."

"Really?" Lori had seen thousands of the bugs in her lifetime— stepped on thousands of their carcasses that lined the beach a few weeks each year. But she had never actually looked at one. She studied the fish fly closely, its shiny, fragile body, long delicate tail flukes, and its big globular eyes. Such a sad, gentle creature. She gently picked it up by its gossamer wings and thrust it into the wind. "Go, enjoy your few hours of life."

"And I'm going to enjoy the next few hours of my life and finish the song I'm working on." Liz picked up the guitar she had brought with her and began to play, meshing together a melody with words, aptly expressing every emotion she encountered in her life.

Meanwhile, Lori listened blissfully to the soft swish of the waves on the shore blending with the melodic guitar, breathed deeply of the pine-scented fragrance wafting from the towering trees, and felt the tender ruffle of wind on her skin. It just didn't get any better than this!

She picked up her sketchbook, flipped it open to an empty page, then leaned back. Finding it easiest to express herself in shades of black and white, she used a graphite pencil to line draw. Hands were often the subject because of the stories they could tell. If the eyes were the windows to the soul, then the hands brought their soul to life. Were they long and slender, short and stubby? Soft and manicured, or calloused and imbedded with grease? Were the joints swollen and stiff, the skin spotted from a lifetime of living? Were they posed, as if talking, folded in introspect, reaching out for help, clenched in anger, open in friendship?

Lori pulled out a pencil and let the charcoal lines spill down the page, still not sure just who's hands they would become.

***

Five o'clock came. Charlie, Eddie, and Peepsight had busted their butts all day long, managing to complete all thirty of their logs. Phil and Kris, on the other hand, had peeled only three. The sweat-soaked and exhausted men quietly packed up their bags, and without a word, headed back to camp. Soon, only Albert and the two boys were left at the worksite.

Albert placed his chainsaw in the bottom of his boat and approached them. "Not a very productive day, eh, boys?"

Phil laughed. "What do you mean?"

"You smart-ass kids. You didn't get no damn work done today. Well you're gonna be finishing the rest of them logs."

"Yeah, yeah, okay, whatever. We'll come back tomorrow and do them." Phil stood up from under the tree where he had been lounging, stretched his arms out in the air, then spit his plug of tobacco into the water. "Come on, Kris. Let's get going. Time for a beer."

"I don't think so." Albert's steely stare pinned Phil to where he stood. "You're staying here, in the bush, and finishing peeling them logs. Right now."

"What? Geez, there's like fifteen logs there!"

Albert dropped his cigarette and ground it out with the toe of his boot. "If you had been working instead of screwing around and playing all day, you would have had your logs done like the other guys. So you're gonna finish the lot."

Kris's eyes grew big. "That's going to take hours! We won't finish till, like, ten o'clock!"

"Yeah. And then you're gonna skid all them logs into the water. Not just your logs, but *all* the logs. Then you're gonna raft them and tow them home."

The two boys stood there, mouths gaping, as Albert hopped into his boat and took off.

Kris turned to Phil. "Weeble, we're not going to get home until, like, really, really late."

Phil groaned. "Or really, really early . . . tomorrow!"

The boys had never worked so fast in their whole lives. Daylight gold dripped into the final crimson movement of sunset as they painstakingly scraped away the bark and inner layer next to the wood from each log with flat shovels. Finally they rolled the completed logs into the water and built a boom by lashing them together end to end with chains. The curtain of night had long fallen on the Stork Lake symphony before they were ready to raft back to the mill.

They slowly trolled along, logs in tow. A slight breeze blew in their favour, encouraging the raft to float home. The pinpricks of a thousand stars, so clear to see against the black velvet sky, shone like tiny nightlights. The moon hung over the lake, huge and orange. Slowly it rose, getting smaller and brighter, changing colour to silvery white. Finally it was high and round, sending a cascade of silver through the sky, spilling a path of molten silver through the rippling dark water, lighting their way.

Stiff with the tension of their muscles, the boys' aching arms and backs cried for bed while their mouths were unusually silent. The black outline of fir trees against the sky seemed to roll on forever before the lights of civilization glittered out of the darkness. They puttered along the back bay behind the camp to the sawmill and tied the logs up to the shore. As they trudged up from the mill and down the hill, Kris finally spoke: "Man, we did it. The old man is going to be really, really, happy."

***

Supper was over; the kitchen cleaned and closed for the night, and the girls had returned to their room. Lori held up her sketchbook for Liz to see. The hands she had drawn that afternoon were of a female, with Lori's telltale ring on the pinky finger. They were holding a straight flush. "What do you think?"

"I think I better rustle up some bucks for the poker game! What about your mom, though?"

"We'll sneak out. What she doesn't know won't hurt her . . . or us."

"Okay. But you know, she checks every door in this place after the last of the guests leave. She seems to think bears know how to turn doorknobs. She'll lock us out, and we'll never get back in."

"She doesn't check the back door by the ice machine. No one ever uses it, so it's always locked. We could leave that one unlocked . . . even a little open. And it's far enough away from her room that she won't hear us come in, no matter what time it is."

The girls waited half an hour until they heard Helen's door close.

"Do you think it's safe?"

"Should be. But just in case, let's stuff thingamajigs in you-know-whats." Lori reached under her bed and pulled out four more pillows. "I grabbed these during supper . . . thought they may come in handy."

"You did think of everything, didn't you?"

The girls moulded the pillows into lifelike forms under their covers, then very quietly crept out of their room, tiptoed through the storeroom, and out the door.

***

Lori had just won her fourth straight pot. She felt relaxed and happy as she chewed on the end of an unlit wine-tipped Colt. Everything was going her way.

"Damn, you *are* having good luck tonight," complained Dennis.

"I am, aren't I?" She smirked back. "See, my book was right."

"Just deal. What's the game?"

"Straight poker, nothing wild," she said, dealing the cards.

Liz scrutinized her hand. "I'm in."

Jeremy threw in his chips. "Me, too."

Dennis glanced around the table then back down at his cards. "I raise ya."

The pot continued to grow till there was a nice little pile of chips in the middle of the table.

Finally, Jeremy said, "Someone has to say it. I call. What have you got?"

Suddenly there was a sharp rap at the door.

"*Lori?* LOOORRI, where are yooou?"

"Oh, Kikawi," breathed Liz.

Helen didn't wait to be invited in. She flung open the door with a vengeance and stood in the doorway. In the dully lit room, her face gleamed from night cream, her fluorescent caftan shimmered; her anger outshone both.

"What do you think you're doing?"

No one moved or spoke.

"I asked you, what do you think you are doing down here in these boys' cabin?"

Lori finally spoke up. "I'm playing poker, *and* I'm winning!"

"You girls, get back up to your room!"

Liz immediately stood up, but Lori remained seated. Her pride was already hurt; there was no way she was going to give her mother the satisfaction of running back up to the lodge with her tail between her legs.

"I want to finish this hand."

The room went deadly quiet.

"I . . . said . . . get . . . back . . . to . . . your . . . room." This quiet tone was deadlier than the shrieking.

Lori slowly stood up. "Count my chips for me, Dennis," she said with false bravado. With a toss of her head, she walked to the door with as much finesse as she could muster and stepped out with an air of belligerent defensiveness.

***

As Lori and Liz disappeared into the dark abyss, the rest of the guys breathed a sigh of relief. "Wow, that's one scary momma!"

Dennis turned Lori's cards over. "Look at that. Straight flush, queen high. Would've beat me. She sure was having good luck."

Jeremy shook his head. "*Was* is the operative word. I think it just ran out."

***

Helen's voice pierced the darkness. "I'm just fit to be tied. Honestly, I don't know what to do with you. You seem to take great joy in worrying me sick. This newest stunt . . . stuffing your beds. What has gotten into your head? Do I have to lock you in your room?"

Lori stopped and whipped around. "Well if you weren't so unreasonable, I wouldn't *have* to stuff my bed."

"You are a fifteen-year-old girl! It's the middle of the night, and you are still out roving around guide cabins. I am not unreasonable!"

"I work every night till 9:00 or 9:30 . . . When am I supposed to go out?"

"Don't be so melodramatic. You can go out. You used to enjoy a boat ride with Alma and Andy. You should still be doing things like that."

"Maybe they don't want me hanging around them every night. You don't."

"Don't get smart with me." Helen's voice had that warning note in it.

"Why don't you want me visiting down here? What do you think is going to happen to me?"

Helen went ballistic. "You don't understand! They are too old for you to hang around with. I'm telling you this for your own good."

"No, it's for *your* own good! What else am I supposed to do at night after working twelve hours? Go to my room? No wonder I'm a recluse!"

"Stop that right now."

"Stop what? Telling you how I feel?"

It was at the moment that Phil and Kris, on the way to their cabin, crossed their path.

"Mom? What are you doing here at this time of night?"

Helen was incredulous. "What am I doing here? *What am I doing here*? I see two young girls here that should be asleep. I see two young boys here that should be asleep, and you ask what I'm doing here? I want all of you in your beds this instant!"

"But—" Phil tried to explain why they were out so late.

"I said . . . *in bed*!"

The kids instantly scattered.

***

Too tired for Heineken and Hot Rods, even too tired to even undress, the boys simply pulled their boots off and fell into bed.

"God, doesn't bed feel the best?" said Phil. "I'm gonna sleep really, really late tomorrow."

***

Up at the lodge, Lori was unstuffing her bed. "Liz, you wouldn't believe it. I had another great poker hand . . . I wasn't ready for bed! You know, we will be going down to the guys' cabin to play poker again, don't you?"

"I know, Sunisquoi. I know."

***

There was a loud rapping on Phil and Kris's door.

"Breakfast! Let's go!" yelled Albert.

Phil ripped open his sandpaper eyes. "No, no, no. We just got home a couple of hours ago!"

The door jerked open, and Albert's short, stocky frame filled the doorway. "Yeah, well, you should have thought of that yesterday. Get your butts out of bed! We have to cut more logs today."

"I couldn't even fall out of this bed right now," cried Kris.

"You're getting up if I have to pull you out with a peavey!"

"Albert, you can't be serious!" said Phil.

"Someone's gotta be serious. You wanna run this camp someday? Then you gotta learn to do a LOT more stuff around here. And you gotta be responsible. Stop slacking off and thinking this is all just a big joke. Someday I won't be here to bail you out."

"Ah, Albert," said Phil as he slid out of bed. "You'll always be here to tell us when we've screwed up."

Lori replaced the hat on the wall then picked up Albert's favourite hunting cap. At eighteen, kids think everyone will be around forever—

1977

Al approached the table with a bottle of Adams Private Stock Canadian Rye Whiskey in his hand. He cracked open the seal and, in true Vanasse tradition, threw the cap away.

"We won't be needing that anymore."

"Usually I drink bourbon, but tonight"—John Batten held out his glass—"tonight, I'm drinking Albert's drink."

"Here here." Helen held out her glass. "Fill me up, Al."

The lodge was quiet on this warm August evening. The empty kitchen was washed and swept out for the night; only the scent of supper still clung in the air. In the dining room, the windows blackened with night reflected just a few faces sitting around one of the knotty pine tables.

John turned to the slim, grey-haired man seated on his right. "It's great to see you, Frank. I've missed you around here these past few years. Though I think Al shouldn't be working you so hard . . . I saw you fixing a doorstep earlier. He should be treating you like a guest!"

At seventy-seven, Al's dad was frailer looking—but as feisty as ever. "I've been twittering these few fingers I have left for too long now. An old bird like me needs to feel useful to feel alive. Nope, it's great to get up here for a few weeks, do a little work, do a little fishing, visit the grandkids. Now this young lady here"—Frank grinned at Elsie—"she's my inspiration. If she can keep working fourteen-hour days, well, I should be able to manage to nail a board or two."

"You got that right!" bellowed John. "What the hell potion do you stir up in that kitchen of yours that keeps you going? You haven't aged in the last twenty years!"

Elsie gave a little giggle. Time had stood still for this short mother of nine, grandmother and great-grandmother to countless more. Her hair was just starting to turn a bit grey, her eyes still twinkled, her smile was as bright as ever.

"It's the booze." She laughed as Al poured her out a shot. "The alcohol has preserved me."

"Well, I'm all for preservation! Everyone got a drink now?" asked Al. All heads shook in agreement. "Then a toast . . . Here's to you, Albert."

They clinked glasses. "To Albert!"

But Albert wasn't really there—he had died the winter before.

John sighed. "Stalwart Albert . . . I still can't believe it. We were here last year, and he was running around giving orders. He seemed like the same old Albert. We didn't even realize he was sick."

"He didn't want any pity," replied Al, "and he didn't want to just curl up in a corner. That wasn't his style. No, just like you, Dad, and you, Elsie, Albert wanted to keep working, keep living, right to the end. He knew it was his last summer. It was like he was trying to settle his affairs, finish up his work. He never worked so hard to complete all his projects, to teach Phil and Dennis all his little tricks on how to keep the place running. Yet none of us caught on. I guess we didn't want to. You never want to think the best employee you've ever had, the best *friend* you've ever had, is ever going to leave you."

"I never met anyone else like him," John stated simply. These few words spoke volumes. The tall, vigorous man was no novice himself when it came to mechanics. His father had developed the first twin disc clutch for farm tractors, and when John took it over some years later, he expanded it internationally by manufacturing clutches for multi-million-dollar ships. John was a man of supreme confidence and throwaway ease, a superb pilot and sportsman, and yet, he had been in awe of Albert. "Elsie, I knew you and Albert for how long? Twenty-five years? Longer?" questioned John. "I've been hunting and fishing these waters long before even you bought the place, Al. Hell, half of the bays, creeks, and falls within twenty miles are named after me or one of my Twin Disc crew, and Albert was with us every step of the way. I learned more about mechanics, men, and wildlife from him than from anyone else in my life. How the hell do you replace someone like that?"

"You don't," replied Al. "That five-foot-five man wore the biggest shoes of anyone I've ever known. No one can fill them. It takes three men just to try and do what he did. I have a carpenter, a head guide, and a mechanic. They are all great, hardworking guys. Dennis apprenticed under Albert, so he knows a lot of his tricks, but he's still no Albert. None of them are."

"What about Roger? Doesn't he have his dad's wizardry with machines?"

"He's got himself a job and a wife in town," answered Elsie. "Besides, he's not inclined the same way as his dad. One of the best guides there is, but he don't care about building or fixing things. Roger's a charmer, and you can't charm a machine."

"I wouldn't say that. Albert could!" Al shook his head in disagreement. "I'll never forget one morning, maybe eight years ago. The guests had been playing poker late, and it was near two before I could get to sleep. Wasn't two hours before I was awakened by a noise, when I got out of bed and peered out my window. I couldn't believe my eyes! The whole Giddings & Lewis Party were up, running around in their pyjamas, or less—"

The Sawmill

Of all the machinery Albert coaxed, begged, and breathed life into, the sawmill was his greatest source of pride. He had designed it, located various spare parts for the components, then assembled it. The heart of the sawmill was a 1928 four-cylinder Star motor. This engine had powered the Star Four automobile, and after its passenger-carrying days were over, Albert had outfitted it to run the mill, which it did, admirably, for many years.

This homebuilt sawmill in the bush was an endless source of fascination for many of the guests, with some of the greatest ovations and accolades coming from the engineers of Giddings & Lewis. As the fourth-largest producer of high precision machine tools in the world, they appreciated just what Albert had accomplished. Every year, when Giddings & Lewis were in camp, their entertainment after dinner was to head to the sawmill for a demonstration. Albert would cut a couple of pine boards and receive a big cheer. This year, however, to their great disappointment, there was no show.

"What seems to be the problem, Albert?" Honore Hubbard and Lee Mitchell, two of G&L's top engineers, had made their way down to the mill to see why Albert's masterpiece wasn't running.

"The Star motor has been acting up for weeks. I get it started, then it stops. I get it started up again, and it stops again. It gets off time and misses. It's frustrating, but I kept hoping it would last till fall when I could take it apart and fix it. Today, though, it just quit dead."

"What do you believe the problem is?"

"The worm gear's plum worn out."

The engine was outfitted with worm gears, which meant a "worm" in the shape of a screw meshed with the gear, which was the shape of a toothed wheel. The wheel part was made of steel, and the worm part was made of brass. The brass worm had worn out first, so it could no longer drive the wheel. There was nothing but lines left, which left no gear at all.

"Geez, sorry to hear that," said Lee.

Albert scratched his head. "It's a bother all right, having to make a new part."

"*Make* it?" Honore's tone was incredulous.

"You can't order parts for a defunct 1928 car engine, so's I have to make it."

Both Honore and Lee shook their heads.

"Albert," said Lee, "I like you and respect you too much to see you waste your time. Our company provides precision tools to manufacturers in over two hundred industries, including airline, automotive, and agricultural. We have the best engineers working in one of the most modern and sophisticated plants in the whole U.S., and I'm telling you right now, *we* couldn't make this gear in our shop. If we can't, nobody in this world can. This is going to set you back a lot of time and money."

Albert disagreed. "Can't afford much downtime and don't have any money. I have to get this mill going in one or two days, max. We have a cabin to finish before fall."

Lee answered, "I don't think you're going to be milling any logs any time soon. Not unless you get a new motor in here on the next plane."

"Like I said, the camp can't afford a new motor."

"Then you won't be milling logs. Look, Albert, we know you can work miracles. This sawmill here is proof of that. But there is a fine line between genius and insanity. You're talking about crossing it. There's just no way to replace that gear."

A loud whine invaded the silence and woke the whole camp. It was not yet 4:00 a.m. Honore and Lee—and the entire Giddings & Lewis crew—climbed out of their cabins into the grey pre-dawn in their undies and shorts and whatever else they slept in to see what the noise was all about. Hair tousled, feet bare in the dew-covered grass, they walked the short path down from their cabin to the sawmill. Albert, with a grin and a cigarette on his lips, had that sawmill fired up and was slicing through a log like it was butter.

"I can't believe this thing is running!" cried an astonished Lee. "You must have had another gear kicking around, Albert."

"Ah, yeah, sure I have another gear. I made it!"

No one believed him.

"You guys get dressed, then meet me in the lodge for coffee. I'll tell you how I did it."

Ten minutes later, the engineers were decent and assembled as Albert had requested.

"Okay, Albert," Lee started. "For the sake of argument, say you did make it. How'd you do it?"

"Well it was the brass gear that was worn out. So I had to find a new piece of brass. If you hadn't noticed, stores are as scarce as hen's teeth 'round here, so I couldn't buy a new piece. When you work at a fly-in camp, you don't throw nothin' out. Everything can be made into something. We pile all of this junk in a big heap back in the bush, called the hardware store. Amazing place. You can find almost anything you need there. And I did. I found a big old brass faucet, just the right size."

"Come on, a faucet? How can you make a gear from a faucet?" chided Honore.

"I'm telling you how. I first cut it down by hand until I got it the shape of a gear. Then came the hard part. I had to create the spiral. That did get me thinking for a minute. How would I do that? Like every gear, it tapered. I didn't have no engineer's drawings of the danged thing."

"Exactly. That's why we couldn't do it in our shop. It's impossible."

"Hard, but not impossible," said Albert. That's when I came up with an idea. I took a real flex hacksaw blade because it could make that wave in the gear—I could flow it through. I started off soft, would get a groove going, and the blade would follow it. It took hours . . . and a lot of patience. Turn it, turn it, turn it, then do the next one."

"My God, that's a lot of work! Didn't your arms get sore?"

"Nah." Albert raised an arm that, while short, was as strong as a troll's.

"How'd you know the pattern?" inquired Lee.

"I had the old gear on a shaft beside me. I could just make out the faint lines on it where the spiral used to be. It gave me the curves. Then I used a file to smooth it out."

"You created a worm gear with no pattern and no proper tools? Just a hacksaw and a file?"

"Took me six hours to carve, but I did it," said Albert proudly.

"Albert, we're all engineers, and we told you you couldn't do it. What possessed you to try?" asked Lee.

"Because you told me I couldn't do it!"

***

"That's all you had to say to Albert," said Al. "The minute you said he couldn't do it, he'd do it. He'd *kill* himself to do it. He didn't care if it was for nothing. He just wanted to prove the point. There was no such thing as no way. And that damn sawmill's been running like a clock ever since!"

"And because of that sawmill, it feels like he's still right here with us—" continued John, waving his hands in the air. "Look around . . . this room is bathed in his visions."

Everyone there did feel his presence—in every multifaceted log, every floorboard, every rafter—everything in the room, painstakingly created by him out of the land he loved. And in the centre of it all, his polished tree, rooted yet stretching toward the sky, symbolized everything he had stood for: wisdom, strength, endurance, *life*.

"Even the sounds around here . . . the tractors, the outboards, the chainsaws . . . all remind me of Albert," said Frank. "And especially the generators. He spent a lot of time making them purr."

"Or just plain making *them*," added Helen. "Because of him, I could finally run my hair dryer, though I also have to thank Elsie for that."

"Oh? How so?" asked Elsie.

"Well, in your own way, you helped him build that generator, didn't you?"

The Generator

"Al, we need a new generator. You're planning two more cabins and a new laundry room. That means more people, more lighting, more appliances, more equipment. That's more power than I can squeeze out of the Witte."

Al didn't hesitate. He trusted Albert. "Then we better start looking for one."

Albert and Al poured over the mail-order catalogues, looking for a new diesel generator. They were all too expensive.

"What are we going to do?"

Albert thought a moment. "Let's contact military surplus. They usually have damn good machines built better than civilian generators. I bet we could pick up a used one pretty cheap."

Sure enough, they had just what they were looking for.

"Albert, this one is a 12-kilowatt with a Perkins engine. Hear they're pretty good," said Al.

"Yup. Should do the job."

"Not a bad price either."

"No, not bad at all."

They soon found out why. When it came a few weeks later, it came in a crate—in too many pieces to count.

Albert stared at the jigsaw puzzle in front of them, then at Al. "Some assembly required?"

"Gawd! What are we going to do?"

"Put it together."

"But Albert—"

"But what? Is there a manual?"

"Yes, but—"

"Okay, then."

Albert walked away. Al didn't understand. How could a manual help? Albert had never worked on a diesel engine before. And, more importantly, Albert couldn't read.

Every night, after a full day of guiding, fixing every and any piece of broken-down, worn-out machinery, repairing doors and windows, or creating new ones, running the sawmill, and keeping the Witte going, Albert headed to his tiny one-room cabin, took off his workboots and socks, and sat back on his bed in his undershirt. Elsie, who had spent the last sixteen hours cooking and cleaning, would sit beside him. Under the light of a bare bulb, she would open the manual, and in her scratchy voice, she would read to Albert, line by line, page by page, how to put the generator together. Albert would sit there and concentrate, memorizing everything she said— every part and its place, drawing schematics in his head.

The next day, when he could etch out a little spare time, he would enter that generator shack. With the diagram he had drawn in his mind, he put a little more of it together. If he got stuck, he would hand Elsie the manual, and she would read that part over to him during their coffee break. Eventually the pieces were put together. By the end of July, it ran the camp like clockwork.

"Just think how much easier it would have been if you could have read the manual yourself," said Al, once it was all put together.

"Wouldn't have been easier at all."

"How can you say that?"

"If I could read, that would mean I'd gotten a book-learning education. That kind of education would have held me back. I'd have known what I was doing was impossible, so I wouldn't have even tried. Where'd we be then?"

***

Al took a sip of his drink, then lowered his glass. "I couldn't argue with the wisdom of that statement."

"So, Elsie, you became an expert on diesel generators, too?" kidded Frank.

"Oh, I don't think so. It was all Greek to me!"

"Would be Greek to most people. But Albert . . . put him in a workshop, and he could repair, improve, or build anything you needed. He prodded conventional wisdom at every turn, rediscovered the old way of doing it, and redefined it in new ways."

"Talking about redefining the way things are done . . . It reminds me about another story about Albert and monofilament line," said Frank.

"Don't try to tell me Albert invented that!" retorted John.

"No, actually as wonderful an invention as it was, Albert hated it."

"Why's that?" John was confused. "I love monofilament line. It doesn't rot in the water like other lines used to. Christ, silk line was only good for about a year."

A small smile appeared on Frank's face. "You know, us hunters and fishermen . . . people think we don't care about animals or their habitat when it's really the opposite. Most of us have more respect for nature and conservation and stronger connections to animals than the average Joe because we see first-hand what happens when you don't take measures to sustain wildlife. Albert was one of the greatest conservationists I've ever met, and that's one of the two reasons he hated monofilament line."

"What was the other reason?"

"Bottom ends—"

Outboard Motors

"Albert, the bottom end of my outboard motor needs fixing," said Frank.

"Don't tell me . . . some goddamn monofilament got wrapped around the shaft!"

"Probably."

"Christ. I'm tired of fixing the bottom end of motors! Got buildings to build, guides to watch over, machines to keep running. I don't got no time to be fixing one or two bottoms a week."

Frank adjusted the brim of his Stetson. "I try, Albert. Lord, I try. But between the wind gusts and the guests' poor casting, lines end up under the boat. Before you know it, it's caught in the propeller."

"It's not your fault, Frank. I ain't blaming you. It's this newfangled line! The old silk, wax-covered cotton or nylon line would break, but this new monofilament line doesn't snap. It just keeps wrapping around the motor. Eventually it burns a groove in the steel of the shaft and cuts the oil seal right out. Then the oil seeps out, and the whole bottom end of the outboard seizes up. That line literally chokes the life out of it."

"Chokes the life out of wildlife, too," agreed Frank.

"You got that right! Every time a bloody lure gets stuck on the bottom of the lake or on a rock, and the guest or guide can't shake it free, the line has to be cut. But because it don't rot, those bits of line float 'round in the water, for what, six hundred years? All sorts of birds get tangled up in it. Geese and ducks, loons, seagulls, herons, and every other bird that paddles in these waters."

"It's sad," added Frank. "I've seen birds with leg amputations, birds starved to death, both because they couldn't break free of the stuff."

"And fish! Fish get caught up in this deadly wrap, too. It winds around their bodies like a belt and eventually kills 'em. Too many times, I seen carnage in the nets we've strung while commercial fishing in the fall. Walleyes, even muskies, cut to bits."

"Most fishermen nowadays are using this line. You can't change that."

"No, I can't. And I can't save them poor fish. But I think I can save a few bottom ends. I been thinking on it, and I've come up with something—"

The next evening, Albert headed to his outboard stand down by the lake. It was the perfect area to work on motors; the old wooden floor soaked up an oil spill without getting slick, the roof kept out the rain, and the three open sides let in plenty of fresh air and natural light with which to operate on the intricate innards of his machines. Albert rolled up the sleeves of his green work shirt, then lifted an outboard onto the sawhorse and secured it in place. "Okay, let's see what we can do with you."

It took Albert three evenings to complete his modification. Finally satisfied, he put the motor back together and placed it on one of the boats.

"Frank! Let's go fishing!"

Never one to pass up the chance to dunk a line, Frank asked no questions but grabbed his pole and away they went, stopping at a walleye hole just behind the islands.

"Okay, Frank, now I want you to purposely cast your line so it gets caught in the motor."

Frank obligingly tossed his jig across the stern, and Albert trolled right into it. The prop picked up the line and then—*snap!* The line was instantly cut.

Frank stared at his lure-less line. "You owe me a jig," he joked.

"If this works, I'll buy you a case of jigs," answered Albert.

"What you do?"

"Grooved the shaft, so it acts like a knife."

Night after night, they tested out the motor, purposely trying to damage the bottom end, but it remained unscathed. By the end of the week, Albert was convinced his invention was a success, and just in time. His target audience was arriving at the camp the next day.

Two engineers from Evinrude Johnson made an annual trek up to the camp for a working holiday, and they always brought two new experimental motor models: a week of "real" fishing was a great way to test out new outboard motors. If they passed the scrutiny of the engineers—and the guides—then they would be released to the public the following year.

"So what'd you bring this year?" Albert asked John, Evinrude's field engineer, as they stood on the dock, admiring the two new motors.

"One 15 horsepower Johnson, one 15 horsepower Evinrude," claimed Bob proudly. "There have been some design changes, so I can hardly wait to see how they perform." He smiled as he looked at the outboards gracing the Stork Lake boats—they were a mixed bag of old motors, all which had seen better days. "I guarantee they'll perform better than the ones you have here."

Albert shrugged. "If you say so."

"We'd like to take them for a trial run in front of the camp before we go fishing. Do you think you could get them on some boats right away?"

"No problem," said Albert, grabbing one and heaving it up on his shoulder. "Anything we have to do to them?"

"No, just bolt them on boats and connect the fuel hoses. They're ready to go," replied Bob.

"You sure?"

"Oh yes, very sure. We know our outboards."

Twenty minutes later, with the new motors hooked up, the two boats roared away from the dock—Bob in one boat and his design engineer in the other.

Frank joined Albert to watch the demonstration. "They sure go."

"Not for long," said Albert.

They didn't even make it past the first island when both boats stopped dead in the water.

Albert was almost peeing his pants with laughter. "A field engineer in one boat, and a design engineer in the other, and neither of them thought to tell me to put oil in the bottom ends of them new motors before leaving the dock!"

The next morning, Albert approached Bob. "I've got a motor you can test out, seeing you's won't be testing out yours."

"Oh?" said Bob, interested. "What type of motor?"

"Just an old one I've made some changes to. Give it a try and let me know what you think."

At the end of the week, Albert pulled his motor with the homespun line cutter out of the water to show Bob just exactly what he had done. There were no signs of wear and no signs of monofilament wound around or melted to the shaft.

"So what do you think?"

"It's not a bad idea, but I don't think it has a practical application . . . at least it's not something we could incorporate into our motors."

It was like a kick in the stomach. Poor Albert was so disappointed. He hadn't made the modifications for money or for recognition. He had simply wanted to come up with a way to solve an ongoing problem, not just for himself but for all fishermen.

***

"You know," said Frank, "It was in the next year or two that some outboard manufacturers featured cutters on their props to shear off monofilament line."

"How did Albert feel about that?" asked John.

"He just said, 'See, it *was* a good idea!' That's all he needed . . . to know he had been right and that his invention was useful."

"You're dry, Elsie. Like another drink?" offered Al, holding up the bottle of rye.

"Maybe a little one," answered Elsie, offering Al her glass. "You know, that there rye bottle you're holding looks kinda like crystal. Reminds me of another bottle. Remember that Count guy? I think you brought him up with you, John."

"Count Josef Meran of Lichtenstein?"

"That's the one. Well he gave Albert a bottle of brandy—"

Count Josef Meran

"Look at that one's fancy pants!" murmured Albert.

"Shh," quieted Al. "Don't offend the very first guests I've ever had before they even step on the dock!"

Al had waited for this moment ever since purchasing Stork Lake that past winter. Finally southern winds melted the pinnacles of jagged ice into the lake. The watery runways of the north were open for business, and so was Al. Eight spring bear hunters now unloaded off the Twin Beech, one of them dressed in a way neither Albert nor Al had ever seen before.

The man wore moleskin knickerbockers, a lode green wool coat, and knee-high socks with his hunting boots. Topping the whole outfit was a bearskin cap. He blew on fingers stiffened from an hour on an unheated airplane, then belted out, *"Was für ein wunderbarer Ort!"*

"Ahh," said Albert, "Hope he knows some English. It'd be a bitch hunting with someone who couldn't take direction."

They soon learned that, though well educated, Josef J. Meran, a Count from Liechtenstein, did not speak nor understand any English.

Al was desperate to make this first hunt successful. If it was, John Batten from Twin Disc had assured him of several more fishing trips during the summer and maybe even a fall moose hunt.

"Albert, you've been doing this for years. I need your help. Every single one of these guys has to get their bear. How are we going to make that happen?"

"Split 'em and spread 'em . . . one guide to each guest, at eight different outposts, in eight different areas. We'll all stay at our outposts until we get our bear. After that, they can return to camp and fish for the rest of their stay."

"Sounds like a plan." Al paused. "I want you to take the Count."

"What? Be alone with a guy that don't speak English for days on end?

"It was your idea, Albert. It was your idea. Besides, you're the best bear guide, and I want him to have the best."

An hour later, Albert and the Count were flown to their designated outpost in South Lake, miles from the camp.

"I'll fly over once a day," said the pilot. "If you need anything, or want to be picked up, spread a white sheet over a rock I can see from the air. That will signal me to land."

At first light on the second day of their hunt, the two men started off across the lake in an old wooden rowboat, headed for an island where Albert had seen bear signs earlier in the week during a scouting expedition. Albert chatted away, and the Count chatted back, neither understanding each other's words, yet still knowing what each other were saying, the way only two men in sync with their passions can do.

Suddenly Albert stopped rowing. "There, on the shore . . . a bear," he said quietly.

The Count inclined his head in understanding, his bulging eyes giving away the excitement he was feeling. "*Ist der gewaltig!*"

"Yeah, and it's really big too. God, it's gotta be over five hundred pounds!"

Albert slowly started to row toward the island, barely breaking the glassy water.

Through the patches of mist still swirling on the lake, the bear could be seen ambling along, occasionally stopping to chew on the frost-coated stalks of last year's grass. Suddenly it looked up, but before it could take off into the bush, the Count calmly raised his rifle, fired one shot, and the bear instantly dropped.

"*Ich habe ihn erwischt!*"

"Yeah, and you got him! Great shot!" Albert was impressed with his accuracy.

They landed the boat and approached the carcass. It looked like a black tent.

"Wow!" exclaimed Albert.

"Wow!" exclaimed the Count. This word they both understood. The Count bent his head and just stood there, silent. Not knowing if he was meditating, praying, in shock, or in awe, Albert quietly stood beside him. Finally the Count raised his head and gave him a huge smile.

"I'll skin 'em out for ya now." Albert unsheathed his knife.

The Count shot a palm toward him in protest. "*Nein!*" He walked over to a nearby spruce and snapped several small branches off of it. One branch he placed in the bear's mouth. "*Sein letztes Mahl.*"

Another branch was placed on the hide, while the third he coated in blood from the entry wound and stuck into the left side of his fur cap.

Silently Albert watched this hunting ritual, thinking it was none too different from some of the old Indians, who thanked their kill and offered it tobacco in gratitude. Even worlds apart, hunters were connected to each other by their respect for animals.

The hunting ceremony now over, the Count turned to Albert. "*Sollen wir dem Bären jetzt das Fell abziehen?*"

"Yeah, and now I'm gonna skin the bear."

Once the bear was skinned, Albert stretched the hide out on the rocks, smoothing all the wrinkles. Then with a tape, he measured it nose tip to tail tip.

"Eight feet, eight inches!" he exclaimed, showing the tape to the Count.

"*Zwei Meter vierundsechzig!*" he repeated in amazement.

"Yep, trophy size!" He then looked up at the darkening sky. "Too late for any planes to fly over. We'll have to bunk down for one more night."

After a supper of fresh fried walleye, they sat around the campfire, and Albert pulled out two mugs. "Coffee?" he asked, pointing to a pot of liquid on the grate that looked more like syrup.

The Count shook his head, then rummaged around in his knapsack and pulled a fancy-looking bottle. "Cognac!" he announced gleefully and poured a couple of ounces into each of the mugs, handing one to Albert, then raising his own mug in the air, "*Prost!*"

Albert followed suit. "Cheers!" he cried, downing his shot in one gulp.

The Count looked slightly taken aback but quickly recovered. He sat there, warming the bottom of his mug with the palm of his hand. He swirled it for about thirty seconds, slowly raised it to his nostrils, closed his eyes, and sniffed it, his nose deep into the mug. He exhaled, lowered the cup, then swirled it again. Finally he raised it to his lips and took a small sip. When he lowered the mug again, he sat back, savouring the sensation.

Albert took the last drag of his cigarette and rubbed it out on a rough poplar trunk. He wasn't used to people twiddling with their drinks. Drinks were, well, for drinking. And this cognac stuff, it was a little woody for his liking, nothing he particularly wanted to linger over. Albert tossed another log on the fire. How long was he going to nurse that drink? It had been a long day, and he was dead tired, yet he couldn't go to bed before the Count—that would be rude. He pulled out his pack and lit another cigarette, and watched the Count continue to sip at his mug. Finally he was done. Albert doused the fire, and the two men crawled into their sleeping bags.

Back at the camp the next day, the bearskin was hung up on the wall of the bunkhouse for its photo op with the proud, knickerbocker-clad Count. His job done, Albert started to walk away.

"*Halt!*" Albert turned around. The Count rummaged around in his knapsack and pulled out a bottle of new, unopened cognac, the same they had drunk over the campfire and handed it to Albert.

"*Danke schön!*"

"Yeah, and thank you. It was an honour to hunt with you."

Later, Albert strolled into the kitchen. "Elsie, that Count gave me a bottle as part of my tip. I don't know what the hell to do with it. I can't stomach the stuff. Why don't you just use it in your cooking?"

Elsie was a marvellous cook, but she rarely added spirits. "What would I put it in?"

"Just use it in the guides' stew."

So that summer, every time Elsie made stew, she'd pull out the cognac and pour a cup in. She finally finished the bottle. "I hate to throw it out. It's kinda pretty. I think I'll have Agnes fill it with some flowers."

Not long after, Al and Albert came in.

Al took a look at the "vase" of late lilies sitting on the staff dining table.

"Where did you get that bottle?"

"Ain't that the bottle the Count gave me?" piped up Albert. "It had some kinda brandy in it. Didn't like it much, so I told Elsie to use it for cooking."

"You did what?" Al rolled his eyes. "Holy cripe, Albert, that was King Louis XIII cognac! Do you know what that cost? About the same as five, maybe six *cases* of scotch! That's stuff's meant to be sipped and savoured."

"Oh!" exclaimed Elsie. "Guess that's why them guides asked for seconds of my stew!"

***

Everyone was finished their drinks—it was time to go retire for the night. Frank opened the door, then stopped.

"Will you look at that?" Everyone crowded around to see.

On this cold, clear late August night, nature's greatest light show, the northern lights, could be seen across the sky. It was rare for them to be so visible at this time of year. The ever-changing curtain of light twirled and danced across the night sky. They almost seemed alive Elsie looked up. "Oh, for God's sake. Look at them lights. Some say they're the spirits of the dead dancing in the sky." She gave a cackle. "Albert's doing a little jig. I guess he heard us talking about him."

Lori hung Albert's hunting cap back on the wall, then took down a leather cap with large earflaps and a chin strap. Albert had always told her you could come up with any solution if you let your imagination soar—

1978

"Was that you who just about took off the top of that poplar tree coming in?" asked Andy, grabbing onto the wing strut of the Cessna 185 as it coasted to the dock.

"Ha-ha, very funny," said Lori, jumping out of the cockpit door. "That was a perfect approach and a perfect landing, and you know it! You'll have to come along for a ride one day, and I'll prove to you just how good a pilot I am."

"Maybe I will if this old heart of mine ever needs a jump start!" Two years before, a stroke had left the right side of Andy's face droopy and his smile a little crooked, but it hadn't ravaged his sense of humour or twisted his bright outlook on life. "What was that there pilot doing while you were terrorizing the skies?"

Ben, the young pilot in question, poked his head out the cargo door. "I was catching a few ZZ's, of course. That's why I take her along!"

"Oh, I see," said Andy, shaking his head knowingly. "I thought you took her because she was good lookin.' My mistake."

From behind his aviator glasses, Ben's eyes brushed up and down Lori's slim figure. "It doesn't hurt that she's not hard to look at," he replied.

"You guys!" exclaimed Lori. "Ben, just give me my bags."

As he handed her two paper shopping bags, he asked, "The 206 will be back tomorrow. We could practice some touch and go's in it tomorrow night, weather permitting?"

Al had run a small niche air service for several years now. Only one plane, the Cessna 185, stayed at the camp full-time. The rest of the planes were based out of Deer Lake, where they were put to work ferrying passengers back and forth to reserves.

"Honest? I haven't flown the 206 yet. It hasn't been here much this summer. That would be awesome, Ben! I'll be ecstatic to point that plane's nose into the wind!"

"Now, how about you point yourself in the direction of that there store, Miss Reid?" quipped Andy. It's twenty to five . . . and I'm feeling mighty thirsty."

"I have to change first. I'll be back down to open the doors in a jiff!"

Taking the stairs two at a time, Lori ran up to her new living quarters, which were on the second level of the lodge. She quickly donned a fresh shirt and clean jeans, ran a brush through her hair, and checked her appearance in the mirror. Her long golden hair framed her oval face that, other than that annoying sprinkling of freckles, was finally smooth and clear. Her large almond-shaped eyes studded with long dark lashes cheekily expressed her every emotion.

"All in all . . . not bad," she commented to the reflection. "Although maybe . . . a different pair of earrings? Where did those silver hoops go?"

Lori knelt beside her bed and lifted the edge of the comforter. "Okay, you guys. Where are they? I know you've been playing with them!"

Four bright eyes stared innocently at her as if to say, "Who, us?"

"Yes, you," Lori answered the silent question. "No one else would come all the way up here to my room, take my earrings off my dresser, and put one"—Lori reached under and pulled out a silver hoop—"under my bed, and the other"—Lori glanced over at a wooden bowl on the shelf—"in *their* bed!"

Trincria gazed away, pretending to look out the window. Medea, however, looked contrite. She lifted her wings and fluttered over, landing on Lori's shoulder. Lifting the small robin onto her index finger, Lori stroked the velvety back. "You and your sister are becoming more and more mischievous! What am I going to do with you?"

But she already knew the answer to her question—she was soon going to have to set her precious little birds free.

Several weeks earlier, there had been a wicked storm; heavy winds tore at the poor skinny birch next to the lodge, violently shaking the robins' home right out of it. The next morning, while Lori brought ice up to the kitchen, she discovered, among bits of broken blue eggshells strewn on the ground, four newborn baby robins, pink-skinned like plucked chicken except for a few tufts of fluff above their ears. Momma robin was nowhere in sight.

"Oh no!" cried Lori, thrusting the ice bucket aside and dropping to the ground. "Please, *pleaaase* be alive!"

She nudged one. It didn't move. She nudged another. Nothing. The other two suddenly held up their teeny heads.

"Thank goodness some of you are alive! Poor wee things. You can't be more than a day or two old, and your family has been destroyed. Don't worry. I'll save you! I'll be your new mommy."

After burying their two siblings in her animal cemetery (where in addition to momma squirrel, now was the eternal resting place of four flying squirrels, a bunny, and a baby loon), the two little birds were introduced to their new home: a Gold Label Ignacio Haya cigar box stuffed with cotton, kept on a desk in the storage room beside the kitchen. Promptly named after characters in a Greek Mythology book Lori was currently reading, Trincria and Medea had voracious appetites, erupting into loud squawking at the mere sound of footsteps travelling anywhere near their vicinity. Soon, not only was Lori feeding them, but everyone that passed by the cigar box would drop a bug, worm, or piece of hamburger into their constantly cavernous mouths. With a whole camp taking care of them, they quickly sprouted feathers and a whole lot of attitude.

It wasn't long before Trincria was attempting to fly, hopping along the desk and floating down to the floor. Medea was a little more tentative and had to be bribed with berries to take the leap. However, soon they both regularly took to the air, zipping into the kitchen to peck at the pies. Chezy looked quite put out when they'd swoop down to sit on the edge of her tinned cat food, apparently not the least bit afraid of the curly tyrant. To her mom's chagrin, they'd jet into her room at cocktail time and land on her dad's shoulder, where he would laughingly offer them a bit a scotch on his finger, though they much preferred straight tonic. Finally, Helen put her foot down when they started fluttering into the dining room. "Lori, we can't have birds flying about, pooping on the guests' heads. What would they think?"

"They'd probably love it."

"Honestly! Now you take those birds and . . . do something with them."

So for the past week, they had resided in a wooden salad bowl in Lori's room, taking afternoon excursions outside. There again, Trincria excelled, tugging for worms and fluttering up to the lodge roof and down again. Medea, however, feared heights. She easily flew up to the roof but would not fly back down. Lori had several times gotten Jeremy to climb up the ends of the logs onto the roof to bring her back down. So while Lori was sure Trincria was a full-grown perch-and-pounce hunter and flyer, ready to be set free, she still had her reservations about little Medea. Was she really ready to strike out on her own?

"Looori! Where are yooouuu?"

"Here we go." Lori placed Medea on the sill beside her sister, then turned around. "Up here, Ma," she called out through the window.

"Where have you been?" puffed Helen as she entered her room, out of breath from climbing up the long flight of stairs.

"You know where I was. We flew into town to shop."

"I just expected you sooner, that's all. Did you get my makeup?"

"Of course," said Lori. She rummaged around in one of the shopping bags. "Let's see, a new badminton set, ping-pong balls, hosiery, a *Cosmo* magazine, books, and"—Lori pulled out a jar and handed it to her mother—"age-defying foundation."

"Oh, good! Maybe this'll work. Seems my face doesn't want to hold up my makeup anymore."

Lori looked at her mother's lineless, perfect skin. "What do you mean? You look amazing!"

Helen shook her head in disagreement. "I swear I've aged twenty years since you started flying."

"That reminds me, I'm going to fly the 206 for the first time tomorrow! You know, you have never seen me fly, ever, never mind flown with me. Why don't you come down to the lake and watch?"

"Oh boy." Helen rolled her eyes, then crossed her heart. "I *can't* watch. It makes me too nervous. Sorry, no, I can't do it. Why on earth do you want to do these crazy things?"

"Crazy? I grew up around planes. I've been programmed to fly. You just don't want me to because *you* have a fear of flying."

"No, it's because I have a fear of *you* flying."

"And I have a fear of *not* flying! I don't want to live that way. Look, Mom, it's not reasonable to think something might happen. I took flying lessons all winter and completed my cross-country with flying colours, no pun intended. And I still always have to fly with one of the pilots. So why would you think something would go wrong?"

"I don't know," said Helen, defeated. "I'm not positive like you. My mother taught me to worry. . . to expect the worst. So no, I just can't watch you."

Lori couldn't imagine being so scared of flying. She loved everything about it: the ground falling beneath her, the winged shadow passing over glimmering lakes that winked in the sun like sparkling gemstones. Even elevator turbulence and weightless downdrafts were a rush. She felt a sudden pang for her mom and for the adventures she was deprived of because of anxiety. Lori threw her arms around her neck and gave her a big hug. "Mom, maybe it's time to stop borrowing trouble. Now, I gotta go. The boats will be coming in any minute. I'll see you at dinner!"

"Hold on!" Helen stopped Lori in her tracks. "Don't forget we are dining with the Lindlarghs tonight, so don't be late. And maybe you should plan to spend the whole night up here with us instead of traipsing down the hill to play pool or go for a boat ride with Alma and Andy. Honestly, you spend more time with them than with your own parents."

"I thought you liked me hanging out with Alma and Andy?"

"Not tonight." Helen was firm.

"Fine. Now I really have to go."

Medea chirped, lifted her wings and glided over to her bowl as if to show Helen just how simple flying really was.

"I wouldn't get so cheeky," declared Helen, shaking her finger at the little bird. "I've seen Jeremy rescue you off the roof!"

A lineup of guides was already waiting outside the store when Lori arrived.

"There she is!" called out Andy. The guides gave a cheer.

"Geez, I'm popular." Lori laughed as she unlocked the door. Twice a day, in the morning before the boats headed out and again at night when the boats came in, she opened the store for business, and it had turned into one of her favourite jobs. It gave her a chance to yak with the guides. Every one of them came in every morning to fill their guests' coolers for the day and came in every night for their ration of two beers, with both stubby brown bottles snapped open to prevent anyone from "stockpiling" beer for a party. No longer frozen with shyness, it also gave Lori a chance to meet and greet with guests one on one, to hear about their day, and hand out congratulations or condolences, depending on what was hanging on the fish hooks outside.

There was a steady stream of business over the next hour. Lori handed out chewing gum and chewing tobacco, bug spray, and aspirin. She loaned out a rod to a guest that had cast his into the lake and picked out a rain suit for a lady who had forgotten to bring one. After helping several more guests select lures for the next day and selling almost every beer in the fridge, she turned to Dennis, who was seated in one of the chairs scattered about the store, reading a magazine. He often kept her company while she kept the store.

Lori picked up an Aero bar off the shelf, unwrapped it, broke off the corner where the mice had been chewing on it, then took a bite. "So how'd your afternoon go? You had a chainsaw in about a million pieces this morning when I was cleaning. Did you ever get it working?" she asked.

"Course I got it working," he smiled, raising a Labatt Blue to his lips. "And the ice machine and the lawn mower, too."

"Geez, didn't I ask you to keep the mower broken another day? If my dad knows it's fixed, he'll want me to cut grass tomorrow, and I don't want to! I have to get the payroll done first thing. Then I want to give the furniture for Cabin 7 a coat of paint in the afternoon."

Dennis flipped her an engaging grin. "What? You want me to take it apart again? Maybe leave the flywheel lying on the workbench, so it looks like it's still broken?"

"Could you? You have no idea how I'm falling behind. I didn't even finish cleaning the workshop! I'll have to squeeze that in tomorrow, too."

"No, you won't. I finished it. There wasn't much left to do anyways. I just had to throw away some stuff and sweep the floor."

"How sweet! You didn't have to do that . . . but I'm *so* glad you did! Sometimes I think I start too many projects at once. I'll be stocking shelves, then decide to type, or shall I say *pound* out, fishing licences on this crappy old Smith Corona. Or I'll start raking the beach and end up stacking kindling. I really have to learn to finish a task before I start the next one."

"You're not regretting changing jobs this year, are you?"

"Not a chance! I'd rather sell tackle than tackle a sink full of greasy dishes any day! Baits, beer, and bars are far more interesting than serving mashed potatoes and gravy. And I like puttering around outside." Lori shoved the rest of the chocolate bar into her mouth.

"You've always been more of a 'chore boy' than 'kitchen girl' anyways. All you need now is a moustache and to learn how to belch properly, and then you'll really be one of the guys!"

"I don't know if that is a compliment or an insult," Lori answered, wiping down the glossy pine counter with a rag. "Anyways, sorry to boot you out, but I'm closing a few minutes early. My family's eating with the Lindlarghs tonight, and I don't want to keep everyone waiting."

"Oh, so you get to act like a guest tonight," said Dennis.

"Yeah, but it makes me uncomfortable. It's weird to have Alma serve me. I feel like I should jump up and help her clear the table, which by the way, I have done in the past."

Dennis laughed. "See you later, kiddo."

***

There was a babble of jovial greetings as Lori slipped into her seat beside her mother. It was a rare occurrence for her to eat in the guest dining room; she could count on one hand the number of times she had done so. However, Paul and Lottie Lindlargh had requested the whole Reid family join them for their last supper there.

From West Germany, Paul was a heavy-jowled man with dark furrowed eyebrows that belied his kind nature. He had first come up bear hunting with his friends, John Batten and Count Meran, and most years since then had taken the long trek over the ocean to pursue his passion for the Canadian fishing experience with his merry wife in tow.

"This has been the trip of a lifetime, again!" glowed Lottie, speaking with just a hint of an accent. "I think I caught two hundred fish today!"

"And shore lunch," Paul patted his round belly. "I feel like I ate two hundred fish today!"

"That's what it's all about," Al said as he poured some wine into their glasses, then sat down. "I'd hate to think your experience here wasn't all you wanted it to be."

"There's no doubt it was everything. Our trips here never disappoint," said Paul, with a sincere depth of feeling. "We have never been anywhere so unspoiled, a place where there's so much left to explore. There's nothing like returning to the wilderness to pursue hunting and fishing. This openness, this vast magnificence for primordial activities is something we lack in Germany."

"I'm glad you still feel that, Paul. Sometimes it starts to feel pretty tame around here for me." Al gazed down the beautifully set table, filled with bottles of fine wine and large platters of mouth-watering appetizers prepared in his state-of-the-art kitchen. "I sometimes wonder if we have modernized the fun right out of it!"

"No, no, it is still very much the best of both worlds," insisted Lottie. "We like peace when pursuing the fish, then we come back to the camp and become social animals again! It is good that everything is so fine here, yah?"

"I agree with Lottie. I'm *done* with wood stoves, Klick, and two-holers!" With that, Helen popped a large shrimp into her mouth.

"Al, you make us feel so special." Lottie patted the back of Al's hand. "We would love to reciprocate the wonderful hospitality someday. We did ask Phil if he would like to come spend the summer with us in Germany. We would be so pleased to show him around not only Germany but also the rest of Europe. He thought about it for about one minute, but then, I think he could not tear himself away from this place. It might have something to do with a girl."

All eyes turned to Linda, a young woman with creamy skin and cerulean eyes sitting beside Phil at the table. The high school sweethearts were now engaged and had not wanted to spend one more summer apart, so Linda had come up to Stork and taken over Lori's old job. Guests loved her wicked sense of humour and bold, no-holds-barred behaviour. Quick on her feet and quicker with her tongue, she instantly had fit into the crazy fishing camp world.

"He better not be thinking about tramping around Europe!" growled Linda playfully. "Expose him to brilliant German girls, flirty French girls, voluptuous Italian girls—not a chance! Nope, he's going to have to make do with only me from now on . . . me, and a white picket fence, a two-story house, and some dogs!"

"Don't worry, I'll love being Mr. Average Joe America," gloated Phil.

Lottie's eyes fluttered. "Of course! Love, that makes it impossible to leave. You must stay with your engaged girl. But you"—Lottie turned to Lori—"do you have a boyfriend?"

Linda smiled up at Alma, who had just placed her meal in front of her. "Thanks, Alma." Then her blue eyes turned and lasered onto Lori. "Yes, do tell. Do you have a boyfriend?"

Both Alma's and Helen's eyebrows shot up.

"Of course not!" Lori answered quickly, shaking her head. "You know I don't."

"Sorry, I just thought maybe there was someone pining for you in Winnipeg. My mistake."

"Good, so you see, no ties," continued Lottie. "When do you finish school?"

"I graduate next year."

"And what are you going to do then?"

"I'm not sure. I haven't figured it out yet."

"This place here, it's beautiful, but maybe you need a change to sort it all out, yah? That's why you must come visit us in Germany. Many teenagers come to Europe to, how do you say . . . find themselves."

"I would love to go to Europe someday."

"Then you must come!" agreed Paul. "We'll show you how we fish there. I have my own private little pond I stock with trout and carp. You will laugh because it is so small!"

"But pretty," continued Lottie. "Of course, you would have to experience our culture, too. We could take you to Bonn to see a concert and to Trier to see the Roman ruins. And shopping in Düsseldorf! After that, our driver could take you to stay in other places: East Berlin, the Netherlands, Austria."

"And while there is no cuisine better than Elsie's"—Paul gestured to the savoury plate in front of him—"it would be interesting for you to try some of our dishes . . . *schweinshaxe* and *spargel*, and of course a little taste of our beverages, such as *Alt* and our famous Mosel wines! We could plan a whole trip. You could come in May, when everything is new and fresh and green, and stay three, four, five months."

"Wow!" Al laughed. "Why don't you ask me to come? I haven't been to Europe yet!"

Linda's voice held a mischievous edge. "Yes, Lori, you should go. Europe would be good for you. After our wedding, of course. You must be here for that. Then you should go. Maybe you'd find a boyfriend there."

Lori watched her mother anxiously shift in her seat and take a swig of her wine in order to swallow her words. Of course she would think it was out of the question and that there was no way her little girl was going to go tramping halfway across the continent to foreign countries among strange people, strange men, far from her watchful eye and availing tongue. However, Lori was hesitant for a different reason. She turned toward Lottie. "You've certainly given me something to think about. It all seems so exotic, so exciting. And it's an amazingly generous offer. The chance of a lifetime! But . . . a summer away from here? I'd have to think about that."

"Of course, of course," said Lottie. "Take all the time you need. Just know you are welcome."

After generous slices of strawberry shortcake loaded with mounds of whipping cream and mugs of steaming coffee, Paul sat back in his chair and groaned, "Time to go home. I've breathed too much fresh air, caught too many fish, and ate too much food!"

The party broke up; Paul and Lottie left for their cabin, and Helen and Al retired to their room to relax. Phil, Linda, and Lori took the gleaming pine stairway up to their suite, and, with a nod and a wink from Linda, Lori took the backstairs back down . . . down to the boyfriend she "didn't have."

***

In order to keep her love life secret from her parents, Lori had spun a web of deception. Some nights she said she was playing pool with the guides. Other nights, she said she was with Linda or on the lake with Alma and Andy, who all kept her secret without question. Tonight she simply snuck out. Heart pounding, eyes darting from side to side to make sure no one was around, Lori crept through the deep underbrush, down the rugged side of the hill, past the old biffy. She rounded the old washstand to the lakeside, then tiptoed through the reeds. Finally, she approached her destination: the cabin on The Point. Gently she knocked on the door.

"Come in!"

"It's just me," she said, stepping in quickly and closing the door quietly behind her.

He immediately sprang out of his chair and came to her. Sliding his hands down to her waist, he brushed his lips lightly across her forehead. Beneath his shirt, she could feel muscles coiled like steel wire.

"Hey, pet, I wasn't expecting you tonight," he whispered in her ear. "I thought you had a dinner thing going on."

"I did. It broke up early."

"Lucky for me," said Jeremy softly, his eyes holding hers.

***

It had been an instant attraction three years in the making. Jeremy had never thought of Lori as anything but a fishing buddy or poker partner. That June, however, she had arrived at the camp, not as the sweet young girl he remembered but as a lovely young *woman*. As she stepped off the plane, she promptly stepped right into his heart.

Stepping off the plane that June, Lori had watched Jeremy walk up the dock to meet her with the easy grace and vitality of a wild animal and wondered: Had he always looked like this? Broad and lean with a washboard stomach and rippling muscles—he looked like a Greek God. How could anyone be so perfect? How come she had never noticed before? And how could someone she had known for so long suddenly make her heart flutter, make Hungarian goulash of her emotions, just like that?

"Long time no see!" greeted Jeremy, almost nervously. "We have to catch up. How about cruising the lake tonight? I found this cool trapper's cabin I think you'd like."

"Sounds like fun. It's a date!" Lori could have kicked herself for the Freudian slip. She was just a friend, "a pet" still to Jeremy.

The puffy clouds had just been set aflame when they took off that evening. The first boat ride of the season was always fun, but tonight, in the company of this new feeling, it was exhilarating. The bumping she felt under her bum as they scoured atop of the shimmering pearly grey waves was nothing compared to the thumping going on in her heart, and even the rush of cool air flowing past her face as they zoomed along could not wipe the flush from her cheeks.

As they continued along through a maze of rocky islands and channels, a bald eagle appeared above them, its outspread wings etched against the glowing sky. Lori watched as it circled round and round their moving boat, never flapping its wings but soaring on a cushion of air.

Elsie would say an eagle above you means something special is going to happen, she thought to herself.

In a quiet bay at the south end of South Lake, Jeremy slowed.

"This is it."

He pulled the boat up into the scrubby willows lining the shore.

"How in the world did you ever find this spot?" Lori asked in amazement after ten minutes of manoeuvring an overgrown uphill trail spiked with spurs.

"Plenty of exploration!" laughed Jeremy.

Finally, among a mixed stand of crooked birch, pine, and poplar, they found the cabin. It was in bad shape. Logs were rotted away, the moss-covered roof had partly fallen in, and the stove was nothing more than a rusty shell, but the intrigue and awareness of another era when things were different remained like a clock.

"Oh, if these old walls could talk! Who did they once shield from the cold? What deep secrets do they keep? What dramas unfolded? Come on, Jeremy, you're a master storyteller. Take me back to their time."

"It belonged not just to a trapper, but a Trapper family," Jeremy said firmly. "The kids slept here." He pointed to two mattresses deconstructed by industrious squirrels. "A boy and a girl . . . Foxy and Beav."

"Foxy and Beav? What kind of names are those for children?"

"Important ones, if you're a trapper. Anyways, the Trapper family was happy in this little home. Every few weeks, Papa Trapper would pick up his gun, his tea pail, and his grub sack and depart on his dog carriole for long treks along his trapline. While he was gone, Momma Trapper kept the home fires burning. She cooked, skinned the animals, taught the kids the art of bushcraft, and waited patiently for her husband's return. When, on some cold clear nights, she could hear the jingle of dog harnesses—"

"Jingle bells were for horses, not huskies."

"The buckles jingled, okay? Anyways, she'd hear him coming and would be so excited she'd run out in her bare feet to meet him."

"Sounds like Momma Trapper had cabin fever."

"And under these very same stars, she would greet him with her undying love and affection, and he would greet her with a tasty moose nose and fur for a new parka. They didn't have much, but they were happy out here, living how they dreamed, with the ones they loved." His tone seemed to veil a hidden meaning.

Slightly flustered, Lori attempted humour. "Wow. Stuck in the freezing bush alone with a couple screaming brats and nothing to amuse you but the voices in your head telling you to skin your husband instead of the mink. I'd run out in my bare feet, too, but I wouldn't stop until I reached civilization."

By the time they got back to the boat, the sun had dipped below the lake, turning the lake to amaranth-tinged mercury.

"Pete's Lunch Spot is just across the bay. We could light a fire and rap a while," suggested Jeremy.

"Sounds good," said Lori, relieved the night wasn't ending yet.

In no time at all, Jeremy had arranged the boat cushions around a cheery, pine-scented fire.

They stared up at the velvet sky, pointing out shooters and dippers, the summer triangle, planets, and satellites. And they talked comfortably about everything, from hockey and planes to politics and school. As Lori watched the firelight flickering across Jeremy's face, she felt in awe. He had always understood her; now it was like he knew her emotions and feelings and tastes inside out.

It wasn't until hours later, their bottoms wet with dew, that they reluctantly doused the fire and headed back to camp.

"Let me walk you home," said Jeremy as he reached down to give her a hand out of the boat.

Lori had never been afraid of the night. Indeed, she loved to roam the camp after dark, when the lights from the cabins were extinguished, and all was quiet save for the gentle hum of the generator. In many ways, the night was less threatening than the day, for the dark wrapped around her like a security blanket. Almost blind, she could easily manoeuvre the tricky ascent up the hill to the lodge. But tonight, it felt incredible to have the tall, darkly handsome figure protectively walk next to her, holding her cool hand in his strong, warm one.

Jeremy glanced down at the girl beside him. Lori stopped for a moment and turned to him, wide eyes dark, full lips slightly apart. That did it. Jeremy lowered his head and kissed her—a kiss that sent a tingling sensation right down to her toes.

They were a match made in fishing camp heaven. Both instinctively were drawn toward the lake, finding it provided both an adrenaline rush and a natural tranquillizer. Every chance they could, they were on, in, or near the water. Waist-high in the cold, clear water, they dragged their boat through three lifts—shallow treacherous channels full of rocks—so they could explore the Bay Cliffs in North Lake. From the base of the cliffs, they climbed up through sunlight-sieved lacy leaves, on the way picking rain-scented, waxy yellow lady slippers from under centenarian jack pine and ripe raspberries growing in tangled abundance. At the top, the cliffs sharply dropped off into the expanse of the glistening lake.

They navigated past countless creeks and numerous islands on through Hell's Pass to the Bathtub, so named because its bowl-shaped granite bottom warmed the waters filling it. They took off their shoes and socks, rolled up their pants, and waded with the minnows, then made their way back to the shore to skip stones and write their names and silly messages in the sand.

They investigated the reef bordering Knuckle Buster. Invisible from the surface, the massive rock formation sat there like an iceberg a mere half-inch under the waves, surrounded with deep, deep water and mystery.

When they weren't exploring, they were fishing. Jeremy would pull out a couple of rods, and they would sit there, snagging rocks, and catching a great many walleye, some northerns, and even muskie, always throwing them all back to their freedom.

"Let it go, Jeremy," Lori begged one evening after she caught a particularly large muskie. "What am I going to do with a dead fish? Take some pictures and mount it on a wall? God knows we have enough pictures, and we have enough trophies. No, I just want to experience the thrill of catching it."

So together, they placed the beautiful creature back into the water, holding it upright, and rubbing its belly, until, with a swish of its tail, it wiggled away.

Sometimes they just sat on a forgotten beach and listened to the stories being told by the gabbing gulls or laughing loons. On rainy nights, they headed to Jeremy's cabin and read, side by side, deeply content in the parallel silence or told each other silly stories and off-colour jokes. As the weeks flew by, Lori felt treasured, complete, content. And with his broad shoulders, perfect white smile, and smouldering eyes, he was one hell of a hunk. Lori still couldn't believe he was hers.

That is, except for fear of discovery—this grandiose relationship had to be wrapped in a conspiracy of silence that even Phil and Linda followed. Everyone at camp knew that if her parents ever found out, Jeremy would be banished on the next plane out, and Lori would be grounded until she was 30.

***

Jeremy led Lori over to the table. "I was just fiddling with the radio antenna before you came. It was a futile effort at best. This thing plays nothing but static."

"I know what you mean. Gosh, I couldn't even name a current song right now. It does make you feel out of touch."

"I have something for you." Jeremy reached up on his shelf and pulled down a hand-carved wooden robin perched on top of a small log and handed it to Lori. The brilliant details of the creation showcased his keen love and observation of wildlife—from the bright eyes to the warm, orange plumage on its chest and down to the white under-tail and rounded wingtips.

"You carved and painted this yourself?" Lori was incredulous.

"Yep. At first, I was going to make a duck decoy, but then you saved those babies. I thought this would suit you better."

"When in the world did you have time to do all this?" asked Lori, running her hands over the carving, fingering the feather ridges, the silkily smooth beak.

"After guiding, while you were working in the store."

"That's why you haven't been coming to the store. You were doing this for me."

"Do you like it?"

"I . . . I think it's the most thoughtful gift I have ever received. Thank you! Although," she added cheekily, "a moose nose would have been good, too!"

"Moose nose *is* good! Don't knock it till you try it. Maybe I'll save one for you if I go moose hunting this fall. Course you'd have to come to me to get it."

"Then I'm afraid it's a delicacy I'll have to do without. I'll be in school. Yikes, fall's fast approaching." She paused a moment. "After tomorrow, the only robin I'm going to have is the one you just gave me. I'm going to let my birdies go . . . even Medea. It's time. They have to get to know some other robins so they can fly south with them." Lori let out a sad sigh.

A sudden breeze ballooned past the faded cotton curtains and caressed Lori's golden hair. A strand fluttered, then settled between her mascara-spiked lashes. Jeremy reached out a hand and pushed it back. His hand lingered on her face, tracing the curve of her cheek.

"I'm sorry you have to let them go. And I'm sorry that soon I'll have to let you go."

Suddenly, magically, Dan Hill's voice streamed in on the radio, crooning "Sometimes When We Touch." They took one look at each other, then melted into each other's arms.

***

Later, Lori quietly stole back up the hill home. She had just rounded the corner to her staircase to safety when she heard her mother's voice. "Hurry up, Chezy. It's cool out here."

Like a beacon, her mother stood in her fluorescent caftan, watching the poodle take a late-night pee. Lori held her breath. If she could just stand still until her mother went back into her room—then suddenly, there was a loud cough behind her that sent her fingertips tingling and caused her brow to break out in a sweat.

"Who's there?" shrieked Helen, eyes scanning. She took a step toward where Lori was standing.

"Just us, Helen. I'm out having a smoke, and Lori's keeping me company." Dressed in a fuzzy nightgown, Linda winked as she passed the statue of Lori, then stepped out from behind the corner to wave at Helen.

"Oh, okay then." Helen breathed a sigh of relief. "Good night, dear." And with that, she and Chezy disappeared back into her bunker.

Linda turned back around and grinned at Lori, the round tip of her cigarette glowing in the dark.

"I don't know if I should thank you or hang you," said Lori. "The way you looked at me when Lottie asked if I had a boyfriend. And almost getting me caught now. Talk about flirting with danger!"

"You know I would never give you away. I was just having a little fun," said Linda with feigned innocence.

"I don't need more drama. What are you doing out here smoking anyways? You quit ages ago. The only time you light up now is when you're drunk or . . . oh. You had a fight with Phil. Okay, so what was it about?"

"Something stupid."

"Isn't it always?"

"I just wanted some me time tonight . . . wash my hair, eat a bowl of popcorn, read a book. But Phil, he always takes that as rejection. Dating is just so intense at a fishing camp. There are no bars, football games, or television to distract the guy, and no girl talk, soap operas, or stores to distract the girl. Your focus is always on one another. You'd think that would be a good thing, but sometimes. . . sometimes you need space."

Lori thought about the few hours that her and Jeremy had eked out together. "I wouldn't know. I'm not big into space right now. That'll come soon enough. And we don't fight . . . about anything! Believe me, there is nothing quite like the thrill and the terror of a secret boyfriend. I'm always looking behind my back, always believing it's the last time we will be together before we are ripped apart. Like I said, I don't need more drama."

"There'd be plenty of that if they found out. Your parents would *never* approve. He's way older than you, he works for them, and in their eyes, he has no prospects for the future. They wouldn't even give him a chance."

Lori knew what Linda said was true. "I know, I know. I don't want the heartache that would come with fighting for him. We'll be apart soon enough. Come fall, I'll be back at school in Winnipeg, and he'll be back in Thunder Bay. Who knows if I'll ever see him again?"

"Who're you kidding? If you're here next year, he'll be here next year. I've seen the way he looks at you. I'm surprised he's not moving to Winnipeg to be near you."

"Jeremy, live in a city? That I would like to see."

"Haven't you heard? Love conquers all. He might just be willing. Just like I'm willing to go upstairs right now and let your brother make up to me!" Linda stood up and ground out her cigarette. "Night girl . . . sweet dreams."

***

"Eat up. From now on, you'll be tugging for your own worms!" For their last supper, Lori had provided a smorgasbord: cottage cheese, strawberries, cat food, and a couple of caterpillars. The little birds pecked away until satiated, then they hopped to their bowl for a little nap.

"Not today, girls. Today you have to find a new place to roost. I better do this quick before I lose my nerve."

She picked up the little birds, marched down the stairs and out the door, and with a final sigh, let them go.

It was like Trincria understood it was time. She thrust open her wings and took to the sky, fluttering from one papery birch to another. She dodged and darted, twisted and glided, then floated down to the ground to peck and prod before racing off again. It was a joy to watch her as nature intended her to be.

Medea, however, flew to the roof of the laundry room. She didn't care that her sister was on a roller coaster ride to freedom. She looked down at Lori with soft little eyes as if to say, "Bring me home already!"

"Medea, I love you, but you have to go. If you don't join the other robins now, you're going to get stuck here. All the rest of the robins will fly south without you. You'll be in captivity forever. You don't want that to happen to you, do you?"

Medea just stared down at her.

"You're just too good a mother." Lori turned to see her mother standing on the boardwalk behind her.

"I don't know what to do, Mom. How do you set something free that doesn't want to go?"

Suddenly another robin with a bright ruddy breast flitted over and landed beside Medea and started to flirt.

Chirp chirp.

"Why I think she's found a beau!" cried Lori. No sooner were the words out of her mouth when the robin took off, Medea not far behind.

"Wow." Lori watched in amazement. Her little bird was not unlike her, braving her fear in the name of love.

***

Helen looked, really looked, at her daughter for the first time in a long time. She was so—grown up. A young woman strong enough and smart enough to know when it was time to let go of those she loved. She realized that sometime soon, Lori would have a someone special in her life—a man that would sweep her off her feet. Then she'd be flying off in more than an airplane—flying away further than Europe. Just like the robins, she'd be flying away for good, and she wouldn't be able to come looking for her.

Helen stepped off the boardwalk and grabbed Lori's arm. "Come on, let's go."

"I can't go anywhere with you right now, Mom. Ben's waiting for me. I'm doing touch and go's in the Cessna 206 tonight, remember?"

"I know. If you can watch your chicks fly off, so can I."

As they set off down the hill, Helen began to hum a little tune.

In a sudden act of affection, Lori flung her arm around Helen's waist. "You know, Mom, I think it's the first time I have realized what a beautiful voice you have!"

Lori hung the leather cap back on its hook. She had learned to fly a plane; now she had to learn how to fly solo. She took a Stork Lake Cap off the wall—

1979

Elsie peered over at Al's teacup. "Oh, look at all that money! Quick, get a spoon and scoop it up."

Al scanned the bubbles floating on the top of his tea.

"Is this money I've gotten or money I'm getting?" inquired Al, rounding up the bubbles in his teaspoon. "Because, you know, I just got a nice big cheque, so that wouldn't be much of a prediction."

Everyone at the staff lunch table grew quiet. They knew what cheque Al was talking about. It was the cheque Boise Cascade had issued for the purchase of Stork Lake. The pulp-and-paper company planned to cut a logging road through the bush that would pass right by Rice Creek, making the lake no longer unspoiled, unattainable. Progress had cursed this blessed little place. They would be closing for good in a week.

"Elsie, why don't you read all our tea leaves? Give us some insight into the future, so we know what we'll be doing next year," suggested Lori, hoping to take some of the tension out of the air.

"Good idea!" agreed Alma.

"I could do that. Everybody got a cup a tea?" asked Elsie.

"Phil doesn't." Linda grabbed the pot and poured him one.

"I don't drink tea."

Linda elbowed him. "Just drink it! I want to know what our future is."

"Okay, okay." He added several heaping spoons of sugar to the cup.

"What are you doing? You have more sugar than tea!" complained Linda.

"Well, I have to make it drinkable, don't I?"

She shook her head. "He's such a baby. What do we do now, Elsie? Do you read the leaves while they're floating around?"

"No, no. Drink all the tea, and when you're done, turn your cup upside down on a plate, and spin it three times. Then turn it upright again. Whatever leaves are left in the cup are the leaves I'll read."

Phil finished his tea in one swallow, dumped his cup, and with his forefinger, quickly twirled it around three times. He handed it to Elsie.

"I'm first!"

Elsie took the cup and squinted inside. "Let me see . . . My goodness, look at them leaves bunched together, with what looks like little fins on the ends. You have a lot of fish in here! Looks like you're still gonna be doing something with a fishing camp. And you're going to have a partner . . . looks like a female partner."

"Well, I'm glad my fortune agrees with my destiny because I'm going to have my own camp someday soon!"

"Do me now," piped up Linda. "I want to make sure I'm the female partner!"

Elsie then gazed into her cup. "Lots of fish here, too. Yes, I think it's safe to say you two will be partners, working in your own fishing camp."

Linda turned to Phil. "You are *so* lucky that's what it said."

"What did you expect? You know you're the only girl for me." He put his arm around her shoulders, pulled her toward him, and kissed her just beside the little beauty mark on her chin.

"Stop slobbering on me!" But Linda's grin was as wide as a Cheshire cat's.

Helen's cup was next. "Come on, Elsie. I need a good one."

"Hmm, there are new beginnings here, in a strange land. And this long line here . . . Well, it means a long struggle in this new land."

"Struggling with a new beginning in a strange land. Doesn't sound like my future. It sounds like my past!" protested Helen. "Sure you got it right?"

"I'm pretty sure. Yep, you can see it right here. Don't worry, though. It'll all come out good again, eventually."

"Eventually . . . gee, thanks," Helen answered jokingly.

"I don't make 'em up—I just calls 'em as I sees 'em!"

"My turn." Alma handed over her cup.

"You have a new beginning, too, only it's connected with your end."

"What does that mean?"

"Looks like this won't be the end of your connection with the Reids. You'll come together again someday."

"I don't know what that means, but if once the camp is closed, I still see you all, well that makes me happy. Maybe I'll work for you again in your strange land Helen!" chuckled Alma.

"Al?"

He shook his head. "I like the fortune you gave me already. I don't want to tempt fate. With my luck, if you read my leaves, there will be something there taking all the money away again!"

Everyone laughed.

"Lori?" Lori handed her cup to Elsie, then settled back in her seat, her leg jumping up and down in anticipation.

Elsie peered into the cup. "My, what a lot of leaves still left in the bottom!"

"Is that good?"

"Means lots of excitement in store. Looks like you'll be with a new person, off to new places far away from here."

Lori smiled secretly at the thought, oblivious that Al's silver eyes suddenly glittered dangerously.

"And this funny little leaf here," added Elsie, "looks like a hat!"

"A hat?"

"Yep, you'll find your answers in a hat."

"Answers to what?"

"The answers you're lookin' for."

Lori shook her head. "I don't get it. I'm not looking for any answers."

"I just calls 'em as I sees 'em. So has everybody had a reading now?"

"Everybody but you, Elsie, and you can't read your own. I'll do it." Lori reached for her cup.

"Okay, then. Never had my fortune told before!" she cackled. "What do you see?"

"I foresee you telling a lot more fortunes, maybe even professionally, for many, many years to come."

"Damned if she ain't right!" chuckled Elsie, her eyes disappearing into her crinkles. "This winter, I was figuring on reading leaves at a little tea place in Kenora!"

"Listen," said Helen, cocking her head. "I hear a plane. M&I's here." As the group got up to prepare for the arrival of the last guests they would ever host, Lori realized that, for the first time, everyone had heard just exactly the prediction they wanted to hear—that is, except for her mom, who was doomed to repeat history.

***

Jack Puelicher casually sauntered into the camp's store. Though short in stature, he had a presence about him that made him seem six feet tall. A third-generation banker, he served as President, Chairman, and CEO of Milwaukee's M&I, Marshall & Ilsley Bank. Jack and his group of bankers had been coming to Stork for ten years, each time booking the whole camp for their own use. So exclusive did Jack want this trip to be that, one year, when he saw an older gentleman with a fishing rod climb into a boat with Phil, he turned to Al.

"Why is there another fisherman here? When I say I want the whole camp, I want the whole camp."

"Well, I'm not kicking my father out!" Al chuckled at his good friend.

Of course, Jack obligingly *let* Frank stay after finding out the interloper was a Reid. Reids were like clan and treated as such. So it was with a fatherly interest that he now approached the much younger member of the Reid family standing behind the store's counter. Through the fat stogie stuck to his lips, he gave Lori a devilish grin. "There's the big man's daughter. How has your year been?" he asked, his eyes searching as if to read her thoughts.

"Great! How was yours?"

"Oh, we made a little money," said Jack offhandedly, grossly understating his company's position. "That's what a little luck and excellent management will do. So what are your plans now that Stork is closing?"

"Well, I finished school, but I'm still trying to figure out my future."

Jack pulled the stogie from his lips. "Listen, I am going to give you some of my sage advice. Figure computers into your future because computers are going to be everyone's future. Our data services division deals in financial technology, and it's expanding fast. Your smartest move would be to get in on the ground floor. In fact"—he tapped his ashes into a deer antler ashtray Gup had made—"you come on down to Milwaukee when you're ready . . . I'll have a job waiting for you."

"I don't know the first thing about computers."

"That's what training is for."

"Wow, that's a really generous offer."

"I mean it. You're a hard worker, and we'd be lucky to have you." His voice was sincere. "Now, be a doll and pack me up my usual and send it up to my cabin, will you?"

"Toothbrush, toothpaste, an assortment of my dad's clothing?"

"Exactly."

"Did you at least bring a jacket?" kidded Lori. Jack always got off the plane with plenty of fishing equipment and plenty of cigars, but not one bag of luggage.

"Why should I when I can wear your dad's? Even his pants fit just fine if I roll the cuffs up. But tell him I want his newest pair of

Kodiak boots this year. Can you imagine . . . last year he loaned me a pair with the soles near worn through."

"The nerve of him. I'll pick out a pair myself."

"Where'd Al get to anyways? We have to have a strategy meeting before we go out."

"You mean he's actually going to guide you? I thought he'd be too busy wrapping things up here around camp."

"He's never too busy for me. Besides, you know I wouldn't step into a boat with anyone but the boss."

"Only because he occasionally lets you run it!"

"You got me there."

Lori smiled. She knew the real reason Jack would only fish with Al was that he enjoyed his company so much.

"So, what are you strategizing about?"

"Obtaining my ultimate angling goal . . . catching that legendary monster muskie that hangs out at the Bridge. That's the only fish in this lake that I've wanted but never got. This is my last chance, and I'm not going home without it. For two years, your dad and I have been trying to raise it. We've seen him plenty of times, his shadow looming in the water, but he won't bite."

"Lots of fishermen have tried to get that one, never with any luck."

"That's because catching this wise old man has nothing to do with luck!" Jack planted his cigar back on his lips. "Time to go. See you later, kid."

Lori watched Jack head out the door. There were so many guests she was going to miss, and this man was one of them. He had never made her feel insignificant—from the time she was small, this powerful banking magnate had always taken the time to chat with her. And now he had just offered her a job!

When she had graduated with honours from high school that June, she had been relieved at the freedom from her old life but scared at the freedom of her new one. Lori had been to Milwaukee the previous winter and loved it. And she had been in Jack's bank, and it was twenty-one floors of, well, *amazing*. She wasn't sure about a job in computers—being behind a desk seemed just a little mundane. But it was nice to know the option was there if she wanted it. Suddenly her new freedom seemed just a little less scary.

***

Lori was closing up shop just as Jeremy came bouncing by on the buggy.

"Need a lift to the lodge?" he asked, stopping in front of her.

"Okay, but I want to drive!"

"Sure thing, pet. I'll ride shotgun."

Jeremy slid over, and Lori hopped on, popped the buggy into gear, and promptly stalled it.

"The girl can fly a plane, but she can't switch gears in a buggy!" he mocked.

After a jolted start, they slowly puttered up the hill. Jeremy crossed his arms behind his head and sat back to enjoy the scenery—that is, the scenery sitting right beside him.

Al was waiting for them at the top of the hill, his silver eyes flashing. He held out his hand and motioned for them to stop. Lori clumsily shifted into neutral.

"Lori, why aren't you working?"

"What?" She couldn't understand the anger in her dad's voice.

"What are you doing joyriding? Don't you have work to do?"

Lori felt like a gutted fish. She had been up since five. She had already put in eight hours of work and wasn't near finished yet. Jack noticed how hard she worked—Why couldn't her dad?

"I'll walk, Jeremy," she said, sliding off the seat. She slunk back up the hill, angry, hurt and ashamed, all at the same time.

***

A winter apart had done nothing to cool down Lori's relationship with Jeremy. There had been a few visits when Jeremy braved the crowds, the cars, and the concrete to come to see her. He never stayed more than a couple of days at a time, and Lori appreciated just how hard he tried not to show how uneasy he felt in the city. They also phoned occasionally and wrote each other often, spilling out their souls in ink. This love affair through secret letters made their relationship even more exciting, underscoring the need to explore their feelings further.

While Lori wasn't yet sure how this chapter in her "love story" was going to end, she did know the Stork Lake storybook was closing. This swansong season had been bittersweet. Lori greedily drank in every sight, every smell, and every sound so that they would be imprinted in her memory forever. She wrote endless pages in her journal and took rolls and rolls of photos, hoping these paper and plastic souvenirs would suffice, but somehow, she knew they would not.

Meanwhile, it didn't seem like losing Stork Lake mattered as much to her mother and father—they rarely even mentioned it. Phil, too, didn't seem to be as upset as she was, probably because he was starting a new life with Linda. She'd listened to them talk in their suite after work, building plans for their life together. Apparently, the future didn't seem so scary when you had someone to share it with. Maybe that was the answer—moving on with someone special.

***

Later that night, Lori and Jeremy returned to his cabin after a staff farewell bonfire. Tomorrow, some of the guides would be leaving permanently.

"Well," Lori sighed, pulling off her Stork Lake jacket. "Just another last on a long list of lasts. I'm going to miss Peepsight and Tommy and all of the gang. It seems so strange that now I'll never know what happens to anyone—if they keep working in camps, fall in love, have kids. Geez, I won't even know if they fall off the face of the earth."

"Talking about falling off the face of the earth . . . I got a letter from you today."

"What?"

"It was written months ago, back in May, but by then, I was moving around so much, it kept missing me. It bounced from Thunder Bay to Redditt to Red Lake and back to Thunder Bay. My sister finally forwarded it here. I can't tell you how that misbegotten letter made my day." Jeremy handed it to her.

Lori quickly read the words neatly written on her lavender notepaper. "I wrote about my upcoming graduation . . . the car parade, the dinner dance, and the riverboat cruise."

"You made it all sound so exciting that I wish I had been there to take you, even though I hate that kind of stuff. My idea of formal attire is buttoning up an extra eye on my jean shirt, but I would have rented a tux just to take you to your do."

"Oh, I couldn't torture you that way, so I found someone to take me," she said lightly, handing the letter back to Jeremy.

"This letter," he said, holding it up in the air, "reminded me of how much I missed you during the winter. To tell you the truth, you fill a very important part of me, and it felt so empty away from you. I treasure the moments we have together, even when I'm tired or into being alone. When I don't feel like seeing anyone else, I still want to be with you. You simply share my peace. You are like part of me. You make me feel settled, quiet, content, not searching for that elusive *something* any longer. You are so beautiful, inside and out, never possessive, never negative." He carefully opened a book and pressed the letter inside. "Can you imagine? We have never even had an argument."

This offhand remark stunned Lori. She realized for the first time they had never had any sort of quarrel, never seemed to have any irritation for each other. She wasn't that easygoing! She certainly let loose on her family—they saw what a little witch she could be! But she never wanted Jeremy to see that side of her. She thought if she kept it hidden, he would never know. Apparently she had done a good job. Was that the only reason they were so compatible? Lori realized she had tried so hard to please him; she had moulded herself to him, believing if she ever disagreed or complained, he would dump her. It wasn't his fault; he hadn't tried to turn her into something she wasn't. She had done that to herself.

Have I ever showed him the real me? she wondered. *Have the few months we've seen each other every summer been nothing more than a honeymoon state, where you can't see through your starry eyes to earthly reality?*

Lori decided to change the subject.

"Jack's such a neat guy, don't you think?"

"Is he ever! Do you know that he ties his own flies?"

"He also does a little thing called running a bank worth hundreds of millions, maybe billions, yet he wears my dad's old clothes. It must be amazing to be so self-assured that you could be so unassuming."

Jeremy looked at her strangely. "You've grown up with all these rich Americans. Did you ever feel envious when you saw all the things they had?"

"Of course not! Okay, okay, not often, anyways. When I was younger, I didn't even realize we were poor. I felt like the richest little girl alive. I had everything. I had my own private beach, my own private lake. I had flowers to pick and all sorts of critters to keep me amused. I had people all around to comfort me when one of these critters died or when I fell and skinned my knees. I had a wealth of knowledge around me, my own specialist in every field. When I wanted to learn to cook, I went to Elsie. Mechanics? There was Albert. Marketing and customer relations? My parents. Canadian culture? Alma or Andy or James or Eddie. And every week, there were different guests, each with their own niche, their own specialty. No, I didn't feel poor. I did know my parents worked hard. I learned that sometimes life was a struggle, that things didn't come easy. But I never equated the struggle with being poor. Later, when we finally had more money, life was easier, but it certainly wasn't richer."

"So money doesn't mean much to you?" Jeremy asked, a hint of hopefulness in his voice.

Lori took a deep breath. It was time to start telling him how she really felt—he deserved to know. "I didn't say that! I enjoy the things money can buy . . . pretty clothes and holidays and nice houses and flying lessons. Don't you?"

"Well, I like that it can buy me fishing equipment." Jeremy hugged her close to him, with arms as hard and polished as oiled wood. "Now, let's not talk about this anymore. I want to just enjoy the rest of the evening with my girl."

***

While most inventory was to remain with Stork—Boise Cascade would open the camp next year for their executives—so the camp still needed to be closed up properly. Unused cabins were stripped, boats laid up, engines winterized, freezers cleaned out, files sorted, personal belongings rounded up. The work was physically and emotionally demanding, so Lori was exhausted when, several days later, she tiredly climbed the stairs up to her room and flopped down on her bed.

Phil peeked in. "Hey, why aren't you working?" he asked jokingly.

"Don't you start, too!"

"Why? Someone call you a slacker?"

"Dad. Can you believe he came into my room this morning and balled me out for sleeping in? It was *ten after five*! You know, normally Mom is my nemesis, but this year she has left me alone. It's Dad who is always as mad as a hornet around me. I can't do anything right. And it doesn't matter how hard I work. He always sees me as slacking off. Just what the heck is his problem?" Lori grabbed Chezy, who was sleeping on her pillow and buried her face in the curly fur.

"What's so unusual 'bout that?" Phil said offhandedly. "He's always made us work harder than everyone else. He's always wanted to prove that we weren't favoured above the staff."

"It's more than that. It's like . . . he hates me. Every time he looks at me, he has this scowl on his face. It doesn't matter what I say or do. He's not happy."

"Maybe it's because of Jeremy."

Lori quickly sat up on the edge of her bed. "You don't think he knows? You didn't tell him!"

"What, you think I have a death wish? Course I didn't tell him! But that doesn't mean he hasn't put two and two together."

"How could he—" Suddenly something dawned on her. "Wait . . . oh God, the letter. He does know."

"What letter?"

"My letter to Jeremy! It came in on the plane that brought M&I in. He would have seen it when he was sorting the mail!"

"Now, just cool it," said Phil calmly. "You don't know that. And even if he does know, would it be so bad?"

"Yes, it would be bad. He would never understand. Neither Mom nor Dad would. Why hasn't he said anything to me? Why's he just picking on me? Why doesn't he just come out with it? I know he's slowly torturing me. He's going to torture me until he moves in for the kill."

"Or maybe he just thinks if he doesn't say it out loud, it won't be true. You're his little girl . . . he wants the best for you. Maybe he doesn't think Jeremy's it."

"It's not his decision," pouted Lori. "God, I'm pathetic. I'm eighteen and still care what my parents think. Whether they agree with my actions or not, it shouldn't matter anymore. They're my mistakes to make."

***

Jack did not like losing—at anything. And most of the time, he didn't. Everything he tackled in his life, he tackled with a vengeance and did not give up until he succeeded. However, it looked like the Bridge muskie might just defeat him. It was Jack's last day ever to fish at Stork Lake, and it had remained elusive.

Frustrated, right after breakfast, Jack called his group together for one last "strategy meeting." The September morning, while clear and sunny, had a definite nip in the air.

"Listen up, guys!" Jack set his tackle box down on the dock, turned up the cuffs on the eiderdown jacket of Al's he was wearing, and then surveyed the men congregated before him. "Al and I are headed for the Bridge this morning. I do not want *any* other boats near there, you understand? I don't want to even see a boat fly by at a distance. In fact, I don't want another boat in the entire vicinity. You all just fish down at this end of the lake. If I even catch a glimpse of you, you're fired. This is my last chance to get that muskie, and no one else is going to catch it, raise it, or even get a glimpse of it."

Armed with their marching orders, the guests in boats set out— seven of them heading west and one lone boat heading south. Al and Jack were unusually introspective as they cruised along, past the numerous rocky shores, heavily treed with pine and spruce. Both men knew this was their last time on this lake.

The Bridge was a large area, about an acre set between two islands with a row of boulders connecting them under the water. Here the winds freely hit the shorelines, blurring the edges of the break lines. With an incredible diversity of underwater humps and ridges, structures and shelters, it created the perfect underwater highway for prowling muskie.

"Okay," said Al, slowing the boat. "We've prospected damn near this whole area. Where do you want to troll today?"

Jack looked thoughtful. "I think I've cast 10,000 times on the outside. Let's reverse it. This time, let's cast into the reef." He pulled a large bucktail out of his tackle box. "Some people say fish are dumb and can't distinguish one bait from the next. I don't believe it. You get a fish hook stuck in your mouth and see if you don't remember what it looked like! No, fish become educated, especially a granddaddy like this one. He's seen every commercial lure known to man, which is why today I'm using this one. I made it myself. Maybe he'll be interested enough to check it out."

As he readied his rod, Jack mused, "I'm gonna miss this, Al. You and me, in a boat, on the water. We've been doing this a long time. Kinda thought we'd grow old together." He was not one to wear his emotions on his sleeves, but this was bigger than his pride.

"Geez, Jack, you make us sound like a bloody married couple," answered Al, adjusting his cap with the Stork Lake insignia embroidered on it.

"It's more than a marriage. After all, a good fishing partner is harder to find than a wife!"

They drifted in a hundred yards while Jack cast the bucktail into the deep water, letting the bait sink before winding it back up. On the third cast, it hit. You couldn't see the fish, just the wake—and it was enormous.

Jack was not one to get excited, but he had never experienced anything like this. He stood up in his seat.

"Al—!" The cigar dropped from his lips and landed at the bottom of the boat.

"God damn!" Al threw his hat up in the air. "You're gonna get him!"

After a few minutes of constant reeling, Jack looked perplexed. "This is too easy . . . this fish isn't even fighting. He's just letting me walk him up."

Al felt uneasy, too. Muskies weren't known for their cooperation. "I don't know Jack—"

Suddenly a large dark shape could dimly be seen under the surge of water. It cruised up, up, up, until its back broke the surface. Still, it did not argue but hovered for a moment before casually gliding under the boat. So massive was it that its head appeared on one side of the boat, with the tail on the other. The two muskie moguls were speechless—never had they seen anything near this size before.

"He's sixty-plus, Al."

"Haul him in."

But it was not to be. The muskie had played him for a fool, and now bored with this game, he simply yawned and spewed the bait from his bucket of a mouth. Without even a flicker of his tail, he sunk back down to the depths like a submarine.

"He . . . just . . . spit my bait back at me," said Jack in shock.

"You did your best."

"It was my job to sink the hook good enough to reel it in." Jack slid his rod across the seats, then dejectedly sat down.

"It's the hunt that matters."

Jack picked up Al's hat and handed it back to him, then bent back down to pick up his fallen cigar. After a quick inspection, he brushed it off then stuck it back into his mouth. Pulling a lighter out of his pocket, he relit it, exhaling a puff of grey smoke. Once again composed, Jack looked over at Al thoughtfully.

"That's what's important to you, Al, isn't it? The hunt? I've always thought it was the prize. But you, you're someone who enjoys the challenge. You know I wondered why losing this place didn't affect you more . . . this place you've worked so damn hard to build. It was the building up you enjoyed, more than the finished product. You're ready for a new project."

"You're right, Jack. I love it here, and I will miss it, no doubt about that. But I am ready for something different. I have a new project in mind, something that stirs me inside again. It's a land development project in Phoenix."

"Phoenix? Hell, I'm opening a branch in Phoenix this fall. Got a home down there, too. We'll get together, have dinner, play squash . . . I'll even spot ya!"

"Spot me? Christ, I'll beat you!"

"And so the hunt will continue." Jack spun around in his seat so he was facing forward. "Come on, Al. Let's catch some walleye for lunch."

***

"That's the last of it." Lori gazed about her.

The desk was swept clean of paperwork, all the files stored in boxes. Every shelf was bare; any remaining lures and leaders, cigarettes, chips, and bars were packed up and stacked in the corner, ready to be flown out on one of the planes the next day. There was nothing left to do now but wait for it all to end.

Linda, who had been helping her pack up the store, straightened up, brushing a rogue curl from her face. "Thank God. My back is killing me."

"It's really going to happen, isn't it? Stork is going to close, and we're never coming back."

"You just realizing this now?" mocked Linda.

"I haven't let myself think about it."

"Well, you knew that even if the camp didn't close, you'd be leaving it someday, didn't you? Either for school, or work, or marriage?"

"Yes, but I always thought it would be here waiting for me, that I could always come back when I wanted to, when I *needed* to. Now, I'll never be able to come home again. And what about Alma and Andy and Dennis and everybody else? When will I ever see any of them? Everyone here is from somewhere else, and that's where they will go back to."

"What can I say? It sucks," said Linda frankly. "Life can be that way. On the bright side, it can also be delicious. Elsie's making turkey with all the trimmings. We're joining M&I in the dining room for the last supper. Come, you'll eat, you'll feel better." Linda firmly believed the answer to woes was food.

"No, I can't . . . there's something important I have to do."

Jeremy peered into the store. "All finished, pet?"

"I see what's so important . . . the last night with your honey for a while," said Linda.

"We're taking one last spin on the lake."

"I've got the boat cushions and the gas tank. All I need is you," said Jeremy.

Linda gave them a devilish grin. "You two be good. Don't do anything I wouldn't do!"

"And what exactly would that leave out, Linda?" cracked Lori.

The sleepy sun was slowly dipping down into its watery bed when Jeremy pulled into Beaver Bay and cut the engine. It was one of their favourite places, named for the fabulous domed beaver house erected where the gentle waves sipped the shore. They sat for a few minutes, rhythmically rocking along with the boat. Finally, Jeremy spoke.

"We haven't talked at all about what happens now."

"You've never been much of a planner."

"I know, but I have made a plan to spend the winter in Thunder Bay."

Jeremy leaned forward, taking her hands in his. "Why don't you gather up your stuff after you leave here and come visit me . . . permanently."

Lori slipped her hands out of his and stuffed them in her pockets.

"I'm going to Europe," she announced, a lump in her throat.

"What?"

"I've decided to take the Lindlarghs up on their offer. I'm going to book my ticket as soon as I leave here, and I have no idea when I'll be back."

Jeremy's shocked face said it all. "When did this come about?"

"I've been thinking about it for a long time, Jeremy, but I just decided today. I have to see what else is out there. I don't know who

I'm going to be or what I'm going to be. I just know what I am right now isn't it. I was so scared when I first heard we were losing Stork. I thought the answer to my fears would be to share them. It isn't. It's to face them, and that I have to do by myself. My God, there's so much out there I want to experience!"

Jeremy stared at her like he had never seen her before. "I thought you loved camp life! I thought you never wanted to do anything else. I had no idea you felt this way. You never said anything."

"Because I was a child. I showed you only what you wanted to see. I was who you wanted me to be, but I can't do that any longer. I'm claiming my confidence, my life. You don't really even know who I am."

"Of course I do."

"Do you know that as much as I love the bush, I don't want to live in it? That as much as I love Stork, I love the hustle-bustle of the city, too? That I want to be somewhere where I can dress up and go to dances? Go to nice restaurants, the theatre, concerts? Do you know that I want a career and not just a job?"

"I thought you wanted to be a pilot! A bush pilot."

"I thought I wanted to be a pilot, too. That's when I thought I only had three choices . . . a guide, a domestic, or a pilot. Now I know those aren't my only options. I am going to travel, then I want to go to university. Maybe after that, I'll go to Milwaukee and take Jack's job. Maybe I won't. What I do know is that I won't be spending the rest of my life at a fishing resort."

"What am I supposed to do now? I thought you were going to be part of my life." The pain on his face was so great she could barely stand it.

"Go live your life! You could attend school somewhere, take a course. I'm sure you could get a student loan. You're so smart. It'd be a shame—" She stopped.

"If I wasted it all? Is that what you think? I'm wasting my life just because I like a simple life?"

"Simple or easy?"

"Wow."

"Jeremy, I'm sorry."

"I don't have to go tripping halfway around the world to get my kicks," he said solemnly. "And I don't have to go to school to get an education. I tried that. I took a ten-month course at the college in Thunder Bay. I lasted through the fall and winter okay, but by March, I just about went nuts! I dreamed of the lake almost every night . . . wishing I could just take a month off. That wasn't too much to ask for, was it? I'd go down to the local tackle shops and lust after all the spoons and plugs and rods and reels. By the time spring came, I was so tempted to go trout fishing, to break out. Finally, by May, the pull was too much. I wasn't able to resist the temptation to pack up my bags and head for open water."

"You almost made it . . . a few more months—"

"A few more fishing months!"

"One summer . . . Would it have been so bad?"

"Could you stand a summer not being here?"

"I'm going to find out, aren't I?" said Lori ruefully.

Pulling her hands out of her pockets, she captured his sad dear, dear face—Jeremy, her Jeremy, who for so many summers had seen her through turbulent teenage years, who had been her sweet first love. Life would never be the same without him, but with sudden clarity, she knew it was time to move on.

As they sat there, in the middle of that lake, they both realized this friendship would never go any further. Like the road that would soon cut into Stork, their roads now intruded on each other's well-being, each other's peace. Everything was changing, and everything would change even more. There was no backtracking. Jeremy was part of this life, and this life was coming to an end. Suddenly a loon cried out, its eerie sound echoing over the crystal waters like a ghostly haunting.

"Let's go home," said Lori.

***

Supper over, everyone retired to the lounge to groan in turkey-stuffed delirium.

"You did a good job carving that bird, Jack. Should have let me know long ago how good you are in the kitchen. We would have put you to work. You could have subsidized that puny salary of yours with some tips, maybe even enough to afford clothes of your own!" teased Al.

"I don't know if I would have tipped him," declared Linda, winking. "I think I found some cigar ashes in my piece. You should have taken that cigar out of your mouth before you started carving!"

"A little scotch will wash that right down. Come on, Al, break out another bottle. We need to celebrate the day's angling achievements," admonished Jack.

"More like angling bereavements!" jested Al, cracking the seal on the Hudson Bay bottle, then throwing the cap into the trash. "We won't be needing that anymore."

***

"Looori!" her mom yelled out. Her voice seemed to be filled with surprise and delight as Lori walked through the door. "Come in here! Are you hungry? I don't think there's anything but turkey bones left, but there's plenty of ham and potatoes and even some Caesar salad."

Lori tentatively entered the room, taking a roost beside Linda and Phil. "It's okay. I'm not hungry."

"I thought you were out on the lake," declared Linda loudly.

"I was. But I decided to come in early. I didn't want to miss this last evening."

"Did you catch anything?" Linda pressed on mischievously.

"Linda." Phil's tone begged her to stop.

"Well, I just want to know . . . want to know if she caught a fish or anything else." Her innocent look belied her intent.

"I did catch something," Lori answered quietly, "but I let it go."

Al speared Lori's eyes with his own. For a moment, her dad stared at her knowingly, his face softened, the war paint removed. Al poured some wine into a stemmed glass then made his way over to hand it to Lori. "Let's raise our glasses, everyone, to new beginnings and new adventures!"

"Here, here!" resounded the roomful.

"I don't know, Al," said Jack. "I love that you're going to start a new business in Phoenix, but what about Helen? Is your poor wife up for another one of your crazy adventures?"

"Jack, are you saying I'm not exciting?" called out Helen. "I'll have you know I can be as daring as the rest of my family. In fact, I'm going to do something right now that I've never done in my whole life, not even as a kid." And with that, she kicked off her shoes, strutted over the large tree in the middle of the dining room, and started climbing it.

The place broke out in an uproar.

"Ah hell," sniffed Jack and scrambled up right behind her.

***

M&I were gone. Alma & Andy were gone. And dear, sweet Jeremy was gone. Only a handful of staff and the Reid family remained, and they, too, would be departing the next day.

Lori hadn't been able to watch those final planes take off that morning. Too much of her was leaving with them. Instead, she roamed over her old haunts: the hill that she used to pretend was her mansion, the woodpile that had been her house. She crept into the icehouse where she had slept hot afternoons away, visited the graveside of her little pets, walked the beach where she had picked up beer caps for her sand cookies.

All day, she reminisced. This place had been to her what no other place could ever be. Who would tend her little garden on the point? Who would run their hands through her tamarack's soft needles, gather the sweet-smelling purple lilacs from her bush? Who would pick the tiny wild strawberries? Save baby birds? What would they do with her grandfather's diamond willow coat rack, with diamonds so deep you could fit your hands inside?

She looked across the sparkle of the lake to the two familiar islands in front. What would they do to this place—this special place? What would a road mean? Would people come in droves and fish until there were no fish left? Would they litter her forests with their campsites, their pathways, their markings? Would the waters be contaminated like Ball Lake? Would cabins be torn down, new, unfamiliar monstrosities built, the isolation, the peace destroyed? How could she bear to see strangers walking down her paths, past her families of trees?

Lori reminisced until the sun started to set over the water. Its gold and tawny yellow patinas stretching across the horizon meant her torturous tomorrow was going to be a beautiful, clear, sunny day. But how could it be? How could the weather not reflect her feelings? Lori had wanted to cry for a long time but never could. She had learned long ago tears were for sad movies or for when someone you cared for died. You didn't sob over disappointments. And yet, this was much more than a disappointment. This felt like a death. It was the end of everything she had ever known. Suddenly the floodgates opened, and the tears came.

Slowly Lori hung the Stork Lake cap back on the wall. Leaving the safety and security not only of this treasured home away from home was scary enough but leaving behind her family and friends was unbearable. How was she going to go on by herself?

EPILOGUE

L ori finally found what she was looking for.
It was the hats. That's what she needed to take with her to make leaving this place okay. Not the physical hats, but what they represented.

They say it takes a village to raise a child. This village, indeed, had raised her. It was a tangible structure of man's spirit: his tenacity over obstacles, his endurance over adversity. Carved out of the ground, often with bare hands and primitive tools, it stood for what we are all capable of, with enough heart, enough determination, and enough vision. And the determined spirits and courageous hearts of those who graced this small village had nurtured her soul and given her the tools and the confidence to continue on her journey. They had taught her that she could handle any future hardships and successes, fears and failures, joys and sorrows. In the future, whenever she was scared or uncertain, she could pull out a hat, and one of them would come to her rescue. This place and these people would always be with her. No pulp-and-paper mill, no plane, no amount of distance could take them out of her heart, her head, or her dreams.

Somewhere inside, she would always retain a part of that storybook girl. However, this magical land was only one stop along the way to the rest of her life. Lori now knew it would be possible to have a happily ever after Stork Lake. Without even realizing it, she had already moved on.

Lori heard her mom calling. "Loooori, where are yoooou? We're ready to take off!" With a slight smile, Lori took off her brown suede cap and hung it on the only empty nail on the wall. Bareheaded, she walked toward the door, opened it, and walked through. She walked straight down the short hill toward the lake sparkling in the midday sun. She walked all the way down the dock to the plane and climbed in. She did not look back.

THE END

Made in the USA
Las Vegas, NV
15 December 2023